RETRIBUTION

COL SEC

BONUS NOVELLA EXTINCTION INISIDE

JAN DOMAGALA

THE
GLO
BAL
— EDIT —

The International division of MEDIA PIRANHA Inc.

RETRIBUTION, with bonus novella EXTINCTION

Copyright © 2021 by Jan Domagala

All rights reserved

Published by The Global Edit, an imprint of Red Penguin Books

Bellerose Village, New York

ISBN

Print 978-1-63777-198-3

Digital 978-1-63777-197-6

This one is for Joyce.

Other books by
Jan Domagala
in

The Col Sec Series

RONIN

OMEGA

DISCOVERY

Contents

EXTINCTION - A Col Sec Thriller

RETRIBUTION - A Col Sec
Thriller

Prologue

―――――――――

|

The large man stood outside the Med Lab looking through the Plexiglas wall at the figure on the bio-bed. His opaline eyes stroked the curves beneath the sheet.

She was asleep now after being moved from the Med Lab onboard the starship that was orbiting Toldax in Alliance space, onto his starship. She was exhausted after all the questioning and tests performed on her, and she had no idea where she was, only that she was alive. It was a fact that she could not deny but one that she realised should be impossible.

He turned away from the glass and activated his NI. 'Inform OMEGA Command that we're on our way, eta two hours,' he said before walking off down the corridor.

Zara Hardy stirred under the sheet. She had heard the clone's words whilst she faked sleep. Who OMEGA was she had no idea, it was a development she was unaware of only having come to light whilst she had been recovering.

Although she was extremely tired from everything that

had happened since her awakening, she had to admit that she felt good; better than good, in fact, she had never felt as good as she did right at that moment. She felt infused with a power that confused her. She hadn't had the time to actually think it through and figure out exactly how this had happened.

There was something else too that confused her, who was this mysterious man and what was OMEGA?

The last thing she remembered before waking in this austere cell was being on the planet Toldax. She had been captured and used as a pawn in an Alliance ploy to capture the man she had grown to love, Kurt Stryder, by an agent named Pavel Norsky who had shot her and caused her death. She was aware of what Kurt was capable of and, to her knowledge, the only one. However, the Alliance had their suspicions, which was why they had captured him in their attempt to learn the truth.

She desperately needed answers to these and so many other questions but was in no position to acquire them at the present time. She was torn between using her newfound health to escape from her current captivity – for that was what this was – and she was certain that whatever plans this OMEGA had for her did not include her being set free, or gathering valuable Intel on whoever these people were.

After careful consideration, she chose the second option mainly because she had no idea where she was being held so an escape plan would not work until she had at least gleaned that snippet of information. So, gathering Intel it was, and whilst she was held in Med Lab there was nothing she could do but wait.

She settled down to do just that and immediately began to wonder what Kurt Stryder was doing now.

II

He felt the rubble being moved and knew he would soon be set free; his agony would soon be over.

He had been buried alive for what seemed like months and with little to live on he had no idea how he had even survived. All that he did know was that his entire existence was pain, agonising pain that saw no end. But that pain was about to end, or so he hoped.

He felt the pressure begin to ease on his arms and legs; felt the weight lift ever so slightly off his torso so that his lungs could inflate a little and he could get more of the much-needed air into his system.

He felt some strength returning to his limbs as the pressure eased; a strength that he never thought possible. With that strength, travelled a rage fuelled by the time he had spent trapped beneath the tons of rubble and the knowledge he had been put there by the actions of someone he worked for.

When the first glint of light reached him through gaps in the rocks and rubble that still lay on top of him, he knew that it was just a matter of seconds now before his release.

He realised from the direction the light struck him that he was lying face down. His pain had been so all-encompassing that there was no way he knew where he was or even which way was up. Consciousness would periodically escape him as the pain overwhelmed him; again and again, this happened and each time he would wake to find that nothing had changed. It would start all over again until he thought he could bear it no longer and that he would surely go insane.

The pressure eased a little more and he could wait no longer. With a herculean effort, he hunched his shoulders and pushed upwards; the muscles bulged in his arms and the rubble began to move.

A primal roar formed deep within his stomach, rising up through to his vocal cords where it could be contained no longer and it burst through his lips. As the rubble slowly fell away from him he pushed harder and raised himself higher until he thrust upwards finally breaking free into the open air, his lungs almost bursting from the force of his primal scream.

Around him were three figures that he instantly recognised as ground workers. They were working on clearing the ground where the facility had stood before the accident that had caused the catastrophic explosion that had destroyed it. He had been on the outskirts chasing Kurt Stryder when he was shot by General Solon just prior to the explosion. The explosion of the facility had covered his body with tons of rubble and it was only now, much later, that they had got around to clearing the site.

In all that time his body had regenerated, much slower than Kurt Stryder was capable of, but nevertheless, as he appeared before the trio of ground workers he was fully healed.

The fury that had built up inside him during his healing process would not be sated; it needed to be released. He stood looking at the startled men, his chest heaving from his exertions, his body bent over as he rested his arms on his thighs as he gave in to it.

In a blur of motion that the ground workers struggled to keep up with, Pavel Norsky attacked them. He reached the first worker and grabbed the sides of his head, twisting it violently, breaking his neck with an audible snap. The second was reached before the first had even hit the ground and a fist struck the man's face with such force that his nose was completely flattened in an explosion of blood. Norsky whirled around and leapt upon the last worker who had turned to run. He landed on his shoulders knocking him to the ground. Norsky grabbed hold of his head and again twisted it, snapping his neck like a twig.

He got to his feet and locked around at the bodies; he felt no remorse, his only thought was how to get off the planet to exact his retribution on those who caused him such agony, starting with Kurt Stryder.

Chapter One

Kurt Stryder had returned to Celeron where he had been born and raised. An 'E' class planet, Celeron was one of the first planets to be colonised by the Confederation over three centuries ago and was where he called home.

His house was a two-storey, white brick villa that had served as the family home until a tragic accident took both his parents from him. Kurt had lived alone in the house since then.

Since his return from Tartaran and the subsequent debriefings, Kurt was allowed some free time. He was given some leeway with regard to regulations considering his status in Col Sec, so he went home until such time he was recalled to duty.

He spent some time relaxing at his villa and did some shopping in Haven, the small coastal town near his home that was a magnet to tourists. Tonight he planned to visit some newly acquired friends.

Kurt drove his Celeron Independent Vehicles Sports Hatch, a pedigree sports car based on the Mercedes design which had stood the test of time for over five hundred years.

CIV had negotiated with Mercedes to use their design and manufacture cars that were in keeping with the Mercedes pedigree. Kurt drove the car up to the Golden Palace in Jacksonville, one of the two largest cities on the planet, the other being Jamestown, both named after the two leaders of the first colonies from over three centuries ago.

The Golden Palace was a nightclub owned and run by one of the biggest gangsters on the planet, Abraham Bane.

Abraham Bane was a large man in incredible shape for someone in his fifties. His salt and pepper hair was combed straight back from a prominent forehead below which deep brown eyes looked out at the world with contempt. He had a long, flat nose that lay close to his face, a testament to a fight he had lost in his youth. He could have had it repaired but had left it as a remembrance of the last fight he ever lost. He became a student of a fighting arts master and learned all he could; using his renowned strength and all his hard-earned knowledge he gained not only revenge but a reputation that helped in his quest to become the leader of the largest gang in Jacksonville.

Although he retained that position, in recent years he had diversified his interests into legitimate businesses making him a very wealthy man.

It had been Bane he had called to see concerning a problem he had just after his enhancements had taken place. The problem concerned an Alliance agent who had kept Kurt under surveillance and ultimately led to him being kidnapped. Tonight though he was there just to relax and say 'Hi.'

He parked his CIV Sports Hatch in the car park opposite the club and walked across to the entrance. He locked the red vehicle via his Neural Interface, which allowed him to do away with mobile devices such as phones or remote controls. He smoothed out his dark blue Armani suit as he stood up to his full height of six feet two inches. His lean, hard frame was that of an athlete and, being a professional soldier from Recon Delta, the elite Special Forces of Col Sec, it was kept in shape through their regular exercise routines. Although, since the experiment that had altered his genetic structure making him virtually indestructible and heightened all his other senses to superhuman level, he hardly needed to exercise anymore. His blond hair was cut short once more now that he was back on active service and his goatee had been shaved off too. His cobalt blue eyes looked across at the Golden Palace as he moved towards it.

As usual, the club was lit up like a Christmas tree with lights strewn all over its exterior. Bane was, if nothing, the opposite of subtle.

The Golden Palace was a three-storey Victorian-style building with a wooden edifice and slate tile roof. The neon strip lights were arranged over the outside frontage to advertise the venue. Bane liked to make a statement and the Golden Palace was his way of saying 'I've arrived.'

On the door stood two burly men with shaven heads each wearing black suits and bow ties to match. A queue had formed waiting to gain entrance to the club and these doormen were the guardians.

Kurt walked past the line of smartly dressed people commandeering scornful glances from those he passed.

'Evening guys, is Abe in tonight?' he said as he approached the two doormen.

'Well, if it isn't Col Sec's finest,' said the one on the left as he recognised Kurt. 'Mister Bane is in every night, sir, go right in Tony will be pleased to see you too,' he added with a smile.

As Kurt walked past them, jeers from the line of people waiting to do the same were thrown at his back.

Kurt walked through the large ornate wooden edifice into

the foyer. A door led to the inner room of the club, which was again guarded by a behemoth in a suit. A nod of recognition from the giant in the suit and the door was opened to allow Kurt to go enter.

The inner room was large, with tables dotted around for those patrons who wanted to eat. There was a small dance floor to the left of him at the far end of the room in front of the tables. The dance floor had a small raised stage where musicians performed. To Kurt's right was a long mahogany bar with bottles arranged on the wall behind. Several bar staff were working behind this bar serving drinks to the customers standing there while waitresses delivered drinks to the guests seated at the tables.

Abraham Bane was in a booth over by the far wall in the VIP section with a huge man standing guard at his shoulder. As Kurt approached them a smile spread across the stony face of the man-mountain, who said, 'Glad to see you again Kurt.'

'Nice to see you again too Tony,' Kurt replied.

Bane looked around Tony to see his visitor and he too smiled. He remembered well the last time Kurt was in his club and he had later described it as one of the more entertaining nights at the club.

'Are we in for more fun and games tonight?' he asked as Kurt came up to his table.

'Can't a guy come to see some friends without being accused of something?' Kurt asked in mock indignation.

'Oh, we're friends now are we?' Bane said.

'Are you saying we aren't because I could always ask my friends over in the Intelligence Division to go over your business dealings? I'm sure they could find something for the local Constabulary to investigate,' Kurt countered.

'No need to be hasty, Kurt. Christ, can't you Col Sec guys

take a joke? Tony, get the guy a drink, he looks like he could use one.'

Before Tony could even move there was a disturbance at the entrance. Four men burst through the guards and pushed their way into the main room.

'What now? Are they with you?' Bane said when he saw the intruders.

'Never seen 'em before but I've got a feeling it's me they've come to see,' Kurt replied. He didn't know how he knew but just that he knew. It was just one of the side effects of his enhancements that he was trying to get used to and understand better.

'Life is never dull when you're in town is it, Kurt,' Bane said, more of a statement than a question.

'You know me, anything but boring,' Kurt replied and then he turned and walked towards the intruders.

As he passed Tony said to him, 'You wait here, keep Abe safe at all costs but feel free to step in if you think I need it.'

'Goes without saying, man.'

'Can I help you guys?' Kurt asked as he approached the small group. Three of the four moved forwards to face him whilst the fourth remained at the rear content to simply watch.

All four newcomers wore expensive suits so they would fit in with the club's regular clients. The three at the front were all large men, standing at six feet six inches tall with powerful, muscular frames. The one at the back had a more natural appearance standing at least six inches shorter than his companions, but they all looked as if they could be brothers, the smaller being the runt of the litter. One feature they all shared which Kurt noticed as they all looked at him was their eyes. They all had opaline green eyes that stared at him with a fierce intensity; he was obviously the reason for their visit.

'We're here to see what you're made of Kurt Stryder,' said the runt as he went and stood over by the bar, confirming Kurt's earlier supposition.

Sensing something was about to happen, the crowd in the room all turned to view the small group. Those seated at the tables all got up and moved over to the dance floor where they assumed they would be safer and could get a better view of the action to come.

Kurt glanced at them as they all left, then looked over his shoulder at Tony and Bane whose expressions had suddenly become hard and extremely serious.

Kurt turned his attention to those facing him and prepared himself for what was about to come.

'Okay boys, let's get this over with,' Kurt said. He stood in a relaxed pose facing the three large men with the hard expressions. He was ready for whatever happened; adrenalin began to flood his system and he felt the world around him fall into slow motion as his senses went into hyperdrive.

The three men were spaced out facing Kurt in a straight line from left to right. Kurt was confident he could handle all three at once if need be, but he didn't want to give too much away about what he was capable of. He wanted to learn what the purpose of this confrontation was and more importantly who had sent them.

The middle intruder came forward first. He swung a straight right punch at Kurt's face putting all his prodigious strength behind it.

Kurt saw the punch coming from the first twitch in the giant's shoulder and simply moved his head to the side allowing the fist to travel harmlessly past. The giant pulled his arm back and threw another punch. Kurt caught this one in the palm of his right hand before it reached his face, twisting it down to waist height effectively locking the arm and lifting the giant onto his toes.

A grimace of pain crossed the giant's face just before Kurt punched him, knocking his head back in an explosion of teeth and blood.

The giant went down on one knee, his left hand on the floor to steady himself and his right wiping the blood from his face.

Kurt faced the other two who came at him one at a time. The one on his right swung a left cross at his ribs but Kurt stepped away from this right into the path of a right cross from the remaining attacker. Kurt blocked this punch by bringing his left arm up and taking it on his bicep. The force of the blow caused him to stagger sideways a step or two forcing him to try and block a savage onslaught of blows from the other attacker.

Kurt dodged and weaved as the two attackers tried to hit him with everything they had. Most of the blows he took on his arms or blocked with his hands; the others missed completely.

The final attacker got off the floor and joined the fray. He picked up a nearby chair and smashed it across Kurt's back, sending him sprawling forwards into the path of the other two thugs. This brought his guard down and they were able to rain more and more punches onto his unprotected face and body until he crumpled to the floor under the sheer weight of them.

His face was cut in several places and blood flowed freely down his cheeks and forehead as he hit the floor.

The attackers stepped back and Kurt looked up at them. When he smiled his cobalt blue eyes were hard and cold. The cuts closed up as new skin miraculously reformed as his body regenerated itself.

Kurt slowly stood up, his face as good as new. The fourth member of his attackers smiled as he bore witness to the event. Kurt looked at each of the three men before him and said, 'Okay, now it's my turn.'

He stepped forward ducking beneath a huge right hand aimed at his head, bringing his right hand up and smashing his fist into the chin of his attacker in a thunderous uppercut that took him off his feet and sent him flying to land heavily on his back.

Kurt then stepped to his right and smashed a right cross into the ribs of the next thug which broke at least two ribs and doubled him over right into the path of a left cross that almost took his head off. The blow snapped his head around sending out a stream of blood from his smashed mouth.

The last attacker reacted with lightning-fast reflexes at seeing his two companions downed in mere seconds. He came at Kurt with a roundhouse kick. Kurt caught the leg against his side wrapping his arm around it, them gripping it tightly he spun the man and threw him across the room to smash into the bar next to the fourth member of the team.

'Seen enough?' asked Kurt as the fourth team member looked down at his companion at his feet.

'It's been most informative, I must congratulate and thank you for your cooperation,' he replied and, with a wave of his hand, he beckoned to the others who got to their feet and walked over to him.

Kurt started to follow them. 'Not so fast, you've got some questions to answer.'

The runt pulled out a pistol from beneath his jacket and aimed it at Kurt who stopped in his tracks.

'Another time no doubt, but right now, we have to leave. We have what we came for and like I said, no doubt we'll meet again soon,' the runt said with a confident air that Kurt did not like.

'I'll look forward to it,' Kurt said as he watched them leave the club.

'What the hell was that all about?' Tony asked as he came to stand at Kurt's side.

Kurt watched the four men exit the club; the smallest of the group backed out keeping his pistol trained on Kurt. The runt waved a hand to Kurt as he passed through the door to the outer porch and the street level.

'I'm damned if I know, but I'm sure as hell going to find out,' Kurt said, his cobalt blue eyes dark with fury. He turned to look at the man-mountain beside him and smiled, 'Now let's go get that drink I came here for.'

Pavel Norsky had left the area where he had been uncovered and headed straight for the nearest landing pad. His clothes were in tatters so he had swapped with one of the dead workers who had been of similar build. The coveralls were just a little tight across the chest and short in the arms and legs but he hoped no one would notice.

As he approached the landing pad there was a shuttle getting ready for departure. He had no idea where it was going but he knew he had to get on board. The boarding ramp was lowered so he made his way up the steep incline. The ramp led into the belly of the shuttle where a row of seats was positioned against the sides of the craft. Several of them were occupied when he entered and he took one that was vacant on the port side of the craft.

A uniformed figure came through from the pilot's section and the moment he laid eyes on Norsky he walked over to him. Placing his hand on the pistol holstered on his hip the guard said, 'Excuse me, sir, who are you?'

Norsky stood up as all eyes turned to look at him and he knew there was no way now of escaping without drawing attention to himself. He held his hands up to show the guard he was unarmed and edged out into the aisle. The guard had backed off a step or two but not completely out of reach, and certainly not for someone who could move as fast as Norsky.

'I'll ask you one more time sir, who are you?' the guard repeated in a more strident tone.

Norsky's movements became a blur. He reached forward and grabbed hold of the guard's hand resting on the pistol with one hand, while the other gripped the unsuspecting man's throat. Before anyone could react, the pistol was free of its holster and aimed between the guard's eyes with Norsky holding both it and the man's throat. Norsky released his grip on the guard's throat and used that hand to jack the slide on the pistol, a Sig P996, a standard sidearm of Col Sec troops, to prime the battery clip.

The sound of the pistol going off in the enclosed space of the shuttle was both deafening and shocking in equal parts. The guard's brains were sprayed down the aisle before he keeled over, and even before he hit the floor, Norsky had turned the weapon on every other occupant inside the shuttle, shooting each one in a similar fashion. In the space of fifteen seconds, thirteen people were dead and Norsky was stepping over the dead guard on his way to the pilot's section.

On hearing the gunfire the pilot was out of his seat and heading back into the passenger section, pistol drawn, to see what was happening. He stopped dead in his tracks when he saw the figure walking calmly towards him, a pistol at his side and the look of the devil on his face.

He brought up his pistol to shoot but before he could complete the act, Norsky had brought up his own Sig and fired. The pulsed plasma bolt caught the pilot in the centre of his chest, sending him staggering backwards into the pilot's section only to collide with the seats before sliding down the back of one, dead. His blood left a trail down the back of the seat he had recently vacated, but Norsky ignored this as he stepped around him to take the empty seat.

Casting his eyes over the controls Norsky was soon familiar with them. The engines had already been primed, a flight plan logged with Flight Control and the shuttle's Nav-Com, so all he had to do was take off.

Once off the ground, he faced another problem. This shuttle would only take him so far as it did not have FTL capability so somehow he had to find one that did. He used his NI to access the onboard computer, which was just a basic model, but it did have the capability to connect to a nearby mainframe. Soon he was scrolling through reams of data trying to find out anything pertaining to the incident that took place on Toldax, concentrating mainly on the destruction of the facility. He knew he was leaving a trail a blind man could follow both in the virtual world and the real one with the number of dead bodies he was leaving in his wake, but he was not bothered. He planned to use that to his advantage. He knew he could not do what he had to do alone so he hoped that those who would follow would help, if not he would destroy them too.

Chapter Two

Col Sec HQ was situated deep underground at Area 15 in the Nevada desert, a few miles from the city of Las Vegas. The underground facility was buried beneath hundreds of tons of rock with the highest security imaginable. It had been relocated there after an attack by the terrorist group known only as OMEGA, who had destroyed the original HQ situated on the site of the old United Nations HQ in New York. General Sinclair was head of the Intelligence Division and his office was in the deepest part of the HQ on level ten.

The office was large yet austere. A thick carpet cushioned your step as you entered and a few works of art adorned the walls.

Sitting behind his large mahogany desk he was dressed in a dark blue suit. His dark brown hair was brushed straight back from his high forehead into a widow's peak. Beneath that his deep brown eyes were unfathomable as was his normal stoic expression. He was still ramrod stiff from his years in Col Sec and, even though he was in his fifties, he was still amazingly fit.

Sitting in front of his desk were two men, both wearing

street clothes. Kurt Stryder was sitting on the left, his striking blue eyes watching the General in front of them with a laser-like intensity. He was wearing a thin, blue, cotton shirt and tan cargo pants. His favourite leatherine jacket had been destroyed back on Tartaran a few weeks earlier and he hadn't had the time, or heart, to find a replacement yet as Sinclair had kept him busy. Sitting next to him was Matt Hawk, the man who had led the rescue mission that brought Kurt back from Toldax. Since their meeting once again on Tartaran they had become firm friends. Matt was a large man, he stood almost three inches taller than Kurt at six feet six inches and had a muscular physique that stemmed from him being born and raised on a planet with a slightly greater gravity than that of Earth. Matt also had short hair cut to a military length, but his was slightly darker than Kurt's. His ice blue eyes looked at the world with a mischievous quality that was sometimes mistaken for indifference, but that couldn't be further from the truth; he cared deeply about things and threw himself into his work with an intensity that bordered upon obsession.

The two of them had been summoned to the office after Kurt had contacted Sinclair. He had told the General about the attack at the club and he had been ordered to return to Earth.

Once in his office Sinclair told them what he wanted them to do.

'You want us to go to the RandCorp HQ to check out how they're doing with the upgrades sir?' Matt asked, a little surprised.

'Isn't that a bit routine for two Intelligence officers, sir?' Kurt asked.

'Does it matter? Gentlemen, you both know the importance of the upgrades to our tec from RandCorp. After the OMEGA incident I think it must be one of our priorities in

Col Sec to get the upgrades as soon as possible and ensure they actually work,' Sinclair said in his usual monotone voice. 'That's why I want my two best men on the job; this isn't routine by any stretch of the imagination. This is our top priority now Kurt and it'll give you the chance to get back into the swing of things once more. All your tests have come back clear. There are no ill effects from your time on Tartaran and the serum does not seem to have been anything but a benefit, so I see no reason why you cannot accompany Matt on this. It'll also give you the chance to meet the Rands. I've got a feeling they're going to be working with us very closely in the future,' he added.

'I see sir, not as routine as I thought,' Kurt agreed.

'Quite. You'll take the Silver Dart; it will get you there as fast as possible. I look forward to your report when you return.'

Matt looked at Kurt and said, 'That's our cue to get going, Kurt,' and he got up to leave.

Kurt followed suit and they both left the office. The express elevator to the upper levels was not far from Sinclair's office and they were soon riding up to the surface.

'I've read your report about the OMEGA incident. Tell me more about the Rovers,' Kurt said as they exited the elevator.

'Well, as you know, the Rovers were the clones that Jonas Wilde had made to populate his army in OMEGA. There were two different types: the basic model and the Rover5s who were the soldiers. These particular clones were built with more muscle mass than your average soldier and were all on the large side. I'm six foot six, and the one I fought was at least as big as me and freakishly strong,' Matt replied. His expression changed, becoming more serious as he remembered the fight in the mall when he rescued Tanya Wilde from the Rover5.

Sensing that the recollection disturbed him, Kurt offered, 'But you came out of it okay didn't you, which proves they are not unstoppable.'

'I suppose so,' Matt said.

'What else is going on here Matt, what's really bothering you?'

Matt looked at Kurt and saw in his eyes that he could trust him. He knew he could tell him something he had kept from Sinclair. 'I couldn't save her, Tanya; ultimately she was doomed. They did it in a way that was certain to send us a message; a message that I got so clearly that it still bothers me to this day,' he said.

'What was the message?'

Matt's eyes darkened as he remembered the last time he saw Tanya Wilde. 'I had placed her in a safe house under guard. When I went to see her to tell her that her father was dead and she would be safe there was a clone waiting for me with a gun to her head. Somehow, even though we had destroyed the Nemesis and cut off the head of OMEGA, they had still infiltrated Col Sec and placed one of their clones right beside her. The bastard waited for me to arrive, he knew I was coming. When I got there he told Tanya and me that her father was very angry with her and she would be punished. Then he shot her in the head, even though he knew this would forfeit his own life; he killed her right in front of me. The message was clear – look at what we can do, look at the lengths we will go to, to fulfil our needs. How are we supposed to combat an enemy with such resolve?'

'Simple.'

Matt waited for Kurt to continue.

'With equal or greater resolve,' Kurt said.

'You make it sound so easy.'

'Isn't it?'

'What do you mean?'

'I mean that we have to do what is needed to ensure they do not succeed. My father once told me that for evil to triumph, all that is required is for good men to do nothing. It's what made me join Col Sec, and it's why I came back after Tartaran. I realised that I was just sitting back and letting others do the work. I can no longer sit back and watch and do nothing, I must get into the fight to make sure that evil will not triumph, and so must you Matt.'

'Is that what you think I'm doing, sitting back and letting others do the work?'

'I think you're in danger of allowing the message to resonate inside your head too long. If you do that then they have won. You start to second guess your own ability and decisions and then you fight below par which is exactly what they want.'

'General Sinclair said something along the same lines when I voiced my doubts at the memorial service.'

'And have you wondered at all why you haven't been on any solo missions since the OMEGA incident? The General is a very savvy man, he knows you have doubts and he won't put you back in the firing line until he's absolutely positive you are back to your best. I suspect this trip is just a warm up to see if you are okay.'

'Kurt, I'm fine, really.'

'Clearly you're not. Now I don't know you as well as the others but even I can see that something has troubled you, knocked you off your game. What you have to do is take the positives from what happened and turn it against the enemy.'

'So you don't believe that OMEGA is finished either then?'

'I believe you dealt them a wounding blow, but anyone who had planned for as long as Jonas Wilde had, I doubt they could be defeated as easily as that. I think we'll see them again and we had better be ready for them.'

Matt realised the truth in Kurt's words and smiled. For the first time since seeing Tanya Wilde killed right in front of him he felt he could go on.

'We'd better go and see the Rands then and make sure that we *are* ready,' he said.

Chapter Three

Jake Riley was walking slowly around the lake; his green eyes surveyed the scene before him. He had had time to cut his blond hair since his return from their last mission and tonight he was dressed casually in shirt, cargo pants and loafers. He had quite a bit on his mind and just being where he was helped clear his mind. It was an idyllic setting, the sun was setting and the orange hues glinted across the surface of the water. Trees rimmed the perimeter of the lake casting shadows as the sun dipped below the horizon. He stopped and looked across the water at the house that lay beneath the tree line; a grand three-storey wooden Georgian style building that was the home of Admiral Garvey and his daughter, Natasha, when they were not at work.

Jake had come to visit Natasha on her invitation so they could try to work out what they had between them, if anything. They had been lovers once, headed for marriage, but Natasha had chosen her career over their relationship. Jake had taken it badly and they had gone their separate ways. They hadn't talked in years until Jake and the rest of the Wildfire Team had been sent to Tartaran to help rescue her, Prince Aswan and Kurt Stryder. The moment they met again, all his old feelings, the emotions he had thought he buried forever came flooding back to the surface once more.

He had believed he would never see her again, then they met at Tartaran and now he was at the family home and they were talking. Where it would all end he had no idea but at least they were talking. Perhaps this was the start of a renewed relationship, he had to admit he hoped that was where it would lead, but it was early days yet. The only decision they had made so far was to talk.

Natasha was taking some time off work while an investigation was undertaken into her actions on board the *Colonial Queen*. The diversion into the Tartaran battlefield, which was a direct violation of an Interstellar Treaty, the subsequent loss of lives and the danger that her charge, Prince Aswan had been placed in were all questions that were being raised. Of course the fact that it was Prince Aswan who coerced the captain of the cruise ship into taking the diversion would be taken into consideration in the investigation, but until it was complete she could not return to work.

'There you are,' said a female voice from behind him. He was so wrapped up in his thoughts and the view in front of him that even his enhanced hearing had not picked up her approach. He turned to glance over his shoulder at her. Natasha stood looking at him, her long, dark hair hung loose around her shoulders; her full sensuous lips were parted in a smile while her dark eyes studied him trying to work out what he was thinking.

'I wondered where you went to,' she added as she walked up to stand next to him facing the lake.

'It really is beautiful here, I envy you for being able to live here,' Jake said.

'I love coming back here and I always regret having to leave but it looks like that isn't going to be much of a problem now. I think I'll be spending more time here as I can't see them lifting my suspension anytime soon,' she replied as she put an arm through his. She leant into him for comfort, an old habit she had when they were together before; it did appear that old habits die hard after all.

'You don't know that for certain,' Jake said, trying to be supportive.

'Come on Jake, you know as well as I do that they'll have to pin those deaths on someone and they sure as hell won't be going after the Prince.'

'They can't charge you with those deaths, they have the official report of the incident, it's on record by now so the most they can do is list your involvement. You did your best to prevent those deaths but it was Aswan's fault, they should charge him.'

'But they won't, you know that, he's just too powerful.'

'Well, whatever they do, it's no use worrying, there's nothing you can do now so why waste your energy.'

'I suppose you're right, you always were.'

'I'll be leaving in the morning; I've got to report back to base. Will you be okay?' Jake asked, his concern for her evident in his voice.

'I'll be fine, besides you'll come to visit the next time you get shore leave, won't you?' she said.

'If you want me to, yes. I can call you when I get back to base just to check in with you and see if you're alright,' Jake said.

'I'd like that,' she said with a smile. 'C'mon, let's go back before it starts to get chilly,' she said and they turned and walked back to the large house.

The rain was lashing against the window of the small cottage as Lieutenant Joseph Vance entered. His outer garments were soaked but he was thoroughly enjoying himself. The walk through the hills and forest of the area had been quite stimulating. Since his return to Earth from their recent mission on Tartaran he had gone through a series of debriefs the same as the others, then allowed some R and R. Being the Team's loner he had preferred to go hiking and his choice of area had always been the Forests of Canto, an E Class planet, highly populated with several huge cities, mountain ranges, deserts and a forest range at the base of the Quad, the largest mountain range on the planet. It was called the Quad simply because it was comprised of four huge mountains called, quite simply Q1 through to Q4. Q1 was the largest counting down to Q4 being the smallest where the forest range ran.

Close by, a series of cottages formed a small community, fulfilling the needs of travellers to the range. Vance had entered one of them, not to shelter from the rain, but to take a short break and grab a bite to eat. He took off the hood of his Berghaus waterproof jacket and unzipped the front as the heat from the log fire hit him the moment he entered.

The interior of the small cottage was rustic with a wooden floor and walls made from logs sourced from the local forest. There was a bar at the far end of the long room where an elderly lady stood serving drinks and taking orders for food from those who chose to visit.

A group of men stood at the bar drinking and they all turned when the newcomer entered.

A sixth sense born of his years in the military forged by combat told him something was not quite right here.

'What do you want here?' asked the largest of the group.

'I was thinking, if it was possible, a nice hot meal,' Vance said with a smile.

'Don't think so buddy,' another member of the group said.

Vance's expression altered from his normal smiling, easy-going face to a stern expression. His deep brown eyes looked at each of the three men in turn. They were large, burly types with weathered faces typical of those who were exposed to the elements; their hands had the calluses of manual workers too. Vance's training told him that these guys would not back down from trouble and could handle themselves in a fight.

Standing at six feet two he was athletically built with a lean hard frame but the serum he had been administered boosted all his physical abilities and some mental ones too, something he was still learning to master. He was confident he could handle these guys but he would have to be careful not to give too much away about what he could do and also not hurt them too much.

'Really, are we really going to do this?' Vance said. 'Tell you what; scrap the hot meal then, how about a nice bowl of hot soup? We can do soup surely?' he added with a smile.

'Nope, you're gonna have to leave,' the third one told him. All three of them leant their backs against the bar and faced him. They were a little surprised with what he did next.

'Okay, I'll settle for a sandwich,' Vance said as he walked towards them.

'What're you doin'?' the largest of the trio asked as he pushed himself off the bar to meet Vance.

'Getting a drink while I wait for my food,' Vance replied. It bothered the three men that he didn't seem intimidated by them. It was something they clearly were not used to.

'What the fuck is wrong with you?' the big man said as he reared up to his full height. Vance stood at around six feet two but this guy was at least three inches taller and had broad shoulders and thickly muscled arms.

'I have been told I'm not a good listener but I think it's a misconception. Of course I listen, I've heard everything you've said,' Vance said with a straight face.

'Are you crazy, if you don't leave here you'll get your ass kicked,' snarled the man in front of Vance.

'Sorry, what did you say?' Vance said with a confused smile.

The large man stepped forward and placed a hand against Vance's chest.

Vance's movements became a blur as he went into action. His senses went into overdrive as the serum he had been administered boosted his output. He grabbed the hand over the top and twisted it off his chest forcing it against the joint. He lashed out with his right foot and kicked the second guy in the centre of his chest, smashing him back against the bar. He followed it up with a roundhouse kick with the same leg to smash it against the third guy who took it on the side of his face and ended up staggering off towards the wall. Vance still had hold of the largest man's wrist. His grip tightened and the thug could not move. A growl escaped from behind his bared teeth as he tried and failed to bring his arm back around in front of him.

Vance simply pushed the arm down then leaned in close to speak into the guy's ear.

'Easy buddy, you'll hurt yourself,' he said softly, followed by, '… and we wouldn't want that now would we?'

The thug ceased struggling when he realised he was incapable of escape.

Vance looked up at the bartender and said, 'Sorry for all the trouble.'

'No trouble at all son, it's about time those thugs were taught a lesson. They've been causing trouble round here for the past few weeks now,' she said in a throaty voice, smiling for the first time since Vance entered the room.

'Really, who are they?'

'Just a bunch of campers who are on vacation; a bunch of bully boys who like to throw their weight around.'

'I don't think you'll have to worry about them any more,' Vance replied, then leaning into the thug once more said, 'They're not going to be bothered by you again.' To emphasise his point he twisted the wrist sending pain shooting up the thug's arm causing him to shake his head vigorously.

Vance allowed the man to get to his feet once more. He looked at the thug's pained expression and smiled as he said, 'Now go and don't come back.' His expression changed from one of friendly charm to that of stern determination.

The bully wilted under Vance's gaze. He hung his head and then gestured to his friends to leave with him.

'Now then, how about that sandwich?' Vance said as he watched the door close behind the trio of bullies.

'I think you deserve more than a sandwich my boy, and it's on the house,' the bar lady replied with a smile. She placed a drink on the bar for him and with a wink of her eye disappeared to fetch the food.

Chapter Four

Lieutenant Angelina Torres stood outside the front door of the modest house trying to get her breathing under control.

The house was a white brick building with a red pantile roof; it had four bedrooms, two bathrooms, two lounges and a kitchen/dining room within its three floors. It was the house she had been born in, grew up in and where her parents still lived.

Every time she returned home to visit she remembered what it was like to live in that house, to grow up there, and it brought back all the uneasy feelings once again.

Wiping her moist palms on the legs of her pants she rang the bell by the front door and took a step back. It was always the same, after she rang the bell she toyed with the idea of just walking away and not bothering to go through with this, but she never did and always regretted it.

'Hi Mom,' she said as the door opened and a frail old woman stood in the doorway. At five feet two inches tall she was six inches shorter than her daughter. Age had taken all the vitality of youth from this woman and she was so wrinkled it was as if her skin had been left out in the sun to dry out. Her body looked so dried out and withered that the floral print dress she was wearing hung off her like a sack.

'Gina, didn't expect you today. You been fired?' asked her mother.

'No, I've not been fired, Mom.'

'Then what you doing here?'

'I'm on leave so I thought I'd come visit, see how the two of you are.'

'Why the hell would you want to do that?'

'Beats the hell out of me! How's he been?' Angelina said, gearing herself up for what was to come.

'About the same; he spends a lot of time out back in the garage tinkering with his tools,' her mother told her.

Angelina walked past her mother into the hallway and into the lounge connected to it. Inside she saw a room steeped in memories from all the years the family had lived there. Photographs adorned the walls and sideboards side by side with bric-a-brac from the years of living in the same house; a life that Angelina had desperately tried to distance herself from and yet was ultimately tied to.

She walked through to the kitchen where a dining table was placed in the centre of the floor with four chairs arranged around it. A sink was over to the left with work surfaces to the left and right of it. A washer/dryer was placed under the work surface to the right of the sink with a tall fridge freezer against the opposite wall.

Angelina walked to the door that led to the garage and placed her hand against the opening control pad. With a deep breath she entered the code and waited while the door opened.

The garage was made of the same building material as the house and was attached to the side with a large sliding door at the front being the main entrance and large enough to drive the family car through. Another door led from the kitchen, which was where she now stood ready to face her father.

'Hi Dad,' she said as she entered. The garage was long, running the entire length of the house and at least eighteen feet wide with a workbench that ran around both sides and met at the far end opposite the main entrance. It had tools arranged on hangers on the wall with storage boxes under the bench holding a variety of other bits and pieces.

A man stood at the far end of the obsessively tidy room. He was around five feet eleven inches tall with a slim, wiry frame that had cord-like muscles running up and down it from years of working with his hands. He wore a dark blue chequered shirt with the sleeves rolled up to his elbows and a pair of baggy corduroy pants that looked two sizes too big for his wiry frame.

At the sound of his daughter's voice he turned his head to look at her. She was wearing her off duty civilian clothes, a loose fitting top in blue cotton and tan pants with walking shoes. It was an outfit she had chosen to accompany the tomboy image her parents had of her.

'Hi Gina,' he replied then returned his attention to what he was working on.

'How have you been?' she asked as she tentatively moved forwards closer to her father. Their relationship had never been an easy one; her father had never made it easy for her to feel accepted for what or who she was. For most of her formative years her nickname had been 'Slugger' and she had been treated like one of the boys, her two brothers. This was part of the reason why she grew up as somewhat of a tomboy and influenced her choice to join the military.

'I've been good. How about you? Been to any new bases recently?' he asked and carried on working, not bothering to look at her.

She felt the usual pain lance through her at the rebuke.

All she had ever wanted was to make her Dad proud of her, but all she ever got from him, no matter what she did, was a lukewarm acknowledgement of her being in the military. In part it was her own fault, because she was not allowed to tell anyone outside of Col Sec exactly what she did. Now that she was part of General Sinclair's new Wildfire Programme it made it even harder to tell them anything, so what she had told them was that she was involved in on-base security. This made for even more problems for her as her father gave her derision at every opportunity about not being a proper soldier and never leaving the base.

'No, Dad, just the usual stuff,' she said, her voice almost catching. She longed to be able to tell him what she actually did; let him and her mother know of all her accomplishments since joining Col Sec. The last mission to Tartaran with her teammates, the Wildfire Team, would have made them sit up and take notice. It would finally give her the respect she desperately wanted from them; it would make them proud of her just like she had always wanted but she had to bite back what she really wanted to say. Instead, she did what she always did and swallowed the hurt and said nothing.

'You know what gets me is why? If you're on the damn base all the damn time why can't you come round more often?' he said, turning to look her in the eye, something she had not expected.

She stopped in her tracks, caught in his stare like a small rabbit in the headlights of a car.

'I have duties Dad, you know that and I can't just leave whenever I want.'

'Why not? It's not like you're a real soldier, you're just a jumped up MP.'

'And there it is, the usual crap I get when I come here. And you wonder why I don't come round more often. That's exactly why I stay away,' she shouted walking forwards to confront him as her anger flared.

'You stay away?' her father asked, a little confused. He was incapable of seeing what he had done, because no one had ever picked him up on his treatment of his daughter, he could see no wrong in it.

'What do you think Dad?'

'I… I don't understand. Why would you stay away, we're family, your family?' he said, backing up a little.

'Are you serious?' she pressed.

'What do you mean?' he asked as confusion contorted his features.

'You really have no idea do you?' she said standing before him with her hands placed firmly on her slim hips.

'I don't know what you're talkin' about Gina,' he added not wanting to see the truth.

'Ever since I can remember you've treated me like I'm nothing, like I didn't measure up to your expectations and d'you know what? I'm sick of it. I don't care if I don't measure up, I like my job and I like who I am and what's more I won't change any of it for anyone, especially you,' she shouted. She turned and walked away leaving her father stunned by her outburst. All he could do was watch her leave.

Angelina stormed past her mother and headed straight for the front door. Her mother watched her leave and said nothing although she had been within hearing distance and a wry smile crossed her lips as the door closed behind her daughter.

'It's about time too,' she muttered to herself.

Kurt and Matt arrived at the RandCorp HQ in Washington DC and were shown immediately to the penthouse suite of offices that Able Rand used to control the huge corporation.

As usual they were allowed to keep their weapons on them being officers of Col Sec. They had passed through the security scans when they walked through the reception and been identified. The RandCorp HQ had no need for security personnel to be on hand in great numbers, the scanners monitored everyone as they entered and ran through a series of detailed identifying scans from full bio scans which included fingerprint and retina and even DNA scans. In this way they did not need facial recognition software as it was possible to change someone's appearance too easily.

As they reached the top of the huge building they were greeted by the sight of two men standing over by the large picture window that gave the building its grand view of the sprawling cityscape. They turned to face them as they entered and the family resemblance was immediate.

'Come in gentlemen, I hope your journey wasn't too tiring,' said the older of the two men. Able Rand was tall and slim and exuded a raw undefined power. His white hair was brushed straight back from a high forehead over piercing brown eyes. His bright and easy smile showed his genuine pleasure at seeing them. His unblemished, smooth complexion belied his true age of sixty-three. He had run RandCorp for the past thirty odd years, taking over from his father just as his grandfather had many decades before. It was truly a family business being passed down from one generation to the next since its inception over five centuries ago.

'It was fine thanks,' replied Matt. He had been here once before just after the OMEGA incident when they investigated the viability of RandCorp being the much needed replacement to MaxCorp in supplying Col Sec's tec and munitions.

'You must be Kurt Stryder,' Able said as the two men came across the room to greet them. 'Allow me to introduce my son, Josh,' Able said, indicating the young man at his side.

Josh was as tall as his father at six three but had a bit more muscle. His turquoise eyes shined brightly from a deeply tanned face framed by tousled light brown hair that had been bleached by the sun and reached almost to his broad shoulders. His goatee, along with the shoulder length hair gave him the appearance of a modern day pirate.

'Pleased to meet you both,' Josh said with an easy smile that mirrored his father's. He extended his hand to shake Matt and Kurt's.

'Josh is in charge of Special Operations which covers a vast array of subjects. Mostly he concentrates on research projects we develop, not only for the private sector but for Col Sec too. His speciality though is the security of these projects for which he has the help of our head of security, Mitch Ryan,' said Able.

'Gentlemen, I'm at your disposal,' Josh said.

'We've been ordered to come and see how the upgrades are coming along,' Matt said.

A look was exchanged between father and son which Josh gave voice to by asking, 'Isn't that something that could've been handled with a call over a secure channel?'

'General Sinclair was a tad concerned so he sent us along to reaffirm his confidence in RandCorp and it was an opportunity for Kurt to meet you too,' Matt replied.

'Concerned about what exactly?' Able asked, becoming disturbed that this visit was not what he had expected it to be.

'I would think they are concerned that we may still have a mole inside the firm, Dad,' Josh said, looking at his father then returning his gaze to Matt and Kurt, adding, 'Am I right?'

'Not so much, no, but we are concerned that the threat of OMEGA isn't over just yet,' Matt said in a non-committal tone.

'What's the basis of your fears gentlemen?' Able wanted to know.

'There's been an incident; that's all I'm at liberty to tell you,' Matt said.

'Look, if you want our total co-operation you have to trust us. I'm not asking for anything that would breach your security, but you have to give us more than that,' Josh said.

'I was attacked by three clones, Rover5s, whilst another watched and assessed,' Kurt said, blurting it out before Matt could stop him.

'From what I've learned of the Rover5s they were bred for battle. You don't appear any worse for wear!' Josh said his eyes going wide with surprise and a little suspicion.

Matt looked at Kurt in anger and Kurt said, 'What? If you want them to work with us, and I do mean *with* us and not *for* us then they have to know something of what we're up against. We have to trust them sometime Matt, it may as well be now.'

'I suppose you're right,' Matt replied, then to the others said, 'Whatever is said in this office must remain Top Secret.'

'Going back to my previous question, you were attacked by three battle bred clones and came away without so much as a scratch?' Josh asked.

'Just lucky I guess,' Kurt replied, which garnered a glance from Matt that said 'see what you get when you reveal too much.'

'Why do I not believe you?' Josh asked.

'Look that's not important at this time, what is important is that we think OMEGA is still active and is planning something so we need those upgrades and we need them now,' Matt said, cutting through the argument.

'The upgrades are ready to be uploaded to the Col Sec mainframe. In turn they will be downloaded to your NIs. The new software will overwrite the existing software and you'll be good to go,' Josh said.

'Sounds good to me,' Kurt said.

Matt accessed a secure comm. channel via his NI and called General Sinclair. 'Sir the upgrades are ready to be uploaded to the mainframe,' he said.

'Okay commence when ready,' Sinclair replied.

'The General says to commence when ready,' Matt replied.

Able said, 'Okay then, but we can't do it from here, we'll have to go to your new base.'

'New base, what new base?' Kurt asked as he looked from Able to Josh and finally to Matt who wore a broad smile.

'Oh you're gonna love this,' Matt said.

Chapter Five

Zara Hardy was pacing around her cell. It was an austere, simple cell with nothing more than a bed as furniture. She had been transferred from the ship she had been on in orbit around Toldax to this present starship. She had an idea where they were taking her but her exact whereabouts were still a mystery to her.

She had been getting used to her new abilities although they were also a mystery to her and the fact that she was even alive was the biggest mystery of all. She could remember getting shot and dying, but if that was true then how was she still alive and what had happened to the hours in between her dying and waking up on the starship that she had no memory of?

Through the hours of questioning and testing she had endured at the hands of her captors, it had given her time to postulate a theory of what had happened to her.

She knew what Kurt Strycer was capable of and had seen him regenerate in front of her own eyes. The Alliance had tried to assimilate his ability by reproducing a serum similar to the one administered to him by using his blood. What she thought had happened was, when Kurt had covered her body to protect her from a fireball during their escape from the facility, they had become trapped on Toldax. She had a few cuts and scrapes on her body from some of the fighting they had endured during their escape attempt and some of Kurt's blood must have mingled with hers when he tried to protect her from the flames. The trauma of the gunshot must have activated the regenerative effect of Kurt's blood when it mixed with hers. It had taken longer for the effect to fully regenerate her than it did with Kurt, but nevertheless it had worked and for that she was grateful. She did not know just how powerful she was but she was getting some idea.

What troubled her at that moment though was something she had overheard in a conversation between some of her captors. They were planning an attack on Col Sec but before that they were planning on capturing Kurt Stryder.

She had to escape somehow and warn them of what was intended but she had to find the right opportunity.

She did have one advantage and one which she would have to use. They had kept her with them for a purpose; they obviously had a use for her and that meant they wanted her alive. That was good because when she made her move to escape they would hesitate in using deadly force against her. Her new abilities would help her in her attempt to break free and it would be a good chance for her to test them. She did not have to wait much longer.

The door to her cell opened and a guard walked in holding a pistol aimed straight at her. She recognised the weapon as a Sig P996, the standard sidearm of Recon Delta Marines of which she was one.

'This way,' said the guard as he motioned for her to exit the small cell in front of him with his pistol.

She slowly walked past him staring him fully in the eye; she stood at five feet ten so she was almost as tall as the guard. She had an athletic figure with a full bosom and her full sensuous lips parted in a wry smile as the guard quickly glanced down to snatch a glimpse of her cleavage. She had been given a one-piece coverall suit to wear with an elasticised waist which showed off her trim waist to good effect, added to which she had undone the top three buttons to show what the guard could not tear his eyes from. That was something she knew she could use later when the time was right.

'Where're you taking me now?' she asked, her voice low and sultry.

'I'm not allowed to say,' the guard replied, swallowing hard as he dragged his eyes away from her cleavage.

'So you know where but you can't say, is that it?' she probed.

'Come on they're waiting,' said the guard, steeling himself against her deep brown eyes which he found strangely hypnotic; not in the truest sense but she was extremely attractive and if he wasn't careful he knew he could fall under her spell.

She exited her cell and walked into the austere corridor. The ship she was on was very basic in design, nothing in the way of decoration so when she walked down the corridor she saw nothing. There was a hatch on the right as she approached the place where the guard ordered her to halt.

The hatch opened and another guard stood in the doorway aiming another Sig P996 at her. He beckoned her forward through the hatchway and into a docking tube, which led into another smaller craft.

She was shown to a seat against the starboard hull where she sat. She never took her eyes off the new guard but her peripheral vision, because her sight had been enhanced, picked up more detail about the small shuttle than any normal eyes could. There was a row of four seats on the starboard side and the same against the port side. Behind her stood another guard who took over from the one who had ushered her to her seat and had now left them and gone forward into the pilot's cabin.

She appeared to be quite relaxed but in fact she was coiled like a powerful spring ready to be released. The guard behind her sat in a seat on the port side so he had a good view of her.

She felt the docking clamps disengage and the shuttle pulled away from the other ship.

Now was the time to make her move.

She turned to face the guard behind her and caught his eye. She bent forward, twisting in her seat to expose more of her cleavage, and smiled as his eyes followed the curve of her neck down into the creek between her breasts.

Before the guard knew what was happening she was out of her seat and rushing towards him. He just had time to look into her face before she struck him with a straight right to the point of his jaw. His head hit the back of the seat as his senses left him and he slumped down in his seat.

'Sleep tight,' she said with a smile as she relieved him of his pistol.

The pilot's cabin was just a few paces away and she covered the distance in less than a second.

The door opened to her touch and the first guard spun around to see who it was. He was standing behind the two pilots seated at the front of the shuttle getting ready to sit down in the third chair. His eyes went wide as her.

Zara put the muzzle of the Sig to his forehead and pulled the trigger. The pulsed plasma bolt blasted the man's head apart spraying a red stream over the backs of the heads of the two pilots.

The man in the right chair turned just in time to see her step over the fallen guard and just before she shot him too.

Zara pulled the dead pilot from the chair and tossed him over the backrest then sat down. The other pilot stared at her, his eyes wide with fear.

She extended her arm towards him aiming the Sig at his face. The pilot mouthed a silent prayer just before the gun went off blowing his head apart. The window at the side of him was painted with his blood before he slumped in his seat, dead.

Zara quickly took control of the shuttle, disengaged the automatic course control and took over the manual control. She turned the shuttle away from the course that had been plotted and went to full burn on the thrusters to get as far away from her captors as she could.

As she checked out the nav-com her eyes stared with surprise. There was a planet close by, well within the range of the shuttle, and it was a planet that she instantly recognised.

It was Celeron – the home of Kurt Stryder.

On the starship Zara had just escaped from, the Rover5 was on the bridge waiting for news of Zara Hardy's departure. He was a clone like all the others on board, but not quite the same. Jonas Wilde had wanted a hierarchy within his warrior clones so he had a few engineered with command protocols built inside. He and his three brothers were part of the first batch and his name was Orion.

A guard came onto the bridge and stood behind him.

'Did she get away as planned?' he asked without turning around.

'Yes sir, she's on her way to Celeron as we speak,' replied the guard.

'Was the sub dermal tracker planted as I wanted?'

'It was sir,' the guard replied.

'Good, we'll be able to keep an eye on her no matter where she goes. Inform our assets on the planet that she's on her way to them,' he said.

'Copy that.'

'I'll inform OMEGA Command of our status,' he said and he turned to leave the bridge. 'I'll be in my quarters, inform me of any new developments,' he added before leaving.

Chapter Six

Jake Riley and Natasha Garvey approached her family home from around the lake. They entered the three-storey building through the large ornate wooden front door and immediately heard voices coming from the study to the left of the hallway. A large wooden staircase spiralled upwards to the upper two floors from the open hallway. The study door was slightly ajar allowing the sound of voices to travel out to them.

'You do realise that if the Alliance gains control of the research it could prove disastrous to the Confederation,' said a stranger's voice.

'There's not a lot I can do, I'm out of the loop since I retired,' replied Admiral Garvey.

'Retired, since when?' asked the stranger.

'Since I returned from Tartaran. I've had enough of this whole thing Miles. Too many lives have been lost due to this and this last sortie almost cost me my daughter. I won't allow that to happen again,' Garvey said.

Natasha pushed open the door without knocking. Her father was standing facing another man of similar age and they were deep in conversation, which was suspended the moment they noticed they were being watched.

'Hi Dad, aren't you going to introduce us?' she said, sensing the tension between the two men.

The stranger turned to look at her and his slate grey eyes showed his anger. He was around five feet eleven tall and had white hair and a stern expression on his aquiline features. He looked about ready to leave when Garvey said, 'This is Doctor Miles Baxter and he's just leaving.'

'Baxter, why do I know that name?' Jake said.

'What's going on here, Dad?' Natasha asked, concern written all over her lovely face.

'You probably know his son better, Jonas Baxter, he was the one responsible for the serum you were given; you and Captain Kurt Stryder,' Admiral Garvey said, turning to look at his visitor.

'What's going on here, sir?' Jake asked, his concern level escalating at the mention of the word Tartaran. He still had bad memories of their time on that planet's surface, bad memories that bordered upon nightmares.

'Miles here is concerned about the Alliance taking control of Tartaran,' Garvey said.

'Why exactly?' Jake asked, suspecting the worst but needing it put into words.

'Be careful what you say here, you know this is classified,' Miles Baxter said, stopping Garvey in his tracks. The latter turned to him and gave him a look of frustration.

'Jake Riley is the leader of the Wildfire Team and has one of the highest clearances in Col Sec, besides he and his team were responsible for rescuing my daughter. They were just on the planet so they have a right to know what this is all about, don't you think?' he said angrily.

'No I don't, but it seems that I won't be able to stop you

so it's on your head,' Miles Baxter said throwing his hands up in frustration.

'Will someone please tell me what you are talking about? What is it about Tartaran that Doctor Baxter here thinks we shouldn't know about?' Jake said.

Garvey paused, then said, 'Fifty odd years ago the Confederation and Alliance fought a war over the planet Tartaran. We sent several scientists down to the planet's surface to observe the indigenous life forms by setting up an Observation Post. We followed what we took to be a herd of creatures but we quickly learned they were a family unit. We also learned from an autopsy on one of them that they were creatures of experimentation – transgenics – but from experiments that took place over thousands of years ago. Whatever had changed them had taken place centuries before, and whoever had carried out those experiments had long since passed away or possibly been killed by their own experiments.'

'How does that tie in with what's going on today?' Jake asked.

'The serum that was developed and administered to Kurt Stryder and then refined before being administered to you, came directly from research gained from the autopsy of the creature from Tartaran,' Garvey said.

Jake said, 'I see why you're worried about the Alliance gaining control of the planet but you needn't worry too much. I was down there and believe me it's the closest thing to Hell that I ever want to get to, so I can't see the Alliance getting anything but a world of hurt from anything down on that surface.'

'I hope you're right young man, I seriously do,' Miles Baxter said.

'I think he's right. I was on the original landing party to set up the OP and the creatures overran us once they'd finished observing us. They allowed us to think we'd gone unobserved but they knew we were there all along. It was uncanny how they did that. I've never seen such naked aggression before and I hope I never will again, it was terrifying,' said Garvey.

'I know what Doctor Baxter means though,' said Jake, 'but I'm sure General Sinclair is taking steps to prevent this from happening,' he added.

'That could be difficult; the last I heard was that you were kicked back home with your tails between your legs from Tartaran by the Alliance who now have a super destroyer on the station there. Unless he's planning on a full scale assault of the planet, I can't see you retaking control anytime soon which gives the Alliance all the time they need to capture a creature of their own and complete the same research as us,' Miles Baxter said, his voice rising in anger.

Jake looked at him and was about to say something then thought better of it. Instead, after a quick glance at both Admiral Garvey then Natasha, he said, 'I'd better get back to base.'

The planet Tartaran was an E-Class world. For at least the past half century it had been considered a Forbidden World due to the story surrounding the battle that took place over the control of it. It was a story that had recently been repudiated by reports of renewed conflict there between the Confederation and the Alliance. The latest news painted the Alliance in a not so flattering light. A statement had been issued by General Sinclair reporting of acts of murder by a group of outcasts known as Outlaws who had taken up residence in orbit above the planet and who had perpetrated upon innocents wandering too close. A group who were in fact, Special Forces of the Alliance, a Black Ops team seconded from the Black Knights, the Alliance's equivalent of the Confederation's Recon Delta.

All these new revelations about the part the Alliance played in the development of the legend of Tartaran did nothing to alter the fact that they were in control of the planet and the surrounding space; a fact that the Confederation could do nothing about but were determined to change in the forthcoming weeks.

General Lokar Tillic stood on the bridge of the super destroyer Cronus which was a variation of the Nemesis design, the starship OMEGA, which used to attack Col Sec HQ not too long ago. His hands were behind his back as he stared at the forward viewscreen; the image displayed there was of the planet below, Tartaran.

'Send down the shuttle, I want covering fire from attack craft that will follow them to the surface. Once there, I want the troops to create a perimeter and maintain it until the survey team have done their job,' he said.

'Copy that, sir,' replied the Captain of the super destroyer, Arvin Dancovic, a ten-year veteran of the Alliance fleet.

The command was given and the craft left the docking bays and headed for the surface of Tartaran.

The shuttle carrying the troops and the scientists was flanked by six attack craft to control interference against any winged creatures that patrolled the skies.

Like all the creatures on Tartaran, they had tremendous strength and a rapacious appetite for destruction, fuelled by an aggression against any interlopers to their domain and something that was terrifying to witness.

As the shuttle entered the atmosphere a flock of the winged creatures came from the treetops of a huge forest to intercept it. They had massive wingspans of over twenty feet each with huge taloned feet. Their heads were sleek and tapered to the front where a wicked huge maw opened filled with razor sharp teeth. The wings and plumage were layers of multi-coloured feathers whilst the body and underbelly of the creature were covered with lizard-like skin. It was a weird mix and yet strangely beautiful.

The attack craft formed a perimeter of protection around the shuttle hoping to fend off the creatures. Pulse cannons fired, blasting a path through the flock for the shuttle to reach the ground.

The creatures were in their natural habitat – the air – and they swooped, twisted and turned to evade the pulsed plasma bolts from the pulse cannons at the same time as attacking the invaders to their domain. At first the attack craft gained the upper hand and blasted a few of the creatures out of the sky, blood, feathers and gore spraying around the sky as they fell. Then the creatures began to anticipate the tactics of the attack craft and the fight became a bit more even.

Within moments the small group of attack craft lost three of their number to creatures that either simply ripped their wings off or moved out of the way causing another of their number to fire on one of their own.

The attack craft kept firing on the attacking creatures but before they knew what was happening another of their number had been torn apart and hurled away, the crew inside screaming as they fell from the small craft to their deaths.

The shuttle increased its speed as the pilot knew their protection was being ripped apart right before their eyes. They had to get to the ground and fast, or they too would suffer the same fate as the attack craft. All those inside the shuttle gripped their seats as the pilot threw the craft into a series of loops, twists and turns trying to evade the winged creatures hunting them. Several of the scientists threw up as the shuttle became a vomit rocket plummeting towards the ground.

Finally, just when they thought they would not make it, the pilot fired the landing thrusters and brought the shuttle in for a controlled landing. The scientists all gave a collective sigh of relief, garnering a few looks of disdain from the accompanying soldiers.

Once the shuttle was on the ground the soldiers exited with weapons drawn to provide the guarded perimeter the scientists needed before they could even begin to start work. The final two attack craft circled overhead to give covering fire against the winged denizens of Tartaran's skies.

The leader of the soldiers stood by the hatch of the shuttle and beckoned the scientists to come out.

'Right, you need to work fast, the clock is ticking,' he said.

Chapter Seven

Able and Josh Rand along with Matt Hawk and Kurt Stryder had taken the express elevator down to the sub basement where they exited into a long corridor.

'What's down here and how can this be a new Col Sec base?' Kurt asked, perplexed at the different direction they had been taken.

'It's not far now Kurt, everything will become clear to you when you see it,' Matt replied.

A glance passed between Able and his son Josh that did not go unnoticed by Kurt. He couldn't help but wonder what was going on down here.

'Yes, not far now,' agreed Able with a smile. He remembered General Sinclair's reaction to seeing what Kurt was about to see and was quite looking forward to it. It gave him satisfaction in knowing his work would be appreciated.

They soon reached the huge doors to the Gateway Project where the two Rand men halted. Matt looked at Kurt who was staring at the huge metal doors, wondering what could possibly be behind them when Able spoke.

'We're here,' he said.

Josh activated the door release via his NI, a secure connection only those with access to the project were allowed to have.

The huge doors began to slowly slide apart with a deep rumbling sound, denoting their weight. Each door was made of compressed ferrite, an alloy that most starships were made from. It was the hardest metal alloy known with incredible tensile strength but with the added advantage of being incredibly light.

'Welcome to the Gateway Project,' Able Rand said as he ushered Kurt inside the huge chamber.

Kurt walked inside and marvelled at the size of the chamber, all the machinery and the actual Gateway at the far end.

'What is this place?' Kurt asked a little breathless at the sight before him.

'The Gateway is like a small hyperspace window controlled by that orifice over there which is connected to an identical orifice inside our lunar base. It's still an experimental technology and one we're all keen to develop further,' Able explained with great pride.

'Can you imagine the potential; picture one of these Gateways in every base on every planet in the Confederation. You could transport instantly between them cutting out the need for starship travel,' Josh said excited by the prospect of their vision.

'The potential is fantastic I grant you that, but the dangers are also massive should an enemy get hold of this and develop it too,' Kurt said, bringing the mood down somewhat.

'That's as may be but we're here today to show you what it can do. Its security will be in your hands soon,' Able said as he walked forward towards the Gateway.

'What do you mean by "soon"?' Kurt asked.

'General Sinclair has delayed the handover until you are

ready to accept it fully. I think there has been a staffing difficulty,' Josh said trying to explain.

'You can ask him yourself when you report back to him
after we're done here,' Able said. He turned to the Gateway
and said to one of the technicians working nearby, 'Activate
the Gateway please, we're going to the Lunar Base.'

Zara landed the shuttle at the nearest available landing area
which was the Jacksonville Space port. Having no money or
any other means to pay for anything she looked around the
parking lot for a vehicle of any description she could use
temporarily until she was back on the grid. She hoped the
tracking chip in her NI was still active but because she
presumed she had been reported K.I.A. there would be no
need for Col Sec to look for her. They may have even taken
her off the grid completely and disconnected her chip and
her NI altogether.

While she was searching for a suitable vehicle she
pondered her next move. She came across a bike, a Yamaha
780cv, a relatively small machine but, if she could get it
started, perfect for her needs.

She tried her NI to see if she could access it. The familiar
tingle told her all she needed to know. She accessed the
onboard computer of the Yamaha and overrode the locking
codes to the engine; within seconds the engine was purring
nicely.

She threw a leg over to sit on the bike and twisted the
throttle control whilst engaging the gears. Selecting first gear,
she released the clutch and rode it off the parking lot heading
into the city.

Whilst she navigated through the streets she accessed a
com channel and called Col Sec HQ on Earth. The second

her call was connected her tracking chip was identified and, because of the nature of her so-called demise, the call was diverted straight through to General Sinclair via a secure channel.

As she drove through the streets of Jacksonville she heard a familiar voice through her com channel.

'Zara my dear, what a pleasant surprise, we were told you were killed. What the hell happened?' Sinclair said.

'That can wait sir, I have some news you may want to hear regarding an impending attack on Col Sec by something called OMEGA,' she replied quickly, pleased to hear the General's voice once more.

'OMEGA, are you sure?' he asked, his voice suddenly becoming professional.

'I'm positive sir. I heard two of the men talking about OMEGA. Strange men, could've been brothers, twins even, they were so alike.'

'Well, that is not good. Where are you right now? We need to get you back in as soon as possible,' Sinclair said, very concerned now.

'I'm on Celeron sir; I'm on my way to someone I hope can be considered a friend, Abraham Bane. Sir, how's Kurt?' she asked, her voice getting softer. She knew her death must have hit him hard and she needed to know if he was okay.

'Your death hit him harder than he would like to admit. He left for a short while but he's back now. Do you want me to let him know?'

'If you could please. If possible sir, if his duties allow, could you allow him to be the one to bring me in, if he wants to that is?'

'Once I tell him you're alive I doubt anything could stop him coming to you my dear. I take it he knows this Bane character otherwise you wouldn't be going there. I'll get in touch with him right away and you stick tight and he'll come to you as soon as he can.'

'Thank you, sir. As soon as I get to Bane's I'll send a report to you directly via a burst transmission through my NI,' she said, then closed the call to concentrate on her journey through the streets of the city. Her spirits had been raised upon hearing what the General had said about how Kurt felt about her. She just hoped he still had strong enough feelings to come and help her for she had a feeling she was going to need his help very soon.

Chapter Eight

The Gateway orifice opened and the energy it created lit the entire chamber up like a firework display.

'The sensation is quite unusual the first time you go through but you soon get used to it though,' Able said as they all watched the miniature wormhole form before them.

A familiar tingle alerted Kurt that a call was coming through to him.

'Hold on guys,' he said as his NI connected the call.

'Kurt I've got some important news for you. There's no easy way to say this so I'm just going to come out with it. Zara Hardy is alive,' Sinclair said.

Kurt was taken aback. Could it be true? Could she be alive and if so, how was it possible? The only way she could've survived the gunshot and subsequent destruction of the facility on Toldax, was if she somehow had the same ability as he did. But how did she acquire it? What should he say? Does Sinclair know about his ability? If his supposition was correct and had any validity at all, did Sinclair suspect or had she told Sinclair how she had survived?

'How is that possible sir, did she tell you?' Kurt said, deciding to play it safe.

'She didn't say, the important thing is she is safe but she also said that OMEGA is planning an attack on Col Sec. She'll tell you all about it when you bring her in.'

'Where is she sir?'

'Celeron, she's on her way to meet Bane, she said you'd know where that was.'

'I know sir. Do you want me to go now?'

'Yes, Matt can handle the Rands on his own. You get over to Celeron as fast as you can and find out what Zara knows about OMEGA,' Sinclair said.

'Copy that sir.'

'Keep me informed on your progress as soon as you reach her,' Sinclair said before closing the call off so that Kurt could get on with it.

'Gonna have to cut this short guys, I'm needed on Celeron. Will you be okay to handle this on your own Matt?' Kurt asked.

'Of course Kurt, what's wrong, is there anything I can do?' Matt said.

'No I'm fine but I've got to go, I've just heard that an old friend has turned up. I have to go to her, there's some OMEGA involvement,' Kurt said.

At the mention of OMEGA, Matt's expression became serious. 'OMEGA, will you need back up?' he asked.

'You finish off here and I'll go on to Celeron then if Sinclair okays it, you can rendezvous with us there,' Kurt said.

'You'd better take the Silver Dart and I'll send for another starship,' Matt said.

Kurt turned around and left the room heading for the express elevator once more.

Jake Riley arrived at Col Sec HQ and went straight to see General Sinclair.

'Jake, how was your trip to the Garveys?' Sinclair asked when he saw him enter his office.

'Quite informative sir, I met Doctor Baxter's father. He was quite forthcoming about the research that led to the serum we were given. He was positive that we are heading for trouble with the Alliance if we don't retake Tartaran,' Jake said.

'He's quite right and I'm working on something to that end but for now I must ask you not to worry about it, we have much more pressing matters to attend to.'

'Such as?' Jake asked wondering what possibly could be more pressing than the Tartaran situation.

'I've sent Kurt to pick up one of our own and I want you and the rest of the Team to follow immediately as back up. There's an OMEGA connection here. The person Kurt will be meeting has just escaped from an OMEGA ship. I'll upload all the relevant data to the Pulsar and you can all access it once on board. I want you to assemble the Team straight away and leave for Celeron.' Sinclair said and his business-like tone told Jake that this was indeed very serious.

'I'm on it sir,' he said and turned and left the office, already accessing his NI to make the call to assemble the Wildfire Team.

The final member of the Wildfire Team, Lieutenant Mack Cooper, was sitting on the beach at Pallisto, an E Class planet that was renowned for its sandy beach resorts. Situated fifty-nine light years from the Solar System it was within a simple one-jump journey from Earth and considered the vacation planet of the Confederation.

The sun was high in the clear blue sky as Mack lay on the sun lounger, his hands behind his bald head. His bare torso rippled with muscles as they bunched under his mocha skin. He had extremely broad shoulders and a trim waist and with his height at only six feet he often looked squat. He was extremely powerful and excelled in sports such as wrestling, pro-football and many martial arts. Today though, exercise was the last thing on his mind. After all the training he and the rest of the Wildfire Team had under-taken recently, followed by the terror they all faced on the planet Tartaran, he was there just to relax and recharge his batteries.

He had picked his spot on the beach with care. He was close enough to the clear waters of the sea if he wanted a quick dip to cool off, yet out of the way of other vacationers so that he didn't warrant any unwanted attention from them. For the first time since he could remember he just wanted to be left alone.

That didn't seem to go according to plan though.

His eyes were closed as he baked in the early midday sun listening to the sounds of the beach all around him as he dozed on the lounger. He could hear the waves lapping up against the shoreline and the sound of sea birds as they swooped in to pick up scraps of food dropped by those down below. He could hear voices all around him from people having fun or simply chatting amongst themselves, which he tried to tune out. He was still getting used to his enhanced abilities, hearing conversations from a distance away was one of the ones he was having the most trouble with.

A football came whistling through the air in his direction and even with his eyes closed he could tell it would hit him. He didn't know how, he just knew. Without looking, his right hand went up and caught the elongated spherical object in mid-air, which brought a gasp from those throwing it.

'Wow man, great catch, you wanna play some ball?' shouted one of the men throwing the ball around. They were showing off their physiques to the young women on the beach in an adolescent display that Mack had no interest in. He tossed the ball back at them, keeping his eyes closed.

'Nope,' he said, hoping they would reconsider and leave him alone.

His disinterest sparked something in them though; the very thing he was trying to avoid was going to happen whether he liked it or not.

'What, we're not good enough for you to toss a ball around with?' shouted the young man, this time slightly angry at the rebuke.

Mack turned his head to look at them. There were eight of them with ages ranging around the early twenties. They all had good bodies and he thought they were jocks on a college vacation, probably some college football team flexing their muscles to impress the ladies. Three of them stepped forward, the one who shouted and two others, the rest were quite happy to stand back and not get involved.

'I'm just here for the sun, buddy, so go back to your game, your friends are waiting,' he said as politely, yet firmly, as he could.

From one of the others who held back, a voice shouted, 'Come on Cody, throw the damn ball.'

Mack held Cody's gaze and the jock said, 'What is your problem?'

'Excuse me, problem?'

'You heard me.'

'I don't have a problem. I came here to top up my tan, relax and enjoy the quiet. I'm not disturbing anyone and I don't want to be disturbed. Now if you have a problem understanding that statement I could spell it out for you, maybe use words with fewer syllables. Would that help?' Mack replied.

The sarcasm was not lost on Cody and he stepped forward intent now on a confrontation.

Mack was on his feet in a flash catching the jock by surprise.

'You don't want to do this, trust me,' he said as Cody slowed down before him.

Mack looked the young man in the eye with his best cold, hard stare. Cody was in good shape, he stood around six feet four with the lean physique of a quarterback. Good bone structure gave him model good looks that at the moment were fixed in a confused/angry expression as he looked down on the shorter man.

'Oh, but I think I do,' Cody said knowing he had two of his friends to back him up should this go south. He also knew that since he'd made his move it was too late to back down and save face in front of them all.

'Do you know me, or anything about me? Do I appear as if I'm going to back down from you at all? For all you know I could be a raving nut job who will rip off your head then shit down your neck. Do you really want to try this?' Mack said hoping he could put this guy off something he had clearly not thought through and seemed intent on doing.

'I agree you're a nut job alright but the rest, I don't think so,' Cody said.

Mack felt a tingle then and he knew a call was being routed to his reception centre via his NI. The familiar tingle also told him it was a battlecom channel so only he would hear the call.

He held up his hand to stall Cody from doing anything rash as he turned his head to listen to the call.

'Mack, be ready for immediate evac, we've got a call. I'll

be with you shortly in the Pulsar, be ready this is a Wildfire priority,' Jake said.

'Copy that,' he replied then turned to a bemused Cody and said, 'Sorry guys, can I take a rain check? I've gotta go,' and he picked up the small bag he had with him and walked off past a startled Cody. When the jock saw the expressions on his two friends' faces he went to grab Mack's shoulder to turn him round.

Mack grabbed the hand on his left shoulder with his right hand and twisted it outwards away from him as he turned to face Cody. This action had the jock's arm twisted against the joint and held in a straight, locked out position, palm facing upwards, with the arm pushing up against the shoulder forcing him up onto his toes. Cody could not move and the pain that lanced up his arm into his shoulder showed quite plainly on his face.

'I said, "rain check" guys,' Mack said.

'Okay, okay you made your point man. Let him go,' one of his back up urged.

Before Mack released him he said, 'A suggestion for you Cody. Think before you let your balls do your talking for you. They sometimes say things that the rest of your body can't back up, do you catch my drift?'

Cody nodded his head rapidly and Mack let go of his hand. 'Enjoy the rest of your vacation,' he said as he left them staring at his back as he walked off across the sand towards his hotel.

Chapter Nine

Orion was sitting in his quarters when the pilot called him.

'The target has touched down, sir,' he said.

'Inform the assets on the surface that I want the target under close surveillance at all times. Assemble the troops, I'll lead them myself and inform me the second he arrives,' Orion replied. 'Inform OMEGA Command we are a go for Phase Two,' he added.

'Copy that, sir,' replied the pilot.

Orion smiled to himself, the thought of the plan coming to fruition pleased him. He knew this plan was a priority for his masters at OMEGA – the first part in their plan to destroy Col Sec. Once this was completed the galaxy would be wide open and ripe for their picking. As their founder had predicted, OMEGA would be the power in the galaxy.

He got up and began to prepare for what he had to do.

Matt, Able and Josh exited the Gateway and if they had not done this before they would have sworn they were still in the same room. Everything about this chamber was the same as the one they had left on Earth.

'So what happens now?' Matt asked.

Josh took control and said, 'We authorise the download to your systems and the upgrades will take effect almost immediately.'

'Is that it? I feel like there should be more to it than that,' Matt said slightly perplexed.

'I know what you mean, sometimes I'm amazed at what today's technology can do too and I feel like it shouldn't be this easy to get such a lot done so fast.'

Able said, 'That's the world we all live in now though so don't rail against it, embrace it.'

'It's not that I don't enjoy what we can do, I just think it's too easy sometimes and that makes it harder to stop the bad guys because it's just as easy for them too,' Matt said.

'Well, with these upgrades your comm. systems should be harder to hack into, also your whole mainframe will be more secure too. Your Neural Interfaces will be able to access and process a lot more data, which will help you in your day-to-day duties. It'll take a few hours, days in some cases, for the upgrades to filter through to everyone. Those further away from the signal will take longer obviously,' explained Able.

'I hope so,' Matt said wistfully.

'What's troubling you son?' Able asked.

Matt looked at the older man and his son. They were two people he could trust implicitly and, for reasons he could not fathom out, they engendered in him a feeling that not only did they understand what he was going through but that they were on his side and he could rely on them almost like family.

He said, 'I've a terrible feeling that a storm is coming, one that we have no defence against. We were lucky with the first attack by OMEGA with the Nemesis but only because they rushed to attack us. They were hasty and were not really prepared fully so we got off lightly.'

'I wouldn't say all those deaths and the destruction they caused was "getting off lightly",' Josh replied.

'Believe me Josh, if they had truly prepared for the attack there would've been no way we could have stopped them. We had no defence against the Nemesis as it was but we managed to gather enough forces to combat her, but if she had been fully functioning and fully manned then we all would have died. Col Sec would have been in ruins and God knows what else would have happened. So when I say we got off lightly, I mean it very literally.'

'So what is your fear now then?' Able asked, his brow creasing in concern.

'My friend has just left to meet a friend and he said there was some OMEGA involvement. They're still out there and if they learnt anything from their first attack then we could all be in big trouble.'

'What do you think their aim is?' Josh asked, sharing his father's concern and understanding some of Matt's anguish better.

'The same as it's always been, the total destruction of Col Sec. I just don't know how or when and that's what troubles me; it's the not knowing,' Matt replied.

'Well the best thing you can do is report back to base and leave everything here to us. You'll feel better if you can be where you can do the most good. The upgrades will go ahead, you have my word,' Able said.

'Thanks, I'm sure they will,' Matt said and although he was reassured by the words he could still not shake the almost debilitating feeling of dread.

Pavel Norsky sat in the pilot's seat of the shuttle he had stolen for his escape from Toldax. He had taken the small craft as far away from the planet as he could and now was waiting for the inevitable to happen.

From the computer mainframe he had gleaned enough data, comm. transcripts and flight records to know that whoever was running the clean-up operation was unaware of what had happened to cause the explosion. That was okay because the less that was known about it the better off he would be. Obviously the Alliance, his old employers, would not want anyone to know what they had been playing at down in the facility, they would want those details kept a closely guarded secret.

Something had disturbed him though, there was a report that said they had found something down in the rubble that they had transported off the planet. What could they have found? Could one of the other soldiers who had received the same serum as him have survived too? He dismissed that theory because he had been given a concentrated form of the serum, much stronger than the team of marines had been given, so he doubted that any of them could show any of the results he had exhibited. Having said that though, it did not give him any idea of what could have been found that was important enough to be taken back to this OMEGA Command, whoever that was.

He hoped the trail he had left was enough that someone from this OMEGA would come after him to make contact.

He didn't have to wait long.

The sensors showed the approach of a large starship that slowed down when it came within hailing distance.

'Ahoy shuttle craft, shut down your engines and prepare to come aboard,' said a voice through the comm. channel.

'You took your time getting here,' Norsky replied.

'Identify yourself,' the voice ordered.

'I don't like your tone so alter it before I alter it for you, permanently,' Norsky replied. He had never liked being spoken to like that and now that he was as powerful as he knew he was, there was no way he was going to allow it. The fact that they could have blown him out of the sky did not bother him in the slightest, he felt like a God and such a feeling was addictive.

The starship came within docking range and activated a tractor beam, which locked onto the small shuttle then dragged it aboard.

Norsky remained seated as comfortably as he could in the pilot's seat as he waited for someone to appear. He heard the docking clamps engage as the shuttle came to rest in the docking bay of the larger starship and he knew they would come soon.

The door opened and he heard several footfalls as three people entered the shuttle. He heard the audible gasps as they saw the dead bodies littered across the passenger section and he got up to greet them.

'Welcome aboard, I'm Pavel Norsky, late of the Black Knights, and you are?' he said.

Standing before him was a large man with the body of a weightlifter. He looked at Norsky with opaline eyes that showed slight surprise and then a smile crossed his rock-like face.

'Pleased to meet you Captain, you can call me Hermes,' he said.

Chapter Ten

Kurt Stryder sat in the comfortable leather seat on board the Silver Dart in preparation as the starship they had travelled in re-entered normal space near his homeworld of Celeron. The thought of seeing Zara again filled him with both trepidation and awe. From what Sinclair had told him she bore no grudge towards him for leaving her on Toldax, after all, everyone thought she had died, which brought him to the awe part. How had she survived being shot at point blank range? He remembered it well, too well in fact. The sight of her being shot in front of him, the pulsed plasma bolt striking her chest, her falling down and seeing the life slip away from her as her eyes dimmed, were images that had been burned into his memory. Every time he closed his eyes he saw the same sequence of events. For weeks he hadn't slept because of this and it came to the point where he didn't know how to carry on. He became a recluse, never leaving his home until he heard of the attack on Col Sec HQ and its aftermath. He attended the memorial service and seeing everyone there, seeing, almost feeling their grief as a tangible thing brought back his own grief. Knowing they would continue he decided he needed to get away to sort through what he needed to do to organise his own life. That was why he booked a berth on the Colonial Queen Cruise liner, which ended up, through no fault of his own, visiting the Tartaran battlefield, the sight of one of the worst battles waged between the Colonial Confederation and the Elysium Alliance and subsequently one of the biggest cover-ups in recent history. What happened on that ill-fated cruise forced him to face the truth that he could no longer turn his back on his destiny. He had been blessed with this gift, also his curse, and he must put it to the best use he could, so instead of going through with his resignation he returned to Col Sec.

A voice came through the internal comm. system, 'We'll be leaving the Vanguard and then landing in Jacksonville Spaceport in a few moments, sir,' said the Captain of the Silver Dart, James Wright.

Kurt operated his harness in readiness for the drop down into the atmosphere on the planet. At the touch of a button on the armrest of his seat, the harness straps snapped into place coming out from recesses in the seat itself, and closed over his chest.

'Thank you, Captain. Can you inform the Captain of the Vanguard to remain on station here until reinforcements arrive from Col Sec, just in case they are needed before they arrive?' Kurt said connecting to the comm. system through his NI.

'Already done sir,' replied Wright.

Kurt felt the familiar lurch in the pit of his stomach as the Silver Dart dropped clear of the Vanguard's docking bay. Captain Wright fired the main thrusters and sped the shuttle towards the nearby planet.

Jacksonville Space Port was on the outskirts of one of the

planet's two largest cities and named after one of the two founding fathers of Celeron.

A call to flight control from Captain Wright soon had a flight path cleared for the Silver Dart to land safely. The moment the shuttle touched down the Flight Attendant came through from the pilot's section. She was slim and very pretty, something Kurt had not noticed as his thoughts were on Zara from the moment he entered.

'I've organised for you to have a car put at your disposal sir,' she said.

'Thank you Lieutenant, what's your name?' Kurt said, noticing the bright-eyed young woman with the beaming smile for the first time.

'Lieutenant O'Neil, sir. Can I say it's a pleasure to meet you Captain Stryder, I've heard such a lot about you?' she replied.

'Call me Kurt please, and don't believe everything you hear. Wait, what have you heard?'

'Don't worry Kurt, it's all good,' she said, her eyes sparkling with a mischievous quality bringing a smile to his lips for the first time since he could remember.

He was on his feet heading for the door when he turned to look at her. 'We'll be here ready for departure as soon as you return. Just call when you're on the way and the engines will be warm,' she said.

He smiled and said, 'Copy that Lieutenant.'

The car she had arranged was parked at the edge of the landing strip and was a sleek Celeron Independent Vehicles Sports Hatch, similar to the one he owned but in black. The CIV Sports Hatch was one of the fastest cars on the roads of Celeron, capable of speeds of up to two hundred miles an hour and Kurt's personal choice.

Did she know or was this just a lucky guess he wondered as he got behind the wheel? He charged up the fuel cell and started the engine; selecting first gear he slipped the clutch and drove away from the landing strip, the tyres squealing on the asphalt as the car accelerated up through the gears.

Putting all thoughts away in a back corner of his mind Kurt engulfed himself in the sensation of driving. Before long he was nearing the outskirts of the city.

The facility was huge, the size of a small city. It was built around a central hub covered by a huge dome and had tubes that radiated out from it connecting other smaller sections to it. Each smaller section was the size of a football field. The whole thing had been erected under the cover of a stealth shield on the lunar surface. No one was aware of its existence on Earth and that was how the inhabitants wanted it kept, until the right time.

Inside the main dome was the heart of the complex, the Command and Control section. One man was standing at the main control console studying the recent reports from the construction crew building the gantry for the launch. He heard the approach of another and turned, his pearly green eyes growing hard as he looked at the man. His eyes were red rimmed due to the fact he had been staring at reports for a fourteen-hour stretch. The two of them could be brothers they were so similar, each standing six feet four inches tall with broad shoulders and muscular physiques, Rover5s, the same as everyone in the facility, except he was in command.

'Are we on schedule?' Apollo asked as the other Rover5 stood to attention before him.

'Everything is progressing as planned,' replied the other clone.

'I want security kept to a maximum; we are too close for anything to go wrong. I want guards put on all exits and around the perimeter of the facility. I want it to be impossible for anyone to even get near to this place.'

'It will be done, sir.'

'I'll inform OMEGA Command of our status. I'll be in my quarters,' Apollo said as he turned to leave relinquishing control of the C and C to the other clone.

Chapter Eleven

Matt reached the foyer of the RandCorp building and exited through the large doorways. As he reached the pavement outside the building where the staff car was parked ready to pick him up, he looked down the crowded sidewalk and saw something that rocked him to his core.

A snatch of long blonde hair cascading around a pair of slim shoulders, a glimpse of the bluest eyes he had ever seen and a smile he thought lost to him forever.

Could it be her? He wondered but then discounted the thought for he knew it was impossible. It couldn't possibly be the person he thought because he had seen her killed right in front of his own eyes.

Before he knew it the figure had gone, lost in the throng of people milling around on the sidewalk.

He tried to dismiss the thought from his mind and started to walk over to the car, but however hard he tried he just couldn't tear his eyes from where he had seen her.

Before he knew it he was walking after the disappearing figure, his pace quickening.

Peering over the bobbing heads and shoulders of the

crowd in front of him he strained to catch a further glimpse of the fleeing figure. Just when he thought he had lost sight of her, he saw a swish of blonde hair swirling around a set of slim shoulders which he instantly recognised as she crossed the street, dodging the traffic.

The traffic was dense as one would expect during the day in this part of the city and when he left the sidewalk to follow her he had to dodge cars from both directions. Not wanting to alert her that she was being followed, it made his task of crossing the wide street a little harder.

Diverting his attention between the cars thundering down the road threatening to squash him like a bug and the disappearing figure of the young woman was not an easy task. He was halfway across when he saw her dip into an alley between two buildings. This was the opportunity he needed to sprint the rest of the way across the road.

When he reached the mouth of the alley he paused, almost scared to see what was down there. Nevertheless he stepped into the mouth of the alley and what he saw stopped him in his tracks.

Standing shoulder to shoulder, less than a few feet away from him were two Rover5s, dressed in smart pinstripe suits but unmistakable due to their similar appearance and striking opaline green eyes. At the far end of the alley was another Rover5 standing next to the female he had followed there. She wore the same expression of pure, unadulterated terror on her face as he had witnessed on that fateful day he saw her die and he felt sick to his stomach. The Rover5 at her side held a Sig P996 to her temple pressing the muzzle hard into her skin forcing her head sideways as tears ran down her face.

Tanya Wilde screamed, 'Matt, help me.'

Matt felt like he was back in that bedroom, weeks ago

watching the same thing again. This time though he was determined the outcome would be different.

He walked forward, his focus on the Rover5 at the far end of the alley. The two clones facing him reached inside their jackets for pistols. Matt caught a glimpse of the gunmetal blue of the pistols in his peripheral vision and he went into overdrive.

Quickening his pace he stepped forward shortening the distance between him and them making it impossible for them to use their weapons. He grabbed the hand of the Rover5 on his left with his own left hand trapping the Rover5's hand before he could draw the pistol. With his right hand he backfisted the other clone with all his might. He remembered the last time he tussled with one of these clones and he almost lost that fight, this time he was up against three of them so there was no holding back.

The clone's head was snapped sideways from the force of the blow as he spat a stream of blood across the alley floor. Matt kicked him with a roundhouse kick to the stomach with his right foot, doubling him up. As he collapsed on the floor gasping for breath, he punched the clone on his left full in the face with his right hand as he kept hold of his gun hand with his left.

As the clone he was holding staggered from the punch, Matt ripped the pistol out of his grasp, a Sig P996. He jacked the slide to prime the battery clip then, as the clone turned to look at him, Matt shot him in the face. He turned to face the clone on the floor who had turned to look at him at the sound of the gun shot, only to be faced with the muzzle of the gun now staring at him. A second gunshot echoed off the walls of the alley, heralding the death of the second Rover5.

Matt aimed down the alley at the Rover5 standing next to Tanya and fired. The pulsed plasma bolt struck the clone high on his chest punching him back and away from Tanya who was still screaming.

The clone struggled back to his feet and by the time he was on his knees Matt was standing by Tanya's side. He looked down at the struggling clone and shot him in the head.

He turned to look at Tanya and was surprised to see her smiling, all traces of fear had disappeared from her exquisite features.

A frown creased his forehead as something niggled at the back of his mind. Something was not quite right here and he didn't know what it was.

'I knew you'd come,' Tanya said smiling.

A sound alerted him to an approaching danger. He turned to see but it was too late. A sharp pain exploded across the back of his head as he was struck from behind. His legs lost their ability to hold him and he felt the ground rushing up to greet him.

The side of his face impacted the dirty alley floor as he fell heavily, lights dancing at the edges of his vision.

He heard two words spoken by the woman he had hoped to prevent from being killed again, 'So predictable,' she said as she and the other clone walked off leaving Matt lying where he fell.

He saw two sets of feet walk off into the shadows just before darkness engulfed him.

Chapter Twelve

Zara pulled up in front of the Golden Palace and she looked up at the garish frontage, all bright Neon lights sparkling and shining as the night grew closer, remembering the last time she was here.

It had been the night Kurt and she had come to visit Abraham Bane and find out who had been behind an earlier attack on them. It was also the night she had been captured by Pavel Norsky an Alliance agent sent to abduct Kurt. Instead he had used her as bait to eventually lure Kurt into his trap. She had been shot and killed in their attempt to escape from the facility they had been taken to on Toldax. Now she was back here, travelled full circle, back to where it had all started.

Suddenly fear gripped her as she thought of Norsky; if she had survived what had happened on Toldax what was to say that Norsky hadn't survived too. If that was the case then they could all be in big trouble. Norsky, if he survived, would be as powerful as she was and maybe even as powerful as Kurt which was something she dared not to think about too much. She had learned in their brief time spent together that he was a very dangerous man.

Putting the bike on its stand she dismounted and headed for the door. A queue was beginning to form as the evening meal crowd were lining up ready to gain entrance. As normal, two huge men dressed in black suits guarded the door, sentinels for the evening's entertainment. As she walked up to them, bypassing all those waiting in line she said, 'Evening boys, is Mister Bane in?'

'Who the hell are you?' one of them said.

'Don't I know you?' said the other doorman.

'I was here some time ago with a friend of mine. There was a bit of trouble,' she replied.

'Yep, thought it was you. Are you here to see the boss then and what's with the coveralls?' he said which brought looks of puzzlement from the first doorman.

'Yes, if he's in. I ... er ... got dressed in a hurry. I need his help for a while,' she said not wanting to give too much away in front of the crowd.

'Follow me Miss, I'll take you to him,' said the second doorman, bringing jeers of derision from those waiting in line to be admitted. Zara simply blew them a kiss then followed the doorman inside.

'Cute,' the first doorman muttered then called for quiet from the line.

The two of them entered the nightclub and it was the same as she remembered it. There was a long passage from the front entrance to the main room, once through this they came to where tables were laid out in a seemingly random pattern on the floor, several of which were now occupied. There was a smallish dance floor over to her left in front of a raised dais where musicians played soft background music. Over to her right, as she walked through, was a long mahogany bar with a mirrored display to the rear displaying an amazing array of bottles stacked in front. Three barmen worked feverishly to fill drinks orders from those seated at tables and those customers who were standing in front of the bar. In front of her, over by the far wall, was a row of private booths designating the VIP area. Bane, as usual, was seated in his own booth, the third from the right.

As she approached the booth, passing between the tables that were still filling up and the bar, she saw Bane turn his head to look in her direction. A smile crossed his hard mouth and he nodded his head to the doorman bringing her to him. A very large man who had been standing guard close by the booth, known to her simply as Tony, caught the nod and walked across to greet her. It was almost like a military handover as Tony reached her, the doorman turned and returned to his post outside.

'Hello again Miss, on your own this time?' Tony said with a slight smile but constantly watching everything going on around him. He was as vigilant as ever, Bane had made many enemies in his rise to power and his job was to keep the man as safe as he could; a job he took great pride in doing extremely well.

'Yes, Tony, but I am hoping to meet someone here,' she replied.

'Kurt?' he said.

She was surprised by his response and excited at the mere mention of his name.

'Have you seen him recently?' she asked.

'I'll let Mister Bane explain, Miss,' Tony said then showed her to the booth.

'Zara you are a sight for sore eyes I must say and after what Kurt told us I never expected to see you again, especially not dressed like that,' Bane said as he stood to greet her.

He took her hand in his and gently kissed the back of it then eased her into the seat opposite him.

'What did he tell you?' she asked as she sat down, concern written all over her face.

'That you were dead.'

'He told you that did he?'

'As a matter of fact, he said he saw you killed right in front of him.'

'Oh!' was all she could think of saying.

'Are you going to explain any of this? If not to me then certainly I think to Kurt. The man was devastated, I could see the pain in his eyes when he told me.'

'Mister Bane, I can't explain any of this to you right now as I'm not sure I understand it all myself yet, but when Kurt arrives, if he thinks it's okay, then I'll let him explain. For now though, I'm here to ask a favour,' she said, the words tumbling out of her mouth hoping to get him on her side before he could refuse and dismiss her.

He smiled and said, 'Abe, call me Abe.'

'Okay, Abe,' she said tentatively, 'I need your help,' she added as she rested her hands on top of the table.

He placed both his hands on top of hers to comfort her as he could see the distress in her eyes. He said, 'Anything.' He had said it as a father would to a daughter and it caught her by surprise a little. She smiled and said, 'If I didn't know better Abe, I'd swear there was a soft heart beating somewhere beneath that rough exterior.'

With a wink of his eye he said, 'And if you ever repeat it I'll have to deny it, of course.'

'Of course,' she added returning the wink.

'What do you need?' he asked.

'Just a place to stay until Kurt comes for me; somewhere safe. There are some men who may come after me, I think they work for something called OMEGA. Have you heard about it?'

At the mention of OMEGA Bane sat up straight. He waved Tony over and as the man mountain bent down to listen Zara heard him say, 'Tony let the boys know we may be in for some company. It could be bad, real bad, so I want everyone carrying.'

'I'm on it boss,' Tony said then walked off to stand guard in front of the booth. He communicated with the rest of Bane's men via a closed circuit comm. channel accessed through his NI.

Bane turned his attention back to Zara and she said, 'So you've heard of them.'

'Who hasn't?'

'I've been away so humour me,' she snapped back, then immediately regretted it considering how welcoming he had been and said, 'Sorry, I didn't mean that, it's been a little strange lately.'

Bane waved her apology off like it didn't matter, he understood a little from what he'd learned from Kurt anyway. He said, 'OMEGA is a terrorist outfit that recently attacked Col Sec HQ on Earth. It was a massive thing, all over the media and GalaxyWeb. Apparently they attacked from orbit in a huge starship, killing thousands and destroying the entire building. There was a memorial service and everything.'

'Was Kurt involved?' she asked, somehow already knowing the answer.

'No, by that time he hadn't returned to Col Sec. He took your death really badly, resigned his commission and decided to live at home.'

'What brought him back?'

'Something that happened on Tartaran, something else

that has been huge in the news. You've missed quite a lot young lady.'

'Tartaran? I thought that was a Forbidden Zone?'

'It was and is again but this time the Alliance is there in force. You've got an awful lot of catching up to do.'

'You said that OMEGA *is* a terrorist group not *was*, by that do I take it that it's still out there and the attack on Earth was just the beginning?'

'From what we were told they were destroyed after the attack on Earth, but I don't think a group with the resources to plan and execute an attack of that magnitude could be so easily defeated. Also the mere fact that you are being chased by men who work for OMEGA answers your own question, don't you think?'

'You're right, of course. I'll never forget the one in charge, big man, at least as tall as Tony, maybe a bit bigger and the strangest eyes I've ever seen.'

'What colour?' Bane asked suddenly getting anxious.

'Opaline green, why?'

'Because when Kurt was last here, he was attacked by four men, all with opaline green eyes.'

The realisation hit her like a starship entering a hyperspace window. This had all been a set up. She had been allowed to escape. They had used her as bait to lure Kurt here, but why?

'Shit! I'd better warn Kurt,' she said then a familiar voice said, 'Warn me about what?'

She turned to see a man standing by Tony. A man she thought she would never see again.

She was out of her seat so fast and running at him Tony thought they would collide and end up on the floor.

She wrapped her arms around his neck and pressed her lips against his, tightly at first, then softer, more gently as they kissed.

Finally, yet reluctantly, she pulled away and looked up into his cobalt blue eyes and knew he felt the same about her as she did about him.

No words needed to be said to clarify what they both felt.

'Kurt, we have to leave, I think this is a trap,' she said.

Chapter Thirteen

Orion stood on the landing strip outside the shuttle as the rest of the team debarked.

'Get in the vehicles, I want to be on station ready to go in less than twenty minutes,' he ordered.

The Rover5s all filed across the plascrete into the three waiting vehicles, Grand Voyager 600s. They all wore battle suits, kevlon blast resistant pads over the vital organs, with Rapier helmets and all carried Remm assault rifles at high port across their chest as they ran towards their rides.

Once inside the vehicles the order was given and the convoy set off leaving the Space Port behind as they left for Jacksonville.

The first thing Matt noticed when he opened both eyes was pain; blinding, searing pain centred across the back of his head. The second thing was a pair of boots close by his head.

'Are you alright, sir?' asked a voice he barely recognised

through the haze blurring his mind. When he realised it was Tucker, the driver of the staff car he replied, 'I've been better.'

He put his right hand to the back of his head and when he felt nothing but a slight raised area he looked at his fingers in the fading light of the alley to see if there was any blood. After finding none he did a quick inventory of the rest of him, checking for any injuries he may have sustained while he was unconscious. Satisfied that he was alright he slowly got to his feet hoping that the sense of nausea was not going to last too long.

'What happened sir, I saw you come to the car but you wandered off. I thought you must've remembered something and you'd gone to do it or go somewhere, but when you failed to return I called out. When there was no response I knew something was wrong so I followed your tracking chip and found you here,' explained Tucker.

'I thought I saw someone I knew,' Matt said, his voice sounding harsh to him.

'And was it who you thought it was?'

'It couldn't have been.'

'Are you sure, sir?'

'Pretty much, yes.'

'Why is that?'

'Because I was standing right in front of her when someone shot her through the head.'

'Wow! Well that makes no sense, sir; no sense at all.'

'You're right Tucker, it doesn't. Let's go, General Sinclair will need to know what happened here today,' Matt said and he slowly headed towards the end of the alley, the nausea already fading as his senses returned thankfully as he needed to focus on what was to come.

As he reached the staff car his renewed grief at seeing Tanya had been replaced by an anger that boiled inside him and would only be quenched when he had the culprit of this insane plot lying before him.

He would have his revenge and it would not be pretty.

Norsky looked warily at the large man with the opaline eyes in front of him. He looked every inch of what he was, a warrior, and although he felt confident he was no match for the new improved version of Norsky he didn't want to get into any protracted conflict with whoever his employer was. He felt that they could be allies and prove valuable to each other's aims and therefore, as much as it pained him to do so, he had to tread carefully.

'Captain Pavel Norsky, late of the Elysium Alliance's Black Knights, specialist in covert intelligence, expert marksman and close quarter combat, need I go on?' Hermes said by way of introduction.

Norsky knew by the résumé that they had done their homework on him but he was completely in the dark as to who they were or what their objectives were. What he did know about them though, was that they wanted the same thing as him, the destruction of Col Sec.

'You seem to know me and although you've given me your name I know next to nothing about you. If we are to work together don't you think it would be wise to share some information?' he suggested.

'What do you want from us?' Hermes wanted to know.

'I want to know what your aim is towards the Confederation.'

'We have no aim towards the Confederation, just Col Sec.'

'What is it you want from me then?'

'There is a plan in place for an attack on their HQ but we need the services of an Alliance officer.'

'That is intriguing,' Norsky said as his interest was piqued.

'Go on, tell me more,' he said as he leaned forward in his seat.

Captain Pierce of the Vanguard called Kurt over a secure channel. The familiar tingle alerted him and he turned his head away from Zara and Bane so he could concentrate on the call.

'Go ahead,' he said.

'We have been monitoring a smallish cruiser that has just taken up a stationary orbit over Jacksonville sir. A shuttle from this craft has just landed at Jacksonville Space port and from our sensor scans we can tell you that there are three vehicles loaded with six men each on their way to your location as we speak. Their ETA is approximately fifteen minutes.'

'Thank you Captain, have you heard from the Wildfire Team?' Kurt asked.

'No, I'm sorry; they're probably keeping radio silence.'

'Okay Captain, thanks for the heads up, I'll keep in touch, please monitor our progress,' Kurt replied and ended the call.

As he faced Zara and Bane once more they looked worried. Bane asked, 'Trouble heading this way?'

'I'm afraid so, eighteen of them,' Kurt told him.

'Like I said Kurt, this whole thing has been a set up from the beginning. I just don't know why,' Zara said.

'I can think of a reason why,' Kurt said. He turned to Bane and said, 'I'm sorry to bring this to your door again.'

Zara said, 'If we leave now, they'll follow us and not come here.'

'How can you be so sure?' Bane asked.

'If we take it that this has been a set up from the start then we have to assume they have eyes on this place watching for either Kurt or me, or both of us. If that's true then we have to also assume that when we leave they will follow us seeing as we are their objective,' Zara explained.

'She has a point,' Bane said.

'I can't take the chance that they won't follow us though, so we'll have to make sure they do. I won't endanger any innocents,' Kurt said.

Bane smiled and said, 'Nice gesture son, but trust me, we haven't been innocent for a long time.'

'I meant your customers Abe; I know you and your boys can handle yourselves but what about them?' Kurt said gesturing towards the room full of people with a wave of his hand.

'You let me worry about them; you need to go now. If these guys are as bad as the lady here seems to think, then you need to go so that me and my boys can do what we have to, to protect my customers.'

Reluctantly Kurt said, 'I suppose you're both right. If we leave now then there's a chance they'll follow us and not bother you and if not then our leaving will give you the time you need to evacuate your club.'

'We're wasting time Kurt, we have to leave, and now,' Zara urged.

'Okay, I have a car outside, let's go,' Kurt finally said. He could see no other recourse but to agree and just hope that everything else worked out.

The two of them left the club as Bane got to his feet to watch them go. He turned to Tony and said, 'Keep watch for those vehicles. If they look like any of them are heading this way, we get everyone out and fast.'

'Yes boss, we can tell everyone there's a fire or something, that'll light a fire under their asses and get them moving, no pun intended,' Tony replied.

'Good idea, go tell the boys and tell them to get ready,' Bane said then moved off towards the bar muttering to himself, 'That guy will be the death of me. I need a drink.'

Outside the club Kurt steered Zara towards his car, which he had parked on the VIP car park across from the club. Zara remembered it well from the last time she had been to the club for it was where Pavel Norsky had taken her captive in his attempt to capture Kurt all those weeks ago. Such a lot had happened in that time and it seemed like it was all connected, almost as if it was the same incident.

As Kurt and Zara activated the harnesses in the seats once they were inside in the car, Kurt looked at her and said, 'Hope we're right about this.'

He started the car and drove out of the car park heading away from the club.

'Are we not going towards the Space port?' Zara asked when she saw the direction they were heading.

'Not unless you want to drive straight towards them. We have to lead them away, make sure they follow us then we can double back and get to the shuttle,' Kurt said as he concentrated on driving the car. He soon had her powering through the streets of Jacksonville hoping that he didn't pick up any unwanted attention from the local Constabulary; being stopped for a speeding violation was the last thing he needed right at that moment.

The clone monitoring Zara looked up from the small screen on the pad he was holding and said, 'They've left the club.'

Orion turned to look at the clone and said, 'Copy that.' He accessed a comm. channel via his NI and called the drivers of the two other vehicles following behind his. He said, 'They've made their move, peel off and intercept.'

Chapter Fourteen

Jake Riley had picked up the rest of his team; Angelina Torres was already on Earth so all he had to do was pick up the other two, Joseph Vance and Mack Cooper en route. With the full Wildfire Team assembled, he ordered the Artificial Intelligence in control of their own starship, the Pulsar, to take them to Celeron. The AI was called Artificial Integrated Intelligence Control Module, a name the Team could not get their heads around so they simply called it Artie.

'We are approaching Celeron controlled space, sirs,' the AI said, its synthesised voice coming through the integrated speakers all through the Pulsar.

'Thank you, Artie. Hail the captain of the Vanguard please and then locate Kurt and his friend for us,' Jake replied.

'Pierce here,' replied the Captain, 'glad to hear from you Captain Riley. We've been monitoring a small cruiser that arrived a short time ago; a shuttle exited it and landed at Jacksonville Space port. Eighteen men got out and into three vehicles which are now heading towards Captain Stryder's location.'

'Okay, we'll take over from here Captain, please inform the pilot of the Dart to return to your vessel and then remain on station to monitor the cruiser. We'll handle the extraction from here,' Jake said.

'Copy that, sir,' Pierce said. Although Pierce and Jake were technically the same rank, that of Captain, but Jake, being in the new Wildfire programme, gave him authority over the rest of the fleet officers.

The Pulsar's AI gave access to every comm. channel available wherever they were to each member of the Team. Jake used his NI to call Kurt.

'Kurt, Jake here, we're coming to extract you and your friend,' he said.

'Sir I've just identified the person with Captain Stryder, she is Zara Hardy, also a Recon Delta Marine but she is listed as Killed In Action,' Artie said.

'I knew he was meeting one of our own but not who it was. KIA you say, I bet she'll have an interesting story to tell us then,' Jake said.

'Good to hear from you again Jake, have you got a lock on me?' Kurt replied as he drove through the streets of Jacksonville.

'Yes, and we're closing on you but it'll take time and you have to know you have three vehicles on your tail, each with six hostiles on board. You need to get to somewhere secluded so we can take out your pursuers,' Jake said as he watched the scanners showing Kurt and Zara's position.

'That might be easier said than done but I'll try,' Kurt said.

'We'll be with you as soon as we can, keep this link open,' Jake said.

Jake turned to the rest of his team and said, 'Let's get in the forward section and take it down there.'

Without a single word the team all walked as quickly as they could into the nose cone section and strapped themselves into their seats.

'Okay Artie, let's take her down, keep monitoring our progress and keep a lock on Kurt and Zara,' Jake said.

'Copy that sir, I will relay visual data to the screens in the forward section and will ensure the comm. link remains open and fixed for your use,' the Pulsar's AI said.

'Right Team, let's go to work,' Jake said as he settled in for the task ahead.

———

Zara glanced at Kurt who was concentrating heavily on driving at speed through the streets, 'Who's Jake, is he our evac?' she asked before quickly returning her attention to the road ahead.

'Jake Riley, he's Recon Delta like us and he heads a special team from a new programme initiated by General Sinclair called the Wildfire Programme. The Team is the Wildfire Team and all four members have received a variation of the serum that was given to me. They haven't the regenerative capabilities that I have and now obviously you too but they do have some enhanced abilities. It looks like Sinclair has scrambled them to come pick us up,' he replied never taking his eyes off the road ahead.

'I don't like this Kurt, it seems like we're being played and I'm not sure why,' she said concern etching her forehead with deep lines.

'The General seemed concerned about this OMEGA group coming back. After the attack on Col Sec HQ a few weeks back they hadn't heard about them but now with the attack following our escape he's sure they're involved in this somehow. If they've heard of the serum somehow then we could be facing a threat similar to the one posed by the Alliance when they captured me to try and duplicate the results on some of their own,' Kurt said offering a supposition.

'Sounds reasonable. How much do you know of this OMEGA?'

'Only what I've read in the reports of the attack. They are a determined group that seek the destruction of Col Sec and Sinclair in particular; you can download it to your NI when we get back to HQ.'

'If we get back, you mean,' Zara said.

'We'll get back, don't worry about that.'

'You really believe that don't you?'

'Yes, don't you?'

Zara thought about that for a moment then said, 'I'm not sure. Since coming back there's a lot I'm not sure of.'

The streets passed by at speed and as Kurt steered the car around a bend he spotted a vehicle coming straight for them.

The Grand Voyager 600s suddenly veered around utilising an emergency braking technique that brought it to a stop across the road, effectively blocking the road off. The side doors slid open to reveal two men aiming pulse rifles at them. Pulsed plasma bolts lanced out at them filling the space between them with destructive energy.

'Shit, I think they've found us,' Kurt said.

'You think!' Zara snapped.

Kurt copied the technique, choosing to ignore the sarcasm, spinning his car around to face the opposite direction. Plasma bolts narrowly missed the speeding sports car and instead struck the ground or other vehicles close to them. The front of a green sedan burst into flames as a barrage of plasma bolts struck its forward compartment. It spun out of control as the driver of the vehicle struggled to bring it to a stop. He finally brought it to a halt and dived out of the door leaving the burning vehicle askew across the road.

Without reducing speed Kurt was suddenly facing the way he had just come and sped off once more. The Grand Voyager was soon giving chase once more as it swerved around the burning vehicle left abandoned in the road.

'That was a close call,' Kurt observed, but before Zara could comment another Grand Voyager 600s appeared from another direction cutting into traffic and positioning themselves right behind them just before the first one pulled in behind it.

'Hold on,' Kurt said as he spun the steering wheel turning the sports car down another street away from the pursuing vehicles.

Unfortunately the nearest Grand Voyager 600s made the turn as well, staying as close to them as they could whilst the other continued along the original road.

Zara looked through the rear window to see how close they were. 'We've lost one, the other has gone past,' she said.

'They're hoping to cut us off further down the block,' Kurt told her.

The Grand Voyager rammed into the rear section of the CIV Sports Hatch rocking those inside from the impact.

'These guys don't give up do they?' she said as she faced front once more.

Kurt gained control of the Sports Hatch from the fishtail motion the impact with the larger vehicle caused. He increased their speed, hurtling down the street at well over eighty miles per hour dodging in and out of traffic on both sides of the road.

Pulsed plasma bolts peppered the back of the Sports

Hatch making it swerve from the kinetic energy from the impacts.

'We can't take many more hits like that,' Zara said.

'This is a Col Sec vehicle; let's see what improvements they've made to her. Perhaps we can persuade them from trying that again, eh?' Kurt said.

He reached down to the centre console and opened a slim panel. Beneath it was another panel, which he accessed via his NI and found a series of hidden functions that could be useful.

'Let's try this,' he said and activated a set of defences built into the car. Firstly he fired an EMP weapon at the vehicle behind them; it was a short range burst hoping to short out the fuel cell and other electrical functions on the vehicle.

The EMP struck the Grand Voyager full in the front grille but had no effect. It carried on chasing them and the two clones hanging out of the side windows continued to fire at them.

'Damn, they must be shielded; bastards came well prepared. We may have to resort to harsher tactics,' Kurt said.

He suddenly steered around another corner without indicating to fellow travellers. He was trying to lose the Grand Voyager and by crossing oncoming traffic he almost caused a crash between at least three other vehicles as they skidded and veered to avoid him. Two mid-sized vehicles almost collided as the Sports Hatch crossed their path. A large bus had to pull up short before it ploughed into them. It jack-knifed and slid sideways to a halt as the driver spun the wheel and slammed on the automatic brakes in an attempt to prevent a major accident.

The Grand Voyager lost ground as it had to negotiate through this new blockade. By the time they had managed to get around the bus that was partially blocking the street, the Sports Hatch was nowhere to be seen.

Kurt accelerated through the gears on the Sports Hatch as he drove the car away into another side road across from the scene. Before he had got too far though the third and final Grand Voyager came into view. It came around a bend in the road barrelling down it towards them. It swapped lanes and was heading straight at them.

Chapter Fifteen

Matt arrived back at Col Sec HQ after going straight back to the airport. Another Silver Dart had been sent by Sinclair to pick him up once their first had been commandeered by Kurt.

He went straight to Sinclair's office, he had given him his report via closed comm. link through his NI and he was interested in what his commanding officer would have to say on the matter.

As he entered the office on Level Ten, he saw Sinclair seated behind his desk as usual.

'Well this is a development we didn't see coming,' Sinclair said as he saw the expression on his agent's face. Matt looked like he'd seen a ghost, which of course he thought he had. The opposite hypothesis was too terrible to comprehend and he had forcefully put it out of his mind, although on the journey to the HQ he found himself considering it more and more.

'I know what you mean sir. There can only be two possibilities as I can see it. Either the first Tanya was a clone or the one I saw today is,' Matt said as he approached the desk and the seat Sinclair offered him.

'Or Tanya had a twin sister,' offered Sinclair which was something that Matt clearly hadn't considered.

Sinclair saw Matt's expression alter as he contemplated the implications of that scenario.

'What I want to know is what is the purpose of all this?' Sinclair said.

Matt looked at him with slight surprise and said, 'Thought that would be obvious sir. It's the same as the message that was delivered to me when they killed Tanya in front of me. It's to mess with us, to show us what they can do. It's almost like they're telling us no matter how many of them we kill there will always be someone, or another of the same to take their place. This must be how Hercules felt when he faced the Hydra. Every time he cut off one head another two replaced it.'

'In that case we can expect an announcement of some kind then,' Sinclair said.

'I don't follow sir,' Matt said.

'Think about it, they went to all the trouble of finding you and making sure you saw whoever it was. They waited for you to follow them ensuring you got a good look at whoever it was so you could positively identify them. Then they stopped you from following them or even asking questions further ensuring the mystery would continue. They left you with this image of a dead girl knowing you would want answers. Now why go to all that trouble if there was no payday?'

'So what announcement do you think they will issue then?'

'That's the mystery, I'm not sure but we'll keep monitoring all news broadcasts and the GalaxyWeb to see if anything gets posted there too.'

'Where is Kurt, did he pick his friend up okay?'

'That's an ongoing situation. We are monitoring it as we speak. So far he has located his friend but there is some opposition to his successful evac. It seems the demise of OMEGA was more than premature, I've sent Jake and the Wildfire Team to assist.'

'You're right sir. If they're involved with the action on Celeron, and it can only be them who engineered my meeting with Tanya earlier, then they are definitely back to their old tricks again.'

'What the fuck are they playing at, are they crazy?' Zara asked calmly even though the larger vehicle was closing the gap between them at an amazing speed.

'Don't worry, they want to stop us not kill us, they'll move,' Kurt replied confidently.

'Give me your gun, let's see if I can persuade them,' Zara said and reached inside Kurt's jacket and pulled free the Sig P999 from its holster. She opened the side window and reached out and fired at the oncoming vehicle. She fired a continuous burst of plasma bolts at the front of the Grand Voyager, three bolts struck the front grille and as the recoil forced the weapon upwards the next four bolts struck the windshield smashing it and striking the driver in the chest and head. Blood sprayed backwards from the kinetic impact of the bolts but the driver didn't care as he died when the last bolt exploded inside his head.

The driver died at the control wheel as he fell forward, locking it over and suddenly taking the large vehicle across the road. Kurt turned the Sports Hatch slightly to the left evading the oncoming Grand Voyager as it slewed across the road to collide with the front of a building. The impact caused the front of the vehicle to crumple killing the front passenger.

Kurt steered the Sports Hatch away from the crash towards the end of the road and almost into the last Grand Voyager that had gone around the block. Seeing the vehicle at the last second he had just enough time to swerve around it.

The driver of the Grand Voyager sent the vehicle into a skidding turn so tight he almost tipped it over. Within a few yards he had controlled the spin and powered the larger vehicle after the smaller, sleeker Sports Hatch.

Behind them, back at the crash site, two of the Rover5s got out of the rear compartment and dragged the front two clones from the vehicle leaving them on the road. One of them got behind the wheel and restarted the engine. The front of the vehicle had been reinforced as the three Voyagers contained some kind of shielding but it had still sustained quite a bit of damage. The engine still worked though and as the second clone got into the front passenger seat the driver reversed it out from the building. Debris cascaded down from the top of the Voyager as it reversed from where it had collided with the front of the building but it did not impede its progress too much. Once it was clear of the building it continued the chase once more.

Zara replaced the spent battery clip in the Sig with a fresh one and continued to fire at the following Grand Voyager. She hit the front grille but this was the vehicle that was shielded from the EMP which offered them some protection against the plasma bolts.

The clones inside the Voyager returned fire by hanging out of the side windows once more. Pulsed plasma bolts struck the sides of the Sports Hatch and those on Zara's side almost forced her back inside. One of the bolts struck the doorframe close to her shoulder and the secondary impact struck her shoulder.

'Agh! Shit!' she screamed as the pain from the wound lanced through her. She ducked back inside and looked at the wound through the damaged clothing. Beneath the torn and burnt coverall over her shoulder she watched as new skin formed where the wound was. Her eyes went wide in surprise as the realisation of her newfound ability hit her fully. She had suspected she had this ability as there could be no other explanation to her resurrection, but actually seeing it with her own eyes was something else. Not only was it awe-inspiring it was also quite daunting. Now she faced the same dilemma as Kurt about her future.

'Will I ever get used to that?' she asked.

Without looking at her Kurt said, 'Maybe.'

'Have you?' she asked.

'Not yet,' he replied.

More pulsed plasma bolts struck the rear of the Sports Hatch as Kurt tried to get away from the clones behind them.

'Where the hell is Jake?' he muttered.

Artie piloted the forward section of the Pulsar down through the atmosphere of Celeron towards the flight lanes above Jacksonville.

'Have you got a fix on Kurt and Zara yet Artie?' Jake asked as he looked through the forward viewport.

'Yes sir, we are approaching them now,' the AI replied.

Seated behind Jake was the rest of the Wildfire Team. To his right was Joseph Vance, to his left and slightly behind was Angelina Torres and next to her was Mack Cooper. Vance said, 'We're not gonna be able to get low enough to pick them up, not unless they get closer to the edge of the city.'

'What about that park? If they got to it we could put down there and pick them up,' Torres offered pointing to the Jacksonville Central Park, a huge area of greenery frequented by holiday makers, visitors and locals alike as an area for relaxation. It was decorated with a wide variety of flowers, shrubs and trees both indigenous to the planet and brought here from other worlds. It was a showpiece of the talents of several gardeners who had worked for many years to bring it to the stage it was at present.

'Jake to Kurt, can you make it to Central Park?' Jake said through the comm. link.

'I'll see what I can do. We're under fire from one of those vehicles you told us about though,' Kurt replied.

'I'll see what I can do to help,' Jake replied, then to the AI said, 'You heard that Artie, let's try and help them.'

The AI said, 'I'm taking us down a little closer sir, do you want manual control over the weapons sir?'

'I'll take them Artie,' Cooper offered and turned his seat to the right where the control panel was. He charged up the weapons and said, 'Weapons are hot. How far do you want this to go Cap, shall I limit it just to pulse cannons or are missiles authorised?'

'Let's wait and see what the situation warrants 'eh before we go around blowing the whole planet up,' Jake replied.

'Spoil sport,' joked Cooper.

The forward section of the Pulsar blasted through the atmosphere and levelled off above the huge city of Jacksonville and the AI said, 'We are approaching the location you requested sir.'

'Can you get a location fix on Kurt yet Artie?' Jake asked.

'I have a fix on them sir, but they are not where you want them to be just yet.'

'Where are they, show me,' Jake ordered and the forward monitor screen displayed an enhanced image of the situation down on the planets' surface.

'There you are,' Jake said.

'How far are we from this Central Park?' Zara asked as they sped along a straight stretch of road between high-sided buildings.

'Too far, I doubt we can make it, hang on,' Kurt replied as he suddenly spun the wheel and turned the Sports Hatch down a narrow alley between two buildings. He was hoping to lose the two vehicles stuck to his rear bumper like glue since the crashed Voyager had caught up with them. The turn down the alley certainly caught the clones chasing them unawares, they had to skid to a stop then reverse and negotiate the turn into the alley which cost them valuable time allowing Kurt to put some distance between them. What he hadn't bargained on was the fact the third Voyager had been in communication with the other two and was running parallel to them so that when Kurt's Sports Hatch emerged from the alley he was waiting for them.

'We don't seem to be able to catch a break at all here,' observed Zara with some chagrin.

Pulsed plasma bolts peppered the rear of the Sports Hatch as the clones inside the Voyager following them opened fire.

'We can't take this for much longer, has this thing got any weapons other than this Sig of yours?' Zara said.

'Nope just the non-lethal variety; the EMP is about it. Apparently it's not a good policy to litter the streets with wrecked vehicles or dead bodies. You'll have to make do with the Sig,' Kurt replied.

More bolts struck the rear compartment of their vehicle and a small explosion erupted somewhere at the back of it sending the car into an uncontrolled rear-wheel spin. The vehicle veered across the road narrowly missing two oncoming vehicles from the opposite direction, which had to swerve to avoid crashing.

'The fuel cell has been damaged, we're losing fuel, we won't get far now, we'll have to ditch this and make it on foot,' Kurt said once he had the Sports Hatch under control once more. He had checked the vehicle's control panel and the readouts told him they only had a few minutes before the fuel cell was completely depleted.

'Are you crazy, make it on foot?' Zara shouted not believing what she was hearing.

'Have you any better ideas?'

'Yes actually. Pull up at the front of that building,' Zara told him.

Kurt wasn't quite sure what she had in mind but he went along with it, he had no choice really, their vehicle would stop of its own accord soon anyway.

He skidded to a stop in front of a tall building that had a double-fronted entrance hall. They both got out; she fired at the clones inside the Voyager that was coming to a stop just down the street from them as they ran up to the entrance.

'Okay, what's your plan?' he asked as he reached the entrance to the building. She came and stood next to him aiming the Sig down the street at the Voyager, firing off the occasional bolt to persuade any clone from exiting the vehicle.

'We get inside and get to the top of the building, perhaps your friends can pick us up from the roof.'

'Sounds like a plan,' Kurt agreed and accessed the control panel at the side of the door via his NI. He had soon hacked into the locking mechanism and had the double doors opened so they could gain entry to the building.

Zara kept watch down the street and occasionally fired a shot in the Voyager's direction in an attempt to delay them. From the opposite direction came the other two Voyagers, both of which came to a screeching halt in front of the building. Clones were firing from open windows at her with pulse rifles as they approached. Plasma bolts struck the ground in front of her and the walls at their side as Kurt attempted to open the doors.

'Okay we're in,' he said as he pulled her through the open door just as a salvo of plasma bolts peppered the doors where they had stood seconds earlier. Kurt locked the doors and pulled her towards the elevator at the back of the hallway. They ran and got into the first elevator available, scattering a few people who were in the hallway shouting for them to get away and hide. Kurt pressed the control panel to take the elevator to the top floor.

As they watched the doors close they saw the doors to the entrance blown apart under concentrated fire from pulse rifles. Kurt and Zara were on the move upwards in the elevator when a group of Rover5s came rushing into the hallway. As they spread out to take control of the area one of them stood in the middle and issued orders.

'You three lock down this hallway, no one in or out. You call the elevators and follow them to whichever floor they took, the rest with me up the stairs. Contact us the moment you know which floor they're on,' he said indicating which clones he meant with decisive waves of his large hand.

Inside the elevator Kurt and Zara watched the LED readout as the floors dropped away as they rose through the building. They were heading for the thirty-fifth floor at the very top.

'When we get to the top, look for a fire escape, we should

be able to get out onto the roof from there. It'll be easier to hold them off from that vantage point as they'll have to use the same point of entry to reach us,' Zara said.

'Unless there's more than one fire escape in which case we're screwed as we only have one weapon,' Kurt pointed out the one flaw in her plan.

'Well if you have any other suggestions what we should do then go ahead, I'm all ears,' Zara chided.

'Let's get to the roof and we'll have a better idea what we're facing. There may be something we can use as a weapon if we need to hold them off from two points,' he said.

The elevator came to a halt and the doors opened and they got out quickly. They looked around for a fire escape and found one at the far end of the corridor they were standing in.

'Over there,' Kurt said and they both sprinted towards it.

Kurt reached the window first and he manhandled it open just as they heard a disturbance behind them. Zara turned to look and saw several clones coming through the stairwell door. They were armed with pulse rifles and brought them up to fire.

She aimed and fired the Sig she was still holding before they had the chance to fire. Three pulsed plasma bolts struck the first two clones as they approached, stopping them in their tracks. They went down instantly, their blood spilling onto the floor where they lay.

'Quick get through the window, get up to the roof,' Kurt said pulling Zara to him.

'You go, I have the Sig,' she replied pushing Kurt away.

'Look, I won't lose you again,' he said grabbing her by the shoulder. He pulled her towards him and forced her to the window. 'Now go!' he shouted.

She was not prepared for the strength he displayed but

when she saw the anguish in his eyes she dived through the window onto the fire escape's steel balcony.

Kurt turned and by this time three clones were close enough to reach out and touch him. A hand clamped down on his shoulder pulling him back. Because he had one foot through the open window he stumbled back into the corridor right into a group of clones. They started to pound him with the rifle butts on his back and shoulders.

He lashed out at the nearest one, punching him in the stomach, doubling him over as all the air was purged from his lungs. He elbowed another in the face smashing his teeth in an explosion of blood. A third received a chop to the throat which crushed his windpipe causing him to drop like a stone as his airwaves snapped closed; his face went blue as he struggled to drag air into his starved lungs.

For a second Kurt found himself free to move a little but then a pulsed plasma bolt caught him a glancing blow to his left shoulder spinning him around. The pain from the shot lanced through him almost bringing him to his knees. He dodged to the side as the clone tried to reacquire his target. Kurt caught the front of the muzzle of the pulse rifle and yanked it from the clone's hands then swung it around his head to smash it into the head of the nearest attacker. It struck the clone's head with such force that it caved in the side where the point of impact was. Blood and brain matter sprayed out from the collision splashing other clones as they too came forward.

Turning the rifle around into the proper grip he rapidly fired at the rest of the clones gunning down at least three more. The corridor was empty by then as any other clones were reluctant to enter the killing field that the corridor had become. Kurt turned and exited through the open window and sprinted up the metal fire escape to vault over the lip of the roof.

'What kept you?' Zara asked as soon as she saw him. She saw the torn and burnt area of his shirt where he had been shot. The edges of the damaged cloth were smeared with blood, his blood, but when she looked closer the skin had reformed over the wound and was as good as new.

'I met some old friends, they didn't want me to leave,' Kurt replied.

'Well, at least they gave you a going away present,' she said.

'Yep, at least now if there is more than one fire escape we have a better chance of holding them off until Jake gets here,' Kurt said.

'Well let's hope they get here real soon because here they come,' Zara said as she pointed to the edge of the roof. A pulse rifle appeared over the edge and started firing. They quickly looked around for cover and realised there was none. They were sitting ducks on the top of this building and were about to face a group of determined well-armed clones.

'Get ready, here they come,' Kurt said calmly.

'They've made it to the top of that building,' observed Torres as they all watched the forward monitor screen.

'Yes, they're in a spot of trouble and if we don't get down there soon we may be too late to help,' Jake said. Without turning from the monitor screen he spoke to Cooper on the weapons control. 'Get ready to take out those hostiles Mack,' he said.

'Copy that,' Cooper replied, his hands ready on the control console.

'Artie take us down as close to the top of that roof as you can and fast,' Jake told the AI.

The Pulsar flew down towards Kurt and Zara as fast as her main engines allowed. As she neared the rooftop the AI pulled up using thrusters to hover over the surface giving Cooper time to make use of the pulse cannons. Kurt and Zara were standing back to back firing at the clones surging over the lip of the roof in attack formation.

Pulsed plasma bolts struck them from above offering back up to Kurt and Zara and the clones fell like rag dolls. Within moments of the Pulsar's arrival Kurt and Zara were standing alone on the rooftop which was now littered with many bodies.

Seeing that the clones were no longer a threat Cooper had ceased his onslaught and all those on board the forward section of the starship breathed a sigh of relief.

They had reached them in time.

A ramp was lowered from the rear section of the craft as it hovered near the edge of the rooftop so that Kurt and Zara could walk on board.

'We did it,' Zara said not quite believing that they were still alive.

Kurt smiled at her and said, 'C'mon, let's go, our ride is here.'

They walked up the ramp, which closed behind them as the craft slowly began to ascend up towards the upper atmosphere once more.

Hiding behind the lip of the rooftop, watching the craft ascend through the clouds, one of the clones, Orion, accessed a secure comm. link through his NI. He said, 'They're on their way; don't make it too easy for them to escape. I'll return to the airport and come aboard the shuttle once they've made the jump back to Earth.'

'Copy that,' said a voice in his ear.

Confident their plan was going forward as they had planned he went back inside the building off the fire escape and headed towards the elevator. His part in the plan was complete and it would now be up to his brothers to continue and bring it all to an end. All he had to do now was return to the Lunar base to await further orders.

The familiar tingle to his NI informed Apollo of a call coming through. He had been in his quarters relaxing after his stint in the C and C.

'Go ahead,' he said as he relaxed on his bed.

'Everything is going according to plan,' said the voice in his ear.

'Excellent,' the clone said.

'I'll give you further sit-rep's as the situation develops.'

'Good, I'll inform OMEGA Command,' the clone said then closed the connection. A hint of a smile crossed his lips as he passed the report on to OMEGA Command.

As Kurt and Zara reached the forward pilots section they were greeted by four smiling faces. At the very front a blond-haired man said to Zara, 'Take a seat, introductions can come later, we're the Wildfire Team and your escort back to Col Sec HQ.'

Kurt returned the smile and said, 'It's great to see you again Jake.'

'Just glad we got here in time Kurt,' Jake replied and then he turned back to face the front of the craft once more. 'Okay Artie, take us up,' he said seemingly to no one which confused the newcomers until a disembodied voice replied, 'Copy that sir, we'll be rejoining the rest of the Pulsar in approximately eight minutes. Welcome aboard Captain Stryder and Miss Hardy, please strap yourselves in this could get a bit bumpy.'

As the two newcomers sat in the two vacant chairs that had appeared from out of the walls Jake said, 'Pulsar to Vanguard, what's the status of that cruiser?'

Captain Pierce said, 'She's just moved out of orbit to intercept you. Do you want me to move to engage?'

'That would be most helpful, Captain. Once we've rejoined with the rest of our ship we'll be heading back to Earth. I suggest you try to delay them then make the jump back to Earth also,' Jake replied.

Kurt looked at Zara who was watching the crew of this ship go about their business with the efficiency of a well-oiled machine. She said, 'It seems we're not out of the woods just yet.'

'Mack stay on the weapons console ready to give the Vanguard a hand should they need it,' Jake said.

'Copy that,' he replied.

Torres turned to the newcomers and said, 'Don't worry, we'll get you home safe.'

'I'm not worried,' Zara said, quite amazed when she realised that she actually wasn't worried at all. She was as calm as if this was a Sunday school outing. She knew she should be concerned, but instead she found herself almost knowing that everything would work out okay.

Torres looked at her not quite knowing if she was putting on a brave face or if she really was such a cool customer. Perhaps she knew something about this situation that the rest of them didn't. Putting those thoughts behind her she turned back to study the forward monitor screen.

Kurt looked at Zara and said, 'You really aren't bothered are you?'

'No I'm not, I don't know why, I've just got this really strange feeling that we'll get back to base. Do you think it's something to do with what I'm going through, do you experience feelings like that?' she said.

'I'm still trying to come to terms with what I can do and I find out new things about it all the time so, yes, it could very well be part of the change. It's something to think about certainly, so I wouldn't dismiss it as a glitch, it could very well be significant,' he said.

'If that's true then why do I feel like that? Are these people that good or is something else going on here we're not aware of?' she said and the longer she thought of the implications of that question the more it worried her.

'Yes, they're that good. I've seen them in action before and it would be a lot simpler if that was true. Unfortunately from what was in the report about OMEGA I doubt this will be over even if we do get back to base safely,' he replied.

The Pulsar burst through the upper atmosphere on full power, her afterburners blazing a trail as they made their way to rendezvous with the main body of the starship. Inside the forward section the AI was monitoring the approaching cruiser that had altered its approach into an attack vector.

Off to the side, the Vanguard was also coming into position to intercept. The Vanguard fired her forward pulse cannons across the bow of the cruiser then hailed the craft ordering it to lay to and allow the Pulsar's forward section clear passage to rendezvous with the rest of her. The Vanguard's hails went unanswered and the cruiser returned fire with lateral pulse cannons. Plasma bolts strafed the front of the Vanguard as the cruiser sailed past towards the Pulsar's forward section. The Vanguard was sent off course by the blasts from the cruiser and by the time the pilot had brought her around so they could follow the cruiser, they were too close to the planet's atmosphere and had to reverse their momentum before they got caught in the gravitational field of Celeron.

Jake and his team watched as this action unfolded and when they saw the Vanguard knocked out of position they knew they were on their own.

What the pilot of the cruiser was unaware of was that the rest of the Pulsar could take action as instructed by the AI.

The cruiser came towards the forward section trying to cut them off from rejoining the rest of the ship and therefore making it impossible for them to make the jump to hyper-space. She fired her forward pulse cannons at the smaller craft in rapid bursts.

The forward section was still coming up on full power with their afterburners flaring behind them. Inside Jake watched and issued orders quickly as he saw the cruiser fire on them. 'Artie I hope you have your shields up. Mack fire a full spread of Hellfire missiles at that cruiser. Artie swing us around her the second Mack fires the missiles.'

Cooper said, 'Missiles locked on target and away.'

'Artie now!' Jake shouted and the AI did as ordered and steered the small craft by shutting off the afterburners and cutting in lateral thrusters to send her sideways around the approaching cruiser. Her own inertia would do the rest now that they were in zero gravity.

The three Hellfire missiles impacted on the cruiser's shields, but the force of the explosions stopped her cold. All forward momentum ceased and she lay motionless in space as Jake and the others on board the Pulsar watched as they sailed around her. By the time the cruiser could manoeuvre herself around into a position to continue her attack, the two sections of the Pulsar would again be one.

The AI used the Pulsar's thrusters to manoeuvre the forward section into position so they could dock once more. Once that was done Jake said, 'Okay Artie, let's make the jump back to Earth. Pulsar to Vanguard, thank you for all your help, I suggest you follow us back to Earth before that cruiser asks for a rematch.'

'Copy that Pulsar, see you back home, Vanguard out,' Captain Pierce replied.

'Okay Artie, take us home,' Jake said and he sat back hiding the relief he felt as the AI did as ordered. A hyperspace window opened in front of them and within seconds they had disappeared through it.

Chapter Seventeen

'Are you sure this will work?' Norsky asked as he stood next to the large man he knew simply as Hermes. They were on the bridge of the Lempinski, an Akiva class starship similar to the Legend-class starships of the Colonial Confederation. It could pass as an Alliance starship, which was exactly what they hoped for. It was fitted with Alliance class defence shields and weapons and had all the Alliance identity codes installed into the mainframe computer. It was to all intents and purposes an Alliance starship except that it was crewed entirely by clones from OMEGA with one notable exception – Pavel Norsky. This craft was identical to those supplied by MaxCorp to the Alliance and with everything installed to Alliance spec's it should pass muster as one of their own.

'There are no guarantees in anything but we have done everything possible to ensure no one suspects we are not an Alliance starship,' replied Hermes.

'Well, I guess we'll soon find out, won't we? We're coming up on the Tartaran perimeter,' Norsky said.

Hermes glanced at him as they stood side by side looking at the forward viewscreen and wondered how he knew where they were. He had no idea, all he knew was they had just come out of hyperspace; as to their actual location he had no idea and neither should Norsky. It was slightly unsettling but he didn't let his concern show.

'Sir, approaching the Tartaran perimeter in three hundred kilometres,' the pilot said.

Norsky looked around at the crew and wondered how on earth they managed to identify each other; to him, they all looked the same. The one standing next to him was called Hermes, but even with his enhanced senses, he could not pick him out if several stood together. All he knew was that they were clones; maybe they were interchangeable taking on the role of 'Hermes' when needed. It was something to ponder on some other time. For now, they had brought him here to do a job and it suited him to comply as the end result was something that suited both their agendas.

'Take us in and hail the command starship,' Hermes said then, turning to Norsky, 'Okay, Captain, time to earn your pay.'

'Alliance Lempinski to command craft, this is Captain Pavel Norsky of Alliance Intelligence acting under direct orders from High Command. I'm here to take command of any and all samples brought up from the planet below. They are to be returned to a secure location for further study. Please have them ready for transportation upon our arrival,' Norsky said through the comm. channel.

He turned to Hermes and said, 'They'll be checking my ID codes now to see if I'm legit. They won't dare contact High Command for fear of looking like fools. The Alliance rules their military with fear, to ensure obedience is a given.'

'That is what we are counting on.'

'What you need from them will be ready when we arrive. You just need to make sure we're ready to depart the second those samples are on board and secure, I don't want to have to explain our mission any further should they decide to question us. Is that clear?'

'You are not in command here, is that clear? We know what we are doing; you do your job and leave the rest to us.'

'You had better know what you're doing because there are at least five other starships out here and I doubt you could hold them all off let alone that super destroyer that's the command craft.'

'It won't come to that if your codes are identified as you said. No one will die here today.'

Norsky looked at him and said, 'I've been dead, that doesn't bother me, failure does though. Make sure you do this right because failure is not an option.'

Hermes looked at him and something in his eyes made him falter. He was scared of nothing; fear was something that had been engineered out of this generation of clones and yet there was still something about this man that troubled him.

'At least we agree on that,' he said finally.

Norsky turned and strolled away, 'I'll be in my quarters if you need me,' he said over his shoulder.

Hermes watched him leave, still feeling unsettled by the man, which in itself was troublesome as he was programmed not to have these sorts of emotions.

'Sir, we are approaching the security perimeter,' the pilot said.

Hermes returned his attention to the task at hand. He said, 'Wait here for them to deliver the samples.' He would remain on the station on the bridge until the handover was complete. He had no reason to leave to relax, or anything of the sort, unlike Norsky. His duty was clear and he would carry it. He had no choice, it was the way he was made; he would carry out his orders or die.

The Pulsar reached the Terran system and slowly entered orbit around Earth. Jake, Kurt, Zara and the rest of the Wildfire Team took the forward section down to the planet's surface and landed at Area 15 where Col Sec HQ was situated, deep underground.

They took the express elevator to the bowels of the huge complex alighting on Level Ten where General Sinclair's office was situated. As they entered they were greeted with Sinclair seated in his usual chair and Matt in another chair in front of the large ornate desk. The two men got up as they saw their friends and colleagues enter.

'I must congratulate you all on a successful mission,' Sinclair said with an uncharacteristic brief smile.

'I'm not sure it was that successful sir, but we are here,' Kurt said.

'How so?' Sinclair asked. 'Before you answer that I must inform you of a troubling development brought to my attention by Matt,' he added.

All attention was suddenly focussed on the general and what he had to tell them.

'When Matt came from RandCorp HQ he saw someone who lured him to an alley where he was attacked,' Sinclair said.

'Attacked, by whom?' asked Kurt concerned.

'I would expect by the same people we just had a run-in with,' Zara offered. Kurt looked at her with a raised eyebrow. She was exhibiting another sign of her extraordinary prescience.

'How can you possibly know that?' Matt asked.

'I'm not sure, I just do that's all. Am I right?' she said.

'Yes my dear, you are indeed, which is something that requires further investigation but not right now. Right now we have more pressing concerns,' Sinclair said before Matt could ask any more questions. He was still rattled from his encounter earlier and it showed.

'So who was it you saw?' Torres asked, sensing that there were questions here that certain people didn't really want asked or answered, so she brought the topic back on target.

Matt looked at the dark-haired beauty and said, 'Tanya Wilde.'

'Wasn't she killed shortly after the Nemesis attack?' Cooper asked.

'Yes, right in front of me and that's what's troubling me.'

Everyone looked at him and saw the anguish in his tortured eyes. They realised some of the hurt he must be feeling at having someone shot and killed in front of them, someone they cared for.

'The trouble is we are not sure why she showed up. Plus, if she is alive now, who was it that Matt saw being killed?' Sinclair said.

'What do you think Matt?' Kurt asked as he went up to his friend and placed a hand on his shoulder. 'Are you okay buddy?' he asked.

'I don't know Kurt, I really don't know. I mean I thought I was getting over seeing her killed but seeing her just recently brought it all back. If this new Tanya isn't the real one then who the hell is she and what's the reason for bringing her back?' Matt said anguish tainting his voice.

'The obvious choice is OMEGA; they are the only ones with the resources and capabilities to clone her. Whether or not this Tanya is the real one remains to be seen, but we have to assume that they have an objective here and that we'll find out what that is soon enough. I'm sure we'll hear from OMEGA before long,' Sinclair said.

'What do we do in the meantime?' Kurt asked.

Sinclair looked at him then at Zara. 'I would like to

know a little more of young Miss Hardy's miraculous escape from Toldax,' he said with a smile.

Kurt knew this was the opportunity that Sinclair had been waiting for to learn just how successful the serum administered to him had been. Now Zara had handed it to him on a plate and there was nothing he could do to prevent the truth coming out. His whole body tensed up in readiness for the revelation that was about to be uncovered.

'I have no idea, sir. I presume that the plasma bolt didn't kill me, obviously. I must've been covered by rubble that somehow protected me from the explosion when the facility blew up. When I woke up I was on board a starship so I can only presume that whoever found me administered medical aid because any injuries had vanished,' Zara said.

Kurt looked at her with surprise. He somehow kept his facial expression neutral so he didn't give anything away.

'They must have put her in a medical coma so that her body would heal itself,' Vance said.

'Yes, that way her body would not register the trauma she had undergone,' Torres added.

'Makes sense sir,' Cooper said.

'What else could it be? I mean the alternative is that her body regenerated itself. We all know that's not possible, don't we?' Jake said and the glance they all gave Kurt did not go unnoticed by Sinclair.

He looked at each and every one of them then glanced down at his table. When he looked up once more it was with some disappointment he said, 'Yes we all know that is not possible.'

Kurt relaxed then, it seemed for a moment then that his secret was about to be revealed; a secret he shared now with the woman he loved. It was also a secret that his friends knew about but one they seemed willing to keep.

'Well, I think you've all earned a spot of rest. I suggest

you all grab a bite to eat and some sleep before the debriefing sessions. I'll schedule them to start tomorrow. For now, people, well done,' Sinclair said.

Kurt said, 'C'mon guys, let's go before he changes his mind,' and he led them all out leaving Sinclair to ponder at how close he had come to learning the truth about Kurt.

Chapter Eighteen

When Kurt woke his first thoughts were of Zara Hardy. They had shared a meal together after leaving Sinclair's office and they had talked long after. When they realised how late it was they left the restaurant and he escorted her to the quarters she had been allotted for the duration of her stay on base. She had invited him in for a drink, which he gladly accepted.

They talked long into the night about their days in Recon Delta, about training, about everything and anything except what had happened to them both. That was the one subject they skirted around and later after he had returned to his own quarters, he could not think of one reason why.

He checked the time and called her quarters to see if she was awake.

'Hey you,' she replied, her voice husky from sleep. The sound of her voice sent a warm tingle through his body, which settled as a flutter in his stomach.

'I was wondering if you'd like to grab some breakfast?' he asked.

'I'd love some. Give me about fifteen minutes to take a

shower and make myself beautiful for you then I'll meet you in the canteen, okay?' she said.

'I'll see you there in fifteen, and you are already beautiful,' Kurt said then closed the connection. As he made his way to the shower his step was lighter than normal.

Norsky came out of his quarters and returned to the bridge a few hours after they had arrived at the Tartaran security perimeter. He had not heard any news of the samples being transferred to their starship since their arrival and was wondering what the holdup was.

'Any news on the transfer?' he asked as he entered the bridge. Hermes was still where he had left him standing in the centre of the bridge looking at the forward viewscreen. The other clones remained at their respective stations and continued with their duties.

Hermes turned to face him and said, 'They're docking as we speak.'

'That's good then, we can return to. Where is it you're taking these samples?' he said suddenly aware that he didn't know what they actually intended, just that they had designs on the destruction of Col Sec.

'Earth, we're taking them to Earth,' Hermes said, turning back to the forward viewscreen.

Norsky felt like he was being dismissed as inconsequential, which was something he was not going to let pass him by without saying or doing something.

He walked up to Hermes and stood right behind him. He clamped a hand on his shoulder and spun him around with surprising strength. As the clone faced him his eyes opened wide in surprise and sudden anger. Before he could raise his fist to strike Norsky reached up and grabbed him by the throat extending his arm, which stretched the clone's neck making him stand on his tiptoes. He tried to prise Norsky's hand free with both of his but failed to even get a good grip.

'I think it's time you showed me some respect. Without my invaluable aid, you would not have been able to carry out this portion of your mission, so when I ask a question it's only polite to offer up an answer,' Norsky said through gritted teeth.

He released him before other clones came to his aid. 'What do you want to know?' Hermes asked.

'What are these samples you've had brought on board and what do you intend to do with them?'

'They are creatures from the planet below, creatures with a propensity for violence. Our intention is to set them loose within Col Sec HQ and wait for them to kill everyone there,' Orion said.

'And how the hell do you plan on getting them inside Col Sec HQ? You'll be shot down before you get within landing range.'

'You've been away for some time Captain but let me assure you that we've taken steps to ensure that our plan will succeed. If you bear with us for a little while longer all will be revealed.'

Norsky looked around the bridge and saw that all eyes were on him. He had to admit that he was intrigued once more. They had persuaded him to help them with the lure of the destruction of Col Sec, now he hoped they would fulfil that bargain and carry out their plan.

'Okay then, I'll wait a while longer but this had better be worth it,' he said.

'Trust me, Captain, it will, you have my word,' Hermes said with a smile.

As Kurt and Zara were just finishing off their breakfast they both received a call through their NIs from General Sinclair.

'Please report to my office immediately,' he said.

The two of them looked at each other and by the tone of Sinclair's voice, they knew it was serious.

They got up and left the canteen without a word. The canteen was on the floor above Sinclair's office so they went straight to the elevator and rode it down to Level Ten. When they entered Sinclair's office everyone else was already there. They were standing around the desk and facing the rear wall where a monitor was displaying an image of a news feed.

'What's going on?' Kurt asked as they entered.

Matt turned to look at them and his expression told them more than any amount of words ever could.

'This came in on every news feed available and it went straight on to the GalaxyWeb,' Sinclair said as he turned to look at them.

'Computer replay news feed,' he said as he returned his attention to the monitor screen.

The image on the screen restarted and showed a young woman standing on the steps in front of the MaxCorp building. Arrayed before her was a set of microphones and cameras to collect and record the event.

The young woman was easily recognised as the woman Matt had seen killed, Tanya Wilde, the daughter of Jonas Wilde, the brains behind OMEGA.

'I've come here today to right a wrong and to clear my father's name. A few weeks ago an attack on the Colonial Confederation Headquarters was perpetrated by an enemy force you called OMEGA. It was claimed that my father, Jonas Wilde was in charge of this group and therefore was guilty of this atrocity. No one stood up for him. It was claimed that he used resources from MaxCorp to fund this group and that Maxwell Eisenhower was unaware of all this. It was in fact Eisenhower who was guilty of all the crimes laid at my father's feet. It was in fact Eisenhower, not my father, who used his own corporation to fund this OMEGA group. Eisenhower killed my father when he learned of what he was doing. My father tried to get Eisenhower to stop his plan and when he wouldn't my father threatened to inform the authorities. That's what got him killed. My father told me all this before he was killed but I was away and couldn't get back in time. I had arranged to come home when the attack happened and my flight was delayed. Then I heard all the claims about my father that were flying about and I remained away until I could gather the proof,' she said.

A voice from out of camera shot asked, 'What is this proof you're talking about?'

'I have a call log of my father's last call to me informing me of Eisenhower's plan. It disagrees with the report from your General Sinclair of Col Sec. It proves that my father was innocent of all the claims against him and refutes General Sinclair's claim. If he claimed to be an eyewitness to the actions he described, you must ask yourself if he was somehow complicit in any of it,' she replied.

'Are you accusing General Sinclair of being involved in the attack on his own HQ?' asked the reporter, his tone telling everyone of his disbelief.

'I would never accuse anyone, all I ask is for an investigation by an independent authority be undertaken because only then will the truth be found,' she said. Then, holding her hand up to stem any further questions, she said, 'I've been asked to take over control of MaxCorp in the meantime by the Board of Directors to which I have agreed. I must inform you now that MaxCorp has ceased production of all products under contract to Col Sec until further notice. The decision to renew any contracts with them will depend upon the verdict of the enquiry I have requested. Production to our other customers will go ahead without further disruption.'

That was the end of the transmission and the screen went blank leaving the room in silence.

'Now we know,' Kurt said.

Chapter Nineteen

OMEGA command was at a secret location known only to those who had business there. It was a sprawling complex built deep inside a warren of caves on the planet RH426. It was a barren world, the 'RH' stood for Roger Humphries, the astronomer who discovered the planet during the early years of the colonisation programme. It was basically a huge rock floating around an S-type star (S as in Sol, our own Sun). It had no indigenous life but at one time did wield an astonishing variety of rare earth elements used in propulsion systems for starships from that time and was just ripe for mining. The Confederation strip-mined it until there was virtually nothing left, especially considering the cost of the project, so they abandoned it deeming it of no further use or value.

Jonas Wilde knew of the planet from his days in Col Sec and once he had set up OMEGA he planned to use RH426 as a base.

There were a series of natural caves situated away from the major deep cast mines that were ideal for his needs and he began a clandestine programme of siphoning off funds to finance and build a base there.

Now, more than five years later, the base was fully functional and was the control point for all OMEGA activity and where Jonas Wilde remained. His face had been broadcast all over the known galaxy as the face of OMEGA and the man behind the atrocity that had levelled the original Col Sec HQ. He didn't mind everyone knowing he was behind the attack. What he did mind though was the loss of the ability to move around freely, but he knew you couldn't have one without the other.

He was a sociopath who would not take the blame for any of his failings, preferring instead to blame others. He blamed Col Sec in general, and Sinclair in particular, for the breakup of his marriage although if he thought back they had never been suited. His wife realised what kind of man he was early on and only remained for the sake of their only daughter, Tanya. As soon as she was able she left the marriage citing irretrievable differences in the marriage. What she really meant was she couldn't bear to be around him any longer. She died shortly after and there was some doubt surrounding the circumstances of her death. It was a road accident, but some thought Jonas had had a hand in her demise. However, due to lack of evidence to prove otherwise any suspicion over his involvement had been shelved.

Wilde blamed Sinclair for him being discharged from Col Sec. They allowed him to resign his commission rather than forcing him out, in that way he could gain employment elsewhere without his record holding him back. The reason for this decision was that his psyche evaluation showed some anomalies that they could not let pass. In other words, he had failed, but it was borderline, hence the offer of resigning so that the failure would not go on his record. They were clear in their instructions though, if he tried to remain they would have to demote him and he would never hold any command rank ever again. Alternatively, they could release him with the psyche failure plainly displayed on his record.

He chose to resign, after which he procured a position at MaxCorp. However, he blamed Col Sec for his undoing, laying the blame squarely upon the shoulders of General Sinclair.

He also blamed his wife for making their daughter soft and for turning Col Sec against him, so when he had had the opportunity he had her killed in front of the agent she had grown so fond of. The new Tanya, who he had grown, was a clone of his real daughter with one major redesign. He had made her like him, a sociopath and therefore much more controllable, or so he believed. She was now truly her father's little girl and together they would take down Col Sec and all those who worked with them.

He watched the news feed once more, revelling in the story he had woven to cause confusion and doubt over Col Sec and in its leader, General Sinclair. They would be running around in damage limitation exercises, wondering what to do if the Confederation turned against them and how they could put things right again. This meant they would be totally unprepared for what he had planned next.

Once he had destroyed Col Sec's ability to function it would be time to turn his attention towards the Elysium Alliance. With the void created with the destruction of Col Sec, it would be the optimum moment for the Alliance to mount a first strike against their old enemies. He could not allow that to happen. His aim was to destroy Col Sec, but not the entire galaxy, by a war that would consume too many planets and their valuable resources. What would be the point in that? No, his aim was to cripple the power structure and replace it with another – OMEGA – with him at the helm.

The next phase of his plan was about to be put into action. This would lead to the endgame. It was a two-pronged attack that would split Col Sec from its most valuable asset and place that asset in his hands while the rest of Col Sec would face their worst nightmare and ultimate defeat.

They would not see it coming; when they did they would not be able to do anything about it because it would be too late.

The endgame would not only cripple Col Sec but cripple Earth's ability to respond as well. It would create a power vacuum in which the Confederation, after being decimated, would be unable to cope with what had happened, giving him the opportunity to step in and fill that void.

Once that had been done his revenge would be complete.

All the focus would be on the attacks on Col Sec, no one would suspect an attack on the Confederation itself. President Takagi would never suspect his government would be put at risk. The attack on Col Sec HQ earlier, which led to the relocation of the HQ and the separation of the Confederation HQ into the Capitol Building, was ultimately his intention. Split the two apart making them easier to attack and destroy; it was an old tactic, as old as battle itself, divide and conquer.

Whilst his troops took care of Col Sec HQ, Norsky would bring Kurt Stryder to OMEGA Command where he would be bled dry so that his blood could be used to help create an army of indestructible Rover5s. Then, finally, the last attack on the Capitol Building would destroy the Confederation government, all supervised from the Lunar Colony.

He had a manufacturing facility here inside the colony where he grew a new batch of Rover5s. It had been from here that the Rover5s used on this mission had been grown. For this new batch, he had named the commanders after the old Greek Gods. Orion was in command of the team dealing with the woman found on Toldax, Apollo was in command of the Lunar base, Hermes was in command of the team looking after Norsky and Hades was in charge of the final assault team which would be leaving soon. He had given them the names to distinguish them from their brothers and to give them a sense of individuality that being grown in a batch robbed them of.

Wilde rubbed his hands with glee as he thought about the expression on Sinclair's normally stoic face when he realised it was over and that Col Sec was defeated. He wished he could be there at the end but he knew because of the propaganda Sinclair had spread about him after the attack in New York, it was impossible for him to go anywhere on Earth without being arrested. It was a situation he was also working on to rectify.

It was all coming to fruition; all he had to do now was wait.

'What do you intend on doing, sir?' Kurt asked once the screen had gone blank. They were all still in Sinclair's office and were still reeling from the message they had just watched.

'We do what we do best, we carry on with our jobs,' Sinclair replied, his face stern. He was determined not to give in to this new threat, this propaganda war started against him and those he worked with. He would face this with the same resoluteness that he faced every threat against the Confederation, and he would win.

'Do you want any of us to go talk to this Tanya Wilde and see what this is all about sir?' asked Jake.

'Oh God no, there would be absolutely no point in that. No, she has made her intentions quite plain in her statement. I can only deduce that she is working for OMEGA now and they are pulling her strings, so to speak,' Sinclair said resolutely.

'So you're sure that OMEGA is behind all this then, sir?' Kurt said.

'I'm afraid so, there can be no doubt now. We were never sure that Jonas died in the explosion that destroyed the top of MaxCorp HQ. It seems obvious to me now that since all the attacks by the clones he dubbed Rover5s and the resurrection of Miss Wilde. We can be certain that he is in control and is planning something truly diabolical.'

'You make him sound like a villain from one of those old spy movies,' Kurt observed with a slight smile.

'Make no bones about it Kurt, that man is a deranged individual, a sociopath who is incapable of taking the blame for any of his actions. He blames Col Sec for everything bad in his life, whether they are real or perceived and me in particular. He is smart, resourceful, determined and capable of getting almost anything he wants. When you couple that with the financial resources he has at his fingertips then he is possibly the most dangerous man alive today. We tried to curb his finances, take away his resources by issuing a statement that held him accountable for the atrocities recently, but it seems he has found a way around that particular strategy. Now he has the full backing of MaxCorp once more and there is no telling what he will do with it.'

Kurt looked around at all the other faces and they shared the same expression. They were all aware of what this person was capable of, Matt more than any of them. It seemed that there were only two people in the room who were not and it was Zara and himself. He was getting a feel for what they were up against more now after Sinclair had explained it fully and he felt the same as they did. This whole situation was dire and they were very much on the defensive. They were relegated to the role of counter-puncher; they could only react to whatever was thrown at them. They could not take an offensive posture because they had no target to aim at. All they could do was wait for what was to come and react against it and hope they had a defence against it.

'I see, I'm sorry sir, I didn't know,' Kurt said.

'No need Kurt, you were not here when it happened so you could not have known.'

'I attended the memorial though after it was over, and I was on Celeron when the attack took place.'

Matt looked at him and said, 'I saw you.'

'I know, I felt guilty about not being here when it went down but I was facing demons of my own. It was later on Tartaran that I realised I couldn't turn my back on you any longer.'

'Water under the bridge now,' Sinclair said as he looked at the two men. He continued with, 'We must look forward and plan for what Jonas throws at us and hope we are as best prepared as possible.'

With a wave of his hand, Sinclair indicated that the briefing was over and he turned to face the monitor once more. As his best filed out of the office he was left alone to think and hope that any preparations they made would be enough in the coming hours.

Chapter Twenty

The Lempinski came out of hyperspace close to Earth but out of range of the sensors of the defence net. Hermes stood on the bridge as before staring at the forward viewscreen, legs wide apart with his hands clasped behind his back. He had remained like that since Norsky had challenged him about their mission and he had to admit the man had a singular focus that he found quite frankly disturbing.

'Okay, we're here. What do you intend on doing? No more riddles or diversions, I want the plain truth,' Norsky said as he came to stand next to the hulking clone. He, unlike Hermes, had paced the width of the bridge waiting for their arrival at their destination.

Hermes turned to face him and said, 'We will take the ship into orbit around Earth. We have codes that will identify her as a Confederation ship and by the time they have realised they are false, it will be too late. We will have, by that time, landed at the new site of the HQ with a force great enough to overcome their defences. We will then penetrate their HQ and release all the samples.'

'About time, let's get to it,' Norsky said eager to get started.

'You have another mission; you will not be coming with us. Ours could be considered a suicide mission as we do not expect to survive.'

Norsky looked at him with renewed respect. These men were laying down their lives for their cause with no thought for their own safety. That kind of dedication required a certain kind of fortitude, or fanaticism. Which one this was he wasn't sure.

'We require you to do something that is vital to our mission's success, without which this whole mission could fall apart and all our sacrifices will be for nothing. It will also give you what you truly desire, a chance for revenge against the one person you hate the most in the entire galaxy, Kurt Stryder.'

At the mention of *his* name, he became focused. Up to that point, he felt a slight disappointment at not being in on the attack, at not being able to vent his fury against Col Sec. On the mention of the man's name and the fact that he would finally get to face him, for once they had his full, undivided attention.

'Tell me what I must do,' he said.

Able Rand was at his desk perusing some files on his computer monitor. It had been a long morning; as usual, he was up at six to exercise then, after a shower, he would go to the office where his working day would begin. It was a routine he had adhered to since he had inherited the Corporation from his father.

He had personally supervised all the upgrades to the tech that they had supplied to Col Sec, all of which had gone smoothly. As the transfer was done wirelessly, as most things were done nowadays, all upgrades would have been complete by the time he sat down for breakfast and that included any tech that needed to be transported across the galaxy. They had used a subspace carrier wave boosted by transmitters strategically placed so that the upgrades would be carried out as fast as possible.

He was just thinking of breaking off for the time being to grab some lunch when a security alarm alerted him to a breach at the ground floor entrance.

Norsky and the team of Rover5s had arrived at the Rand-Corp Headquarters building in a shuttle from the Lempinski. Norsky had alighted at the foot of the steps of the great building after rappelling from the hovering shuttle along with the clones. They alighted at the steps of the great building to amazed looks from the bystanders and pedestrians. Once they were on the ground the shuttle lifted back up into the air towards the top of the huge building where it put down. The pilot kept the engines turning over to keep warm for a fast take-off and departure. Norsky and the Rover5s walked up to the door as he accessed the security cameras that covered the entrance via his NI and shut them down. As they entered through the huge double doorway they were greeted by two security guards dressed in dark suits with tell tale bulges beneath their left armpits, telling Norsky they were armed.

They couldn't believe what they were seeing and for a moment they were frozen to the spot from the absurdity of it all. What was an armed group of huge muscle-bound men doing invading the lobby they thought? Then their training kicked in and they pulled out their pistols, Sig P999s.

'Freeze!' they both shouted at the intruders as they aimed their weapons at them.

Norsky turned his head to look at them and they seemed to move in slow motion. He was supremely confident in his abilities and since waking up on Toldax he knew exactly what he could do. He knew he was in no danger from the guards. He knew he could not outrun a pulsed plasma bolt but he could anticipate when it would be fired and in that way actually move out of the way in time.

Before they could fire he had brought up his Remm assault rifle and fired a stream of pulsed plasma bolts at the guard on his left, cutting the guard almost in half. Blood sprayed in a lateral arc from the guard's guts as he was sent sprawling backwards. His arms went up and he fired his Sig sending a burst of plasma bolts up into the roof of the building.

The second guard turned to look at his fellow guard as he was cut down, his eyes wide in disbelief.

How the hell had he moved so fast?

He watched his friend's guts spill out as he was sent flying backwards from the salvo of pulsed plasma bolts. He watched his friend die.

By the time he returned his gaze to his attacker the Remm was pointing at him too.

Norsky fired a second burst at the other guard, the bolts stitching a line up his chest as he fell backwards, dead.

By the time the second guard hit the floor everyone in the foyer had run, scrambling for either the exit or some kind of cover. Panic ran through the lower level of the building like flames through sun-dried tinder.

The Rover5s had remained immobile whilst Norsky strutted his stuff. The moment the two guards had been dispatched and panic erupted in the lobby, they shot anything that moved. The staff who worked in the lobby ran towards all the emergency exits but were cut down by the plasma fire from the Remm assault rifles.

Norsky brought the Remm up to his shoulder and fired at all the cameras he could see. One shot for each camera was all it took, rendering the security feed for the foyer blind.

He then turned the assault rifle on the main desk and fired, salvo after salvo until it was completely destroyed. He spun around and looked at the carnage. There were still a few people who didn't have the time to get to safety, all of whom were gunned down mercilessly by the Rover5s. Soon the foyer was littered with the dead bodies of RandCorp workers along with the two security guards.

The alarm was raised the moment a single unauthorised weapon entered the premises and the foyer was locked down. By the time Norsky and his team had finished killing all those present, all the doors leading to rooms off the foyer and elevators leading upwards were locked. Norsky used his NI to access the building's main computer hacking through several levels of security and firewalls. He was an agent of the Alliance and his skill at hacking was second to none so it only took him moments. Once he had access he unlocked one elevator for his use only, the Express elevator. This was the only one that could reach the Penthouse. He kept the rest locked down so that no one could escape from the upper levels. There were several people up there he needed to gain control of. While he was getting to them he wanted to cause as much mayhem as he could. If that meant slaughtering as many people as he came across then he was okay with that. He had no compunction in killing; they would be considered collateral damage, nothing more, a means to an end.

He entered the elevator and looked at the nearest Rover5. He still could not tell any of them apart so he said, 'You know what to do,' and then ordered the elevator to go to the Penthouse. As the elevator doors closed he ejected the battery pack from the Remm, replaced it into the charging pouch on his ammo harness and replaced it with a fresh one. He racked the slide of the rifle on the underside priming the weapon so that he was good to go.

The elevator arrived at the Penthouse and the doors opened.

———

Able Rand was concerned when he saw how the feed from the security cameras went down in the foyer. The Penthouse covered the entire top floor of the building and had several large offices and it was the hub of the entire MegaCorp. It was where Able ran his business aided by his son and daughter, Josh and Jennifer. What worried him most about the alert was that they were in danger. He wasn't afraid for his own life as he had lived a long, incredibly fruitful and productive one and if it ended today he would have no regrets. What he could not face though was having his children in danger. He would walk through hell and back to ensure they were safe. That was why he had installed all new security features in the Penthouse and had all personnel who worked on this floor supplied with sidearms, trained by the security staff on how to use them effectively.

He opened his desk drawer and took out a Sig P999. He ejected the battery clip and checked its charge; there was a small LED indicator on the side showing either a 'red' or 'green' light. The 'green' light was on meaning it was carrying a full charge. He inserted it back in the butt and jacked the slide to prime the pistol and he was ready to rock and roll as the ex-Marine who instructed him would say.

'Josh, Jess, are you both armed?' he said through the comm. channel his NI had accessed.

'Yes Dad,' Josh said, then added, 'I'm going to Jess' office now. Don't worry I'll keep her safe, you make sure your office is secure.'

'Don't you worry about me son, just make sure your sister is safe okay?'

'Will do. This is a great opportunity to test out those new security measures we installed,' Josh said with enthusiasm.

'I've set the silent alarm for everyone on this floor, they should be heading for the hidden exits as we speak,' Able said.

'Good, now you get into your pod and get out of there now Dad,' Josh said, his voice exhibiting concern for his father.

When Josh received no reply from his father his heart jumped into his mouth. 'Dad, are you there?' he said, his voice rising.

Nothing, he could tell the carrier wave the comm. signal used was dead. That could only mean one thing.

His father was in trouble.

Norsky exited the Express elevator, his Remm assault rifle up at his shoulder as he aimed down the barrel. Several people were running past the entrance to the elevator so he shot them. Bodies went flying down the corridor, recipients of pulsed plasma bolts that cut them down as they tried to escape.

When he had hacked into the building's computer he had learned of all the security procedures evident in the building, including the recent improvements to the Penthouse. It also afforded him a schematic layout of the floor so he knew where all the offices were and who worked in them.

He headed for the main one, where the head honcho worked, Able Rand himself.

Stepping over dead or fallen bodies he made his way along the corridor to the end where it veered to the left, ending at a pair of huge double doors. He aimed the Remm at the doors and fired. The plasma bolts blew a huge hole in the doors and as he stood in the shattered remains of the doorway the look on the tall, old man's face was quite funny to see.

'Knock knock,' Norsky said with a sinister smile. 'What? Oh, you thought your new security measures would prevent me or anyone else from getting in here?' he asked. Then with a dismissive wave of his hand said, 'I disabled them on the way up.'

'Who are you?' Able Rand asked remarkably calmly in the face of such danger.

'Take a seat Mister Rand, and I'll tell you while we wait for him to arrive,' Norsky said.

'Wait for who to arrive?'

'Why, Kurt Stryder, who else?'

Chapter Twenty-One

Sinclair got up from his desk and, placing his hands in his lower lumbar region, he arched his back stretching out the kinks he felt knotted there. He walked over to the cupboard to the right of where he had been sitting and picked up a small glass tumbler. He placed a few ice cubes in the bottom of the tumbler then picked up the bottle of Jameson Special Reserve single malt whisky and poured a measure on top of the cubes. He picked up the tumbler and raised it to his nose allowing the aroma to waft up to his nostrils. He took a sip letting the amber liquid slide over his tongue and slip down his throat. He closed his eyes, savouring the warmth as it spread outwards from his stomach.

A familiar tingle alerted him to a call coming through his NI.

'Go ahead,' he said.

'Sir, an alert has just come through from RandCorp HQ. An 'Intruder Alert' alarm has been raised,' said a voice in his ear. It was the Communication Section that handled all calls in and out of the HQ.

'What exactly do we know?' he asked, suddenly

concerned. Normally he would not be too bothered as Rand-Corp had beefed up their security with ex-Col Sec marines but since the recent events concerning OMEGA, he could not take anything for granted.

'Not a great deal sir, just that the alarm has been raised. All the security feeds from the entrance to the building have been cut off.'

'I want what we have before it was severed and rerouted to my office right now,' Sinclair said and he put the tumbler down and turned to the monitor. The security feed from the secure cams from RandCorp HQ began to play on the large screen. What it showed chilled his blood.

Via his NI he accessed a comm. channel. He said, 'Kurt, I need you in my office right now.'

Kurt and Zara were down in the armoury testing out the new Sig P999 when the call came through to him.

'Copy that sir, I'm on my way,' he said.

Zara saw the concern on his face and asked, 'Everything alright?'

'Not sure, Sinclair wants me in his office right away, it sounded urgent,' he replied. He ejected the battery pack from the pistol he had been using and placed it into the charger then replaced the pistol in the rack. 'I'd better go,' he added and kissed her lightly on the cheek before leaving her to her practice.

He quickly made his way to Sinclair's office and when he entered Sinclair turned from the monitor to face him.

'We have a problem,' he said without preamble.

'I'm listening sir,' Kurt said, then he noticed the monitor screen behind the general. It showed a scene from the front of a huge building frozen in time. He recognised one of the figures entering the building. 'Pavel Norsky,' Kurt uttered the name of the man who handed him over to the Alliance back on Toldax.

'Yes, it seems he has gained entrance to the RandCorp HQ building in Washington DC. As you can see he is armed and has shot and killed the guards as he arrived with a small assault force of armed men before destroying the security cameras. We have to assume he is still there and he has a purpose. What that purpose is we have no idea just yet, but we have to assume it involves violence considering how well-armed he and his men are.'

'Those are the same men who attacked me on Celeron sir. Does that confirm this OMEGA involvement?'

'I'm afraid it does, yes,' Sinclair confirmed.

'We have to do something, sir. Has the local Constabulary been alerted? Is a SWAT Team en route?' Kurt asked urgently.

'Yes, to all of those questions. I totally agree, we have to do something and…' Sinclair held up a hand to indicate he wanted to halt the conversation. His expression altered as he listened to something.

'What's up, sir?' Kurt asked.

'I have just received a call from the Communication Section, they are rerouting something to the main monitor,' Sinclair replied and he turned to the huge screen where another image replaced the security feed from RandCorp they had been watching.

The image changed to that of two men standing in an office. One of them was holding a Remm assault rifle to the other man's head. The older man had the confident demeanour that came from wielding power and the knowledge that he could handle anything life would throw at him. The other man had a slightly manic look in his eyes, which made them worried for the older man's safety.

Norsky said, 'Hello General Sinclair and is that Kurt standing next to you? Good to see you both. Bet you never thought you'd see me again did you, Kurt?'

'What do you want?' Sinclair asked before Kurt could say anything.

'Straight to the point I see. I've heard that about you General; direct. Well, straight to the point then, I want Kurt to come here. We have unfinished business and I think it's time we got it settled,' Norsky said, looking straight at them through the video feed he had accessed via his NI. He had isolated one security camera when he had found the office he wanted and used it for this conference call.

'I'm sorry Pavel but I cannot allow that to happen. You are a professional like me and you know that we do not negotiate with terrorists. If our positions were reversed you would do the same,' Sinclair said steadily, not wanting to agitate him any further.

'There is one huge exception though that you are not taking into consideration. You are not me, you would not do this,' Norsky said as he pressed the assault rifle hard into the temple of Able Rand's head. Before he could fire Kurt shouted, 'Okay Pavel, you win, I'm on my way.'

Sinclair spun around to stare at him, his eyes cold and hard. 'What?' he said through gritted teeth; clearly he was not used to being disobeyed.

'See General, Kurt knows me better than you. He knows what I'm capable of, he has just saved this man's life,' Norsky said with a smile of victory.

'Let's get one thing clear Pavel, if you hurt anyone else, I will kill you,' Kurt said calmly without any emotion.

'That I would like to see,' Norsky said, then added, 'I may kill a few more up here just to see you try.'

'You may think you are in control at the moment Pavel but you're not. You are in a position that is not easy to defend. You have hostages, granted, but they are only valuable to you if you keep them alive. The moment you hurt any of them all bets are off, you have to know that. You have to know that we can take that Penthouse any time we want. You are just one man, a small force could storm your position in seconds and you would not be able to stop them. So please don't think you're in control, you're not,' Kurt said calmly, almost condescendingly.

'Nice speech Kurt but we both know that if you send any size force in here against me you must expect to find a lot of dead bodies. There is only one man who stands a chance against me and that's you, Kurt. So shall we spare all those other lives and just keep this between you and I?'

'If that's what you want Pavel, I'll be there,' Kurt said. He glanced at Sinclair and shook his head slightly.

'I'll be waiting Kurt, and don't keep me waiting too long, you don't want me to get bored and start killing people,' Norsky said as the video feed was cut off before anything further could be said.

Kurt looked at Sinclair and shook his head. 'I have to do this, sir,' he said.

'I agree, I just did not want him to think he had forced our hands into doing what he wanted.'

'You know I can't take any backup, he'll see it coming a mile away. I have to go in alone,' Kurt said. He was testing the General to see how far he could push this, how much he would trust him to get the job done.

'You'll have backup waiting at the limit of his range. You can call them in when you have the situation under control or if you need them.'

'Jake and his Team?'

'Yes, at the moment they are on board the Pulsar in orbit over us. I'll instruct them to go and wait in high orbit over Washington so they can drop down when needed, they can leave shortly after you. If he has eyes on you approaching I don't want them seen approaching at the same time or he may start killing hostages.'

'Give me one hour's head start then tell them to follow sir,' Kurt said then turned to leave the office.

'Kurt, I don't understand what he meant about you being the only one who stands a chance against him, but I have my suspicions. If they have any validity then he is a very dangerous individual so be careful. Good luck son,' Sinclair said. Kurt nodded his head and left the office.

Chapter Twenty-Two

Standing on the bridge of the Lempinski Hermes was keeping an eye on the scanners targeted at the area in Nevada where the signal from Zara's subdermal tracker was originating.

'Sir we have a jet fighter leaving a base out in the desert over where the tracking signal is coming from,' said ops.

'Prepare the assault team, I'll lead them myself,' Hermes said, then using his NI to access a secure channel he called Norsky.

'He's on his way, you know what to do,' he said, closing the connection without waiting for a reply.

A smile crossed his lips as he strode off the bridge. When he reached the docking bay he was greeted by his assault team of thirty Rover5s. The samples were preloaded into the shuttle that was sitting in the docking bay. They had been sedated with neural suppressors clamped onto their heads. At the moment they were deep in REM sleep but the moment they were turned off they would wake immediately and with a thirst for revenge and a fury to fuel that need. Anyone standing in the samples' path would not stand a chance.

All the Rover5s were dressed in battle suits with patch pockets on the arms and legs that carried extra battery clips for the Remm assault rifles and the Sig P996s they all carried. The moment they saw Hermes approach they all filed into the shuttle and strapped themselves into their respective seats ready for departure.

Hermes joined them and sat down strapping the harness around him. The shuttle's pilot released the clamps holding the craft in place then operated the docking bay doors. The shuttle dropped free from the docking bay and the pilot fired the main engines sending it hurtling towards the planet below.

Josh Rand knew his father had gone off the grid. He knew the only reason that that would happen would be if he were in trouble.

His heart jumped into his mouth at the mere thought of that happening and he found himself rooted to the spot, unable to move, to even think.

'Where's Dad?' a voice asked from behind him. He turned to see his sister standing there. She was almost as tall as her brother standing at a little over six feet and had the same turquoise eyes, but her hair was lighter, a true blonde. It hung down over her broad shoulders, almost to her waist, in a cascade of wavy curls. Her normal friendly open expression had been replaced with one of concern. She wasn't afraid for her own safety, Able had reared them both to be independent individuals and, because of their upbringing, nothing much scared them. Yes, she was worried for the safety of everyone on this floor and in particular her father, but she wasn't scared. She was too busy being pissed off to be scared.

'I'm not sure, last I heard he was in his office,' Josh replied.

'We have to help him,' she said, reaching for her pistol. She racked the slide priming the battery clip then walked towards the door. They were in her office; she helped with the day-to-day stuff while Josh was in charge of Special Projects. Mitchell Ryan was the head of security, an ex-Recon Delta Marine. He was on the same floor as them and was organising the evacuation of the other workers into the escape chutes, special elevators built into recesses of the outer wall of the building. Ryan was standing by the chute furthest from Able's office on the far side of the building.

'I was waiting for Mitch to finish up with the staff before trying anything,' Josh said standing in the doorway blocking her path. She was more impulsive than him and quite capable of rushing to their father's aid without thinking and end up putting both of them at risk.

'We can't afford to wait, Josh, we've gotta go help him.'

'Sis, we have to wait for Mitch. He knows how to do this stuff, we don't. If we go in there we could get Dad killed, not to mention us too. Is that what you want?' Josh said, trying to placate her.

Jess shook her head, declining to say anything. She knew her brother was right but it burned to admit it.

'Mitch'll know what to do; he's got years of experience in this sort of thing.'

'Tell him to get his ass over here quickly then,' she snapped. She was worried that her father could get hurt by their delay and was furious at the temerity of the man who had come here and attacked them.

'Sis, calm down. Mitch is doing his job, you know, what we pay him to do. He'll get here as soon as he can.'

She tried to access a comm. channel through her NI but found that something was jamming transmissions. 'I can't reach him, something's jamming the comm's,' she said. She went over to her desk and said, 'We'll have to do this old school.' She activated the intercom on her desk; it was a hard line system with connections in every office and at strategic locations around the floor. She said, 'Mitch, the bastard has Dad in his office. What shall we do?'

'Nothing, I'll be there right away,' said a voice that was calm yet firm.

Mitchell Ryan was in his mid-forties with short, jet black hair. His deep brown eyes were intense and his jaw firmly set in determination. He had his game face on as his old training had kicked in the moment the alarm had gone off.

There were still a few of the staff who needed to get away from the Penthouse but now his priority had to be getting Able Rand away from the man who had attacked them all. He waved the rest of the staff into the chute and said, 'I've gotta go, just get into the chute and the compressed air will ensure you get to the ground floor safely. There will be members of my security team that will meet you down there, just follow their instructions and you'll be okay.' As soon as he knew they understood his instructions he left them to it and headed for Jess's office. Luckily he didn't have to pass by Able's office on his way to where the two Rand siblings were. When he entered the office Josh turned towards him and the relief at seeing him was spread across his face.

'Mitch, am I glad to see you,' he said.

'About time too,' Jess said which garnered a stern look from her older brother.

'Sorry,' she said when she saw her brother's expression. 'What can we do?' she added.

'Look he wants your father alive, he's a hostage and his only value is him being alive. That's the good news, he'll keep him alive as long as he thinks he's gonna get what he wants.

Do any of you know if he's contacted anyone with his demands?' Mitch said.

'If he has he must've done it before the jamming device was initiated,' explained Josh.

'What about the SUT?' asked Jess.

'The Single Unit Transporter? What about it Jess?' Josh asked wondering where his sister was going with this.

'What's a single unit transporter?' Mitch asked, slightly confused.

Josh turned to his friend and said, 'The SUT was a device we were developing; it enabled a person to transport from one place to another. We dropped it from development because we found it too dangerous.'

'Too dangerous, in what way?' Mitch asked, a plan forming in his mind.

'We found that the person using it was subject to cellular degradation. It was so severe that after three trips the damage was so great that it was irreversible and the subject died in agony shortly after. Since then it's been put on hold until we can figure out how to find a way around this problem.'

'How dangerous is it to use just once?' Mitch asked.

'I know what you're thinking Mitch. Use the SUT to get into Dad's room behind the terrorist before he knows what hit him, but it won't work, trust me,' Josh said.

'Why not, I'm willing to risk the damage to myself to save your father,' Mitch said.

'You don't understand Mitch. The first time anyone uses it there is severe disorientation, so you see if you did get in behind him you'd collapse and wouldn't be able to do anything to help anyway. You'd just be handing him another hostage,' Josh explained.

'Damn!' exclaimed Mitch angrily. 'Thought we had something there,' he added.

'We may have,' Jess said. As they turned to look at her she had a smile on her face.

'What're you thinking Jess?' her brother asked, knowing that look on her face.

She smiled then told them her idea.

Chapter Twenty-Three

Before Kurt took a modified F215 Hornet from Area 15 to Washington, the Wildfire Team took the Pulsar's forward section up to the main body of the craft in orbit. The Hornet was the fastest fighter jet in Col Sec's armoury and had a passenger seat fitted behind the pilot's. Once he was airborne the shuttle left the Lempinski heading for the airstrip Kurt had just taken off from.

On board the Hornet, Kurt was strapped into the rear seat by a harness that crossed over his chest and fastened in the middle. The 'G' forces from the take-off pressed him firmly in place in the seat as the afterburners sent them hurtling through the air.

He accessed a comm. channel via his NI and called the Pulsar. 'Jake, I want you to coordinate your drop with my arrival at RandCorp HQ. When I land on the roof I want you and your team to go in the front and take care of the hostiles in control of the lobby,' he said.

'Copy that, Kurt,' Jake's voice said in his ear.

The trip to Washington would take less than two hours at their present speed and Kurt was prepared for his arrival. He was fitted with a parachute and when he was over the general area he would be jettisoned out.

He had no idea what he would face on arrival, whether it would be a force of Rover5s or simply Norsky on his own, but face it he would. He was prepared to meet whatever lay ahead and knowing that his regenerative powers were at their height gave him the confidence to proceed. The fact that he faced Norsky, someone who quite possibly had the same abilities as himself, did not faze him. It just meant that the odds would be equal for both of them.

He had come prepared with a Sig P999 and a Remm assault rifle, which he would take with him. He was wearing a battle suit of Kevlon blast-resistant body armour and had the Sig strapped to his right leg in a holster and the Remm strapped across his chest. It was uncomfortable as the harness and the G force pressed the weapon into his chest making it harder to breathe, but he was willing to put up with it all to complete his mission. He knew that Jake and his team had his back so everything was in place to complete the mission successfully.

Things could go wrong with any mission and this was no exception, he just had to trust his abilities and skills and those of the team that would be helping him.

All he could do for now was sit back and wait until he was ready to get into the game. He closed his eyes and centred his mind; the time would come soon enough for him to spring into action, until then it was best he remained calm.

The shuttle containing the Rover5s and the samples swooped in low over Area 15. Pulsed plasma bolts from the forward-mounted pulse cannons strafed the ground. Guards had emerged from the complex that was Area 15 only to be cut down mercilessly by the attacking shuttle. Blood stained the ground where they fell, their weapons discarded.

Landing thrusters controlled the docking of the shuttle allowing it to land softly near the base. The moment the shuttle hit the ground the doors opened and the Rover5s poured out, assault rifles up at the shoulders ready to fire on anything that moved. They moved like a well-oiled machine covering each other as they approached the complex. The doors were soon unlocked and a squad of Rover5s stormed inside. Several marine guards were waiting for them. They fired Remm assault rifles at the clones; plasma bolts scorched the air between the two battling parties. The Rover5s ducked behind whatever cover they could find and continued to return fire.

The guards tried to hold off the advance but their limited numbers meant that they were outnumbered and outgunned. They tried to contact the base below, but all comm. links had been jammed by the shuttle on its descent.

The guards were effectively cut off, on their own.

Before long the other clones joined the fray firing from all angles, catching the guards in a deadly crossfire. Within a few seconds of them joining the battle, it was over and all the guards lay on the floor, dead from the wounds inflicted by the assaulting forces.

Once the complex was secure, Hermes called to the shuttle for the clones guarding the samples to bring them to him.

The Rover5s back in the shuttle herded the three samples out of the shuttle towards the complex. Hermes watched the three creatures slowly lope across the ground from the shuttle towards the complex. Three octo-felines from the planet Tartaran with the neural inhibitors strapped to their broad, flat heads came out of the shuttle. Their heads moved from side to side as they sniffed the air, tasting it, using their enhanced sense of smell to locate and recognise all the clones around them. Their bodies were long, around thirty-odd feet long with a long tail that whipped from side to side. Two sets of forelegs at the front had paws the width of a man's head with claws as long as the average finger. At the rear of the beast were two sets of hind legs each as powerful as those at the front.

A throaty roar grumbled from each beast as they approached the complex. Their nature was to hunt and kill but the inhibitors kept that nature under control, keeping them calm and sedate. The trio of beasts reached the complex where Hermes was waiting for them.

Pointing to three of the clones who had come across with the beasts he said, 'Take them down, reduce the neural inhibitor's control and let them loose.'

Turning to the shuttle where a small contingent of clones had remained behind he said, 'Get the defences set up.'

Chapter Twenty-Four

'I doubt any of us would get close enough for that to work,' Mitch told Jess after she had relayed to them her plan.

'Don't dismiss it though, we could use it as a fallback option maybe,' she argued.

'Perhaps, but for it to work we'd need a diversion, and I mean one that will really concentrate his attention away from what we're trying to do here. At the moment we just don't have that,' Josh said.

'I agree with Josh on this, so for the time being we'll just have to try and stall him until help arrives,' Mitch said.

'I'm not following,' Jess said, her eyebrows knitted in confusion.

'There's a purpose behind all this. You just don't walk into a MegaCorp building like this one armed with the weapons he has knowing all the security measures in place without having an agenda. Trust me this guy wants something and all this is his way of getting us to listen,' he explained.

'So you think they'll send someone to deal with this? I thought all comm. links had been jammed?' Jess said.

'That's just so the right person gets to come to the party. He doesn't want gatecrashers busting their way into his little party especially after he's gone to the extra trouble of sending out the right invitations. All we have to do is make sure everyone else is safe and bide our time until the guest of honour arrives, then the fun really begins,' Mitch said.

'You're enjoying this aren't you Mitch?' she said anger building inside her.

'I must admit it brings back memories from my days in Recon Delta.'

'This isn't a game Mitch, my father is in there with that mad man,' she raged.

'Sis, Mitch didn't mean anything and I'm sure he's as concerned as we are over Dad's safety,' Josh said, stepping in front of his sister.

'You don't have to intervene on my behalf Josh,' Mitch said, stepping around him. 'I know your father is in there,' he said as he stepped in front of Jess, then continued with, 'and I'll do everything I can to ensure that mad man does no harm to him, even if it means laying down my life. I'll do it, not just because it's my job description but because Able is my friend.'

'I'm sorry Mitch, it's just I can't stay here and do nothing,' she said, her anger and frustration almost boiling over.

Mitch looked her in the eye and softly said, 'Yes you can because if you try to do anything you will get your father killed. You could get killed too, so yes, you can stay here. You will stay here and play nice until it's time to not play nice, okay?'

She looked deep into his eyes and slowly she got herself under control again, forcing her fear for her father back down where it would remain under guard. She nodded her head in agreement fearing that the quaver in her voice would give away the fear she still battled.

'Good,' Mitch said then added; 'Now we wait.'

Jake and his team were all suited up and ready to go. They all wore battle suits similar to Kurt's and they were on the flight deck of the forward section on the Pulsar.

'Sir, I'm reading a small craft attacking Area 15,' the Pulsar's AI said, the automated voice coming from the integral speakers making it sound like it was all around them.

'Can you elaborate a little Artie?' Jake asked.

'Certainly sir, a shuttle has just landed at Area 15 after attacking the guards stationed there. Once it landed a force of soldiers entered the complex followed by three creatures.'

'What sort of creatures?' Torres asked.

'I believe they are from Tartaran, sir.'

'Can you put a visual up on the monitor?' Vance asked. Within a second the image of the three octo-felines slinking towards the complex was on the forward monitor.

'Holy fuck! I hoped I'd never see those bastards again,' Cooper said.

Jake said, 'Artie contact Colonel De Boer at Fort Bragg, it's no use trying anyone at the bases closer to us, there will be communication blackout over the entire area. Inform him of the situation at Area 15 and ask him to get some reinforcements over there asap. Let him know what he'll be facing, they need to be prepared. It looks like it's an all out attack on Col Sec HQ.'

As the AI was complying with that order, Torres said, 'Jake, are you thinking what I'm thinking?'

'That this whole thing is a diversion to get us and Kurt away from HQ while they attack?' Jake replied.

'It does seem a tad suspicious Jake,' agreed Cooper.

'What do we do boss?' Vance asked.

'Our jobs, we back Kurt up like ordered then we get back to base to help the Colonel,' Jake said.

'Sounds like a plan,' Torres said.

'Artie take us down,' Jake said.

Chapter Twenty-Five

When the call from Artie came through to Colonel Anton De Boer he was just about to sit down at his desk in his office to review the recent performance reviews of his men. The data from the AI was sent in a burst transmission direct to his NI and it hit him like a bullet to the head.

He cried out in shock as his NI received the data and he almost fell to the floor, his face contorting from the intense pain.

An aide came bursting into the room when he heard the colonel cry out. 'Sir, what's wrong?' he asked as he ran around to the side of the desk to him. It took a few moments for the pain to ease enough for De Boer to be able to speak. His eyes opened and his vision cleared enough for him to realise he was not alone.

'Are you okay, sir?' the aide asked once more when De Boer looked up at him.

De Boer waved a hand at his aide to reassure him he was alright, while his NI assimilated the amount of data it had just received. The pain finally subsided enough for him to be able to talk and he looked at his aide, his expression that of deep concern.

'Scramble the men, immediate departure for Area 15. Col Sec HQ is under attack,' he said.

———

Kurt was getting ready for his arrival in Washington when a call came through to his NI from Jake.

'Kurt I think you should know that this action is a diversion. Col Sec HQ is under attack from an assault force of Rover5s and three of those huge creatures from Tartaran. I've contacted Colonel De Boer at Fort Bragg to send reinforcements to help out,' he said.

'Go secure,' Kurt said, his voice a little shaky as he scrambled the call via his NI.

'Copy that,' Jake said as he complied wondering what had got his friend so spooked.

'I think this is not just a diversion, I think it's a two-pronged assault on Col Sec. The guy I'm going to face at RandCorp HQ is just like me. He has the same regenerative capabilities as me and he's taken control of the Rands to lure me out. He must be with OMEGA which means that this situation has just got a whole lot worse,' Kurt told him.

'So are you saying that they've sent him to kill you?'

'If anyone could, I'd bet it would be him but I think that there's something else going on here.'

'Are you saying that you think they want to capture you?' Vance asked, joining the conversation.

'Could be yes. Think about it, Norsky and I would be more or less evenly matched so we would cancel each other out and that's where the Rover5s come in,' Kurt said, sharing his theory.

'Yes, they would give this Norsky an advantage I guess,' Torres observed, also joining the conversation.

'That's why it's vital you take care of the Rover5s at the lobby, you can leave Norsky to me,' Kurt said, adding grit to his voice as he anticipated the battle to come. It was time to settle the unfinished business between the two of them like Norsky had mentioned and he was determined to end any further threats from this quarter.

'If this is a plan to capture you, Kurt, then my guess is that they must have an evac strategy in place. You need to consider that too,' Cooper said, mentioning something the others had missed.

Kurt thought about it for a moment then said, 'They must have a shuttle parked on the roof of the building ready to take off, which also means they have a starship in orbit.'

'You're right, all these troops must have come from somewhere, I'll get Artie on it right away. If we can identify it then we can take measures to prevent it escaping,' Jake said.

'Good idea, you take care of that end and I'll sort out the shuttle from this end,' Kurt said.

'Copy that,' Jake said then added, 'We'll see you at the party and good luck.'

'You too,' Kurt said then the call was ended. Kurt said to the pilot of the Hornet, 'I've just received news that Area 15 is under attack. There are reinforcements en route to that location and as soon as you drop me off I want you to return there and give them whatever assistance you can. Coordinate your actions with Colonel De Boer, he'll give you further orders.'

'Copy that sir, we're coming up on the drop zone so you'd better get ready. Good luck, sir,' replied the pilot.

'You too,' Kurt said.

With that, the pilot pulled the lever that operated the canopy above Kurt's seat. It slid back to reveal Kurt's section to the open air. The sudden inrush of air would have taken his breath away had he not been wearing a Rapier battle helmet with a full facemask. The second he saw the canopy slide back he felt the sudden kick up his spine from the rockets blasting his seat into the air. He soared high over the rapidly disappearing Hornet's trajectory as the pilot followed his orders and spun his aircraft back towards Area 15.

He had a wild idea on how to deal with the shuttle on the roof of the RandCorp building. It meant him doing a modified HALO jump. HALO or High Altitude Low Opening jump usually meant the jumper would jump from a high altitude of around thirty thousand feet, then free fall at terminal velocity and open the 'chute at a low altitude around seven thousand feet or lower. Kurt's idea was to do the same without the high altitude. He had been ejected from the Hornet at around five thousand feet and once he was free from the confines of the flight chair he positioned his arms by his sides and began his descent. He hurtled towards the ground at an alarming rate and soon reached terminal velocity. He knew he didn't have long before he reached the rooftop and had to act fast. He accessed the onboard computer of the shuttle via his NI and switched off the jamming device.

He could see the shuttle getting closer every second as his speed ate up the distance between them. He calculated the time he needed to open his parachute. If he opened it too soon the pilot of the shuttle would spot him and have time to shoot him down, if he opened it too late he would die on impact.

It would be tight and the margin for error would be almost impossibly difficult to calculate.

He waited and waited and then, hoping he had got it right, pulled the ripcord to open his 'chute.

The fabric of the parachute billowed out above him snapping him upright with such force his head snapped back almost rendering him unconscious. His speed slowed dramatically but as he saw the top of the RandCorp tower approaching he knew it wasn't quick enough, but he hoped he'd got his calculations right.

He slammed into the top of the tower with such force his legs broke just before the rest of him impacted with the roof.

He was dead on impact.

The pilot of the shuttle got out of the cabin as he saw Kurt approach the roof. When he saw him crash into the roof a smile crossed his rugged features.

'What an idiot,' he said as he approached the body lying close by. He leaned down so he could check the pulse just to be on the safe side. He knew there was no way this idiot could've survived that fall but he had to make sure. He couldn't see what all the fuss was about this guy, if he was dumb enough to foul up a simple parachute jump then he wasn't the big threat they all thought he was.

As he reached down to check for a pulse Kurt's hand snapped up and caught the Rover5's wrist. He had regenerated just in time, his broken bones had reset, his internal injuries healed and his skin had reformed over all his cuts and lacerations. The look of surprise on the clone's face was almost comical as he saw Kurt's eyes open.

'Boo!' Kurt said and pulled the clone over his head to fall on the floor behind him. Kurt flipped himself back onto his feet and turned to face the clone who combat rolled to his feet also. Both of them went for their weapons but Kurt was faster by far. He had his Sig out of his holster and aimed before the clone's hand had even reached his pistol. Kurt fired the Sig blowing the top of the Rover5's head apart. The clone was sent backwards to land on the floor and Kurt replaced his Sig in its holster. Leaving the body where it was he walked over to the door that led to the interior of the building.

Once the door was opened he walked down the stairs that led to the Penthouse, stopping just before he reached the next door. Now that the jamming device had been switched off he knew he would be able to contact those left inside, particularly Able Rand.

Using his NI he contacted Rand directly, NI to NI. 'Don't react to this call in any way, your very life depends upon it,' he said. When he got no response he accessed the other's NI to check his vital signs. From the elevated heart rate, he knew that Able had received the call. To make it easier for Able to communicate with him he said, 'Swallow once for yes and twice for no. Are your son and daughter on the same floor as you?'

One swallow. Good. Switching from Able to both Josh and Jess, something he had never attempted before, he said, 'My name is Kurt Stryder and I'm here to help. I need you to remain where you are for the moment. The man who has your father is a very dangerous man and if you interfere you could get him and yourselves hurt or worse, killed. Please allow me to do my job.'

Jess told him of her idea of using the SUT and Josh said, 'Leave it, Jess, let him and Mitch do their jobs.'

'Mitch, Mitch Ryan, is he there with you too?'

'Yes, he's our chief of security. He made sure everyone on this floor evacuated before he came here to us,' replied Josh.

Kurt tried to envelop Mitch in the conference call. When he knew he was also involved he said, 'Mitch Ryan, I've read your record in Recon Delta, it's very impressive.'

'I'm afraid you have me at a disadvantage, I know nothing about you, not even your name,' Mitch replied.

'Kurt Stryder.'

'I have heard of you, rumours mainly from buddies of

mine who still have contacts in Delta. From what they tell me you're the new hotshot in town which means Able's chances of survival have just increased.'

'Curb your enthusiasm Mitch, you don't know who we're dealing with here and trust me you don't want to. He's as bad as I am good if that makes sense?'

'It makes a great deal of sense; he's the yin to your yang.'

'Sort of, yes, only I can go up against him because if you try to take him, you will most definitely die. I'm not bragging when I say that, it's just a fact.'

'Okay, what do you want us to do?'

'Jess' idea may have some merit, but we'll only have one shot at this and the timing will be crucial so you'll have to be ready.'

'Don't worry about us, we'll do what we have to,' Mitch said, speaking for them all.

'Okay, here's what you need to do.'

Chapter Twenty-Six

General Sinclair heard the alarm blast through the HQ and reached for his service weapon from the drawer in his desk, a Sig P999 in a soft leatherine holster. Through his NI he accessed the computer to see what had triggered the alarm. When he received the signal from the video feed delivered directly to his visual cortex he was shocked to see the Rover5s leading the three huge octo-felines inside the upper complex. As he was placing the weapon around his waist the door to his office opened and Matt walked in.

'Sir we're under attack,' he said. He looked at the general's face while he read the reports from the computer.

'Yes, we are,' Sinclair replied, passing on the video signal to his NI making him also aware of the severity of the threat. After a pause he went on with, 'It seems that this may be their endgame. Everything that has gone on before this has been setting us up for this attack.'

'We'd better get the rest of the staff out of here so we can defend it properly sir,' Matt said with grim determination.

'Initiate the evacuation protocols then see who is available to form a defence force.'

'Copy that sir,' Matt said.

Zara appeared at the door; she had been on her way up from the firing range after Kurt had left her there when the alarm had sounded. She had rushed up to Sinclair's office just in time to see Matt enter.

'What's going on?' she said bursting through the door.

'We're under attack,' he said and he included her into the video loop shared by him and Matt, it was the fastest way to bring her up to speed and he needed her at her best now more than ever. 'This has been their plan all along. We have to get everyone out so we can defend the HQ,' Sinclair said as he saw her eyes focus after receiving the signal.

'Let me help,' she said.

'Oh don't worry, we need every able body we have and from what I gather, you are probably more able-bodied than all of us, with the possible exception of Kurt,' Sinclair said.

Zara's expression was one of complete surprise. *How did he know, who had told him?* she thought. 'I don't know what you mean sir,' she said, glancing at Matt who wore the same surprised expression.

'We all know what I am referring to Zara but we can discuss this further once this is all over. The time for subterfuge is over I think, don't you?' Sinclair said, looking her straight in the eye, holding her gaze like that of a cobra before striking.

'I have no idea what you're talking about sir, but I agree that you need every hand you can muster,' Zara replied as calmly as she could. She held his gaze, determined not to blink first. She knew of Sinclair's reputation and she didn't want to fuel his already loaded suspicions.

'First things first, as they say,' Sinclair said.

Matt said, 'I'll get the evacuation underway, sir.'

'Get comfortable Able. Can I call you Able? Of course, I can, I have the gun. Take a seat, it won't be long now,' Norsky said.

Able Rand had met most of the high rolling company CEOs from most of the huge MegaCorp's from around the galaxy, but this man was showing confidence that was unheard of. It was almost like he knew he could not fail, or worse still, he could not be hurt. It was a dangerous character trait for it led him to believe he was deranged, unbalanced. This led to other questions such as what were his chances of survival. He made no assurances to Kurt that he would let anyone go free so what exactly was this man's plan? After receiving the call from Kurt he knew that rescue was at hand, he just hoped he knew what he was getting into.

Able sat at the desk and tried to relax. He had been in high-pressure environments before, so he knew how to remain calm under duress but never one where his very life was at stake. He found this whole thing stimulating in a perverse way.

'That's better; Kurt should be here very soon. He won't keep me waiting too long, there's too much at stake here,' Norsky said.

'What exactly is at stake here? I mean, what is your plan? You do have a plan don't you?' Able asked, wondering what was about to happen. If this man was as deranged as he suspected then there could be more to this than just a terrorist attack. He wondered what the motivation was when Norsky called Col Sec HQ and wanted Kurt to come here. Was this just personal between the two of them? He thought not, like he had said, there was too much at stake. But what, exactly, was about to happen?

'My plan is none of your business,' Norsky said, smiling that slightly manic smile of his.

'Oh, I see,' Able said, nodding his head slightly. 'You really are in trouble now aren't you?' he added.

Norsky's smile faded as he took in what had been said. He walked over to the desk and, as nonchalantly as he could, leaned against it and said, 'And what do you mean by that?'

'Your statement earlier about your plan being none of my business is usually what someone who has no plan says; someone who has bungled his way into a situation that at the time seemed like a good idea, but when it came down to it, left them royally screwed. Let me guess, this whole thing wasn't your idea at all, was it? You're acting under orders from someone else who actually holds the power, aren't you?'

Norsky pushed himself off the desk to stroll off towards the window. Those words had had a sting of truth in them and he found them hard to come to terms with. Instead, he said, 'You have no idea what you're talking about, old man.'

'Oh, I think I do. I think I hit the nail on the head with that one.'

'You may be right about this not being entirely my plan, I'll grant you that, but I'm still in charge here.'

'Are you, really? Think about it for a minute, you have to know that what Kurt told you was right. You are not in control here; at best you are trapped with several people that, if injured, will bring you life imprisonment in a penal colony. The mere act of how you came here was a violation of so many Confederation codes and laws that you will end up in a penal colony for the rest of your natural life, that's if you actually survive this. That being said, you have to ask yourself one question, what is really going on here?'

Norsky's eyes blazed with a passion and hatred that made Able sit back in his seat. 'I'll tell you what is going on here; I'm going to face off against the one man who has ruined my life, Kurt Stryder. He's coming here to try and stop me from killing you and whoever is left up here. I couldn't give a damn about any of that. All I care about is getting to look him in the eye before I take him away and hand him over to those who are running this operation. You were right, I am following orders and those people who issued the orders are attacking Col Sec as we speak so there will be no rescue, no one will come to help Kurt or stop me from doing what I set out to do. Kurt will come willingly with me, you'll see, because at heart he is what you would call, a good man. He won't allow me to harm you or anyone else here so he will unthinkingly sacrifice himself for your lives. My victory will be complete when I hand him over knowing what they have in store for him.'

Able was speechless for a moment, this had been a diversion all along for the main strike against Col Sec. This was another incident like the Nemesis attack that devastated New York not so long ago. How many more lives will be lost in this new attack, he wondered.

'Do you feel any better now that you know?' Norsky asked, his smile returning but this time a little more manic and a little more unsteady. It was clear that his grasp on his sanity was a tenuous one at best and Able thought better of antagonising him further. He simply stared at him and hoped that Kurt was prepared for what Norsky had in mind for him.

Chapter Twenty-Seven

Matt had set the evacuation in progress by triggering the silent alarms that were sent directly to the NIs of the staff working in the HQ. Everyone who had been working there filtered down through the levels to the very bottom where the evacuation tunnels were situated. These were a precaution that had been built into the base after the attack on the Confederation Building in New York by OMEGA. Sinclair thought that should another attack occur then they would need an escape route, one that was easy to access and that took them away from the danger. The system consisted of five tunnels situated on the deepest level of the new base. These five tunnels ran horizontally away from the base for a mile where they ended at a huge elevator that took the evacuees to the surface. Each elevator could hold fifty people and was powered by a series of hydraulic rams that pushed the elevator to the surface where those inside could climb out through a hatch in the roof via a ladder. The elevator would stop level with the surface and a concealed cover over the shaft would slide open revealing the hatch in the top of the elevator. In this way, the evacuation tunnels could not be detected by scans from above.

By the time the staff from the upper levels reached the tunnels, those who had been working on the levels below them had already evacuated so there was no backlog. Matt, General Sinclair and Zara, along with a detachment of Recon Delta Marines who were stationed at the HQ as security, were the only ones left there. It was up to them to defend it.

When Matt was sure everyone in the base had received the signal and were on their way to the tunnels he turned to Sinclair and said, 'Sir they're on the way to the tunnels. There is no one left in the path of the Rover5s.

As Hermes and his team of Rover5s entered the upper levels of the HQ they encountered moderate resistance from some security staff armed with small arms and then suddenly everyone just seemed to vanish.

'Where is everyone, this place is supposed to be teeming with people?' he said. The Rover5 next to him held a portable tracker that he was using to scan for life signs inside the building. 'Everyone is moving down through the lower levels towards the bottom,' he reported.

'Excellent, they're making it easier for us,' he said with a vicious smile. Through his NI he contacted the Rover5s left on the surface. He said, 'Deploy the device; I want this entire base sealed off. No one gets out, ever.'

Colonel De Boer was sitting on the troop carrier, a Hurricane C230, with the rest of the troops he was taking with him from Fort Bragg. He was anxious because the time it would take to get to the HQ was prohibitive of effectively mounting a defence for it. He knew that, the troops also knew that, but they all appreciated that they had to try. The C230 was the fastest troop carrier in their arsenal, with a top speed of over six hundred miles an hour but it would still take them just under three hours to reach the HQ. An awful lot could happen in that time and that was the basis of his fears.

They were still over an hour and a half away from their destination and he used his NI to contact the flight commander of Red Wing, one of the fighter wings that were also stationed at Fort Bragg. They had been scrambled at the same moment that Colonel De Boer had alerted his men to the attack. They would have used a Wing based at Nellis, a much closer base but comm. links were down in that area, obviously to give the attacking forces more time to execute their plan.

'Commander what's the status of your men?' he said using his NI.

Commander Mark Travis was one of the youngest fighter pilots to ever have earned the command of a flight wing. At the age of twenty-four, he had been in command of Red Wing for the past three years. Of medium height, he was slim but incredibly fit and his eye-hand coordination was still one of the top three in Col Sec. His boyish good looks had earned him a string of admirers amongst the female population on Fort Bragg's huge complex, which he dismissed with the normal self-deprecating humour belying his enormous self-confidence. Blond hair, so fair it was almost white, was hidden at that moment beneath his flight helmet as his bright blue eyes glanced across the instruments of his F215 Hornet through the visor. His NI was tuned into the flight controls of the plane helping his already awesome hand-eye coordination speed in any combat situation. In a calm voice, he replied, 'We're less than half an hour away from our destination Colonel. We'll soften them up ready for your arrival.'

Kurt reached the Penthouse at the end of the corridor away from where Norsky was holding Able Rand in his office. He took off his helmet and placed it on the nearest table inside an office he was passing by. Then he continued towards the far end of the corridor. He could hear voices not too far away and if he tried really hard he could even pick up the sound of heartbeats. Four of them sounded normal under the circumstances, a little fast maybe but that was to be expected concerning the stress they were under. These were Able, Josh and Jess Rand with Mitch Ryan. The fifth heartbeat was strong and steady and unnervingly calm considering how much hatred there was in it. This was Norsky's; it had to be. Only someone with the same abilities as he had could have a heartbeat like that.

He stopped and waited; the timing for what he had planned was vital, everything had to be in place before he could continue.

Jake and the rest of his team were about to drop from the forward section of the Pulsar. The craft hovered over the RandCorp HQ building ready for them to rappel down to the ground. The entire area had been cordoned off by the local Constabulary and armed constables lined the perimeter waiting for them to arrive.

'Okay Artie, you know what to do,' Jake said as he applied the line to his belt and stood facing the interior of the craft in the hatch. Torres, Vance and Cooper all stood next to him ready to drop.

'I do indeed sir,' replied the AI.

The Wildfire Team pushed off and rappelled down to the ground, all of them eager to get this mission underway.

Chapter Twenty-Eight

The Lempinski was in stationary orbit above the Nevada desert over where the shuttle had landed at Area 15. They were ordered to remain there should the ground forces need covering fire until they had completed their mission.

Artie approached the starship under a stealth shield so that the Pulsar could remain undetected. On the approach, the AI had scanned the ship for her defence capabilities and what her armaments comprised of. With all the data compiled, the AI dropped the Pulsar's stealth shield and attacked.

The main body of the Pulsar was not quite as big as the Lempinski but her battle capabilities far outweighed those of the OMEGA ship.

The moment the Pulsar became visible on the larger craft's scanners they began to raise their defence shields, but by that time it was too late. The Pulsar's AI had already fired a brace of missiles from forward missile tubes and they were seconds away from impact. The target had been the shield generators and when the two missiles impacted on the hull the resulting explosions tore huge holes in the hull which destroyed two decks, the shield generators and, more importantly, anyone in the vicinity.

The Pulsar's forward pulse cannons raked the side of the Lempinski with high energy pulsed plasma bolts creating further damage to the ship.

Explosions erupted up and down the flank of the Lempinski where the bolts struck. With the shields being down, the ship was easy prey to the faster, more powerful Pulsar.

On the bridge of the Lempinski the captain was barking orders out to the crew. 'Get those shields up; we're sitting ducks here. Helm, take evasive action, get us away from that craft. Weps, return fire with everything we've got,' he shouted as he moved from one station to the next. Inside the craft, with all the explosions erupting throughout the vessel, the crew were being thrown around like rag dolls as they attempted to go about their duties.

Missiles were fired from the Lempinski's aft missile tubes. The Pulsar's AI saw them being fired and fired countermeasures, a series of small missiles launched from a rotating barrel similar to a Gatling gun from four centuries before. The small missiles targeted the incoming fire from the Lempinski and blew them apart before they had time to get close enough to cause any damage. Once they were destroyed the AI moved the Pulsar around the Lempinski and began firing from a different angle. The engines were disabled with a salvo from the Pulsar's forward pulse canons followed by a brace of missiles. The resulting explosions almost tore the rear off the starship, which left them dead in space.

Escape Pods were jettisoned shortly after from the flanks of the disabled craft, which was heading towards the planet below. Artie extrapolated the trajectory of each Pod and knew where they were all headed.

'Commander of Red Wing you have incoming,' Artie told the commander of the fighter wing about to reach their objective.

Commander Mark Travis' NI recognised the signal as a Col Sec Priority coded communication so he acted upon it. He immediately warned the rest of Red Wing to watch for enemy action as they all approached the target area.

The onboard sensors swept the area before them and picked up ground forces that had set up Anti-Aircraft pulse cannons around a shuttle that was parked on the landing pad at Area 15. These would be the priority targets and they would have to take these out first so that when the Colonel arrived with reinforcements they could deploy safely.

Suddenly, as they were about to make their first attacking run the sensors indicated a threat from above. When Travis saw the threat he knew exactly what the signal had meant and ordered his men to take the appropriate action.

The entire wing all veered off from their attack run to avoid being hit by the plummeting Pods that slammed into the ground. Onboard inertial dampeners had prevented the occupants from being crushed by the impact with the ground and the Pods opened to deploy a further contingent of clones all armed with Remm pulse rifles. They all ran towards the defence forces that had been set up and began firing at the fighter jets as they turned back to continue their initial attack run.

Withering fire from the ground struck the first F215 Hornet as it swooped too close. The plasma bolts raked down the length of the sleek craft causing damage wherever they touched. The kinetic force from the impacts threw the trajectory off and sent it into a vicious spin that the pilot could not control. The small craft was too close to the ground to power out of the dive and it smashed into the dusty desert a few hundred yards away from Area 15 in a fiery explosion that could be seen for miles.

Travis and the other four pilots managed to avoid being hit by any more ground fire as they turned away to rethink their attack. Travis spun his F215 Hornet back towards the target area and immediately fired two Hellfire missiles the second the target was picked up by the onboard computer. This act was copied by the rest of the wing and within seconds of them firing, the eight missiles were streaking towards their targets.

The ground forces tried to lock onto the incoming missiles with the Anti-Aircraft pulse cannons but the Hell-fires had been equipped with tremblers, a new development by RandCorp, which distorted any signal that attempted to lock on to them.

Three of the missiles slammed into the first of the ground forces defences destroying it in a paroxysm of flame and exploding shrapnel, blood and bone as two more struck the shuttle blowing that apart too. The last three missiles struck another of the Anti-Aircraft pulse cannons with a similar effect as the first.

Travis and his wing came in fast firing pulse cannons at the ground forces that had remained incredibly focused, refusing to run in the face of utter destruction instead choosing to remain and fight. Any commander would have been proud of the spirit these clones displayed; they showed true bravery.

Several of the clones were torn apart by the incoming fire from the F215s while others fired back scoring direct hits on two more of the attacking jets. These jets were sent spinning off into the desert to crash as their comrade had done earlier. That left Travis and two more F215s who, after reaching a safe distance, once more fired Hellfire missiles at the ground forces. The six missiles soon covered the distance between them and the target, destroying what was left of the valiant resistance the clones had put up.

As Travis flew over the wreckage that was left of the clones' attacking forces, he called Colonel De Boer on a closed channel. 'Colonel you are cleared to land,' he said. Although his part of the mission had been a success it had cost them dearly and what was about to come would cost even more lives. This was a sobering thought he took with him as he, and what was left of Red Wing, returned to base.

Down in the upper levels of the HQ Hermes, the Rover5 designated as the leader of the mission had been in constant contact through his NI with the forces up on the surface. When they came under attack from the Red Wing, the forces who had arrived in the Escape Pods had rushed into the complex that led to the interior entrance for Col Sec HQ to reinforce those forces who were readying the device. They needed to be ready for the next wave of Rover5s coming.

He contacted the Rover5s who were just below the surface getting the device ready to be activated. The device was a thermobaric earthquake bomb, so powerful that it would seal off the entire base from the surface. Whoever was left below the surface would not escape alive. They would die from the heat and shockwave the explosion created, leaving the base ripe for the picking.

The originators of this plan could see no possible way that those inside the base could survive when the charge exploded. They had thought of every conceivable escape scenario and had a contingency plan for each of them. Col Sec was doomed.

'Start the countdown, one hour should be enough time for us to reach the rest of them, and just enough time for the Colonel to arrive but too late to help,' he said. With a wave of his hand, he urged his men forward towards those trapped beneath.

Chapter Twenty-Nine

The local Constabulary had formed a perimeter around the RandCorp building and when the Wildfire Team rappelled down from the forward section of the Pulsar, they made sure no one encroached on that perimeter.

Jake and the team landed lightly at the foot of the steps to the building and immediately released their cords, which were spooled back inside the Pulsar before the AI took her back into the air.

Swinging their Remm pulse rifles from their backs they brought them up to their shoulders aiming down the barrels ready to fire.

The forward section of the Pulsar had turned to face the front of the building and the second the Wildfire Team had brought up their rifles, Artie fired the forward pulse cannons. Pulsed plasma bolts peppered the front of the building with continuous fire; the windows, doors, in fact, the entire front of the building, was decimated under the barrage from the pulse cannons.

Jake and the rest of the team ran forward towards the smashed front of the building and the second they were within reach of entering, the pulse cannons ceased firing. The timing had been immaculate, they had trusted Artie to get it right and everything they had gone through together in the past few weeks had cemented that trust.

They burst through the smashed front of the building and the Heads Up Displays on their helmets had already targeted the Rover5s so each member shot and killed one of them.

The remaining clones were not fazed by the swift retaliatory action and came out from behind their cover firing their weapons. The Team knew where the clones had been hiding and so when they emerged they were already moving out of the target area. Having reaction times point five faster than that of normal humans, including the clones, meant that they were already targeting as soon as they had moved. Pulsed plasma bolts stitched a line of death across the chest of one clone sending it flying across the room whilst another had its head blown apart. The last two were cut down before they had the chance to return fire after missing with their first salvos.

The entire action took less than a minute from start to finish.

Jake looked around at the mayhem caused both by them and by the clones before them. He said, 'What a mess.'

'Copy that,' Cooper said.

'These people were cut down with no regard for the fact that they were non-combatants. For fuck's sake they weren't even armed,' Torres said angrily.

'Let's finish this,' Jake said with a grim determination. He contacted Kurt via his NI and said, 'The lobby is secure. We're on our way up to the Penthouse.'

'I'll try and give you a distraction as I'm sure Norsky will be monitoring the elevators,' Kurt replied as he readied himself for the next phase of the operation.

'There's no need Kurt, we've got it covered. I just hope the Rands don't mind what we're about to do to their building,' Jake replied who then broke the connection leaving Kurt wondering just what he had meant.

'Artie, you know what to do,' Jake said as he connected to the Pulsar's AI.

'I am in position now, sir, waiting for your command,' the AI replied.

'Okay, let's do this,' Jake said and they headed for the elevator.

Matt and Zara had armed themselves with Remm assault rifles along with the Recon Delta Marines who had been stationed at the HQ. They knew they had a fight on their hands; if it had just been the advancing force of the Rover5s it would have been bad enough. The enclosed spaces of the corridors, offices and labs would make it hard enough to formulate a defence strategy, but when you added the element of the three beasts from Tartaran the odds against success plummeted. Nevertheless, they would do what had to be done to ensure the safety of the HQ. Sinclair would not allow another Headquarters to be destroyed. He still had nightmares about the attack in New York, the dead and dying whom he had been powerless to save and which still haunted his dreams. The massive cost of losing the building and having to relocate was something he could live with, but the cost in lives was something he would not put up with. It was something he knew would stay with him until their deaths had been avenged.

'Sir, I would feel safer if you would go with the others into the evacuation tubes,' Matt said.

'I am not leaving Matt, you will need every able-bodied

person available and I intend to help in any way I can,' replied the General.

'Sir, we can do our jobs more effectively if you are not here. Your being here puts an added strain on our resources,' Matt argued.

'How so?'

'If we have to concentrate on keeping you safe then our attention is divided between what is considered important. Your safety is a priority, you are the head of Col Sec and our duty is to keep you from harm. We can't be as effective in defending this place if we are continually worried about you. You have to go, sir,' Matt said.

Sinclair stood back and looked at the faces of those around him. They all wore concerned expressions. He knew that the task before them was an almost insurmountable mountain to climb and the last thing he wanted was for his presence to add to its difficulty. He had hoped that his being there might in some way spur them on to greater efforts but it seemed he had read it all wrong; in reality, he was putting them in even more danger he realised.

With great sadness, he nodded his head and said, 'Okay, the last thing I want is to be a hindrance so I'll accede to your wishes, but I have to say it is with great reluctance,' he said and turned to leave. As he reached the door he turned and said, 'Good luck to you all.'

Norsky was getting impatient with all the waiting around. Surely Kurt should have arrived by now he was thinking as he tried to connect with the clones down in the lobby. When he found no connection between his NI and any of the clones he realised something was wrong. Somehow they were all dead, somehow they had been overpowered, but by whom?

Perhaps Kurt was already here and he had come with some backup after all. If that was the case then he had to get ready for his arrival.

He used his NI to connect to the building's intercom system and said, 'Are you there Kurt, come on now, don't be shy? Come on out so we can get this game started.' His voice boomed out of all the speakers that were hidden in the walls throughout the building.

Able tried to remain calm, the final confrontation was getting closer with every second and now clearly this gunman thought that his adversary was hiding from him. He didn't say or do anything; he thought it best he didn't antagonise an already inflammable situation so he remained seated and waited nervously.

Kurt accessed the same speaker system to reply. 'What's the matter Pavel, are you missing me?' he said as he walked into view.

Norsky saw him at the end of the corridor and brought his Remm assault rifle up to fire. However, before he could pull the trigger, the window behind him imploded, showering him with millions of shards of crystallised Plexiglas as it was struck by a multitude of pulsed plasma bolts. Outside the building, the forward section of the Pulsar had flown up and hovered in position then opened fire with the forward pulse cannons once the AI had scanned the interior to locate Norsky. This was the diversion Jake had talked about.

Norsky threw himself on the floor the moment it happened, not sure what the hell was going on.

Kurt had contacted Able as before to warn him that something was about to happen and, when it did, he was to run towards the door and escape. The head of RandCorp bolted out of his seat as the chaos exploded inside the room leaving the gunman on the floor in a state of total confusion. By the time Norsky realised what was happening it was too late to do anything about it. All he could do was watch his hostage escape through the door towards his nemesis, Kurt Stryder.

He was filled with a rage of such intensity that he sprang to his feet; a bellow of pure hatred spilling over his lips which echoed throughout the corridor as he ran at Kurt.

The moment Kurt saw Norsky get to his feet and start to run at him he brought up his Remm assault rifle to fire. He had to wait for Able Rand to clear his line of sight first, but the moment he was clear he opened fire on the former Alliance agent.

A stream of pulsed plasma bolts lanced through the air between the two of them finally impacting on Norsky's blast-resistant vest. The damage to him was minimal but the kinetic effect from the bolts stopped him in his tracks as it knocked the breath out of him.

'Go, get to your children, they're in an office close by,' Kurt said as Able ran up to him breathlessly. He never took his eyes off Norsky. He had watched him go down as he was hit by the stream of plasma bolts but he knew it would not stop him for long. The body armour he wore would protect him from harm and his regenerative powers would help him recover more rapidly from the kinetic effect of the blasts than a normal human.

He allowed Able to get around him while he kept his assault rifle trained on the area where he had seen Norsky go down.

'Is that the best you've got Kurt? Is that how you want this played out, trying to kill me from a distance?' said Norsky as he got to his feet, shrugging off the effects of the shot to his chest.

'The thought had crossed my mind,' Kurt replied.

'I thought you were a soldier, a warrior. I thought you would want to look me in the eye when you tried to kill me; you know, up close and personal,' Norsky said, throwing his arms wide in a gesture that said 'come and get me'.

'You thought wrong,' Kurt said and shot him again.

As the ex-Alliance agent was flung backwards off his feet once more, Kurt turned and left the corridor. He caught up with Able who by that time was in the office with his son and daughter and Mitch Ryan, their security chief.

'Right, is everything set?' he said when they all turned to look at him.

'We're all set,' Mitch said, his jaw set in determination. 'Are you sure you want to do this?' he added.

'I can think of no other way, can you? Besides, you don't know this man like I do. Trust me, there is no other way,' Kurt said and he held out his hand to Jess who handed over the small device.

'Is it set?' he asked and she replied with a simple nod of her head. 'Good, now go, get out of here, it's me he wants not you. I don't want you near when he comes after me,' he added and ushered them out of the room towards the escape chutes.

'Come on there's one at the rear of this office,' said Josh and the four of them entered the small opening that Mitch had activated. They were soon falling towards the ground on the outside of the building riding down on a cushion of air. If it had not been for the danger they had just faced, Josh for one would have loved the ride. As it was he was just glad to get his family and Mitch away from the danger and hoped that Kurt could handle things without their help. He didn't know the man but he had a feeling they would work together pretty soon.

Kurt waited for them to leave, then he turned back to face where he had last seen Norsky.

Suddenly there was a blur of motion before him and he just had enough time to make out the shape of a man, Norsky, rushing at him. The ex-Alliance agent hit him with the force of an express train forcing both of them into the wall. The speed he hit him with was enough to kill a normal man but because of their enhanced strength, they survived the collision, which was more than could be said for the wall. A man-shaped crater appeared at the point of impact with cracks spreading out from the gaping hole. Plaster and chunks of the wall rained down on them as they struggled, each trying to gain the upper hand.

Norsky was the aggressor, pushing Kurt further into the already damaged wall. Then he slammed a knee into his midriff forcing the air out of his lungs in an audible 'whoosh!' As Kurt's head went down from the force of the blow, Norsky brought up his other knee into his face. There was an explosion of blood from Kurt's nose as the blow impacted it. Norsky continued his frenzied attack by lifting Kurt's face up level with his own, his left hand around his throat. Then he smashed his right fist into his already bloodied face repeatedly until Kurt's knees sagged. Norsky stepped back and as Kurt slowly slid down the wall he pummelled him some more from above.

Kurt felt his senses leaving him and he fought to keep awake. Shrugging off the effects of the blows he reared up, using the strength in his legs he pushed Norsky off him sending him staggering across the corridor.

Norsky could not believe that he was still awake, that he still had any fight left in him and his anger exploded fuelled by frustration at being thwarted once more.

He sprang back at him. Before Kurt could react fully Norsky was on him again raining blows down on his face, chest, anywhere he could hit. There was no reason or tactic to his attack just pure frenzied hatred.

Kurt covered up and regained some composure but under the attack, he could not do much except defend himself. Seeing an opportunity when Norsky brought his hand back to strike once more, Kurt smashed his own fist into the unprotected throat of his attacker.

Norsky immediately fell off him clutching his crushed throat as he desperately tried to drag air into his lungs but found he could not breathe. He writhed on the floor as panic gripped him and his face turned blue.

Kurt took the time to regain his composure and his own breath. His face regenerated rapidly, the cuts and bruises healing as new skin formed over them. He knew he had not killed Norsky, if his regenerative abilities were similar to his own then he knew his throat would soon heal and the attack would continue. Sure enough, he saw Norsky's throat begin to fill out once more and the bruising slowly disappear as it healed. The colour of his face returned to normal and he got to his feet staring at Kurt. A smile crossed his lips and he said, 'You're going to have to do better than that Kurt.'

Chapter Thirty

The Recon Delta Marines, the security detail in Col Sec HQ, were led by Captain Mykal Trent. Six feet four of hardened muscle tempered by a fierce intelligence he was a well-liked officer. His hair was so white and cut so short it made his head appear bald and his piercing laser-like eyes made him a formidable sight.

He led his men up towards where the Rover5s were coming down. They had no idea what their intentions were but whatever they were it was not good news for those in the lower levels.

'You know the drill guys. We stop them at the first opportunity or we die trying,' Trent said through his internal comm. channel filtered through his Rapier battle helmet to only those in his squad. He had a squad of twelve marines, not enough for what faced them but they had no choice; it was them or nothing. The only consolation in their favour was that they also had Matt and Zara on their side.

Through the HUD in his helmet, he received sensor data about the approaching bio signs. What he saw furrowed his brow, he could handle the bio signs of the clones but it was what came with them that worried him. What were those things? He turned to Matt and asked, 'What the fuck are we facing here Matt?'

Matt's expression told him everything he needed to know and what he said confirmed it. He said, 'Your worst nightmare.'

Trent checked the sensor data once more, which told him they were close. 'Okay guys, this is it,' he said as a sound reached them from around the corner in the corridor; a sound that chilled the blood, the deep-throated roar of the octo-felines.

They had arrived.

Norsky rushed at Kurt once more, feeling more powerful than ever. He knew there was nothing that could stop him. Oh, he could be hurt, he could still be injured and feel the pain from it but it wouldn't stop him. He knew he would regenerate and be able to fight on and that his strength and speed had been increased. He had noticed this earlier, but it was during this fight that he finally realised just how powerful he had become.

He was a God; there was nothing he could not do, nothing that could stop him.

When he had done what he wanted with Kurt he would turn his fury on those clones that brought him here. Those clones who thought they controlled him; they would soon learn who the true master was.

The two of them collided once more, rolling on the floor of the corridor, each punching the other in an attempt to gain the upper hand. Norsky shrugged off each blow with contempt as his confidence rose to epic proportions. Kurt fought with the ease and grace of a skilled fighter, carefully warding off blows that would kill a normal human and dodging others.

He pushed Norsky from him but the ex-Alliance agent refused to go as he grabbed hold of Kurt's arm. Twisting around and under Norsky he bent his arm around his back and grabbed him around the neck with his free arm around Norsky's back. Bending at the knees Norsky slammed an elbow into Kurt's ribs hearing a satisfying snap as two of them broke. He then reversed the hold he had on him, throwing him over his shoulder to land on his back in front of him.

Norsky jumped up to land on Kurt's midriff with a knee but his prey was aware of the tactic and rolled free at the last instant. Norsky's knee impacted with the floor smashing right through the surface.

Kurt was on his feet in a flash and aimed a series of blows at his attacker who performed a backward roll out of the way after blocking the first three punches.

With his head down Norsky ran at Kurt catching him around the waist, then he picked him up only to slam his back down into the floor again with such force that the floor gave way slightly. Kurt's broken ribs had healed but after this latest assault, his back almost broke. Kurt managed to get his feet under Norsky's chest to push him from him, sending him across the room once more.

Norsky regained his feet and ran at him aiming a haymaker right cross at Kurt's head. Kurt brought up his left arm to block the punch then smashed his right fist into Norsky's stomach. His attacker doubled over from the pain from the blow and Kurt grabbed his head and still holding Norsky's other arm he threw him bodily against the wall. The impact almost sent him through into an adjacent office, but instead, he fell to the floor at the base of the damaged wall.

Norsky was off the ground in a flash leaping on top of

Kurt smashing his fist into the side of his head. Kurt saw stars dance before his eyes for just a second from a blow that would have caved in a normal skull. That second though was all Norsky needed to get him on the floor.

Just as he rolled on top of Kurt, bringing up his fist to smash into his face, he heard the sound of the elevator arriving. He turned to look in that direction, giving Kurt the opportunity he needed.

Kurt punched Norsky squarely in the face which eased him off enough to give him the room to bring up his legs to kick him off him. Norsky went staggering across the room just as Jake and the rest of the Wildfire Team exited the elevator. Jake saw what was happening and brought up his assault rifle and shot the ex-Alliance agent as he flew across the room.

The salvo of pulsed plasma bolts struck Norsky in the centre of his chest tearing through his already damaged body armour to strike flesh.

His anger flared as he saw the odds tilt against him. His chest was regenerating, healing, as he looked at the newcomers, but the focus of his anger was still directed at Kurt Stryder. Ignoring the Wildfire Team he rushed at Kurt once more. Kurt was ready this time though, clearly, he had just been waiting for the others to arrive as his stance was more confident and self-assured.

As Norsky approached, Kurt sidestepped then as his attacker rushed by he snapped out a ridge hand strike catching Norsky in the throat. The speed of the strike was such that not even Norsky's enhanced reflexes could see it. When it impacted his throat his head remained in place but the rest of his body continued moving forward. His legs went up in the air as his momentum carried him on then he crashed down to the floor on his back.

Kurt was on him in a flash snapping the SUT on his

wrist. Light exploded around Norsky as the SUT was activated and, within a flash, quite literally, the light imploded disappearing to a pinprick. When it vanished Norsky was no longer there.

'Now Artie,' Jake said.

Norsky appeared above the RandCorp building exploding out from a burst of light so intense that onlookers thought a new sun had flashed into existence before disappearing just as quickly.

Norsky had felt something snap onto his wrist and before he could react blinding light engulfed him. With it came the sensation of total disorientation. He had no idea which way was up or where he was. His head spun and wave after wave of nausea washed over him making it impossible for him to focus. The light disappeared just as suddenly as it had appeared but the sense of disorientation remained. When his eyes had cleared and the pain vanished he saw where he was. This caused further confusion for he was somehow outside the building in mid-air.

'Oh shit!' he said when he saw what was about to happen.

On the command given by Jake, the Pulsar's AI fired a Hellfire missile at the figure that suddenly appeared. The resulting explosion blew the unsuspecting Norsky into smithereens. He saw the missile being fired but could do nothing to prevent what was to come next. All thoughts of Godhood were extinguished in the explosion.

His body was ripped apart by the force of the blast

sending body parts outward in every direction in a shower of blood and gore.

Kurt looked at Jake and his team and smiled. This part of their mission had been a success. A major threat to the safety of Col Sec had been eradicated but this was just the start. The major battle was still being waged and they were too far away to help.

'It's not over yet guys,' Torres said which ended their short-lived celebration.

'Artie meet us on the roof, we need to get back to HQ and fast,' Jake said and without another word, they all headed for the roof.

A protective cordon on the edge of the building had been formed into officers of the local Constabulary. They made sure there were no encroachments inside what was now a crime scene. A tall man approached the cordon dressed in coveralls with 'Forensic Unit' emblazoned across the back. He was accompanied by five other men, all similarly dressed, a fact that did not go unnoticed by the officer as they approached.

'We've come to process the scene,' the tall man leading the group said, his opaline eyes looking straight at the officer.

The officer inspected the credentials held out by the tall man and he glanced at all the others with him. He said, 'Okay, it's all yours.' As he allowed them through the cordon he asked, 'Are you all related?'

The leader said over his shoulder as they continued on towards the building, 'We're brothers.'

The body parts that littered the ground and the fallout from the Hellfire missile that exploded above everyone's heads were gathered up by the forensic unit members and placed into sealed containers.

Without saying a word, and once all of Norsky's remains had been collected, the forensic unit disappeared inside the building where they made their way to the Express elevator. Once they reached the Penthouse they exited the elevator and walked to the door that led to the roof. The shuttle was still there even though the pilot was dead. They all got inside and one of them sat in the pilot's chair. He fired up the engines and before long the shuttle was rising into the air before the pilot turned her away from the building and pointed her up towards the upper atmosphere.

Down on the ground, the officer who had allowed them through the cordon saw the shuttle take off and he called his headquarters using his NI.

When the call was put through he said, 'Sir something weird has just happened over at the RandCorp building.'

'What sort of weird are we talking here?' asked the Commander. So the officer told him what he had seen in detail, including the eye colour of the men.

'I think you're onto something there but I also know it's out of our jurisdiction so I'll inform the right people. Good work son,' the Commander said before breaking off the connection.

His next call was to Col Sec HQ but because of the attack all comm. lines were down so the call was logged by an automatic receiver and stored for further inspection. The Commander came off the line unaware that his call had not been heard at that point, so he went about his business thinking that it would be taken care of.

Chapter Thirty-One

The first of the three octo-felines poked its head around the corner of the corridor. When it saw the prey they had been tracking it threw its massive head back, opened its huge maw of a mouth and let out a huge roar. The sound reverberated through the corridor echoing off the walls warning the Recon Delta Marines what they were up against.

'Holy shit, you weren't kidding about them being my worst nightmare,' Trent said as he brought up his assault rifle to aim at the huge beast.

'No, I was not. I only knew of them through the reports from the Wildfire Team and Kurt Stryder but seeing them I can now believe what they said,' Matt said, never taking his eyes off the approaching beast.

'What did the report say?'

'That they were virtually unstoppable.'

'This day just keeps getting better and better,' Trent said just as another roar filled the corridor heralding the arrival of the second beast.

'Holy crap,' Trent said as he looked at the second beast then consulted the sensor readout on his helmet's HUD.

'There are three of the fuckers!' he said, not quite believing what he was seeing.

'And quite a few Rover5s to back them up,' observed Matt as he also accessed the computer sensor readings via his NI.

'Talk about your back to the wall,' Trent said. Then, setting his jaw in grim determination, he said to his squad, 'You've all seen what we're up against, you know how important our job is here today. Colonel De Boer is on his way with reinforcements so we just need to hold our position here and not allow the enemy to gain a foothold in this base. I know you won't let me down so let's do this.'

The first beast sniffed the air recognising its prey and locked its front set of eyes on the men and woman before it. Its powerful muscles in the front two sets of legs bunched up, bulging beneath the skin as the rear two sets of legs prepared to pounce like massive coiled springs.

Before it could move Trent fired his assault rifle, a short burst of pulsed plasma bolts struck the beast squarely in the chest just as the beast raised its massive head to roar prior to an attack. The smell of burnt fur and flesh filled the confined space in the corridor along with the beast's bellow of pain and rage. The salvo of gunfire had wounded the creature but, more importantly, it had enraged it beyond its capability to control. It sprang at the marines catching them completely unawares. Even though they had been keeping a close eye on them they were unprepared for the speed and ferocity of the creature. Its massive mouth closed on the arm of the nearest marine clamping down hard then, with a twist of its head, it ripped the man's arm from its socket. Blood trailed through the air as the marine's heart pumped it out of the open wound. Even though he vainly tried to hold it in with his other hand it was futile, he fell to the floor weak from the massive and rapid blood loss. The creature swallowed the arm whole then turned to attack another marine. It smashed its head into the chest of another marine tossing him high into the air. He smashed into the ceiling then came crashing down right into the open mouth of the creature who bit down hard on the marine's midriff. The jaws were so powerful that with one single bite it severed the man in two. It tossed one half into the air to catch it in his mouth while the rest of the man fell to the floor to be pinned by a massive feline paw.

The other two creatures attacked after smelling the blood. The marines had to fall back as they could not fight in close quarters with this enemy.

Trent bellowed at his men trying desperately to be heard over the roars of the huge beasts. He told what was left of his men to fall back where they could attempt to regroup.

Matt and Zara had watched the first encounter with the octo-felines and they were as afraid as the Recon Delta marines, but like the other marines, they refused to allow it to show.

They made their way back through the corridor, backpedalling as they went. They fired their assault rifles futilely at the great beasts. The pulsed plasma bolts struck the creatures but their fury was such that, even through the pain, they continued to surge forward. Their skin began to regenerate slowly, not nearly as fast as Kurt or Zara, but it still healed far faster than anything they had seen before.

Behind the creatures the Rover5 who was leading the others, Maguire, said to the rest of the clones, 'Stay back, now they have the scent of her there should be nothing to stop them.'

'We have to split up and try to make them follow us. If we can divide their forces we may have a chance to whittle them down,' suggested Matt to Trent.

'We can try but I think our best option would be to fight on a united front,' replied the commander of the marines.

'How did they know where this place was?' asked Zara, voicing something that had been bothering her since the attack had begun.

'Excuse me?' Trent said, wondering why the sudden change of tack.

'How did they know where this base was? I thought it was supposed to be top secret, yet they found it with no trouble. It was almost like they followed something here, tracked it here,' she said.

'Are you suggesting that we have a mole in here?' Trent asked.

'No, but I think I know where she's going with this,' Matt said looking at the Captain. He turned to Zara and said, 'You escaped from their ship didn't you, how long were you on board, have you any idea?'

'None, I just remember waking up and being transferred to their ship. We made several jumps and then I escaped close to Celeron where Kurt picked me up. At the time I thought it strange, almost too easy and I never figured out why we were at Celeron anyway but now I'm thinking it was all to get me here.'

'They tracked you, you have a sub-dermal tracker implanted,' Trent blurted out when the realisation dawned on him what they were talking about.

'What does that mean though?' he added when Matt and Zara looked at him.

Matt smiled and said, 'It means we now have a plan.'

'One thing's been bothering me since this whole thing started,' Jake said as they sat in the forward section of the Pulsar. Kurt turned to him and asked, 'What's that?'

'How they found the HQ so easily, well at all really,' he replied.

'Isn't it obvious sirs, Miss Hardy has a sub-dermal tracker implanted which they followed,' the AI interjected.

'Just what I was thinking,' Jake added.

'How do you get to that?' Kurt asked looking around for someone to talk to; he was not as comfortable as the Team were yet in conversing with the AI.

'I have been running extrapolations on the events as they unfolded, Captain Stryder. Miss Hardy escaped from a starship in orbit around your home world. There was no explanation as to why they were there so we must assume it was to force you to come to her aid,' Artie said.

'But they tried to stop us; they tried to recapture us both and we only got away by the skin of our teeth,' Kurt said.

'All the more reason for you to ensure you took her to a place of safety; somewhere they would not be able to find her.'

'Somewhere they would not be able to find either of us, somewhere like the HQ,' Kurt said as he saw what the AI was suggesting.

'Exactly, sir, with the sub-dermal tracker in place they were then able to locate the Headquarters below ground and attack once Norsky had lured you away.'

'Are you then saying that this whole thing was to destroy the base? If that's the case then why lure me away, what was their idea to have me battle Norsky, what did they hope to achieve?'

'Because Norsky had a contingent of clones with him I believe they were there not to prevent anyone gaining entry to the building but rather to act as backup for him to enable him to capture you.'

'To what end?'

'Did you not report that on Toldax the Alliance took samples of your blood to use in their own plan of re-creating the initial experiment that gave you your abilities?'

'They wanted me as a source for their own experiment on creating a sort of super clone?'

'I do believe that is correct, sir. If their plan to destroy Col Sec HQ is a success and they had captured you it would have seriously inhibited Col Sec's ability to defend against such an enemy.'

'Have you come up with a theory as to how they plan to destroy the base?' Jake asked.

'The most effective way would be to force the personnel deep into the base then explode a thermobaric device. It would cause quite some damage and the shockwave generated would travel through every level killing anyone trapped in there.'

'Zara and the rest of Col Sec are down there. We have to do something,' Kurt said and the anguish he felt was evident just by looking at him.

'I doubt very much that, according to the timing of their plan, they would allow us to reach the base before they detonated the device, sir,' the AI said.

'Are you saying there's nothing we can do to help them, Artie?' Torres pleaded.

'We have to warn them at least, tell them to get the hell out of there as fast as they can,' Kurt said.

'I am attempting to contact General Sinclair now, sir, but I fully expect a jamming cordon to be in place,' Artie said. He then added, 'It seems I was wrong,' and then he connected the call.

At that very moment, Sinclair was walking away from the base through one of the escape tunnels. When the call came through to his NI he thought at first it was an update from those he had left behind.

'Jake, give me a sit-rep,' he said once he recognised who was calling him.

'General, I don't have much time so please listen very carefully. The Rover5s are going to detonate a thermobaric bomb that will collapse the top levels of the HQ, sealing it off. Sir, the shockwave will fill the entire HQ, which means no one will be safe. You have to get everyone out of there as fast as you can. We don't have a time frame for when it'll go off just that it will.' Jake said quickly trying to get as much information across as quickly as he could.

'Most of the personnel have already been evacuated through the escape tunnels but Matt, Zara and a small detachment of marines are still up there trying to defend the base until Colonel De Boer arrives with reinforcements,' Sinclair replied. He felt a wave of defeat wash over him then as the reality that Col Sec and he personally had been duped. He had been confident in their power to defend the Confederation and now he was faced with the reality that they clearly were not. His overconfidence had cost them dearly, not only in the lives that had been lost this day but in their ability to respond to further threats that were no doubt on their way.

'They won't get there in time, sir. All you can do is evacuate your people now,' Jake urged.

'Leave it with me, Jake. Rendezvous at Evacuation point Alpha,' Sinclair said then closed the connection. He contacted Matt directly and when the call was connected he said, 'Listen, Matt, you have to get to the evac tunnels a.s.a.p.

They have a thermobaric bomb with them, which they plan to detonate sealing the base off. There is little time and it is doubtful you will be able to get to it to defuse it so your only alternative is to get out.'

Matt had stopped in his tracks when the call came through as he listened intently to what was being said. Before answering he connected to the main computer via his NI and used the base's sensors to look for munitions not listed on the base's inventory. The sensors would log any munitions that were not supposed to be in that location and sort through the database to categorise its specificity. When he received the data through his NI he was shocked. It wasn't that he doubted the General's statement but he had to check anyway, standard operating procedure, one never assumed anything to be fact until one had ascertained its authenticity. There was indeed a huge thermobaric device timed to detonate and considering what was between it and them he tended to agree with Sinclair that he would not reach it in time to defuse it.

They had no choice but to retreat to the evac tunnels.

'We will evac as soon as viable, sir,' he said.

'Now Matt, I do not want any heroics from you or the others, is that clear? Just get all of you to the tunnels now, we will deal with the ramifications of this day later when we have regrouped and we can have our say on the matter but to do that I need all of you out of there safely.'

'Trust me, sir, we'll be there,' Matt said then closed the connection so he could brief the others on the new situation.

The shuttle that had left the roof of the RandCorp building exited the Earth's atmosphere and engaged a stealth shield. This enabled it to pass through all the security blockades set in place due to the attack on Area 15.

Their destination was the OMEGA facility on the Moon where they hoped their precious cargo would be greeted with enthusiasm.

'Can we get any more speed out of this thing?' Kurt said. He gripped the armrests of the seat he was in. All he wanted to do was get there as fast as possible. He had to get there, he had to help Zara, having already lost her once he would not lose her again.

Artie answered for Jake who the question was clearly aimed at. The AI said, 'I am getting as much speed out of the engines as possible, sir.'

'We're not going to get there in time, are we?' Kurt asked, his words dripping with despondence.

'No sir, we are not,' the AI replied. Kurt was chilled by the cold tone the answer was delivered in.

'That's just not good enough,' Kurt blasted; his anger could no longer be contained.

'I agree, sir, and that is why I am taking us to the evacuation point, it is all we can do at this time,' Artie said, his words consoling even though the tone was still cold.

'You know, we've been on the back foot ever since this thing began. Isn't it about time we took the fight to them?' Cooper said fed up with being on the defensive all the time and letting it show.

'Good point Mack but we've got more important things to think about at the moment,' Jake said as he looked at Kurt. He knew the anguish and frustration that was going through him for he felt the same emotions when Natasha was trapped on the surface of Tartaran and he was racing to get to her before the worst happened.

'That's just it though Jake, it's something they would

never expect,' Vance added bolstering his colleague's argument.

Torres said, 'I agree, we have to do something to let them know this won't go unpunished.'

Kurt had been listening even though it appeared he was lost in his own thoughts. He turned to look at them and asked, 'What do you suggest?'

Chapter Thirty-Two

When Matt contacted Zara she was off to one side of a corridor hoping to lead the beasts away from the marines and into an ambush.

'This could get messy then,' she replied once Matt had filled her in on the situation.

'You have to get to the evac tunnels as soon as possible Zara, we have no idea how long we have before they detonate the bomb,' Matt said urgently.

'I may need some help with this, I think they may have blocked my exit off,' she said. As she waited for a reply from Matt who was obviously thinking of the best way to help her she thought *What good is the ability to regenerate if I'm trapped down here? Could I regenerate from such a blast or would it obliterate me beyond my capacity to regenerate?'* Even as that thought filled her mind she knew the answer, she remembered seeing Kurt regenerate from a ball of flame that filled a corridor when a generator blew up on Toldax. He saved her by covering her with his body, shielding her from the intense heat from the flames. She remembered seeing his flesh sear off then miraculously regenerate into new skin right before her eyes. That was when their blood had transferred from one to the other and how she became what she was today. If Kurt could survive that then she would survive whatever this day brought.

Matt contacted Trent who was in a different section of the corridor with the marines. They were getting ready for when the creatures went by, Matt told him of their dilemma.

'What do you want us to do Matt?' Trent asked. After being told about the bomb he could not see a way out of their situation and was resigned to go down fighting if need be.

'We need to make a run for it and hope for the best. Is there any way you can get to us?'

'We can lay down some covering fire for you; draw their attention away from you. It might just give you the chance to get away,' replied Trent.

'Sounds good but make sure you leave enough time for you to get to safety also.'

'Don't worry about us; we know what we have to do.'

Matt paused as he hoped that didn't mean what it sounded like. Having no other option though he acceded to his suggestion, he said, 'Okay then, we'll wait for you at the evac tunnel entrance. Try not to keep us waiting too long, I wouldn't want to have to come back and drag your sorry asses out of there.'

'We'll be there, don't worry, sir. You just get ready to move when we make our play,' Trent said then broke the connection.

Matt tried to put out of his mind what he thought Trent was about to do. Enough lives had been lost already and the thought of losing even one more deadened his soul. He hoped that one day soon there would be a reckoning when he would get the chance to pay OMEGA back for everything they had done this day.

'Hang tight, I'm coming to you,' he said to Zara.

The corridor Zara was in stretched out for several yards and had three sections that veered off to either side with an assortment of doors leading to offices and the like. She had positioned herself in the doorway of one of these offices at the far end of the corridor. It was a dead end. The idea being that the creatures would follow her into the corridor and once in the enclosed space the marines and Matt would attack from the rear catching them all in their crossfire.

It was a good plan in theory, but now that she was in position waiting for them she had her doubts.

With the thermobaric bomb just waiting to detonate and three angry octo-felines with a squad of Rover5s between her and her exit, she had a knot of fear running through her that they would not get out of there alive.

At the end of the corridor, she saw the first of the creatures appear and then suddenly the sound of gunfire from behind it.

The creature tried to turn around but its sheer size made it difficult to manoeuvre. Pulsed plasma bolts struck the creature from the side enraging it as the heat distribution through the skin threatened to overwhelm its senses. Matt appeared from another doorway halfway between her and the creature. He began firing at the creature, also aiming at its head. The creature reared up baring its long, razor-sharp fangs and bellowed its rage at them both. Matt continued firing his assault rifle until the battery clip was depleted. The creature had sustained multiple hits to its head and upper torso and as Matt was in the process of replacing the battery clip in his Remm it collapsed in front of him.

Zara came out of the office doorway and ran to him. 'We have to help Trent and his boys,' she said.

'They're giving us a chance to get away while they hold

them off. We have to move now,' Matt said as he looked at her through pain-filled eyes.

'We can't leave without them, we have to help them,' Zara said, her voice pleading as she looked deep into his blue eyes.

'We have to go, Zara, we don't have time for this,' Matt said more sternly this time. He had to get her moving as they couldn't afford the time to argue.

She was about to say something else and he interrupted with, 'I made a promise to Kurt to look after you and to get you out of here safely. Don't make a liar out of me.'

At the mention of Kurt's name her whole demeanour changed. She tempered her decision to stay with her need to see Kurt. Knowing that if she survived this she would be able to fight on and her only desire at that moment was to see Kurt and together fight on against this insidious threat to the Confederation. They had dealt them a bitter blow this day and one that she vowed to return in equal measure.

Against her better judgement, she said, 'Okay, let's go,' which brought a huge sigh of relief from Matt.

'Follow me,' Matt said and he led her to the end of the corridor.

Trent and the rest of the marines had managed to get behind the creatures and the Rover5s and had started firing at them with all the firepower at their disposal.

In the first wave, half of the Rover5s were cut down by rifle fire. When the creatures were also hit they turned away from the scent they had been following, Zara's, so they could attack whoever was firing on them. It took them a while before they could twist their long bodies around to face the other direction and when they had they stormed after the marines.

Trent saw two marines on either side of him get hit by the hulking monsters. Their jaws tore apart the two men sending body parts flying across the corridor, blood splattering over the walls. Trent fired at the creatures and clone soldiers alternatively. His squad was down to three men by now after the creatures had attacked them. He knew he had to hang on long enough for Matt and Zara to get away, so he forced himself to fight on. He ducked beneath the lunging head of one of the last two creatures and rolled under its forelegs firing his Remm assault rifle up at its belly. Blood splattered the ground from the wounds he had just inflicted on it. As he rolled clear he fired another salvo at the creature's flank tearing open a savage wound that caused blood to spurt over the walls and floor. As he got to his feet he continued firing at the head of the creature as it tried to turn around. Pulsed plasma bolts struck the eyes, burning them beyond the creature's ability to heal. It thrashed around when it realised it could not see out of half of its eyes. Trent shot it again in the head with a continual stream of plasma bolts. Blood poured from every wound as the massive head was snapped backwards from the kinetic force of each bolt.

The creature knew its life was waning and it made one last effort to crush the man before it.

Zara turned to look at the struggle between the marines and the creatures. All she had to do was turn and leave but something stopped her. She knew she had been given these abilities for a reason and if it wasn't to help people then what for?

Seeing Trent was about to lose his life was all she could take. She could not leave knowing someone was about to die when there was something she could do to prevent it. She ran at the huge creature jumping at its massive head grabbing its mouth by wrapping her arms around it, snapping it shut and forcing it away from its intended victim. She slammed the head against the wall giving Trent time to move out of the way.

'Knife!' she shouted and he threw his K-Bar knife towards her after ripping it from his forearm sheath. She snapped out her arm to catch it in mid-air then twisted beneath the head so she could use it. With all her strength she rammed the blade up into the creature's lower jaw and up into the upper jaw pinning it closed. Blood ran down her arm from the wound she had just inflicted on the beast. She released the head and it fell to the floor. The beast was dead.

The other two creatures roared their fury at seeing their kin cut down. They thrashed around as they forced their way through the corridor, desperate to reach the puny creature that had killed one of their own.

The two remaining marines had ducked inside the nearest doorway when the clones returned fire. They kept well hidden as a withering barrage of pulsed plasma bolts peppered the doorframe. The clones were no fools, they covered each other's fire so they did not have to change clips at the same time and in that way they kept the marines pinned in the doorway.

Matt saw this and picked up his own assault rifle and fired at them. By the time they realised what was happening two of them had fallen to Matt's gunfire. As the rest of them turned to see what had happened, the marines saw the opportunity and caught the remaining clones in their crossfire.

Within a few seconds, the clones were all lying on the floor dead. All that was left was the threat from the two huge creatures.

Zara stood facing the two beasts. She had the K-Bar knife in her right hand, it was still dripping with blood from the first beast and in her left hand, she held a pulse rifle she had retrieved from a dead marine.

She glared at the two beasts, her eyes blazing with fury. Too many had died because of her; it ended here and now.

No more would die here, not if she could help it and she knew she could.

The two beasts lowered their heads as they eyed her. The muscles in their shoulders bunched as they prepared to attack. They bared their fangs as they opened their huge mouths to roar their fury at her.

Zara knew what was coming and she was prepared. She stood with her legs apart as she balanced herself and got ready for the assault.

There was not much room in the corridor but somehow the two beasts were able to stand shoulder to shoulder. When they began to move though, there was nowhere for Zara to go. She had no choice but to meet the attack head-on.

She had no desire to run, she was going to stop these creatures here and now. They would hurt no one else, of that she was determined. She had to give in to her intuition about her newfound abilities. For a while now she had thought, no she had known, that she could do what no other human could do. She was aware of her strength and speed and hints of mental abilities that only others could dream of. She had to allow these abilities to come to the fore, allow them to flourish, in that way she would be able to do what she had to.

She leapt into the air over the head of the octo-feline to her left and twisted in mid-air to land facing front, straddling the beast as she landed on its shoulders. She plunged the blade deep into the flesh at the base of the neck causing a spurt of blood to gush out. She twisted the blade sideways as she tried to sever the spinal cord.

The beast reared up on its hind legs as it attempted to throw her off. Zara hung on with her knees and used the rifle to shoot the other beast to her left. Pulsed plasma bolts strafed the beast's flanks causing blood to spray out onto the floor.

She clung on with her knees riding the great beast as it bucked and tried to shake her free. Again and again, she stabbed the blade deep into the neck of her steed. Blood jetted out from each wound she inflicted on the beast, covering her hands and arms. Finally, the wounds were too much for even the great beast and it slumped to the ground, its huge mouth open as it panted its last few dying breaths. As it landed on the floor Zara leapt from it somersaulting in mid-air to land in front of the last creature. She spun on this already wounded creature stabbing the blade deep below the neck several times, her movements nothing now but a blur to those who watched. With her pulse rifle, she fired several shots into the head of the creature before her and, even though the speed of the Tartaran beasts was blindingly fast, even they could not keep up with Zara's hyper-accelerated movements. The pulsed plasma bolts struck the creature's head before it had time to move away, destroying the front set of eyes. As the creature lunged for her with one of its forepaws, she danced effortlessly to the side then stabbed the knife into it causing the beast to withdraw with a howl of pain. Zara jumped onto the paw then up onto the head of the creature where she slammed the blade through the cranium, splitting bone, deep into the brain, sending a spurt of blood several inches into the air. Zara remained astride the head as it dropped to the floor, then stepped calmly from it knowing the battle was over; all the creatures were dead.

Matt had been staring at her in awe. His jaw was slightly open and his eyes were wide in surprise. Her display of raw naked power and balletic coordination was something he had never seen before.

As she came up to him stepping around the corpses of the creatures she said, 'Job done.'

Trent and the last two marines had finished off the

remaining clones and had had just enough time to also see Zara strut her stuff; they too could not believe their eyes.

'What just happened?' Trent asked, voicing the thought running through all their minds.

'I saved your asses is what just happened and before you all get on moral high ground saying things like "Why didn't you help out earlier", my abilities were supposed to have been kept secret. I couldn't let any more people die though and I don't care who knows anymore either. If I've been granted these abilities then it would be wrong not to use them, no more than that, it would be irresponsible.'

Trent looked at her and simply said, 'I was just going to say thanks.'

Zara looked down at her feet, ashamed at her outburst and as she looked up they were all smiling at her, relief on their faces.

One of the marines said to his buddy, 'Sure glad she's on our side.'

'I'd like to get on...' the other started to say but was quickly stopped by receiving an elbow in the ribs to stop him from finishing his remark.

Matt walked over to her and said, 'We have to go.'

'Where is the bomb?' she asked which threw him completely. He looked at her, his brows knitting together. 'Why, what're you thinking?' he asked.

Chapter Thirty-Three

General Sinclair reached the end of the evac tunnel and was greeted by the rest of the personnel who had travelled the same route.

'General, glad you could make it, sir. Where are the others?' said Lieutenant Franks. He had been put in charge of looking after the evacuees.

'They should be right behind me, I hope,' Sinclair replied as he glanced over his shoulder to look down the tunnel.

The evac point was at the end of the tunnels, a mile away from the edge of the underground base. The five tunnels each had an evac point of their own as each tunnel radiated out from the base in different directions.

'Sir, when are the evac transports going to arrive so we can get everyone to safety?' Franks asked which brought the General's head around to look at him. Sinclair's eyes momentarily showed the anguish he must have been feeling at not knowing how his people were faring deep in the bowels of the base. Regaining his composure once more he said, 'They should arrive within the next few minutes. An automatic signal went out to the nearest bases the moment the evacuation was signalled.'

'Let's hope they get here in time to board the transports sir,' Franks said.

'We will not be leaving without them Lieutenant, of that you can be sure,' Sinclair said and he turned back to look down the tunnel, willing them to appear.

———————

Kurt was pacing the forward section of the Pulsar. He was anxious to reach the HQ and see Zara again. The rest of the Wildfire Team were also anxious but for other reasons. Jake wanted to see Natasha once more but he also wanted to get back into the fray. They were desperate to get back into action, to deal OMEGA a telling blow instead of riding the punches all the time.

'Has anyone any suggestions on how to take this fight to them?' Kurt asked as he turned to face the rest of them. He had his hands on hips as he spoke, not sure what to do with them. What he really wanted to do was wrap them around the neck of whoever was responsible for all this mayhem and the frustration at not being able to do that was ripping him apart.

They all looked at him with blank stares, clearly, they had not come up with anything either. Just then a voice cut through the deadlock of silence.

'If I may, sirs, I do not think this is over yet,' the AI said.

'What do you mean Artie?' Jake asked with concern etched across his face.

'I have been running further extrapolations to our enemies' attack strategies and I think I may have come up with another attack they may try.'

'You've gotta be kidding me, they're gonna attack somewhere else?' Vance shouted in anger, voicing everyone's rage at being battered by the forces of OMEGA. They wanted to fight back but were constantly held on the defensive.

'I do believe, sirs, that whilst the forces of Col Sec are busy fending off the attack at our Headquarters and the RandCorp building, the Capitol Building would be a prime target. I do believe that the entire government of the Confederation would be in attendance pending such attacks we are facing at the moment, to form the Defence Committee.'

'I hate to say it but he's right,' Jake said as it dawned on him what could be about to happen.

'It's too late to get any help over there. They'll be sitting ducks,' Cooper said slamming a fist down on the armrest of the seat he was in.

'Let's not go off half-cocked. Artie, can you scan the area over the Capitol Building to see if there's any unusual activity and in the meantime turn us around to head over there, just in case?' Kurt said.

Artie came back straight away with. 'I have several crafts heading towards the Capitol Building, three attack helijets and a troop carrier, sir. I have changed our trajectory, sir; our new destination is the Capitol Building.'

'Artie, what's the eta of those crafts and how far behind will we be?' Jake asked, holding his breath while he waited for the answer.

'They should arrive at their destination in seventeen minutes, sir. We will arrive six minutes after that sir,' the AI said. Jake was perturbed by the cold tone in which the times were delivered, and he had to remind himself that Artie was actually an unfeeling machine even though by now they all thought of it as part of the crew.

'You can cause an awful lot of chaos and mayhem in six minutes,' Jake said.

'Let's just hope they can hold on until we can get there,'

Torres said echoing the hope they all held close to their hearts.

'I have attempted to contact them, sir, but it seems there is a communication blackout in place,' Artie informed him.

'Standard operating procedure, cut off the comm. channels before any attack so they can't call for reinforcements,' Kurt said, something they were all well aware of.

'I just hope they realise before it's too late,' Jake said.

The rest of the journey was spent in quiet contemplation while they were all lost in their own private thoughts.

Zara turned to Matt and said, 'They're coming here. We have to get to the evac point.'

Completely bewildered by her turnaround, Matt just nodded his head and said, 'C'mon, it's this way,' as he indicated the direction they must take.

'We wouldn't have got there in time, not with the troops guarding it. Best we get the hell out of here and regroup with the others,' she said as she picked up her pace.

'That's about the most sensible thing you've said in a long time,' Matt said.

'Hey, I have feelings you know,' Zara retorted with a hurt smile. She said, 'I may have given us some time anyway.'

'What are you talking about Zara?' Matt asked, his brows scrunched together as he tried to figure out what was going on with her.

'I accessed the main computer and initiated a complete lockdown of the facility. The blast doors will secure each section and give us a bit more time to get clear when the bomb goes off.'

'How the hell did you do that, it takes top-level clearance. If what you say is true, you may just have killed us all, you certainly will have trapped us.'

'Don't be such a twonk, Matt. Don't you think I already thought of that? I can get us through the blast doors by inserting the access code via my NI when we reach each door. It'll open up just long enough to allow us to get through. As for the top-level clearance, it wasn't too hard to hack into the computer.'

'Well it should've been, I helped oversee the installation of the new security measures when we moved into the base after the attack in New York.'

'Chalk it up to the upgrades then,' she said with a smile, she was clearly enjoying her new capabilities. Matt was concerned about how she was handling this situation but knew it was a conversation for another time.

'Yep, those are some mighty awesome upgrades,' he finally admitted, allowing a little smile to cross his lips. It had felt good to smile. He couldn't remember the last time he had, probably sometime before Tanya was killed. That memory still burned deep inside him but no matter how much it hurt, he was not ready to let it go just yet. He would nurture it, allow it to fuel his rage and then expel that rage against the enemy he knew he would face one day. That day could not come soon enough though.

She winked at him then turned to the others and said, 'C'mon, we've got to get our asses in gear and get the hell outta here.'

'You'll get no argument from us on that score Ma'am,' one of the marines said.

'Don't call me Ma'am soldier, I'm Recon Delta, just like you,' she said with a wicked grin.

'I think you're far from like us Ma'am,' Trent said. When she turned to look at him, her brows furrowed, he smiled, 'I mean it in the nicest possible way.'

'Let's get moving guys, we've no time to waste,' Matt said, putting off any further chatter as they ran for the nearest exit.

Sinclair was pacing up and down away from the staff that had made the journey through the escape tunnels. He was becoming worried about how long it was taking Matt, Zara and the rest to reach them but he would never allow anyone to see or even suspect the anguish he was going through.

In the distance, he heard something that made him take notice. It was the sound of helijets approaching at speed.

A sudden wave of unease washed over him as he realised what it was.

'Everyone, take cover, we have incoming,' he shouted and they all rushed back towards the entrance of the tunnel.

Hermes ordered the clones guarding the device to go up to the surface in preparation for the arrival of Colonel De Boer and the reinforcements. There were thirty-five of the clones all armed with Remm pulse rifles, a Sig P996 each and an assortment of grenades.

They used whatever cover was available and set themselves up behind it.

'Get ready, the device is set to detonate in less than five minutes. They should arrive around that time so let's get ready,' said the clone commander.

Before preparing to greet the incoming reinforcements they had secured the entrance to the underground Headquarters so that when the device detonated the blast would not resonate above ground. All the destructive force would be channelled downwards into the lower levels.

In the distance, the sound of approaching aircraft could be heard. The sound steadily got louder as they came closer and the clone commander said, 'Get ready, here they come.'

Sinclair and some of the survivors huddled in the darkness of the tunnels once more. The sound of the approaching helijets was almost ear-splitting in intensity. Two helijets armed with missile pods slung beneath their stubby wings and pulse cannons front and rear, each able to rotate through a small yet effective arc, making them able to target most airborne enemy aircraft.

They hovered twenty or so feet off the ground by which time Sinclair calmly walked out from the entrance. He waved to the rest of them and said, 'It's okay, they're ours.'

At that moment Zara, Matt, Trent and the other marines caught up with them.

'Sir, is everyone alright?' Matt asked as he emerged from the darkness of the tunnel. Sinclair's normally stoic expression flashed a smile for a brief moment. He was clearly pleased to see they had escaped safe and sound.

'Yes, we are all fine. It seems the automatic signal was delivered to the nearest base which sent out these to help us home,' Sinclair said as he gestured to the hovering helijets which were by this time accompanied by a larger craft that was coming in to land, a Sikorsky CH-555 Super Stallion.

'Gentlemen, our ride has arrived,' Sinclair said and this time he allowed himself a hint of a smile.

As they all filed out from the seclusion of the tunnels Matt asked, 'Will a Super Stallion be sent to every evac point sir?'

'Yes, they would be automatically deployed with two attack helijets as wingmen to ensure the evacuated parties return to safety unharmed.'

'Well, sir, we need to get back to HQ to help the Colonel retake it,' Matt argued.

'I don't think that would be wise,' Sinclair said, putting up a hand to dissuade any further argument.

'Wise or not Zara and I are going back to help out.'

'Count us in too, sir,' Trent added as he came forward much to the chagrin of Sinclair.

'I can see that arguing would do neither of us any good. What you plan on doing has some merit so I suggest you all hop aboard one of the helijets and ask them to give you a lift back to base,' Sinclair said, not bothering to argue with them anymore. Clearly, they had made their minds up and he admired their loyalty to their comrades. He added, 'I will go with the others to set up a forward base of operations where we can coordinate with Kurt and the Wildfire Team.'

'Sounds like a plan sir. Keep us updated soon as you can,' Matt said, waving to the others to follow him. He was out of the tunnel and waving to the pilot of the nearest helijet for him to land and give them a ride.

Chapter Thirty-Four

President Takagi was sitting at the head of the Confederation table. He was chairing a meeting of the Security Council at the Capitol Building.

To his right was seated General George Wallace, who represented the military arm of Col Sec just as Sinclair did the Intelligence Division. Across from him, on Takagi's left, was Alvin Moore, the Chief of Staff. On Wallace's right sat Colonel Abraham Gemmell, who was Sinclair's right-hand man in the Intelligence Division and the one person he relied on to handle things when he was unavailable. The remainder of the table was taken up by other members of the Council: representatives of the Diplomatic Corp, the Med Division, the Science Corp, the Constabulary and Transport. Those who represented other sectors in the Confederation were noticeably absent. This was an emergency meeting of the Defence Committee and therefore did not require a full Council meeting.

The meeting had been in order for the past half hour after everyone had assembled in the large, secure room in the Capitol building. All Confederation business had been relocated to this location after the catastrophic attack in New York recently on the Col Sec Headquarters building there.

Takagi looked at Gemmell and asked, 'What's the latest Intel on the situation?'

Abraham Gemmell was a career officer who had dedicated his life to the service of the Confederation. He was the man Sinclair relied on the most in the running of the Intelligence Division. Standing at six feet five he was slim and lean and for many years had set an example for the officers beneath him by regularly going on training exercises with them to keep abreast of the latest training regimens. Sharp grey eyes focused his keen intelligence on any task given him, which he faced with a fierce tenacity that bordered upon obsession. The dark lustre of his black hair, cut to a military length, had lost none of its colour even though he was in his late forties. When he spoke, his voice, like everything else about him, was even and measured. He said, 'I've not heard from General Sinclair since the attack began, sir, but I'll try to contact him as we speak.' He turned his head away as he accessed the comm. channels via his NI in an attempt to call Sinclair. When he turned to look at the President once more his expression had darkened.

'Sir, I cannot call him, or anyone. There seems to be a blackout on all communications either entering or leaving this building,' he said.

General Wallace caught on immediately to the implications and said, 'That could only mean one thing.'

Gemmell looked at him and said, 'Exactly.'

Wallace and Gemmell were on their feet in a flash, 'Sir we have to get everyone to the bunker, immediately.'

Takagi looked from one to the other, his gaze uncomprehending. Gemmell said, 'Sir we are about to be attacked.'

Colonel De Boer had received the update on their eta from the pilot of their transport. He knew they would arrive within a few minutes and he ordered his men to complete their final checks of equipment and armoury.

The Hurricane C230 they were on board was making its final approach to Area 15. The huge engines went into reverse thrust as it came in to land.

On the ground, the countdown on the thermobaric bomb had reached zero. It exploded beneath the surface and the force of the blast actually lifted the top of the ground, like a huge bubble expanding underground. The buildings sitting on the surface shook as the ground lifted beneath them. Pieces were shaken loose and masonry and sheeting fell as the shockwave hit.

All this was visible from the air as the C230 approached for landing.

De Boer watched as the shockwave lifted the ground from the detonation and uttered a one word expletive, 'Damn!'

On the ground, Hermes gave the command as they rode out the ground wave, 'Open fire.'

Pulsed plasma bolts from the clones' rifles struck the engines of the incoming C230 blowing them to bits. The resulting explosions threw the huge plane off its trajectory and without the power from the engines to control its descent it came in too fast.

'Brace for impact,' shouted the pilot as he vainly struggled with the controls to regain some kind of control.

The nose of the plane slammed into the ground at an alarming speed crushing the entire forward section killing everyone inside. As it concertinaed back into the rest of the plane the soldiers in the passenger section were thrown around like rag dolls. Explosions erupted inside the plane as vital systems shut down or overloaded causing further danger to those left alive. The plane's momentum carried it forward as it ran parallel with the buildings that were Area 15. By the time it had slowed down to a halt, there were a few small fires in and around what was left of the fuselage. It had cracked open in several places and broken apart into three sections.

The second it stopped the clones opened fire once more.

Colonel De Boer got to his feet, blood dripping from a gash on his forehead. His vision was blurred from the impact but he knew he had to rally the troops into some semblance of order. Luckily for him, these were Recon Delta Marines and were the best Col Sec had to offer.

He had them organised in seconds. Any injured men were placed in a position to relieve any pain and to keep them safe whilst the rest arranged themselves around the edges of the open areas ready to return fire.

It did not take long for any of them to realise that their position was hopeless. They were pinned down in the burning fuselage of a crashed plane. If the fires that were building inside didn't finish them, the clones waiting outside most certainly would.

Hermes allowed a cruel smile to cross his thin lips as he said, 'Kill anything that moves.'

Matt, Zara, Trent and the other marines had commandeered one of the helijets and were approaching Area 15 when they heard the thermobaric bomb detonate.

'Holy shit,' Zara said as she looked at Matt. His expression was as stern as the rest of them on board the small craft.

In the distance, they could just make out the C230 carrying the Colonel with the reinforcements. When the plasma fire destroyed the engines and they all saw the massive plane go down with flames billowing out, Matt said, 'Get us there, and fast.'

By the time the helijet was close enough to see the damage, they knew the worst. They could all see the clones firing on the plane and the trapped soldiers inside.

'Shoot those muthafuckas,' Matt shouted with real venom in his voice.

The helijet opened fire with Gatling gun-type pulse cannons mounted on the front of the craft. Pulsed plasma bolts chewed up the ground as the pilot fired on the clones. In seconds the cannons had targeted the soldiers attacking the downed plane and, as the helijet manoeuvred around in the air, the clones' cover counted for nothing. They were now the targets of the withering fire from above and plasma bolts of high intensity destroyed them where they stood. Blood and gore covered the ground where the clones fell, victims of the fire from above and then it was over; not one clone was left standing.

Matt had watched with a grim smile on his face, pleased finally to get some payback on those who had caused so much pain to his friends. When it was over he said, 'Take us down now, we have to get those marines out of there before the entire plane goes up in smoke.'

Once the helijet was on the ground Matt said to Trent, 'Make sure those bastards are all dead, Zara and I will give the Colonel a hand.'

'It'll be our pleasure,' Trent said and he and what remained of his squad were off and running towards where the clones lay. They took no chances, they each had their Remm assault rifles up and ready to fire the second they saw any movement from any of the clones. They checked each body as they went, covering each other just to prevent being caught out.

Matt and Zara sprinted over to the plane where the

Colonel had already organised the evacuation of the wrecked plane. They had just got everyone out when a huge explosion ripped the rest of the plane apart. Flames from one of the many small fires had reached the fuel cells and ignited causing the explosion. A huge fireball reached out up into the sky spreading flames and shrapnel over the escaping bodies as the shockwave from the blast knocked them off their feet.

When it was over and they started to pick themselves up off the ground, Zara looked at Matt and with a smile said, 'Shit, that was close.'

He returned her smile by simply nodding his head, unable to talk just yet as he was still recovering from the effects of the shockwave that had just pummelled him.

They quickly took inventory of their situation. There were several soldiers injured in the crash-landing but nothing life-threatening. Medical supplies onboard the helijet would see to the injured until they could be taken to a hospital, but the main concern was the Headquarters. They hadn't reached it in time to prevent the thermobaric bomb from going off. OMEGA had succeeded in their plan to destroy it.

The injured soldiers were put on board the helijet with orders for them to be taken to the nearest base hospital. Matt used his NI to contact Sinclair.

'Sir, Area 15 is secure but we couldn't prevent the thermobaric bomb from detonating. I'm afraid until we get a team over here to inspect the damage there's no way of knowing just how bad it is,' he said as he walked away from the rest of them to make the call.

'I'll get a team assembled post haste, Matt. In the meantime I will organise transport for you, Zara and the Colonel to return to our temporary base,' Sinclair replied.

'Where would that be sir?'

'Nellis Base, we're coming in to land as we speak. I'll set

up our temporary base here then we can coordinate with Kurt and the rest of our forces.'

'We'll be ready when they get here, sir. I'll leave Captain Trent in charge of the security of this place until he can be relieved,' Matt said then closed the call. He went back to the rest of them to inform them of the new orders.

'This is getting to be a habit, us being on the back foot against them, and it's a habit I'm very keen to kick,' Zara said.

'Well, maybe we can organise something when we're all back at the new base. If we put all our minds to this we should come up with some kind of plan against these fuckers,' Matt said, almost spitting the words out. He was incensed at how they had been attacked constantly with no sign of any way of fighting them. It was not what any of them were used to; they were all rattled by the constant battering they had taken.

The war was not over though and although they may have lost a few battles they were still in the fight, and they were determined to remain in it until they had won.

Chapter Thirty-Five

The attack squadron of helijets and the troop carrier arrived at the Capitol Building and immediately opened fire. The helijets were a variant of the Apache attack helicopters from centuries before. It had four rotors that were the main engines with jets mounted along the side of the vehicle that could be rotated through a forty-five-degree arc for either forward thrust or vertical lift-off. In front of these engines were mounted missile pods that held Hellfire missiles and in front of the craft were pulse cannons. Each craft had a crew of three: pilot, co-pilot and weapons officer or gunner.

Each of the helijets opened up with a brace of Hellfire missiles first. Each missile slammed into the Capitol Building exploding on impact; six detonations rocked the building to its core showering the surrounding area with chunks of debris.

The security staff had seen the attack craft approaching and the moment the Hellfire missiles were launched they moved everyone deep inside the building and closed the blast shields over all the doors and windows.

Another brace of missiles fired from each helijet caused more devastation to the walls of the Capitol Building. Pulse cannons began to fire, strafing the already damaged walls and blowing holes through them. In a few short moments, the outside of the Capitol Building was breached as holes appeared in the walls as the assault from the missiles and pulse cannons destroyed most of it.

The CH-555 Super Stallion landed on the front lawn of the Capitol Building and disgorged its troops. Rover5s, led by Hades, the last of Wildes' four new commanders, all armed with Remm assault rifles, ran out across the lawn towards the almost destroyed building. They were intent on one thing, the destruction of the Defence Council.

Inside the Capitol Building, Colonel Gemmell had organised everyone to get down to the bunker deep underground. There was a contingent of marines who acted as escorts to the party as they ran headlong down the corridor to the elevator at the far end. Two marines stood guard by the door as the Defence Council got in the small cubicle. The doors closed which heralded the start of the journey down to the sub-basement.

Another section of the marine contingent greeted the Defence Council as they arrived on the lower level of the Confederation Headquarters building. Captain Summers came forward as they all exited the elevator and said, 'If you'll follow me, gentlemen.'

He led them down the corridor towards the huge ferrite double doors at the far end. The doors were so massive they filled the entire wall at the end of the corridor. On the door to the right was a panel that had a palm print reader on the front with an Iris reader just above. Summers reached the doors first and placed his right hand on the palm reader panel. A blue light bar ran up then down the length of the panel as it read the details of his palm. He then leant forward and placed his right eye against the Iris reader, which then scanned his eye. As he leant back again the computer voice told him that access had been granted.

'Old school or what,' said one of the marines as the massive doors swung open slowly. They could hear the huge motors working to move the massive weight of the doors

'You'd think that this place would have normal access via an NI,' commented another.

Gemmell turned in the doorway allowing the others to enter and he looked at the two marines who had spoken. He said, 'This building dates back over six centuries. The bunker hasn't been used in over four centuries so the security measures haven't been updated yet. As you know the Confederation business was moved here after the attack in New York recently. We never expected another attack, not this soon anyway. The security may be old school but it works.'

'Yes sir,' replied the first marine.

'We never meant anything disrespectful, sir,' added the second.

Gemmell nodded his head then said, 'Hold this position soldiers, no one gets in here, right?'

The soldiers both saluted and marched off towards the opposite end of the corridor. Gemmell turned around and entered the bunker.

The décor was spartan; there were a few seats around the outside edge of the first room. At the rear were other rooms designated for various purposes: one was a kitchen for the preparation of food and drinks, another was a bathroom.

Gemmell looked around at those present and saw fear on

every face. President Takagi looked at him, trying his best to retain a calm exterior. 'What are our chances Colonel?' he asked, his voice steady and calm.

Gemmell glanced at everyone trying to gauge their reaction before speaking. 'This bunker was built from the best materials possible at the time, sir. We are several hundred feet underground encased in steel walls over three feet thick. This place was built in the days when nuclear war was a possibility so adding all that together I would say that we should be okay until help arrives,' he said.

'And what if it doesn't; arrive I mean?' asked Peter Brinkley, the Director of the Diplomatic Corp. He was a career diplomat and had never served in the military let alone been in combat. He was possibly the most fearful one in the bunker and Gemmell knew he would be the one to break first should they spend any lengthy time down there.

'Think about this situation Peter for just one second,' Gemmell said, calmly trying to ease some of the terror he was facing. 'We are in the Capitol Building during a Defence Council meeting. Our whole reason for being here is because of what is happening out there with Col Sec. As soon as they realise they can't reach us they will be on their way here with help. There is no reason to worry,' he added, walking over to the smaller man and placing his hand on his shoulder to ease him into one of the seats in an attempt to get him to relax.

Gemmell closed the doors to the bunker then and sealed them all in. The doors closed with a resounding thud followed by a whoosh as the seal became airtight.

'We are now on our own energy and air supply, completely self-contained,' he said hoping that would reassure them.

'What if they manage to cut off our supply, we'd suffocate,' Brinkley said, voicing what had suddenly occurred to all of them.

'Let's just hope that does not happen then,' President Takagi said, taking the lead.

They all took a seat and were quiet, lost in their own private thoughts.

Chapter Thirty-Six

'Our eta is less than one minute, sirs,' the Pulsar's AI said.

'We should be in range by now; target the attack helijets and fire,' Jake said.

Everyone sat forward in their seats eager to get into the fight.

'Does that place have a safe room of any kind?' asked Kurt.

'The building is equipped with a bunker in the sub-basement deep beneath the ground level, sir. It dates back at least four centuries but it should still be serviceable,' Artie replied.

The Pulsar was equipped with a dazzling array of missiles and on the order given it fired three tenth-generation Phoenix 94s. Their advanced guidance systems enabled them to be fired from a long-range and lock on to a variety of signals in the target ranging from electronic to infrared signatures. They were the epitome of the 'fire and forget' ordinance.

The trio of missiles sped through the air closing the distance between them and the target within seconds. The pilots of the helijets were warned of the threat through their onboard sensors and they began evasive manoeuvres by first ejecting chaff, which the missiles were designed to recognise and ignore, and then pulling away from their station to gain higher airspace.

Before they had moved far enough away the missiles impacted on each craft blowing them all out of the sky. Blazing wreckage rained down on the lawn of the stately building causing minor fires and scattering the clones guarding the parked Super Stallion.

Before the explosions had finished reverberating around the sky above the Capitol Building, the forward section of the Pulsar arrived and strafed the troops still there with her forward pulse cannons. Bodies were sent flying in every direction, as they became the targets of the pulse cannons; before long no clone was left alive.

A Hellfire missile destroyed the Super Stallion, blowing it up into a million pieces of fiery shrapnel.

Ziplines were thrown out of one of the hatches as the large craft hovered over the smoking ruin of the troop carrier. Kurt Stryder and the Wildfire Team were soon sliding down the lines towards the ground where they alighted with grace and power. They had their Remm assault rifles up to their shoulders ready to target the first threat they saw as they made their way to the building's entrance.

'How long do you think it would take for help to arrive?' asked Brinkley, his voice still a little shaky. He had got his fear under control somewhat but he was still obviously jittery.

Gemmell was dreading a question like this one. There

was no clear cut answer that would appease those trapped inside with him. After some thought, he finally said, 'That's something you know I can't answer, it has too many variables. All we can hope is that help will arrive soon and be secure in the knowledge that we'll be safe in here until they do.'

He hoped that would suffice but he doubted it.

'Our best response time is under ten minutes, depending upon the threat level. If the Constabulary responds it could take longer, but if the threat level is sufficient to require a military response then the times drop again depending from which base the responders are dispatched from. As you know there is a communication blackout so we have no way of knowing if this attack has been reported to Col Sec, but I'm sure that by now the media is all over this so whatever is going on outside will not be kept quiet any longer,' he said to elaborate when he realised that Brinkley was not satisfied with his first reply.

This seemed to calm the diplomat down a little as he realised that his worst fear would not present itself and help would be coming after all.

When he saw the tension ease from the man's face a little he glanced at the President who gave him a slight smile and a nod of his head to say 'good job'.

As he glanced away he hoped that his words proved to be true.

Kurt was the first to reach the front entrance to the building; his hyper-accelerated senses working at their maximum. He knew what was at stake here and was pleased to finally have a clear objective and be able to strike back at their enemy.

He stood at the entrance, his back against the wall as he waited for the rest of his team to catch up. The Wildfire Team were capable of feats that were beyond normal humans, but Kurt and now Zara were both far beyond what any of them could hope to achieve. Even so, they reached the door seconds after him and after a quick glance all around they knew what action to take.

Kurt allowed Jake to take command, after all, he was the leader of the Team and he would gladly follow his orders.

A few hand signals and they were on the same page. Kurt would go straight ahead, Jake and Torres would go right, Vance and Cooper, left.

They burst through the shattered doorway into the rubble-strewn foyer blasting any clones they saw. Pulsed plasma bolts lit up the interior of the building as they made fast work of any resistance they met.

The interior of the building was littered with bodies of the marine contingent who had put up a valiant struggle to defend the President and the Defence Council members. They were simply overpowered by sheer numbers though, which was evident by the number of Rover5s still present.

Taking cover behind an overturned desk, Jake opened fire on a group of clones who were systematically searching every room. As they exited the latest room the pulsed plasma bolts caught the first one high on his chest knocking him back into the nearest one to him. The others reacted with blindingly fast reflexes bringing up their own assault rifles and returning fire.

Torres and Vance fired on these Rover5s from a flanking position, cutting them down before they could retreat into the room for cover.

Kurt, Cooper and Vance found another group of Rover5s doing the same in another corridor and, using the same tactic, made short work of these clones too.

As they made their way deeper into the damaged building they found more and more clones and after killing several more they realised they had wandered into a trap of sorts. They had entered a corridor and as they got halfway down they were suddenly surrounded by at least ten clones all with assault rifles aimed at them.

'Do not move or we will fire,' a voice said from behind the group of clones, obviously the one in command of this group, Hades.

The sight of the clones had caught them all off guard. They were momentarily unsure of what to do and they began to lower their weapons resigned to the sudden change in their situation. Kurt, however, had other ideas. Before the clones could do or say anything he moved. Bringing his assault rifle up he shot the clone in front of him in the face. The plasma bolt at such close range destroyed his head but also threw the rest of them into complete confusion. They certainly were not expecting any form of resistance from their captives considering the predicament they had stumbled into. Kurt slammed the butt of his Remm into the side of the clone's head to his right then slammed the muzzle into the chest of another to his left before firing. The kinetic energy from the plasma bolt threw the clone back against the wall giving the rest of them time and space to move.

The confines of the corridor made it impractical to use plasma weapons so they had to resort to close-quarter combat.

Moving at hyper-accelerated speed, Kurt kicked a clone in front of him between the legs, doubling him up in agony. He didn't have time for anything too fancy, just fast, direct moves. An attacker came at him throwing a punch to his face, which he managed to block before knocking the arm down and delivering a series of fast blows to his head and torso that culminated with a blow that crushed his windpipe.

He then blocked an attack from the side and ducked beneath a follow-up blow and smashed a fist into the clone's groin. Standing up he butted the clone in the face, which put him on his back. An elbow strike to the side of the head felled another while he spun away from another clone intent on destroying him. His movements were a blur to the Rover5s who could not keep up.

Kurt's focus was total; he was lost in the combat, a slave to the energy of the battle. The sound of bare-knuckle on skin was music to his ears as all the frustration of the last few hours from being chased, shot at and having the lives of all he held dear put in danger, came flooding out in a wave of pure fury.

He glanced around to see the Wildfire Team also lost in the combat as they waded through the ranks of Rover5s with as much ease as a hot knife cuts through butter.

Within a matter of seconds, all the clones lay on the floor either dead or unconscious.

'That felt good,' observed Vance with a smile of satisfaction mirrored by the rest of his teammates.

'Let's get moving, this isn't over yet,' Kurt said and Jake waved them on towards the elevator.

They all piled in and pressed the button for the sub-basement.

The Rover5 in command of this operation had placed guards at the elevator doors at the sub-basement level. The second they saw the light go on indicating the elevator had been called up to the ground floor, they went on full alert.

'The moment the doors open we open fire. Kill anyone inside,' ordered the Rover5 in command. He left them to return to the bunker doors where the last of his men were attempting to open the huge doors.

The two guards watched as the lights on the control panel above the elevator lit up showing its descent. They braced themselves taking a wide-legged stance, readying their assault rifles against their shoulders and aiming down the sights as they prepared to fire.

The second the doors began to open they started to fire. Pulsed plasma bolts peppered the inside of the elevator destroying anything inside. The clones kept firing until the battery clips on their weapons were depleted. As they stopped firing to replace the clips they noticed that the cubicle was empty.

The startled expressions on their faces were soon replaced by ones of shock when they saw a figure drop down through the open hatch in the roof. What they had failed to notice was that the escape hatch in the roof had been open and was where the former occupants had climbed through on the journey down. When Kurt appeared in front of them it was too late to do anything about it.

Kurt fired his assault rifle gunning the two clones down in a hail of plasma bolts. He walked out of the elevator whilst the rest of his friends joined him through the hatch.

There were thirteen clones in the corridor facing him at that moment, their attention was grabbed the moment their comrades began firing inside the elevator.

'Hi there guys, wanna play?' Kurt said and he ran at them.

They were completely caught off guard by the rash actions of the newcomer. This was not something they had expected or planned on so they did not actually move until Kurt swiped the first one with the butt of his rifle, caving in his head.

By that time it was too late and he was among them

punching and kicking, knocking them down with the brute force of his frenzied attack.

Before the rest of the team had emerged from the elevator, five of the thirteen clones lay on the floor either dead or senseless.

Jake ordered them to open fire on those clones that presented a clear target and to illustrate he picked off one who had worked its way around Kurt's back. He died as he raised a hand to strike from behind.

It didn't take long for the four newcomers to add to the list of dead and dying and Kurt looked around to see the floor littered with their dead.

'We did it,' Cooper said almost in disbelief at their success.

'Did you ever doubt it, man?' Torres said, high-fiving Vance.

Kurt smiled for the first time since the attack had started and finally felt relief. He waved to them then walked up to the huge doors and viewed the locking mechanism. Turning to Jake he asked, 'Have you ever seen anything like this?'

'I've read about them, they're really old, a couple of hundred years at least,' he said when he saw what Kurt meant.

'Try around four hundred years old,' Torres said. When everyone looked at her in disbelief she said, 'What? I read books too, you know.'

'Okay, but how do we get in there?' Cooper asked.

Jake had an idea.

Stepping away he accessed the pulsar comm. links via his NI. 'Artie has the communication blackout been lifted?' he said.

They all looked at him as if he'd gone mad. This deep underground there was no way he could reach their vehicles AI, or so they thought.

'I am glad to report it has, sir.'

'Great, see if you can reach anyone in the bunker and tell them it's safe to come out now,' Jake said with a smile.

Turning back to his friends he said, 'It stands to reason that anyone entering a bunker like that would have to know how to get back out again. There must be the same locking device on the inside so they can open the door when the danger is over.'

'Good point,' Kurt said.

The sound of the doors opening caught all their attention as they watched the huge slabs of metal slowly swing towards them.

From inside walked a tall man they all knew.

'Colonel Gemmell, so glad you're all okay,' Jake said, stepping forward to greet him.

'I think the same goes for all of us too,' he said and he waved the others forward.

President Takagi walked out and looked in amazement at the bodies littering the floor then at those who were standing in front of him for they looked like they had done nothing more than take a stroll in a park on a sunny afternoon.

'Gentlemen, I must congratulate you on your efforts on our behalf,' he said. When he saw Torres he bowed and added, 'Forgive me, Miss, I meant no disrespect.'

Torres returned the bow and said, 'None taken Mister President. I am first and foremost a Recon Delta Marine, sir, gender does not come into it.'

Takagi spotted Cooper glancing at her behind and quietly said, 'I think you may have to remind some of your teammates of that.'

When Jake heard this he scowled at the offending teammate, receiving a shame-faced glance from him.

'Shall we all get out of here and get you to somewhere a little less damaged?' Kurt suggested.

Jake said, 'Yes, Mister President, I think you'll all be better off at our temporary base until we get this whole thing sorted out.'

'I think we all agree on that score,' Takagi replied again, looking at the amount of dead bodies lying on the floor. 'Lead on, please.'

Chapter Thirty-Seven

Nellis Base was a southern Nevada installation that had been used by the military since the mid-twentieth century. It had always been used by the Air Force as a Tactical Wing deployment facility, although now it was a Col Sec base. It stretched over twenty square miles and was one of the largest remaining air bases in the United States.

The moment the Pulsar arrived at the base, the defences were already up and running at full battle alert. The arrival of General Sinclair and the rest of the staff evacuated from Area 15 had brought on the full alert status.

A fighter wing of Hornets was primed on the runway for immediate take-off and the anti-aircraft missile pods were all armed and actively scanning for any incoming threats. The anti-aircraft pulse cannons were all manned and locked into the base's computer system to help with the active scanning target system.

The Pulsar's forward section touched down inside the perimeter security fence on one of the many runways. News of the success of their mission had been forwarded to General Sinclair and as they were coming in to land a security detail of Recon Delta Marines ran out from the main complex to greet them.

'Welcome to Nellis Base, Mister President, if you and your party would please follow me I'll show you all to your quarters,' said the marine in command of the security detail.

Takagi turned to Kurt and the Wildfire Team and shook each person by the hand. He said, 'Thank you all for your efforts today, we literally owe all our lives to you. This will not go unnoticed or be forgotten, you have my word.'

'Thank you, Mister President, but we were just doing our jobs,' Kurt replied.

Takagi nodded his head slightly and followed the marines towards the base with the rest of the Defence Council in tow.

'Just doing our jobs? Now if we're going to work together Kurt some things are gonna have to change my friend,' Vance said, slapping Kurt on the shoulder.

'What? What did I do wrong?' Kurt wanted to know.

'Well, for starters we had an opportunity there to get some extra R and R, a pay raise maybe, even better food in the canteen, but you screwed the pooch with that comment,' Cooper said, joining in with the ragging.

'I'm sorry guys, I never thought…'

'That's your problem isn't it, Kurt, you never think,' Vance said keeping his face straight.

'We'll have to change that won't we Joe,' Cooper said seriously.

Torres stepped forward and put her arm through the crook in Kurt's elbow and said, 'Never mind these mindless morons, Kurt, you did good. They're just joshing with you.'

Kurt realised then what was going on here and smiled. 'Good one guys, you had me then,' he said.

'Gina, you spoilsport, we could've had him going for a week at least with that one,' Vance said, pretending to have hurt feelings.

'Come on guys, let's go get debriefed and see what the General has in store for us next,' Jake said.

They walked across the airfield feeling relief at a job well done possibly for the first time since this whole thing began.

When they got inside the main complex they were shown to the Conference Hall, which General Sinclair had taken over as his Command and Control centre. As they entered he was standing over by the far wall where a huge monitor had been erected where visuals were being played.

The closer they got to the screen the more they saw. Kurt could see everything in startling detail from across the room the moment he entered due to his enhanced sight.

'Isn't that the Moon?' he said as they went and stood next to him.

'Yes, Kurt, it is. It seems we have another problem,' Sinclair said. He glanced around to see that they were all present before he continued.

'A message came to my attention just after I arrived here. I had a Comms tec going over all the calls that were logged in when the blackout went into play. One such call stood out; it was from Washington. Someone reported that a forensic team picked up the remains of Norsky and took them into the RandCorp building but they never came out. We think they went up to the roof with his remains and took off in the shuttle that was left there,' he said once he had their full attention.

'What does that mean, sir?' Kurt asked. He was concerned about the fact that there had actually been anything left of the ex-Alliance agent who had tried to capture him.

'I'm not sure but we are trying to find where that particular shuttle went once it took off.'

'Have you identified its engine's energy signature, perhaps that might help?' Torres suggested.

Sinclair nodded to the tec who was working away reading the sensor logs and he recalibrated the sensors to look for that particular engine's signature.

'Sir, that was no ordinary shuttle, it had FTL capability, short-range I assume, but nevertheless, it could take it to the Moon in just one short jump,' he said.

'Are you saying that it went to the Moon?' Kurt asked him.

'It seems to be so, sir, yes,' the tec said.

'Okay, if no one seems to want to ask the obvious question then I will. Why the Moon?' Cooper queried.

They all glanced at each other searching for answers. Torres said, 'They must have a base up there. It would account for how they've been one step ahead of us in this. They have been monitoring our every action and directing their agents accordingly.'

'Even if that was true, what can we do about it?' Kurt asked, not convinced that was the answer.

'Sir, I've just completed a detailed scan of the lunar surface and there seems to be an area that is reading as blank,' the tec said before any of the others could reply.

'How?' Sinclair wanted to know.

'I used the orbiting satellites that scan for starships approaching us and recalibrated them, redirecting them towards the Moon. I managed to boost their range and these are the results,' the tec explained as he pointed towards the large monitor screen where his results were being displayed.

'That has to be it, hidden beneath a stealth shield,' Vance said as he looked at the screen.

'Look at the size of the damn thing,' commented Torres.

'Do you think they'll still be there?' Cooper asked.

'Are you suggesting we go up there? There is no way we could get anywhere near that base without them seeing us,' said Kurt.

Sinclair turned from the screen and said, 'I think I may have a way.'

———————

The Rover5 in command on the lunar colony, Apollo, was standing in the Command and Control centre when the forensic team arrived with the remains of Pavel Norsky. He had been monitoring the events on Earth closely and was dismayed at how things had turned out.

It seemed that once again the enemy had been underestimated and they had managed to survive. The only positive consequence of the recent actions that he could see was that they were able to salvage Norsky's remains. If he was able to regenerate from his present state then they may be able to go ahead with the plan they had for Stryder – substituting Norsky for him.

There was one task he faced now though that he did not relish and that was contacting OMEGA Command and giving a sit rep. Knowing he could not put it off any further he went to his private office to make the call over a secure channel.

Jonas Wilde's face appeared on the small monitor screen on his desk. 'I hope you have some good news for me, Apollo,' he said, his face devoid of emotion.

Apollo sat straight in his chair, bowed his head slightly and gave his report. 'I am afraid things did not go as planned, sir,' he said.

'Elaborate.'

'It seems we underestimated their abilities and their resolve sir.'

'We managed to detonate the thermobaric charge inside their underground Headquarters but the casualties were not as high as we'd hoped. Most of the staff escaped through tunnels we knew nothing about. It will take them a while before they can use the base again. Our plan to capture Kurt Stryder did not go as planned either. He escaped and somehow managed to destroy Norsky, but on the *plus* side, we were able to collect his remains and bring them here. With time he may be able to regenerate enough for us to implement the plan we had for Stryder. Finally, and because Stryder escaped in Washington, he and some others went to the aid of the Defence Council. They prevented our troops from fulfilling their objective.'

There was a pause as Wilde collated all that he had heard, putting it into some perspective. When he spoke his voice was calm and steady almost as if the failure of his teams meant nothing, but inside he was seething. His anger was building and at that moment it had no outlet so he thought it best to keep it contained until that outlet presented itself and he could give it full rein.

He said, 'While Norsky is regenerating, administer the additional serum we gleaned from the samples we rescued from Tartaran. Let's see if it will speed up the process any and then see what results we get. As soon as you can take a viable sample from him I want it given to the first batch of Rover5s. Try it on the first ten, no more; if it works then administer it to the rest. Keep Norsky in stasis so we can use him. His ability to regenerate will give us an endless supply of his blood that we can use for our troops. Col Sec will fall.'

'At your command, sir,' Apollo said and the screen went blank as Wilde ended the call.

Chapter Thirty-Eight

'We use the Moon base that RandCorp set up for Col Sec. We get there through the Gateway portal they have designed,' Sinclair said. He was smiling to himself, a bit like the cat that swallowed the cream.

'Okay, I admit that would help but how do we get from there to the enemy facility without them seeing us coming?' Kurt asked.

Sinclair held his smile in check then said, 'The SUT can get you and Zara inside without being detected and once there you create a diversion so we can organise a coordinated attack from orbit.'

'What's a SUT?' Zara asked not sure what was going on here but suspected there was some subtext she was not privy to.

'It's a very dangerous device,' Matt said, then elaborated with, 'It stands for Single Unit Transporter. It can slip a person through a dimensional portal from one place to another but it causes such damage to the wearer at a cellular level that the Rands stopped research into the device. After three uses the wearer is condemned to an agonising death.'

'But you and Kurt have no need to worry on that score,' Sinclair said.

That comment took them all by surprise; they all stared at the General wondering what made him say it. They knew that he had his suspicions about Kurt's abilities but they all thought that he had managed to keep the truth hidden from him. If his comment was anything to go by they could all be wrong on that score.

'Excuse me?' asked Zara, playing along hoping to bluff it out.

'Oh, come on now, Zara, don't you think it's time we ended this charade. I know that Kurt has the ability to regenerate. I'm not sure exactly how far this ability extends but looking at you I would say that he, and now you, are practically indestructible. I am assuming that his blood transferred into you through open cuts on your body when you were both in jeopardy on Toldax. What happened, Zara? Did he shield you from something? Anyway, in his report, he clearly states that he saw you gunned down in front of him. Now I know he skated over some details in his report but along those lines, something so traumatic he inadvertently reported the truth. He saw you killed in front of him and yet here you are, alive and kicking. What other conclusion should I draw from this? Before you answer, it was a rhetorical question, you see I already know the answer. The experiment was a total success.'

There was nothing any of them could say that would sound convincing so they said nothing.

'What, no denial? I thought at least one of you would say something. Well, if we are all finally on the same page here can we continue with this mission?'

'What do you intend on doing?' Kurt asked as he walked up to Sinclair. He felt his anger rising, he had tried to keep his abilities from Sinclair in the hope that what he most feared would not happen. Now though he could see all his efforts were falling apart.

'Completing this mission, what else?'

'You know what I mean, after that?'

'We regroup and rebuild then carry on,' Sinclair said.

'Why are you evading my question? What do you intend to do with this knowledge? What does it mean for Zara and I?'

Sinclair looked deeply at Kurt, all traces of a smile vanished. He said, 'You went to a lot of trouble to keep this from me and I have no doubt you had good reasons, but the changes in you can help a lot more people. Some already have benefited from the results of the experiment and many more can also, but you have to trust us.'

'Trust you to make an army of soldiers like me? How will that benefit anyone? All it would do is prolong war,' Kurt spat the words at him.

'When I said trust us I meant it. You have to trust that we would use the information wisely. Yes, the temptation to make an army of soldiers like you would be enormous but I agree that it would not benefit either side in this and that is why we have to destroy that base on the Moon. If they have Norsky there, and if he is anything like you, then we could be in real trouble,' Sinclair said calmly.

Before Kurt could reply Jake said, 'That's as may be but what you want of them is basically a suicide mission.'

Sinclair turned from Kurt to look at Jake, 'Not at all,' he said. 'We need them inside that base to learn just what OMEGA is planning in there. With that Intel, it may give us an idea of what they are doing elsewhere. It is vital we learn what they are doing and stop them. This may be our first and only opportunity to get in front of them in this. Kurt and Zara are the ideal agents for this,' he added.

Kurt looked at Zara for confirmation, she nodded her

head and he said, 'Okay, we're in. We can sort out our future when this is done.'

'Right, let us sort out the details,' Sinclair said.

Kurt held up a hand halting him. 'Before we go any further I think you should know if you plan on doing anything stupid, and I think you know what I mean, then don't. If I even get a sniff of a hint that you plan on anything against us then we're outta here and you won't be able to stop us. You have no idea what we can do and trust me, General, you don't ever want to, especially if it's turned against you.'

'And I suspect that Norsky has similar abilities which is why it is so important you get across there and get the Intel we need so we can stop them,' Sinclair said, not intimidated in the least by Kurt's thinly veiled threats.

Kurt had hoped that Sinclair would have at least have paused to consider what he'd told him, but the man seemed fearless. Instead, it was he who paused. Whatever happened next at least the cards had been placed on the table so everyone could see. All he could do now was play the hand he had been dealt and hope for the best.

'Okay, we are agreed then. Let's do this,' he said.

Apollo stood outside the hyperbaric chamber looking at the figure immersed in the healing fluids. Norsky had been placed inside so that his severed limbs could rejoin with the rest of his damaged torso and begin the regenerative process.

They had taken a sample of his blood and genetically spliced some of the modified DNA from one of the captured octo-felines from Tartaran to it. Once the splicing process had been completed they had transfused the blood back into Norsky.

The addition of this new DNA wouldn't take effect until

Norsky's body had reformed and the regeneration had begun. Once that started the new blood would mix with the old and the changes would start, or that was what they had hoped.

As Apollo watched he saw the limbs begin to knit together. He was fascinated by the process; it was like watching something magical. During his growing process, he had learned that what was once thought to be magic was now considered science. What he was watching at that moment though was beyond each discipline and a strange mix of both, a sort of arcane science.

It would be hours yet before the process was complete and to prevent him from regaining consciousness there had been a sedative added to the fluids in the hyperbaric chamber.

He turned from the chamber and said to the guard standing watch close by, 'Inform me the moment anything changes.'

The guard nodded his head in compliance and Apollo walked on by and left the room.

Chapter Thirty-Nine

'What backup can we expect?' Kurt asked.

They had been working on the details for a few hours. This was their last chance to gain any sort of advantage in this war. So far they had barely survived each attack but now it was their chance to go on the offensive.

'None this time I'm afraid. You and Zara will have to go alone. Any other troops, even the Wildfire Team would be spotted. I am sure that even now they have all of our bases under surveillance from their base and any troop movements would be spotted. We cannot alert them to our intentions. Once you have the information you make the call and get out of there. You will only have a few moments to get clear because I will have the Odyssey on standby on the dark side of the Moon. The second your call is logged they will come in to attack. They have orders to obliterate the base. I have given orders that nothing is to be left, not a molecule, so let us be clear on this Kurt. If you are still in that base once the attack starts, you will not get out alive,' Sinclair said.

Kurt smiled.

'What do you find so amusing?'

'If you knew what I had survived you might have chosen your words a little more carefully, that's all,' Kurt said.

'Quite.'

'If that's all, sir, Zara and I had better get going,' Kurt said.

'That is all. You have transport at your disposal, you can leave whenever you are both ready,' Sinclair said.

Kurt and Zara turned to leave the Command and Control Centre, which was occupied only by staff working there. Everyone else had left to carry out their new orders.

'Good luck to you both,' Sinclair added as they reached the door.

Apollo had returned to the Command and Control Centre to monitor events on Earth. They may have failed in their recent plans but they kept the Col Sec bases under close scrutiny.

The Rover5 monitoring comm. channels said, 'Sir, I'm receiving a lot of chatter about troop movements.'

'That coincides with what I've been monitoring from Nellis Base and Fort Bragg, sir. There seems to be a large massing of troops from both bases. They seem to be preparing for some mission,' agreed the Rover5 on the sensors.

'Where are they heading? Have they learnt of this base?' Apollo asked.

'According to the comm. chatter they are grouping the troops together. I think they are waiting for transport on a starship but as yet I have no idea of their destination, sir,' replied the comms officer.

'Keep an eye on them, at this late stage in the game we can't afford to be caught napping,' Apollo said.

'Yes, sir.'

Kurt and Zara were smuggled out of Nellis Base in the midst of a transport convoy the moment the subdermal tracker had been identified and removed from her body. They left the tracker active so that anyone monitoring the signal would think they knew where she was.

They were put aboard a Silver Dart at McCarran International Airport and sent to Washington where the RandCorp building was located. A vehicle was waiting for them at Dulles International Airport, a Grand Voyager 600si, one of a fleet of cars that Col Sec owned. It was specially equipped with sensors and armed with onboard pulse rifles mounted on the front of the car, hidden in recesses close to the headlights. It also had small missile pods that were housed just to the rear of the front wheel arches.

Kurt got behind the wheel and drove to the RandCorp building. He parked in the underground parking garage where a space had already been allocated for them. The local Constabulary was still in evidence policing the cordon that was still in place around the damaged structure. They had been forewarned that a vehicle would be arriving and to allow them through to the parking garage beneath the building.

There was an elevator close to where they had parked that took them up to the Penthouse.

Kurt exited the elevator and walked up the corridor. He remembered the layout from his battle with Norsky and as he walked he looked at the damage the fight had caused.

'Kurt, glad to see you again,' Able Rand said from the

doorway to his office. He was leaning his tall frame against the doorframe, his arms folded against his lean chest.

'You too, Mister Rand. I must apologise for the state I left your offices in the last time I was here,' Kurt replied.

'Oh, don't worry about that, this place needed redecorating anyway; you just forced us to do what we were putting off until we had the time. We'll have to make the time now, and call me Able,' he said with a dismissive wave of his hand.

'Only too glad we could help then,' Kurt said with a self-conscious smile.

Able walked up to him and Zara and said, 'Why are you here, what is it you want?'

Kurt glanced at Zara then said, 'What I'm about to tell you is classified beyond top secret.'

'Go ahead,' said Josh as he came out of the office. Kurt or Zara had not seen him in there but the second they heard his voice their senses told them there were more in there.

'You can all come out now as well, you may as well hear this too,' Kurt said.

Josh saw Zara and smiled, clearly he was not expecting the beauty that greeted him.

'Down boy, I'm here on business,' she said with a smile of her own.

Jess and Mitch Ryan emerged as well and stood all together just behind Able.

'Go ahead Kurt, we're listening,' Able said.

'We have detected a base on the Moon where OMEGA has been directing their offensive against us from. The thing is we can't reach it without being detected ourselves, at least not in force and not from in orbit. What we intend on doing is planning our own mission to gain access to the base using your base; the base you offered to Col Sec as a staging ground,' Kurt explained.

'You will still have the same problem even from there I

would assume. They would detect your approach across the surface of the Moon the second you set foot outside the base,' Josh offered.

'We have a way around that, we think,' Zara said.

'You want to use the SUT,' Jess said.

Chapter Forty

The Gateway opened a portal to the Moon Base, which Kurt and Zara stepped through, accompanied by Able, Josh, Jess and Mitch Ryan.

They could not see a way to keep their secret from them. The Rands and Mitch knew all about the SUT and the effects it had on the user in intimate detail. They knew the first volunteers who had tested the device and had watched them die in agony while they attempted, fruitlessly, to find a way to reverse the effects. So for them to use it, a full explanation had to be forthcoming, or Able had frankly refused to allow it no matter how important it was.

He argued that he had seen too many die because of something he had done or set in motion and he would not stand by and see others suffer needlessly. After a brief discussion, Kurt and Zara had agreed to tell them. It had made sense to give them details of the mission they had sworn to keep secret. Able had insisted he accompany them to the Moon Base to help keep their secret from the staff working at the base, some of whom were Col Sec while the rest were still RandCorp employees. The transition to Col Sec personnel had not yet fully taken place. His children and Mitch would not allow him to go alone so they went too, arguing that the more of them there were it would be easier to keep prying eyes away from what they were actually doing.

Kurt and Zara were supplied with combat suits; the new edition of Remm M25 assault pulse rifle along with a Sig P999 each. They also had a K-Bar knife strapped to their forearm in a quick-release sheath. In the combat suit were patch pockets where extra battery clips were stored. They had enough ammo for what they intended, or at least so they hoped. They both wore the new Rapier battle helmet with a HUD display on the inside of the visor.

They had the coordinates of the OMEGA Moon base, which they had obtained from sensor sweeps from the Odyssey that had been ordered into long-range orbit. The sensor sweeps were conducted from just beyond the horizon whilst the starship was concealed under a stealth shield. The Odyssey remained on station ready for the command to fire.

The coordinates were programmed into the SUTs before being strapped to Kurt and Zara's wrists.

'Where exactly will we appear in that base?' Zara asked as the final preparations were made for their departure.

'Good question and one I've been asking myself since this idea was first aired,' Kurt added, looking from the woman beside him to the Rands who were standing close by. They had been with them, along with Mitch Ryan, every step of the way; Josh making sure their equipment was all working at full specs, while Mitch ensured that security was tight even though Recon Delta Marines were everywhere; Able and his daughter Jess were overseeing everything else.

Jess fielded that particular question, 'Because we haven't been able to penetrate their stealth shield there is no way of knowing exactly where you'll show up. What we've done, therefore, is aim your landing site as close to the edge of the structure as we can. Admittedly, a lot of it is guesswork but we're confident that we have the maths right on this,' she said.

'How close?' Kurt asked.

'You do mean inside the structure, don't you?' Zara added not liking the sound of this at all.

Jess looked from one to the other before replying. 'A few feet and, yes, we do mean inside. It would defeat the object of the exercise somewhat if we dropped you off outside the base, don't you think?' There was a hint of sarcasm to her tone which did not go unnoticed. Zara took a step towards the young woman, anger flaring in her eyes briefly but was halted by Kurt who placed a hand on her arm.

'Obviously, Miss Rand, but we have to ask these questions, after all, it is us who are taking the risk here and not you,' he said.

Jess saw the look in Zara's eyes and knew she had overstepped a boundary. She said, 'Of course I understand, and please call me Jess. We may not be military but we do know what we're doing here. You can trust us to do everything we can to ensure this mission goes ahead as you want it to. The second you arrive inside the base you'll be able to access their computer via your NIs and you can get a layout of the interior displayed on your HUD. Once that happens you'll know where to go.'

Kurt looked at Zara to see if she was indeed ready for this. It would be the first time she had put her trust in something other than her own abilities, which she was still coming to terms with, and he needed to know she could go through with it and not baulk at the last second. One look in her eyes told him everything he needed to know

She was ready.

'Okay, let's do this,' he said.

Apollo stood watching as the lab tec went down the line of Rover5s administering the new serum to each of them via a hypo gun.

'How long before we have any results?' he asked once the task was completed and the tec had returned to him.

'It's hard to say; this part is not an exact science. It could be minutes, it could be days, who knows?' the tec said as he placed the hypo gun on the table before him. Apollo grabbed him by the shoulder and spun him around, 'That's not good enough,' he said staring directly down into the face of the smaller man.

'What do you want from me? I've done everything you asked. I manufactured the serum like you ordered and I've given it to your men, what more can I do, the rest is out of my hands. You'll just have to wait to see if there are any changes, but like I told you from the start, this may not work at all, there may not be any improvements,' the tec said, his voice almost pleading. He was afraid for his life and with good cause, he had seen some of the things these Rover5s were capable of and had heard of other things that had chilled his blood. He had agreed to work with them because his contract with MaxCorp would have been terminated otherwise but he never thought for one second that he would be involved with anything like this. Fearful for his life didn't quite cover how he felt, he was terrified.

Apollo glared at the face before him; he actually took pleasure in watching the colour drain from his skin. In that second he knew this man would do anything he told him for abject fear was guiding him. He would do almost anything now to save his own skin.

He released the man's shoulder and stepped back giving him a little space. 'Keep monitoring their progress, I want hourly updates. In the meantime ensure Norsky is kept in stasis, I do not want that thing waking up, do I make myself clear?' he said not needing to add emphasis, his words were enough on their own, the man's terror would do the rest.

The lab tec nodded his head vigorously in compliance, not daring to speak for fear his voice would break and further indicate his terror. He watched as Apollo turned and walked away. He waited until the huge clone had left the room before he allowed himself to breathe a sigh of relief. When he turned to look at the Rover5s who had received the treatment they were all glaring at him the same way as Apollo had and he knew the masters of his terror were all around him; not just the clone that had left the room.

Kurt and Zara activated their SUTs and were immediately engulfed by a bright light so intense it burned them to their core, or so it seemed. Everything around them disappeared as the light took over; it was all-consuming. A sudden feeling of disorientation struck Kurt and Zara who had no idea where they were. There was no difference between up or down to them as their entire existence had become a total confusion. Wave after wave of excruciating nausea washed over them and it was a struggle to retain the contents of their stomachs.

Just as suddenly as the light appeared, it was gone leaving them with the same sense of disorientation. Their surroundings had changed which further enhanced the strangeness of the event.

Zara staggered and Kurt grabbed her by the arm, not only to steady her but himself too. She took comfort in his touch and when she looked at him she smiled. 'We made it, it worked,' she said, amazed at how fast the feelings of disorientation and nausea were facing.

Kurt winked at her and she knew he too was feeling better. What they had just endured would have put any normal human on the ground writhing in agony, but here they were ready to continue as if they had just had a stroll in the park.

'Okay, let's see what we have here,' Kurt said as he dropped the visor on his helmet. He accessed the computer via his NI. There didn't appear to be anything major, just basic functions as he called up the base's schematics, which were then relayed onto his HUD on the inside of his visor. Zara did likewise so they were co-ordinated.

'Got it,' she said and they set off.

Chapter Forty-One

They had appeared in one of the outer pods on the base in an empty corridor. When they moved off they kept their senses tuned to hear any movement nearby. A corner loomed in front of them and they slowed down as they approached it.

Kurt heard movement from around it, the sound of someone approaching. He also heard three heartbeats, strong and steady.

He held up three fingers to indicate how many hostiles there were and for Zara to be ready. She nodded her head in understanding. She was ready; she brought up her Remm M25 assault rifle to her shoulder, sighting down the length of the weapon.

Kurt counted down mentally as the hostiles got closer and when they were close enough he motioned to Zara to make their move.

As one they moved out into the corridor in front of the three-armed clones that were on patrol. Pulsed plasma bolts from the Remm M25s struck each of the three figures squarely in the torso knocking them back several steps. The firepower of the new improved M25s was sufficient to overload the combat suits Kevlon body armour the Rover5s were wearing. They died instantly.

'They either knew we were coming or they made preparations just in case,' Zara said. Each of them had sensor readings of bio signs of the clones inside the base relayed to their battle helmets so they knew what to expect and where the resistance would be. They also knew that by the time the first clone went down the alarm would go off and they would be looking for them.

'I've said it before and I'll say it again,' Kurt said, and Zara joined him in finishing off the famous quote: 'It's not just a job in Recon Delta, it's an adventure.'

'Come on let's see what we can find out,' Kurt said.

'I know what we'll find and we won't have to look real hard either, and that's a whole lot of trouble,' commented Zara.

Kurt glanced across at her and she had a smile on her face. She was actually enjoying herself.

Back on the Rand-built Moon base, those left behind were still in the Command and Control Centre. Able Rand was seated in a chair at a control console – lounging would be a better description – with his long legs stretched out before him. His elbows were perched on the armrests and his fingers steepled together beneath his chin as he watched the monitors for any signs to indicate something was happening over there.

'How can you be so relaxed?' Josh asked as he paced across the C and C deck. He found his nervous energy was difficult to contain.

'It comes with years of experience, son; you should try to

relax before you wear a trench in the floor,' Able said without looking away from the monitors.

Jess and Mitch were at other stations around the room; Jess sitting staring at a bank of monitors whilst Mitch leant against the wall over by the door keeping a watchful eye on the whole room.

'Any word from Kurt or Zara yet?' asked Jess as she glanced around at her father.

'Not yet,' he replied.

'You have to give them time to complete their mission, these things take time trust me, I know. If they go blundering around they could get captured before they have time to do anything, or worse, get themselves killed,' Mitch said.

'You heard what they said, I doubt very much they could get killed,' Jess said.

'I doubt that very much. I've seen shit all over this galaxy but I've never seen anyone who could not die,' Mitch said.

'For all our sakes, Mitch, I hope you're wrong about that,' Able said without taking his eyes from the monitors.

Back on Earth at Nellis Base Sinclair was standing in the centre of the Command and Control Centre. His eyes were constantly scanning the monitors for any news of the progress of this new mission. Nothing so far had come through since the communication from the Lunar Base to inform them that Kurt and Zara had left.

He hated to admit it even to himself but he was worried for their safety. Since they had confessed that their abilities were far greater than they had originally professed, he thought he would have felt safer in sending them on this latest escapade. Taking into consideration their ability to regenerate and their

enhanced senses, on paper this looked like a fairly straightfor-
ward affair. He knew, though, that these things rarely worked
out as they had been planned and that was why agents needed,
above all, to be adaptable. Being able to think on their feet and
plan for any contingency that they may encounter was a
prerequisite for any agent and, although he knew Kurt and
Zara were fine soldiers, they had not been trained in covert
affairs. He just hoped their training in Recon Delta was enough
to see them through whatever they faced inside that base.

'Any news yet on their progress sir?' Matt asked as he
entered the room. He had taken the time to grab a quick nap
then showered before returning to the C and C.

'Not yet, I was just thinking that it has been some time
since their last report. We should have heard something by
now, don't you agree?' Sinclair said, his voice sounding tired.
The man had been on his feet for the best part of the day and
desperately needed a break.

'Sir why don't you go take a break, grab something to eat,
take a nap or something. There's no need to work yourself
into the ground, I'll inform you the moment I hear from
them, you have my word.'

Sinclair looked at him and nodded his head, 'Perhaps a
bite to eat and a shower would do me some good,' he agreed.

'Are Jake and the Pulsar on station sir?' Matt asked as the
General turned to leave.

'Yes, they are in geostationary orbit over the base just
waiting for the signal from Kurt or Zara to extract them
before the Odyssey opens fire.'

'Get some rest, sir, I can handle this. I'll let you know as
soon as anything develops,' Matt said as the General walked
past him on his way out.

Matt stared at all the monitors and the personnel milling
around doing their jobs and he felt frustration rising. He felt
like he should be out there doing something instead of being

stuck in here waiting for something to happen. He was used to being proactive in missions and this present role he had been given did not suit him at all. Unfortunately, there was nothing he could do to alter it now, he had to simply sit back and allow the others to take centre stage for this one. He knew they were capable but that didn't stop him hating not being able to lend a hand.

'Come on Kurt and Zara, get the job done so we can finish this once and for all,' he said to himself.

Sitting on the command deck of the Pulsar in geostationary orbit five miles above the lunar surface, Jake Riley and the rest of the Wildfire Team were also feeling the same frustration as Matt was down on Nellis Base.

'How long has it been now since we got word they had entered the base?' asked Vance

'Ten minutes since the last time you asked Joe. For fuck's sake you're like the kid going on holiday with his parents who keeps asking "Are we there yet?" every five minutes,' snapped Torres, clearly the frustration was getting to her too.

'Ten minutes, not five,' Vance corrected her.

'Joe, leave it,' she warned.

'You two knock it off and do your jobs,' Jake scolded them both.

'Artie, have you been able to isolate Kurt and Zara's trackers now they're inside the structure?' Jake asked the Pulsar's AI.

'It has been difficult, sir, trying to isolate the two frequencies through all the layers of interference being used to jam communication signals, but I believe I have a lock on them both,' the AI responded.

'That's good then, keep locked on to them at all times

Artie, we may have to pull them out at a moment's notice,' Jake said.

'Strictly speaking sir we will not be pulling them out they will have to input the coordinates of this vessel into their Single Unit Transporters and then activate them to travel here themselves. We will not be doing anything to aid their travel sir,' the AI corrected pedantically.

'You're not helping Artie,' Torres said.

'Indeed Miss, is that not what I have just pointed out?' the AI said not understanding her point.

'Never mind, Artie, we'll just have to be ready for when they arrive so we can leave without any trouble from the base below,' Jake said, hoping to put an end to the discussion.

'When we get back home I'm putting in an order to have his logic subroutines overhauled,' Torres said to Jake.

'My logic subroutines are performing to within the required parameters, Miss, there is nothing wrong with them,' Artie said.

'Can we at least have him recognise humour or what about sarcasm?' Vance said.

'Humour is a difficult concept to fabricate, sirs,' Artie offered in his defence.

'Clearly,' Torres said.

'Obviously,' Vance added.

'You can say that again,' Cooper joined in not wanting to be left out.

'Okay, sirs, humour is a difficult concept to fabricate,' Artie said.

'Who said he didn't understand humour?' Jake offered.

'I am sorry, I do not understand,' the AI said.

'I rest my case,' Torres said with a smug grin.

Vance asked, 'Are we there yet?' to which Jake just rolled his eyes in submission.

'I don't think we're gonna get any closer than we are now to their command centre,' Zara observed as three more clones appeared.

'Don't give up just yet,' Kurt said as he brought up his Remm M25 and shot the first of the three clones. A single pulsed plasma bolt struck the clone's head blowing it apart in a shower of blood and gore which alerted the other two behind him.

Kurt shot the next one in line before he had time to aim his own weapon and, as he collapsed, Zara shot the third and last one.

'Who said I was giving up?' she said annoyed at the very idea she would concede defeat.

'I just meant…' Kurt stammered

'I know what you meant and I'm not giving up, I was going to suggest an alternative to storming the command centre,' she fumed.

'Go on, I'm listening,' Kurt said, hoping to relieve the tension.

'We find a remote access point to the computer and download the relative data Sinclair needs,' she suggested.

'Can't you access the computer remotely via your NI?' Kurt asked.

'I can but to gain full access to the computer files we need I would have to log on to a terminal. I can do that via my NI but if I attempt it from here I'll only gain minimum access, we need to get in deeper to find out what they're up to,' she explained.

'Cyber ops were never my thing, I'm basically just a grunt,' Kurt told her.

'What made you agree to the experiment then?' she enquired.

'They told me it would change the military forever and what I did today would rule out the possibility of another war. I fell for the bullshit hook, line and sinker,' he said.

'So you were hoping to better the Confederation then?'

'It's why I joined the military. My father always told me that for evil to succeed all that is required is for good men to do nothing. I wanted to do something so that wouldn't happen and this seemed like a good idea at the time.'

'I see.'

'Right, let's go,' he said as he stepped over the nearest body.

The pod they were in was connected via a series of corridors that were basically tubes, to other similar-sized pods. Each pod had several rooms that were used for a variety of purposes none of which were helpful to either of them at that time.

'Let's see if we can reach another area closer to the centre of this place, to see if we'll have a better chance of finding out what they're up to,' Kurt suggested as he neared the opening of a corridor to the adjacent pod.

'This place is huge, we could search for days before we learn what we need to,' observed Zara.

Kurt stopped at the entrance to the corridor and turned to her. 'You know what, you're right. We need another strategy here,' he said, his cobalt blue eyes shining as an idea formed.

'What do you suggest?' she asked. When she saw the look in his eyes she said, 'Uh oh! This is gonna be bad, real bad,' she added.

'What did we say earlier? Life in Recon Delta isn't just a job...'

'...it's an adventure,' she finished for him.

Chapter Forty-Two

On the Bridge of the Odyssey Captain Tyler Biggs was standing in front of the command chair. Despite being filled with nervous energy he nevertheless gave the impression of perfect calm. His stance was wide-legged with his hands clasped firmly behind his back as his dark eyes studied the forward viewscreen. When he spoke, his deep bass voice filled the bridge, 'Any news on the agents' progress?' he asked the officer at ops.

'None yet, sir, I'm monitoring all channels although there does seem to be a blanket jamming of all comm. links still in place,' replied the officer keeping his focus on the instruments before him.

'I want all the missile tubes loaded ready for firing and all pulse cannons targeting the area the second we move above the horizon; keep it passive though. I don't want to alert them in that base to our presence or intention,' Biggs ordered. As he turned and sat down in his chair he added, 'Inform Captain Riley on the Pulsar that we are ready to engage on his command.'

'Aye, sir.'

'Helm I want to be in position over that base the moment we get the signal to go,' Biggs said as he relaxed into the chair.

'Course plotted and laid in sir, awaiting your command,' replied the pilot.

'Okay people it seems there's nothing more we can do until we get the go signal. So stay frosty and stay prepared, we are about to give OMEGA a valuable lesson in payback,' Biggs said with a wry smile.

Kurt and Zara appeared out of the intense bright light that had suddenly burst into existence. They had their Remm M25s up and ready to fire and the moment the light imploded upon itself revealing them standing back to back, they opened fire.

Those in the C and C were caught unawares. Everyone in there was momentarily blinded by the starburst that exploded in the centre of the room and by the time it had gone, it was too late.

A blistering barrage of pulsed plasma bolts scythed everyone down as Kurt and Zara turned in a full circle. Within a few seconds, the entire command deck crew were lying dead on the floor.

'Right, we only have a few minutes before they find out what happened in here so work fast,' Kurt told Zara once they had ceased firing and surveyed their handy work.

She moved over to the ops station and accessed the main computer via her NI. No subtlety this time she just powered through all the firewalls and went straight to the files she wanted. In a matter of less than a second she had downloaded all she needed to her NI and then turned to Kurt to ask, 'Fast enough for you?'

Before Kurt could reply the alarm sounded throughout the entire base. Her intrusion into the computer main server had raised the automatic alarm and within moments the C and C would be crawling with security personnel looking for the intruder. They had nowhere to go. They were trapped.

Kurt looked at Zara and said, 'Time to go.'

Both of them activated their SUTs once more and were gone in a flash.

Apollo heard the alarm sound and rushed from his quarters back towards the C and C, grabbing a weapon on the way. He burst onto the command deck, his pistol held in a two-handed grip as he searched for a target. What he saw chilled his blood and confused him at the same time. Dead bodies littered the blood-splattered floor; all the staff working there had been slaughtered.

How could this have happened without anyone knowing?

Accessing the comm. channels via his NI he called the lab where the test subjects were still being monitored.

'What is happening, sir?' asked the lab tec running the experiments.

'We've had an intruder, are the test subjects ready?' Apollo asked.

'I can't guarantee the serum has been successful, sir, we haven't had enough time to monitor any results. I haven't had the time to run the proper tests anyway,' the lab tec said.

'Are they ready to go or not?' Apollo asked bluntly. He was not interested in excuses, just results. There had been a serious breach in their security and he was going to do anything that was necessary to rectify that problem.

'Yes, I suppose they are, sir.'

'Good, send them out now to the C and C,' Apollo ordered, then closed the call.

Kurt and Zara appeared out of another starburst of intense light this time inside one of the interior pods. They had appeared on a balcony overlooking a vast area that housed hundreds upon hundreds of containers, each the size of a human being. Row after row of these containers were lined up on the floor filling an area the size of a football field.

'What the fuck are they?' Zara asked and without tearing his eyes from the floor below Kurt said, 'Cloning vats.'

'You're kidding right?'

'I wish I was.'

'There must be thousands of them,' Zara said, her voice almost breaking under the enormity of the discovery.

'Yep, with this setup they can have an endless supply of troops to send against us,' Kurt said, his face cold and hard.

'If they have Norsky up here and they somehow duplicate what was done to him and us, what's to say they won't try to make those things also like us?' Zara said with real fear in her eyes.

'My thoughts exactly. We have to destroy this entire facility, and fast,' Kurt said, accessing a comm. channel via his NI.

'Jake, we have what we need, blow this place to hell,' he said once the call was connected.

Jake Riley heard the call from Kurt and turned to the rest of his team and said, 'Right here we go, Artie take us into position ready for Kurt and Zara to come aboard. Captain Biggs, we have the go signal for your assault.'

The Pulsar's AI steered the huge craft into a lower orbit to make it easier for their two expected guests to come on board.

'Here we go people, payback time,' Jake said with a certain amount of satisfaction in his voice. A sentiment that was echoed by his team as they all replied, 'About time too.'

Captain Biggs had been waiting patiently for the signal from the Pulsar and when it finally arrived he said, 'Right people, this is what we've been waiting for, let's raise some hell.'

The huge battle cruiser's engines fired, sending her up and over the lunar horizon towards the target area. The second they were in firing range they would open fire which gave Kurt and Zara less than ten minutes to get aboard the Pulsar and for it to remove itself from the danger zone.

They could afford no delays.

Chapter Forty-Three

Kurt and Zara looked at each other. They had to make a decision and fast. Should they bug out and get to the Pulsar and allow the Odyssey to blast this place off the surface of the Moon, or should they try and learn if Norsky was located here first?

'What do you think? Do you think they'll have kept him here or moved him to another location?' Zara asked when she saw the hesitation on Kurt's face.

'If they're using his blood to formulate a serum, like they were trying to do with me on Toldax but to enhance these clones, then it's a possibility. If they have taken samples of his blood to store for that purpose then they may have moved him to another location to do the same there. Either way, we have to destroy what they were doing here, we can't take the chance that anything of this experiment will remain and we can't take the chance that the bombardment will do the job on its own,' he replied after a moment's pause while he formulated his response. He knew he was asking a lot of this young woman, but deep inside he knew she would not disappoint him.

'Okay, let's go find him, but before we do, what do you intend on doing when you find him?' she asked.

'We don't really have a choice; we have to make sure he doesn't bother us ever again. Are you okay with that?' he said.

'Definitely, I just wanted to make sure you weren't going to try and take him back with us so the General could use him instead of us in any experiments,' Zara said, bringing up a point that had not occurred to him. Shaking his head he dismissed the thought before it could grab hold in his mind and form into a plan. He dreaded that happening to him or Zara so much, in fact, he would not wish it upon his worst enemy. At the moment Norsky had that potential so he had to remove it before it became a real threat.

'No, definitely not, we have to stop them using Norsky and if it means totally destroying him then that is just the way it has to be,' he said with a tone of finality that brooked no further comment from her except to say, 'Okay, let's do this.'

Before they could move, a Rover5 appeared in the corridor through a door behind them, one they had passed on their way to their present position. The Rover5 was accompanied by three other clones all of whom were armed with Remm assault rifles.

'Freeze!' shouted the lead clone, but before he could react Kurt and Zara had turned, firing their own assault rifles, cutting him down in a hail of pulsed plasma fire.

The remaining clones had already aimed their own weapons on the two figures before them but as they fired, their bolts passed through empty air as Kurt and Zara had gone into a combat forward roll to come up on their knees. Their Remm M25s were already at their shoulders firing as any opposing fire passed harmlessly over their heads.

The three clones were cut down in seconds leaving Kurt and Zara free to get to their feet.

'We'd better get moving, this place is only gonna get more crowded the longer we remain here,' Kurt observed.

'Kurt, where are you and Zara? We only have a few minutes to get you both on board before all hell breaks loose,' Jake said through a battlecom comm. link. Artie had already informed the Wildfire Team that the Odyssey was en route to their location and that her weapons were locked and loaded. If they did not vacate the area within the next eight minutes they would come under fire from their own people.

'There's something we have to do first, stay on station as long as you can and we'll get to you,' Kurt replied, not giving too much away. Jake thought better of enquiring as to what he had meant, instead leaving him to get on with whatever was so important so that they could make the rendezvous on time.

'It seems we'll just have to wait and ride it out,' he told the others.

'Is there nothing we can do to help them?' Vance asked in frustration at having to sit and wait.

'I agree, I'm sick of sitting on my ass while they put theirs on the line for us,' agreed Cooper echoing the sentiment.

Jake looked at Torres, raised an eyebrow and asked, 'You want to get in on this too?'

'They're right Jake, and you know it. If the shit's hit the fan down there what's stopping us from joining in and adding to the mayhem?' she replied, getting to her feet and standing in the middle of the bridge.

'Orders, that's what's stopping us from going down there, our orders. Look I don't know why Kurt has changed the game plan but I'm guessing it must be something really important for him to even think about it.'

'What if they aren't back in time, are you really going to sit back and let the Odyssey level that place knowing two of our own are down there?' Vance asked, getting up to stand next to Torres. This was rapidly turning into a mutiny and Jake had to regain control fast before it all went pear-shaped.

'You've seen what Kurt can do, I don't think anything that happens down there would do anything more than slow him down a little,' Jake said keeping his voice calm so as not to agitate his team any further.

'What about Zara, we have no idea what her abilities are? If they aren't as advanced as Kurt's they could be in real trouble because I can't see that man leaving her behind to die,' Torres said.

'She came back from Toldax after being shot dead and having the facility destroyed around her according to the report, so I think she'll cope,' Jake said.

'Let's hope so then,' Cooper said.

'What's that supposed to mean?' Jake asked rounding on the only member beside himself still seated.

'Well if she doesn't make it out of there I wouldn't like to be the one to tell Kurt that we just sat on our asses up here and did nothing to help,' he elaborated.

Jake turned away from Cooper's blazing stare and said, 'We follow our orders, now everyone get back to work.'

As the other two sat down Torres said, 'How would you feel if it was you and Nat down there and we were up here and did nothing, just following orders?'

'You don't get it, do you?' Jake said, turning to face them all. 'Sinclair wanted them on this op on their own for two reasons; first, they are the best people for the job and second because they have a certain skill set – they can't be killed – which makes them expendable,' he added.

'Isn't that a bit of an oxymoron, saying someone can't be killed but they're expendable?' Cooper asked.

'You know what I mean, they are the future of Col Sec. They can be sent into ops that would be certain suicide for anyone else but they can get the job done. Sinclair's known this from day one, he just needed Kurt to come back voluntarily. Now he has two operatives and I wouldn't bet on him trying to make a few more either in spite of what he may promise Kurt.'

'Bottom line is, we do nothing to help them then,' Vance said through gritted teeth; clearly, he did not like how this conversation had turned out.

'I'm afraid so, yes.'

'That's just fucking great,' Cooper said slamming his fist down on the armrest of his seat in anger.

Chapter Forty-Four

Apollo had re-staffed the command deck after the massacre there. He stood in the centre of the large room as the new clones took over the stations vacated by their predecessors. Although he had holstered his weapon at his hip he remained alert for any other intrusion and he turned as the ten enhanced Rover5s entered the C and C.

'What kept you? Never mind, we have to find the intruder and by 'we' I mean *you*. Get out there, access the interior sensors and locate whoever it is and bring them to me,' he snapped at them.

Without comment, the team simply turned and left the room.

'Have you located the intruders yet?' he asked ops. He could feel his frustration rising once more. How could anyone gain entrance to this location never mind wreak the havoc they had in this, the most impregnable section of this secure facility was beyond him. He was determined though to learn how they had done it and to make them pay.

'Not yet, sir, it's difficult to lock on to them,' replied the clone.

'Why, what is the holdup? You have the most sensitive sensors available and you can't pinpoint one intruder. I find that amazing or is it something else, are you incompetent?' Apollo shouted, his frustration taking control of him.

'Sir, there are two signals that we are trying to track but they keep disappearing then appearing elsewhere. If I didn't know better sir I'd swear they are teleporting.'

'Impossible.'

'I know, sir, but check the readings yourself,' offered the clone at ops and he stood up from his station stepping over the dead body at his feet.

Apollo stepped forward to do as was suggested. After checking the results of the scans he stepped back, his mind rapidly trying to work out what to do to compensate. Finally, he said, 'Recalibrate the sensors to locate just these two signals, and then try to work out if there is some sort of pattern to them, we might be able to predict where they'll go next. In the meantime double the guards on the cloning vats and Norsky. One thing is certain, whoever they are they are working for Col Sec. I don't know how they learned of this base but I'm certain they won't leave before they have what they want.'

Suddenly another alarm sounded at the ops station. The clone sat back down to read what the problem was and said, 'Sir, we have a starship coming into our section. Sir, it's the Odyssey and their weapons are charged.'

Apollo could see his command coming apart at the seams as everything seemed to be against them. His mind raced trying to formulate a plan, working out possible strategies until finally, he said, 'Man the defences, I want to be prepared if they attack. Find those intruders and just in case prep the ship. If we can't save this place we'll leave and blow it to hell.'

Kurt and Zara stepped out from the blinding light into a lab and fired their Remm M25s killing everyone in the room before they could react. In front of them, in the centre of the large room, was a hyperbaric chamber and suspended inside, wired to controls on the outside of the chamber, was a lone figure. He had a full-face mask covering the front of his head supplying oxygen to him even though he was sedated.

'Norsky,' uttered Kurt as he recognised the figure in the tank.

Before they could take any action five armed clones came rushing through the door. A withering barrage of pulsed plasma bolts filled the room forcing Kurt and Zara to dive for cover. The walls and floor were peppered by plasma bolts causing debris to be thrown into the air and because the two of them had been standing in front of the hyperbaric chamber when the shooting started it took several hits also.

From his prone position on the floor behind a desk, Kurt watched as the transparent ferriplex covering the hyperbaric chamber began to star at the sites of impact. Cracks began to appear, stretching further and further away from the initial target areas. Fluid from the chamber started to seep through the cracks as the damage became irreversible.

'We've gotta get out of here, that thing is gonna blow any second,' Kurt said quietly to Zara lying next to him.

'Where do you suggest? I'm all ears,' she replied as she craned her neck around the desk they were hiding behind. Plasma bolts continued to pick off bits of their cover as the firing continued; the clones seemingly oblivious to what was happening to the chamber close to them.

Kurt saw the ferriplex begin to shatter and the fluid from the hyperbaric chamber begin to pour out. The clones became aware of the severity of the situation as the fluid flowed around their feet. Their attention was suddenly diverted away from their prime targets giving Kurt and Zara their chance.

Inside the emptying chamber, Norsky was beginning to wake up. His eyes opened and he took in his surroundings. The memory of his last moments struck him like a thunderbolt from the blue. He recoiled as the memory filled his vision and obscured what was in front of him.

Kurt watched his enemy come round. The recognition of his surroundings slowly registered on his face along with the fact that he had survived the missile attack.

Norsky looked around the room. He saw the Rover5s in front of him and then his gaze landed upon the two figures being threatened by the clones.

Kurt Stryder and Zara Hardy, he had no idea how they had got here, he had no idea even where 'here' was, but he did know that no one was going to harm Stryder and Zara. No one except him, that was.

The clones turned to view what was happening behind them one after another until they were all facing the now empty chamber.

As Norsky's senses returned the changes wrought on him via the addition of the alien DNA began to manifest themselves. As he stepped out of the chamber he began to grow. It was as if he was exploding from within, his limbs began to pulse as his muscles started to spasm. To accommodate this new growth his arms and legs lengthened whilst his torso widened so that when he stepped onto the floor he stood at least a head taller than all the Rover5s.

He glowered down on them, then his fury exploded in a flurry of frenzied movements as he ripped into the stunned clones. He picked the nearest one to him up by the throat with one hand and then gripped the clone's waist with his other hand and with terrifying ease ripped his head clean off tossing it across the room with utter disdain.

'Holy crap!' Zara uttered after seeing the head come flying across the room in their direction. Both she and Kurt watched in stunned silence as Norsky destroyed the rest of the clones in a similar fashion, ripping arms off and punching holes in chests in a display of primal fury that was devastating to see and all before one single shot could be fired against him.

When it was done and all the clones lay at his feet, Norsky turned his attention to them.

Zara said, 'Well, Kurt, if you have any ideas I think this would be a good time to try them out.'

'I'm working on it,' he replied calmly.

'Can I suggest you work faster?' she added not daring to take her eyes off the monstrosity that used to be Norsky.

Before he could reply the huge figure of Norsky rushed them and they knew it was too late.

Chapter Forty-Five

On the bridge of the Pulsar, the tension was palpable. The team were not happy with what Jake had said but they had to admit it made sense with everything that had happened and how this new Wildfire programme had progressed. They were all professionals though and just because he had pointed out an unassailable fact they would not hold it against him. They had a job to do and no matter what their personal feelings were about the situation, they would complete the mission to the best of their abilities or die trying.

'What's keeping them?' Vance muttered under his breath. The waiting was beginning to get to him, to all of them really, it was just that he was the first to vocalise it.

'We just have to give them time to do what they have to do,' Jake said.

'I just wish they'd get on with it, this sitting around and not helping is getting on my last nerve,' Torres said, more frustrated than angry.

'Approaching target vector, sir. We'll be in range in five minutes,' ops said on the bridge of the Odyssey.

Captain Tyrell Biggs sat forward in the command chair and said, 'Lock weapons on target and prepare to fire on my command.'

In five minutes the immense firepower of the starship would be concentrated on the facility on the lunar surface. It would completely obliterate it and any living soul left within its confines.

Kurt and Zara had even less time to get clear or get caught by the awesome destructive forces about to be unleashed.

Norsky slammed into Kurt and his momentum carried them both into a wall. Norsky's increased strength meant that the wall didn't stop them; they smashed right through into the next room.

Zara had been pushed out of Norsky's path by Kurt to ensure her safety, which incensed her. She gathered herself up and followed them through into the next room. Kurt was being pressed against the floor where they had both landed with Norsky on top. He was using his greater mass to pin the smaller man beneath him while he pummelled him with anvil-like fists.

Zara leapt onto Norsky's back and wrapped her right arm around his neck forgetting she had an assault rifle on a sling over her shoulder. All she could think of in that moment was that she had to help Kurt; she had to pull his attacker from him.

Norsky felt her land on him with the same annoyance as if she were a fly on his arm and he reached one hand to his neck and effortlessly tore her arm away and tossed her over his shoulder. Zara collided with the wall opposite them, her back taking the full brunt of the assault. It was when she hit the wall that she remembered the assault rifle. She got to her haunches, shrugging off the quickly receding pain and pulled the Remm M25 around and fired. The pulsed plasma bolts struck Norsky full in the chest and threw him backwards off Kurt giving the latter time to get to his feet. He went over to Zara who was still staring at where Norsky had landed.

'Thanks,' Kurt said as his face rapidly healed from the beating he had received a few seconds ago.

'Don't ever do that again,' she said through gritted teeth, not looking at him, her focus firmly on the spot where Norsky had fallen.

'Do what?'

'That Sir Galahad crap, I'm just as strong as you and I have the powers too so don't think of me as the weak woman here, we're equals okay?'

'Okay,' Kurt conceded with a smile.

Norsky sprang to his feet, the effect of the gunshot almost completely healed, and he stared at the two of them. He was still undergoing some kind of metamorphosis and whatever his body was going through, his already psychotic mind was returning to some kind of feral state. His psychosis made his grasp on reality even more tenuous and therefore the changes had an even greater effect. There was no doubting he had retained his hatred for Kurt Stryder, even his love for Zara had now been tainted because she had helped his enemy, so in his twisted mind she too was now regarded in the same light as Kurt.

His only purpose now was to kill the two of them.

'Got any ideas, or are you still working on it?' Zara asked.

'I've a slight problem,' he replied.

'Problem, what problem?'

'Killing Norsky would be a good idea, I'm just not sure how, is the problem,' he explained.

'Oh shit, as usual, you men are useless when it comes down to it. Leave it to a woman to come up with the solution,' Zara said, as she released her Remm M25 letting it swing around her back on its strap as she reached inside one of the many pouches on her combat suit.

'What the fuck are you up to?' Kurt asked when he saw what she was doing.

'Saving both our asses, now cover me,' she said as she moved off to the side away from Norsky.

Artie said, 'Sir, the Odyssey is almost in position, their weapons are all charged and they have a lock on the target area. They will commence firing in less than two minutes. I suggest we either contact Captain Stryder to update him or move to a safer distance.'

'Okay Artie, I'll do it now,' Jake agreed. He called Kurt using a battlecom channel via his NI, 'Kurt what's the delay, you're cutting this very close to the wire buddy,' he said.

'Hold on,' Kurt replied then the call was disconnected.

'What's happening?' Torres asked.

'I'm not sure, but I trust he has the situation well in hand,' Jake told her.

At the precise moment, Jake had called him Kurt was being attacked once more by Norsky. He had watched Zara edge her way around him and his befuddled brain had not been able to comprehend her purpose but when the focus of his hatred, Kurt Stryder, had shouted his name, he had quickly forgotten her and rushed towards him with renewed fury.

This time though Kurt decided to meet that rush, head-on. He ran at Norsky hoping to keep his attention on him so that their fight would give Zara the time she needed to complete whatever she had in mind.

The two of them collided with a bone-crunching impact that sounded like a thunderclap. Norsky's greater mass and strength quickly overpowered Kurt's resistance and the latter found himself once more being forced back across the room. As he felt his back impact with the wall Kurt tried to push Norsky away to give himself room to move. He saw a huge fist come straight for his face and managed to move his head to the side just enough so that it missed. The punch went through the wall mere inches from his head and would have caved it in had it connected. Norsky pulled his hand free from the hole in the wall and brought it back to strike once more. The balled-up fist loomed high in the air above Kurt's face and because Norsky had changed his grip with his other hand to Kurt's throat, there was no way he would miss next time.

The look of triumph in Norsky's face was quickly turned to one of disbelief as from somewhere behind him a razor-sharp blade severed his raised arm sending a bloody fist flying through the air.

Zara had approached from behind unknown to the giant Norsky and as he raised his fist to strike she used her K-Bar knife to slice through the arm with all her prodigious strength. As the bloody appendage was sent spinning through the air she leapt on Norsky's back once more and as he howled in pain and frustration she pushed the item she had plucked from her combat suit deep into the giant's mouth.

'Fire in the hole,' she screamed as she hurled herself from

Norsky as he thrashed around spraying blood over the room from his severed stump of an arm.

The incendiary grenade she had slammed down Norsky's throat was about to explode and the two of them huddled behind whatever cover they could find.

Norsky's head was suddenly engulfed in a white-hot fire as the grenade exploded inside his throat. All of a sudden the room was lit up with a phosphorescent heat, which was destroying the giant from the inside. It was such an intense heat it burned like a mini sun, engulfing the flesh that attempted to keep it contained.

Norsky fell to the ground, a mound of charred flesh and totally unrecognisable as a human being.

Zara looked at her handiwork and said, 'That ought to do it.'

Kurt said, 'Time to go.'

***

'Come on Kurt,' Jake said under his breath and as the words escaped his lips a bright light exploded in the middle of the Pulsar's bridge. Kurt and Zara stepped through the light as it faded and Kurt said, 'Well, what're you waiting for, get us out of here.'

Jake, with a broad grin on his face, said, 'You heard the man Artie, take us home.'

***

'Open fire,' Captain Tyrell Biggs said on the bridge of the Odyssey as they moved into position. They were completely unaware of the Pulsar as she moved out of range of the larger craft. Their part of the mission had been completed so they moved off allowing Biggs and his men to finish things off.

The Odyssey opened fire with all her pulse cannons and missiles. The destruction to the facility on the lunar surface was immediate and total. Too much attention had gone into the stealth properties of the base and not enough into her defences. Overconfidence in not being detected had been their ultimate downfall and when the cannon fire and missiles struck there was nothing except the basic shields to withstand the onslaught. To say it was ineffective would have been a massive understatement and within moments the base was reduced to rubble.

Unknown to the crew of the Odyssey, one small shuttle had escaped before the attack had commenced. Apollo had foreseen what was about to happen and he had used the same shuttle that had arrived with Norsky's remains to escape to freedom. The shuttle was equipped with both FTL and stealth capabilities so his departure went undetected.

The last thing that Apollo did before leaving was to initiate the self-destruct programme. It was a small but powerful nuclear device positioned beneath the reactor core so that any residual radiation would go undetected with it being so close to the reactor. The countdown had begun the moment the attack started and could not be stopped, even with a total shutdown of power to the base because the device had its own backup power source. The countdown gave Apollo just enough time to get to a safe distance before it would explode.

'Sir, I'm reading a massive build-up of radiation somewhere deep in that facility,' ops said. Biggs went over to the ops station to examine the readings. When he saw them he turned to the helm and shouted. 'Get us out of here, now!'

The massive engines fired and the huge starship began to move away as the device wound up to critical mass before exploding.

'Engines to maximum thrust, put as much distance

between us and that base as you can,' Biggs said as he ran to the command chair and activated the harness that would strap him securely into it.

The startled expressions of those on the bridge asked questions that they would have the answer to very shortly.

As the Odyssey moved away as fast as her engines could push her through space the bridge crews' eyes were glued to the viewscreen that displayed a rearview image of the base on the lunar surface as it receded into the distance. Suddenly a bright light filled the screen as the device exploded returning it and everything it contained to their base atoms. A massive shockwave flew through space chasing the Odyssey as she tried to escape.

'Here she comes, brace for impact,' Biggs said calmly. The Odyssey was already facing away from the wave so she was in the best possible position to ride it out. Her deflector shields were strained to the max as they attempted to deflect the massive energy away from the ship, but added to the distance they had managed to put between them and the base, it was enough for them to survive… just.

As the wave passed them by, dissipating with every inch it travelled they were relieved to still be in one piece.

'Damage report,' Biggs said and was answered by reports coming through from every area of the ship. Apart from some shield failure and a few buckled hull plates they were remarkably unscathed. Repairs would go ahead as they returned to Earth and the ship would not need to be dry-docked for a while.

When all the reports were in and assessed Biggs contacted Sinclair on Earth. His message was short and to the point.

'Mission completed, sir, we're coming home,' was all he said.

Chapter Forty-Six

The Pulsar's forward section returned to Nellis Base while the main body remained in geostationary orbit above.

Kurt, Zara and the Wildfire Team waited patiently for their arrival.

'Welcome back, I'm glad to see you all made it back safely,' Sinclair said.

'Did you ever doubt it?' Cooper asked with a smile.

Sinclair ignored the quip and continued with, 'We can consider this mission a total success and I must commend you all on your exemplary service.'

'Does that mean we get extra R and R for all the shit we just went through, sir?' Cooper asked, pushing his point.

Sinclair looked at Cooper then at every member of the team and, with an uncharacteristic smile, said, 'I suppose we could arrange that, it's the least we could do.'

Cooper turned to Kurt and said, 'See, that's how you do it.'

Kurt laughed as he remembered the roasting he had received after not requesting concessions from Sinclair the last time.

'I bow to your expertise,' he said with a mock bow.

'What happened to the lunar base sir? We saw a massive explosion after we got away, was that the result of the Odyssey's attack?' Jake asked.

'That is something we will have to investigate but initial readings taken by the Odyssey have revealed a larger than normal amount of radiation in the area.'

'What about our base on the Moon sir, is that safe?' enquired Zara.

'I suspect so; I have been assured they were beyond the range of the blast.'

'What happens now then, sir?' Kurt asked, looking intently at the General.

'You all get debriefed and then take some well-earned rest, a holiday perhaps,' Sinclair said, returning Kurt's gaze but giving nothing away.

'You know what I mean General, what happens next to us?' Kurt said again this time more forcefully.

'Well, I have some suggestions on that score. Firstly, if you would agree to allow the Med-lab access to your blood then I am sure we can learn an awful lot from it and put it to good use. We have already used some of it to manufacture the serum that your friends standing beside you had taken and to great effect, I might add. If you are in agreement then I can see no reason why you cannot continue your duties with the Wildfire Team.'

'And what if I refuse?'

'Then you would leave me no choice but to return you to Recon Delta normal duties, but at the farthest outpost I can find where the Alliance would not be able to find you. It would be for your own good but I still think you would be an enormous asset to this group and I'm sure they would agree with me.'

'So what you're saying is that if I refuse to allow you to

take samples of my blood then you would honour my decision?'

'Did I not say you would have to trust me?'

'You did, but I never thought that given the opportunity I offer that you would allow it to slip through your fingers without at least trying to prevent it.'

'I have always been a man of my word Kurt so that when I say to trust me I mean every word.'

'Then I agree, sir,' Kurt said finally.

'Then it's agreed, you are now an official member of the Wildfire Initiative.'

'What's that, sir?' Jake asked, a little bewildered.

'It is the new group formed from Recon Delta with special abilities such as yourselves. You, Jake, will spearhead this new group with your team and Kurt and Zara here will be roving assets. We will recruit new members as and when we feel the need, but for the time being you are *it,* people. You will have an open-ended budget as discussed with President Takagi earlier who was very impressed with how you handled the attack on the Defence Council.'

'That sounds like a plan,' commented Vance.

'Does this mean we get a raise, sir?' Cooper queried, which brought a harsh glance from Jake. 'What? I'm just asking, you don't get if you don't ask,' Cooper added.

'Sir, is there any news on the sudden reappearance of Jonas Wilde's daughter?' Kurt asked, hoping to deflect any argument the two men might have.

'To address Cooper's question, the budget does include an increase in pay for you all, whether you will live long enough to spend it is anyone's guess. As to Miss Wilde's sudden reappearance, I am afraid we have no news on the matter but we are monitoring the situation with avid interest I can assure you.'

'Oh she'll turn up sooner or later, a bad penny always does,' Torres said.

Epilogue

Tanya Wilde stormed into her father's office, her long hair flowing behind her like a cape in the wind. She was dressed in a white blouse and tight-fitting pants. Over her blouse, she wore a pink jacket that was fastened at her waist.

She was furious and she was not afraid to let it show. She walked up to her father's desk at the far end of the large room and stopped in front, her fists bunched and resting on her slim hips.

'What the hell went wrong?' she asked, her voice rising to illustrate her anger.

'Calm down dear, it's only a minor setback,' Jonas said, waving her to sit down in the chair opposite.

'I won't calm down and what you call a minor setback I call a debacle of epic proportions,' she screamed as she paced across the front of his desk.

Jonas couldn't help but be pleased with his daughter's reaction to recent events; this daughter was the daughter he had always wanted. She was just like him, he thought as he watched her pace across the width of his office, her anger almost too powerful to contain.

'We need to take a new approach with this,' she said as she passed by the desk for a third time.

'I'm always open to suggestions my dear,' Jonas said, smiling broadly.

'What do you have in mind?' he asked.

As she came close to the desk for the fourth time she brought up a Sig P996 from out of her jacket and fired. The pulsed plasma bolt took the top of her father's head off in a shower of blood and gore which splattered the wall behind where he sat.

'A new leadership and a new direction I think, with me at the helm. After all Daddy, I am your daughter,' she said without a trace of remorse.

The door burst open and the Rover5 who had been standing guard, entered, his sidearm drawn and ready to fire.

Tanya turned to face him and calmly said, 'Clean this mess up.'

She walked behind the desk as the Rover5 watched with a dazed expression. She tipped the body of her father onto the floor and took his seat. She looked up at the Rover5 and said, 'It appears that I have inherited the family business.'

Fin

EXTINCTION - A Col Sec Thriller

In the early twenty-first century, the US Marine Corps defin-
ition of Red Teams was 'to provide the Commander an independent capability that offers critical reviews and alternative
perspectives that challenge prevailing notions, rigorously test
current Tactics, Techniques and Procedures, and counter
groupthink in order to enhance organisational effectiveness.'

By the mid-twenty-fifth century, Recon Delta employed
this notion but the Red Teams had evolved into a unit that
was virtually autonomous and could act independently
should the need arise.

This is the story of one of them.

Prologue

Tarsus II, 2433CE

Colonel James Lydecker stood overlooking the chamber through the Plexiglas wall. The chamber was huge with equipment lining the walls and spreading over the worktops. There was a group of men wandering around inside the chamber, seemingly unfocused, all dressed in the uniform of Recon Delta Marines. Lydecker was concerned that they could damage the delicate equipment and/or themselves and was just glad they were not armed.

He was in the process of formulating a plan to deal with the present problem when another person entered the small room he inhabited.

"Any changes?" asked the newcomer. He was a small man standing only five feet seven, which meant the colonel was a good head and shoulders above him. He had thinning hair the colour of windblown sand, and eyes that were so dark and troubled that the colonel was worried for the sanity of the man. It had been his program – the fallout – with which he had to deal at that moment.

"None that I can make out, but then again I'm no expert in this sort of thing. I'm just here to clean this mess up," Lydecker said a little angrily.

"I'm still working on how to isolate them from the rest of the troops. If we can't we could be looking at a disaster of epic proportions," the lab-coated newcomer said once he'd gotten over the rebuke from the colonel. He knew all this was his fault and he was desperately trying to rectify it as fast as he could, but so far with no luck.

"Don't worry Doc, that's why I'm here, I'll handle this. You can go back to your research, just make sure you destroy all evidence of this program and I mean *all* of it. I don't want this to resurface some years from now and I don't want anyone stumbling across it in the future by accident. Is that clear?" Lydecker stared intently into the eyes of the smaller man.

"It's perfectly clear, Colonel."

"Good, I don't want any misunderstandings here. There has been a monumental fuck-up and I'm here to make sure it stops here and now and, more importantly, that it doesn't happen again, ever." Lydecker turned away from him to look down into the chamber once more.

The only way to handle this as far as he could tell was to kill everyone in the chamber below. It was harsh; it was extreme, but he knew the doctor was not joking when he had said about the disaster being of epic proportions and so the measures he was about to take were necessary.

"Doc, I hope there's nothing in that lab you need because they are wrecking everything in sight," Lydecker turned to look at him as he reached for the control panel in front of him. It had a manual release circuit for the toxic gas he was about to use on the test subjects enclosed in the chamber. The circuit was operated by a big red button, which he pressed with the palm of his hand.

From hidden nozzles inside the vents for the air conditioning units, a clear gas escaped that quickly filled the room. The effect of the gas on those inside the chamber was clearly visible as they began to clutch at their throats finding it increasingly difficult to breathe. Pretty soon they were all collapsing one by one, lifeless on the floor of the chamber.

"I'll give them a few more minutes then we go in," Lydecker said with a grim finality.

Doctor Henkel, the lab-coated newcomer, stood back from the window wall in shock. He had hoped to find some solution whereby they could resolve the mess they found themselves in. Looking at the cold, hard look in the colonel's eyes told him they had gone far beyond the point of no return and now it was a case of damage control. It was imperative that what had just happened here must not be allowed to get out to anyone else.

After what Lydecker deemed a requisite amount of time he summoned three of his men.

"Sidearms only; shoot the head at the back where the Neural Interface is implanted. Make sure the head is totally destroyed. We go in, side by side in a skirmish line and we clear the room. Any questions?"

When there was no response Lydecker said, "OK, let's do this."

As they operated the control panel to the air-lock doorway of the chamber another figure entered the room. He just had time to see them enter the air-lock as he said, "Colonel Lydecker, I have some information you will need to see sir."

"It'll have to wait, Sinclair, we're on a tight schedule here, this needs to be done now," Lydecker replied before closing the door behind him and his three men.

"But sir…" Sinclair tried to get the colonel's attention

once more but it was too late, he had already opened the inner door to the chamber.

Sinclair turned to the doctor, spearing him with a steely gaze. "Why did you do it, Doctor Henkel?"

Henkel spun around from the chamber's huge window to look at the captain, staring deep into his eyes.

"I… er… I don't know what you mean," he stammered, tearing his eyes away from him, unable to look into those deep brown eyes any longer.

Sinclair pulled out his sidearm, a Sig P990 and aimed it at the side of the doctor's head.

"You will tell me what I want to know, Doctor, right now, or I will blow a hole in your head large enough to fly a shuttle through. Do I make myself absolutely clear?" he said calmly and with absolute certainty that he would do what he promised.

Slowly Henkel turned his head to look into the muzzle of the weapon held to his head. He saw the certainty in the young captain's eyes and also his own death for there was no way out of this for him. If he didn't give Sinclair what he wanted then he was sure he would shoot him, but if he did then those he served would definitely kill him too.

"I'm running out of time Doctor, I need to know what it was you did and right now before they get any further into the chamber," Sinclair said urgently.

Henkel swallowed hard before speaking, "I did as I was told – use the NI to stimulate certain areas of the brain to increase testosterone production and endorphins that would mask pain and also help increase the healing process. It was the super soldier syndrome we've all searched for these past few centuries. I almost had it too," he said.

"What do you mean Doctor, 'almost had it', had what?" Sinclair enquired.

"I almost had it; I succeeded in creating the right impulse

that would target the correct areas of the brain but I was ordered to target another area too."

"I don't understand Doctor, that doesn't explain what you meant by 'almost had it', what exactly *did* you do?"

"I had it; I had the process down pat. I could produce the supersoldier but that wasn't enough, oh no, they wanted the perfect killing machine too. So I was ordered to target another area simultaneously to increase aggression and that was what caused the results you see now. Unfortunately, the test subjects became increasingly difficult to control. They are controlled by an inner rage that causes them to lash out at anyone near. What good is that if you can't direct it at the enemy?"

"Who did… who ordered you to do this?" Sinclair asked, but he had a sinking feeling that he already knew the answer. He had thought that the Alliance had somehow coerced Henkel into sabotaging his own program but after what he'd just heard he had a horrible feeling it was someone closer to home, much closer.

"General Metcalf, your boss," Henkel said.

Sinclair's mind raced trying to comprehend the consequences of this act but there was one detail that didn't seem to fit.

"That having been said, what can you do to stop it and why was the Colonel so determined to keep those test subjects isolated?"

"Because in the initial program I wrote a certain code into it that would transfer the new data to other soldiers, like the Bluetooth from centuries ago but via neural impulses. I thought it would help the process along, make it go faster once we had succeeded. One supersoldier could pass along the program to others via his or her NI, very much the same way they would access a comm. channel or a computer onboard a shuttle or starship, except I made it almost self-seeking, it would search for other NIs and communicate independently. Unfortunately, that code was locked into the program and when I altered it to include the new parameters General Metcalf wanted the code included. Now if any of those infected soldiers get out from there the code will seek out other NIs and transfer the program to the new recipient."

Sinclair's head snapped around as he looked into the chamber again. He had been alerted to something not being quite right by the sound of a gunshot. He saw Lydecker aiming his weapon at one of the soldiers flanking him. He had fired and killed him and was about to do the same again at one of the other soldiers when his expression changed to one of abject fury.

"Oh my God, now they are infected too," he said as the reality of what Henkel had told him was being played out in front of his very eyes.

"Yes, and if they get out, you, me and anyone else within range of their NIs will also be infected. You have to stop them, you have to seal off that chamber and destroy it," Henkel urged him.

Sinclair looked around at the control panel, uncertain what to do.

"Do not access any of the computer's controls just in case the program has transferred to it. If any of them have used their NIs to access anything then that computer could be infected too," the doctor explained.

"What… you mean like a computer virus?"

"Exactly like that. We have to destroy everything in this facility just to ensure it does not travel to the outside," Henkel said, his voice getting more and more strident.

"That is somewhat harsh, don't you think Doctor?" Sinclair asked.

"What other choice do we have? If one person leaves this

facility with that program locked into their NI then the whole of the Confederation could become infected too."

"How many are infected at the moment, is it just those inside the chamber?" Sinclair asked, a plan quickly evolving inside his mind.

"So far, yes. I've managed to isolate the chamber from any access points. As far as technology is concerned, and apart from basic life support functions such as heat, air and lights, that chamber is back in the twentieth century."

"Good, get everyone out, get your staff onto the shuttles. I am ordering the evacuation of this facility. This place has to be put under quarantine until further notice," Sinclair said.

"What about them?" Henkel asked indicating Lydecker and the one remaining soldier who by this time were locked in mortal combat, trying to choke each other.

"That should do it," Sinclair said as he operated the toxic gas release control. The room soon filled with the clear gas killing those struggling to destroy each other inside the huge chamber.

"Are all you Recon Delta types the same, cold-blooded killers?" Henkel was clearly disturbed by the seeming ease with which both Lydecker and now Sinclair had assigned death to those in the chamber so calmly.

"What would you have me do Doctor, leave them inside there to rip each other apart and then to slowly starve them of oxygen once we had departed? Believe me, sir, what I did was far kinder than that," Sinclair replied angrily. "And besides, you had the chance to stop the Colonel from entering that chamber but you chose not to. His death is on your conscience Doctor, not mine. I simply put him out of his misery," he added.

He then reached for the manual override controls to the locking mechanism on the air-lock. He accessed the controls by inputting a random series of numbers into the control pad, thereby scrambling the code making it almost impossible to get the door open again by that method.

"No one enters there now," he said and turned to leave.

Within a matter of minutes, the alarm had been given, Henkel used the comm. systems manually and spoke into the system giving the evacuation order. All the science personnel were filing on board the waiting shuttles. Sinclair and the rest of Lydecker's squad followed shortly once the young captain had explained the severity of the situation and the need to get clear. Once aboard the shuttle they headed for Tarsus Prime, the 'E' Class planet that Tarsus II orbited the same as the others.

Sinclair sat alone, his mind going over what he had done and what was to follow. General Metcalf was in charge of Col Sec Recon Delta operations and it was to him he must report his actions and those of Colonel Lydecker. He was unsure of the outcome of that meeting but one thing he was clear on was that no one must enter that facility ever again and he just hoped that he could persuade the General to see the truth of the matter. He hoped he would leave Tarsus II, a quarantined moon, and not pursue what Doctor Henkel had begun for fear of unleashing a horror that could engulf the entire Confederation or even the whole galaxy.

With that thought firmly implanted in his mind, he sat back, closed his eyes and tried to get some sleep, well aware that horrific dreams would invade his nights from then on.

Chapter One

MaxCorp HQ Earth

2454CE

Jonas Wilde was sitting at his desk in the huge building that was the Headquarters of one of the most powerful megacorps in the Confederation, if not the galaxy.

Around five feet eleven tall he was of average build yet still trim and fit, a testimony to his years in Recon Delta. His features were nondescript, and his dark hair and eyes made it easy for him to blend into a crowd. This was something he was also used to, as in his later years in Col Sec Intelligence Division it had become an asset to his work. He was ruthless and determined with a leaning towards sociopathic behaviour.

He was working his way up the corporate ladder and by this time was the second in command to Maxwell Eisenhower, the owner of MaxCorp and secret leader of a criminal cartel called OMEGA. It was Wilde's intention to wrest control of OMEGA from Eisenhower and turn the organisation into a terrorist group whose target would be the focus of his unbridled hatred of Col Sec. At the moment he was consolidating his power base and something had come to his attention; something that he could use as a final throw of the dice should this game of chance he was playing go against him.

During his years in the Intelligence Division, his security clearance gave him access to a number of sensitive files. One such file caught his attention and he made it his business to learn everything he could about the subject. It concerned an incident that took place on Tarsus II over twenty years ago. It was classified as extremely delicate and given the highest security rating possible, which made his interest even more intense. He managed to hack into the file without being detected and made a copy for his own use.

The subject mentioned in the file was a Doctor Henkel and he learned where he had gone once he left Tarsus II. After what had happened there he resigned from Col Sec and worked in the private sector. When Wilde also left Col Sec and began working for Eisenhower he kept Henkel's name in his memory. The moment Wilde was in a position of power he made it a priority that Henkel come and work for him. He offered him a package he could not refuse and once he was at MaxCorp Wilde made sure he would remain there.

It was not long before Henkel was calling Wilde his 'friend' and their relationship blossomed. Wilde finally learned what he needed from him, all the details of the incident on Tarsus II that had been deleted from the security file for safety reasons. As soon as that happened he had no further use of him and the unfortunate scientist had a fatal accident.

Now he had all the information he needed to implement the plan that would be his failsafe option should his campaign against Col Sec be unsuccessful. In a few years' time, he would be in a position to wrest control of not only MaxCorp but OMEGA too from Eisenhower's ageing fingers.

All he had to do was wait.

Chapter Two

Canto

2458CE

The three men were enjoying the hike through the Forests of Canto. It was an 'E' Class planet, highly populated with several huge cities, deserts and mountain ranges. The largest range was called the Quad that consisted of four mountains ranging in size and called simply, Q1 through to Q4. The forest was at the base of the smallest in the range, Q4.

The trees were huge deciduous monsters with trunks that reached hundreds of feet into the sky forming a canopy that blotted out most of the daylight. The air was filled with the aroma of flowers that covered the ground in a sparse blanket of colour where the sunlight managed to penetrate. Birdsong could be heard from high up in the foliage and the calls of monkeys and other small animals filled the air as they trekked through the forest.

They had travelled there on Rest and Recuperation leave

from Col Sec after their recent mission with a fellow officer, Matt Hawk, to Toldax to rescue another Marine Kurt Stryder who had become an important asset for Col Sec.

What they had witnessed on that mission they had been sworn to secrecy over. General Sinclair personally had permitted the extension of their leave from the normal two weeks to a month, something the three men had wondered about with some trepidation.

"So do you think we'll get canned then?" asked John Wayne, call sign 'Cowboy'. At six feet two, he was slightly smaller than the largest member of the elite group but was almost as broad. He was in good shape but that was understandable as all three were Recon Delta Marines. His dark blond hair was cut short in a buzz cut as per military regulations. Dark eyes scanned the terrain ahead as the trio walked along the forest floor. There was no one around for miles so they could talk openly about their recent experiences. It was always Cowboy who started it. The moaner of the group, he had a tendency to voice his concerns more than the others, something they had grown used to during their long acquaintance.

"I have no idea. Why are you worried?" replied Captain Tony Storm, call sign 'Guardian' and the leader of their team. At six feet four and with impressively broad shoulders he was by far the largest of the team. His brown hair was also styled in the military fashion of a severe buzz cut and his steel-grey eyes glanced across at his companion to gauge his concern.

"Of course I'm worried. You two saw what Kurt could do. I didn't, I was too busy flying the shuttle, but if what you say is true then there's no way that Sinclair will not find out. What's he gonna do, retire? He'll have to get away from Col Sec because he could never carry on with his duties and keep something like that a secret. And when Sinclair finds out we kept vital information pertaining to an operation from him too, what do you think will happen? I'll tell you what'll happen, he'll fire our asses."

"Don't mince your words Cowboy, tell us what you really feel," joked William Ives, call sign 'Hacker'. He was the smallest of the team at six feet one with dark hair and deep blue eyes. Although his speciality was gaining intel and the team's tech expert, he was also somewhat of an adrenaline junkie. Although he was enjoying the hike for the fresh air and exertion he would have preferred free climbing one of the mountains in this range. Being so close to them and not being able to make even one ascent was torture to him.

"Don't tell me you two aren't worried because I won't believe you. We've been a team for too long for that."

"I think you're reading too much into this Cowboy," Hacker said, hoping to ease his friend's fears.

"Oh come on now, you must feel it too. Why else would Sinclair elongate our R&R to a month if not to get things in place for our early retirement?"

"You're really spooked about this aren't you buddy?" observed Hacker.

"Damn right I'm spooked. Recon Delta is my life man, without this, I've got nothing."

"Why don't you tell him we've got nothing to worry about Guardian?" Hacker said, turning towards the big Marine.

"Yes, why don't you tell me, Guardian? You've been quiet on the whole subject. In fact, you go out of your way to avoid talking about it, why is that?" Cowboy asked.

"Look, I'm as much in the dark as you two are. I have no idea what Sinclair will do or say about any of this. All I know is we gave our word to keep Kurt's secret and that's what we'll do," Guardian said calmly, refusing to join in or add to the paranoia that Cowboy was channelling.

"You gave your word, I didn't," Cowboy muttered.

"Hey, we're a team, remember?" Hacker said, placing a hand against his friend's chest to halt him. He stood in front of the larger man staring deep into his eyes. "We stand together or we go down together as a team, right? Haven't we always had each other's backs? Kurt is Recon Delta too, he's one of us man, so we have to have his back as well," he said.

Cowboy had to agree with that, it was a basic tenet of 'Soldier's Law' unwritten or otherwise. They looked after each other both on the battlefield and off and for him to turn his back on that after saying that Recon Delta was all he had, would be to deny everything that he was, or believed in as a soldier.

"OK man, you're right of course. I was just being an ass," Cowboy said rather sheepishly.

"No change there then," Hacker agreed.

"Yep, why change a habit of a lifetime right?" joked Cowboy.

"OK then, now we have that sorted let's move on. We'd better let Hacker go climb something or he'll turn as grumpy as you, and if I have to contend with two grumpy bastards then I might just retire anyway," Guardian said, hiding a wry smile.

Hacker almost cheered with boyish glee at the prospect of making an ascent and he quickened his pace forcing the others to jog just to keep up.

Chapter Three

Col Sec HQ, Area 15

Guardian was standing at attention in front of General Sinclair's desk. He stared out above the general's head as he waited for him to speak.

They had been recalled to Earth once their R&R had finished and had arrived at the new HQ with some trepidation; finally, they would learn what was in store for them.

General Sinclair was the head of Colonial Security Intelligence Division and Recon Delta. He was still ramrod stiff from his years in Col Sec, which belied his fifty-odd years. His brown hair was receding from a high forehead into a widow's peak under which deep brown eyes looked up from the terminal on his desktop to look at Storm. His eyes were unfathomable as was his normal stoic expression and it had been said many times that with such control he could have been a powerful poker player. Secrets were his trade and he had kept many, one of which still haunted his dreams from a quarter of a century ago.

"At ease Captain, you look ready to burst something," Sinclair said.

Storm smiled briefly then altered his stance.

"I must commend you and your team's actions recently on Research Station Five and the subsequent mission to Toldax to help rescue Captain Kurt Stryder. If it had not been for you and your team it could have ended in disaster," Sinclair said.

"Thank you, sir, I'll pass it on to them but we cannot take all the credit, Captain Stryder had a big part to play," Storm replied.

"Can you add anything to your report about Captain Stryder's actions on the station?"

"No sir, he acted above and beyond like I stated in my report."

"And what about his actions down on the planet Toldax, have you anything to add about those?" Sinclair asked, locking his steely gaze on the young captain.

"I can only reiterate what was in my report, sir," Storm said, beginning to feel like this was turning into an interrogation.

"I admire your loyalty to your fellow officer Captain, but I know there is more to it than what you stated. For now, though, I'll allow it to pass."

Storm continued to stare ahead without comment. This was what they had talked about on Canto, they had all given their word to keep Kurt's secret, now it was time to pay the consequences.

Sinclair said, "Now on to other matters. I trust you and your team are well rested from your recent R&R?"

"We are sir and on behalf of my team I would just like to say we are sorry we could not help during the attack on the old HQ."

"Think nothing of it Captain; it was not your fault. I

must say though, we could have used good men like you and those in your team on that day."

"Thank you, sir," Storm said.

"Now down to business, because of your recent actions I am giving you new duties. In fact, I am changing your status within Col Sec. You and your team will be designated Red Team from now on and your duties will be to act as independent agents for Col Sec."

"I'm honoured to continue the fine tradition, sir."

"The first order of business will be to find another recruit for your team. I want a team that is four strong, that way it will be better balanced. There are some excellent prospects training right now on Tarsus Prime. I suggest you and the rest of your team get over there right away. You have complete autonomy where authority resides; the only person you answer to is me, is that clear?"

"Perfectly clear, sir," Storm said, then stood to attention once more. "If that's all, sir."

"Yes, Captain, good luck and keep me informed on your choice. Once your team is up to full strength I'll forward you your new orders."

At that Storm turned on his heel and left the office. He had arrived prepared to face some form of investigation and came away with a promotion.

Things were looking up.

Chapter Four

OMEGA HQ

RH426

OMEGA HQ was in a secret location known only to people who had business there. It was a sprawling complex built in a warren of caves on a desolate world known only as RH426. The 'RH' designated Roger Humphries, the astronomer who discovered the planet during the early years of the colonisation programme. It was a barren world, basically a rock in space that had no indigenous life but it did yield an inordinate amount of rare earth elements used in early propulsion systems on starships.

Once it had been strip-mined of all its assets it was abandoned and deemed of no further use.

Wilde knew of the planet during his time in Col Sec, although it was no secret. However, once he was in control of OMEGA he began siphoning off funds from MaxCorp to build a base there. There was an extensive series of tunnels away from the deep cast mine shafts that had been used once strip mining had yielded everything possible from that depth, which he utilised to build his base. It was also the centre for his cloning operations.

After the debacle that had recently happened with the attack on Col Sec HQ at Area 15 and the failed attempt on the Defence Council, he decided there was only one option left to him.

Standing in front of him was a Rover5 clone, one of the warrior classes. Lately, he had designated names to some of his team leaders and this one would be no different. This one had but one purpose. He would lead a team to Tarsus II and complete something that he had dreamed of since he had the idea to destroy Col Sec. To this end, he had picked a name that suited the mission. This time, this leader would succeed where others before him had failed.

"You know what you have to do Nikolas?" Wilde said, his anger at the recent news of another failure still seething beneath the surface.

"I do," was all the answer that particular question required.

"Then go, and success go with you," Wilde said melodramatically.

As he watched the clone leave his office he sat back in his chair and began to relax. Soon all would be done and he would have won. Col Sec would be destroyed once and for all.

What his psychotic mind failed to realise was that the plan he had instigated, if successful, would cause the extinction of the human race and his life would also be forfeited.

Before he had the chance to ponder that thought his daughter stormed into his office.

Chapter Five

Col Sec military base, Tarsus Prime

11.05 am

Two days after Tanya Wilde had stormed into her father's office, Guardian, William Ives, Hacker and Cowboy were on the planet Tarsus, an 'E' Class planet that had been colonised almost a century before. It had over twelve million people living in the two main cities and several smaller communities dotted around on the outskirts. The climate was stable and the colonists thought it was paradise.

They were too far from Earth and already on a mission when OMEGA's attack on Col Sec HQ in Area 15 took place and therefore were unable to render any assistance. Their only option was to continue with their mission.

They had been watching the Marines training for the past few days and one of them caught their interest.

The person they had singled out was training in close-quarter combat with another Marine. They had watched this particular Marine's progress with avid interest over the last few days.

The indoor gym was massive and was where all the exercise routines were practised. In the centre of the floor was a mat for the close quarter combat training. Marine against Marine they would test their skills against each other and today two such Marines were about to engage in this very same ritual combat.

The two Marines in question were Private Jo Pope against Private Mike Gains. The two of them began circling each other looking for a weakness in the other's defences. Gains made the first move by grabbing hold of Pope's left wrist and pulling it to drag his opponent off balance to enable a throw. Pope countered by reversing the grab and twisted beneath the arm initiating a throw. Gains went with it rather than have his shoulder dislocated. He rolled forwards and came up on his haunches to look at his opponent with a smile of respect. They began to circle one another once more and Gains, ever the aggressor, went once more to grab a wrist. Pope twisted, slipping the grab, then initiated another counter-attack, knocking the hand wide before striking Gains' chest with a series of rapid punches ending with a punch to the face which rocked him back on his heels. Pope then grabbed Gains by the shoulders and twisting at the hip tossed him over to land on his back. The impact of the fall came so quickly after the blows to chest and face winded him so that when he looked up at Pope he knew he was in trouble. Pope still had a hand on Gains' wrist and within a few seconds had the arm extended and pulled against the joint. Pain streaked up his arm into his shoulder paralysing him. There was nothing he could do, Pope's legs were wrapped around his neck holding him in a grip of iron, his arm was extended and the slightest move exaggerated his pain; it was over and he had lost. Pope could end his career if he resisted so he tapped out before the worst happened.

Standing on the balcony overlooking the mat area the three members of Red Team were impressed.

"Let's go, I've seen enough," Storm said and he led them down onto the mat.

The two Marines were waiting for them when they arrived, standing to attention at the edge of the mat.

Storm went to Gains first.

"Well done Private, you put up one hell of a fight," he said then went over to the Marine standing next to the loser of the contest.

"Private Josephine Pope, call sign Hellcat. I can see why they call you that, you don't take prisoners do you?" he said.

"Could never see any reason to sir," she replied, her sparkling brown eyes looking straight ahead at the tall officer's chest. She was around five feet eight tall with a lean athletic figure and light brown hair that was cropped short. Her olive skin tones were the heritage of her Mediterranean forebears. She was attractive yet went out of her way not to appear so.

"And why would that be Private?" he asked.

"My father once told me never to start a fight but if I ever had to, make sure I ended it. It's a philosophy I live by, sir."

"A good one too. Now grab your gear, you're coming with us," Storm said then turned and walked off.

Chapter Six

Tarsus II

11.10 am

The large, well-muscled man named Nikolas sat next to the pilot of the shuttle. His opaline green eyes scanned the sensor readouts for what he wanted.

"There," he said, indicating an area on the moon's surface. "Put her down there," he ordered calmly. His lips parted with a half-smile, he had found what he had been sent for. Now came the hard part; obtaining what he had been sent for would be far more dangerous than anything he had ever done before in his short life. That was not important though, what was important was that he succeeded in his mission, anything else was not an option.

On the forward view screen, an image was relayed from the sensors, an image of a huge facility that sprawled across the lunar surface of Tarsus II. Around it were placed beacons that issued a warning signal to anyone travelling close to avoid the area due to a virulent infection. Inside these beacons was a security shield, in effect a defence perimeter that protected the abandoned facility from intruders.

Long ago it had been decided, once the report from the then Captain Sinclair had been read and discussed, that the danger was too great for anyone at that time to go anywhere near it. The risk of being infected by what was deemed the HADES code was just too great so they quarantined it until something could be done, except that nothing had been done and the danger remained.

Nikolas watched as they approached the facility and he readied himself for what he had to do.

As the shuttle approached the facility on Tarsus II an alarm went off in the command centre of the military base on Tarsus Prime. The same alarm was sent to Col Sec HQ, directly to General Sinclair. When he received the call through his NI it was something he had both expected and dreaded for a quarter of a century. Someone was about to breach the quarantine on the facility and put everyone in danger.

His nightmare was about to come true.

Chapter Seven

Col Sec military base, Tarsus Prime

11.30 am

"Where to now, sir?" asked Cowboy.

Cowboy, along with Hacker, were two of the best Marines Storm had ever served with. Now they had Pope, Storm hoped this new team would go on to great things together.

"Well, I suppose it's back to Earth unless the General has anything for us," Storm said.

"Where's our transport?" Hacker wanted to know as they entered the spaceport.

"Our ride is parked right where we left it," Guardian said as he indicated the small craft parked over by the far side of the landing pads.

Josephine Pope was bringing up the rear as they walked across the plascrete, her kit bag slung across her back. They were all wearing their Col Sec Recon Delta uniforms as they were on duty and it was a military base. Their ride was a Cessna C210; one of a small fleet owned by Col Sec for executive use and codenamed the Silver Dart. It was known by this name because of its swept-back wing formation and sleek profile. It was basically a shuttle but it had an FTL capability making it possibly the fastest shuttle in Col Sec. Based on the Cessna design that has kept aircraft in the air, and more recently in space, for the past five centuries.

"Are we going in that?" she asked when she saw the sleek luxury craft, her eyes widening with shock.

"Oh yeh, no more riding in military transports for us girl, five-star rating for us from now on," Cowboy said with a lopsided grin.

"What no complaints Cowboy? You're slipping, you're usually the first to bitch and moan about ops, about shore leave, about food, in fact, everything," Hacker commented.

"I'm trying to be nice to the new girl," Cowboy replied.

"Are you guys always like this?" Hellcat asked as she caught up with the two of them.

Guardian said, "They're a regular double act but when the shit hits the proverbial you want them by your side. As for your other question about where to next, I suppose I'd better check in with the General when we get aboard."

They continued walking across the plascrete to their ride and Guardian couldn't help but notice an increase in activity around the base. People were running and everything seemed to have an increased sense of urgency about it.

"Let's get aboard now people, something's wrong," he said and began to jog towards the Cessna. Cowboy and Hacker didn't need telling twice and they double-timed it too. Hellcat followed suit and fell in step with the rest of the team. She hadn't had the same amount of time with the team as the rest so her actions were always going to be a beat slower in anticipating what Storm wanted, but she was a good soldier and a fast learner.

As soon as Guardian had climbed aboard the Cessna he threw his kit bag down and took a seat in the comfortable passenger area. Immediately he accessed the onboard comm. unit via his NI and re-routed a signal directly through to General Sinclair.

By the time the signal had been connected the rest of the team were aboard the Cessna too. Hellcat's eyes widened at their opulent surroundings as she gingerly placed her bag on the floor and took a seat. Cowboy and Hacker shared a smile at her surprise and concern. They knew she was beginning to realise that the military did not lash out on expensive toys for its personnel unless they were either higher-ranking officers or the team was very special. She knew, as did Cowboy and Hacker, that they were not higher-ranking officers so that meant their team was special and by special it meant they undertook specialised operations or the most dangerous missions. As she got comfortable she began to wonder just what the hell she had been seconded into.

"General Sinclair, Captain Storm reporting as ordered, sir," he said, his expression hard and unreadable.

The flight crew were in the pilot's section and the flight attendant was on hand standing in the doorway awaiting her orders.

The General's voice came through loud and clear and sounded as if he was in the room with them. "Glad to hear you are up to full strength, Captain," he said. "We have a problem where you are at the moment. A potential disaster has arisen so I want you to remain on board the Silver Dart for now and await instructions, is that understood?" he added.

"Copy that, sir," Guardian replied. His mind raced as to what could have happened that was so disastrous. It obviously had something to do with the increased activity on the base.

The General went on to say, "As you are aware, your status within Col Sec has been updated to that of Rec Team, and you are also aware of the recent attacks on Col Sec by OMEGA. These recent events have made it necessary for us to take certain precautions where security is concerned. One of those steps was a total upgrade for Neural Interfaces. Highest levels of personnel undertook these upgrades first and then the frontline personnel such as Recon Delta. While you are on board I want to ensure that all members of your team have received these upgrades before you go any further. This is vitally important and is connected with what is happening close to you right now, is this also clear?"

"Perfectly clear, sir," Guardian replied, his concern level now jumping to that of dread.

"These checks will take but a second but are vital so please remain where you are and await further orders," Sinclair said and broke the connection.

Cowboy asked, "What the hell was that all about?"

Guardian looked at him, his steel-grey eyes hard and unfathomable and said, "I'm not sure, but it doesn't sound good."

_____

Chapter Eight

Col Sec military base, Tarsus Prime

June 15 11.30 am

In the Command and Control centre of the base, the base commander, Colonel Jerome Parvo, was striding around the large room trying to remain calm. At sixty-eight years old he was close to retirement and he had hoped this posting would be his last. Somewhere to while away his few remaining years in Col Sec as his time drew near and he could leave while still in relatively good health.

He had been on the front line for many of his forty-odd years in Col Sec and this posting, so far away from where the action was, was supposed to be nothing more than a training posting. Somewhere he could pass on his valuable experience to scores of raw recruits as they came close to finishing their training. There were also a few soldiers who came there to undergo extra training away from the prying eyes and ears of the Alliance in preparation for certain covert ops, but generally, this was nothing more than a step up from boot camp. Now, this had happened, the proverbial had somehow reached all the way across the galaxy to hit his particular fan and it was up to him to clean it up.

"OK! What experienced combat troops have we got available?" he asked his second in command Major Donald Sanderson who was standing in front of the large view screen that displayed all the various troop movements in and around the base. Standing at six feet he was just a little taller than his commanding officer, who was a little stooped over due to his advancing years. Eyes as dark as night, studied the screen as he wondered what all the fuss was about. Why was Col Sec HQ so worried about a shuttle approaching a facility on the largest moon of this planet? He wasn't even aware they had a facility up there but since checking the data files surrounding this unknown base he was even more confused. *What was so important about a facility on a moon that it had to be quarantined?* he wondered.

"Not many sir, there are detachments of Recon Delta twenty-third regiment on an extended tactics and manoeuvres course but the rest are just trainees more or less straight out of Boot."

"Get them ready to deploy. I want a squad to go up there and see what it was that set off the alarm. Let's see what has got the panties of the top brass at HQ in such a tight bunch, shall we?" said Parvo.

"Copy that, sir," Sanderson said and he issued the order.

Captain Mike Ford was in command of the detachment from Recon Delta 23rd Regiment. A young man in his mid-twenties he was career orientated and lived for Recon Delta.

When Major Sanderson contacted him with his new orders he was only too glad to spring into action.

Within seconds he and his ten-man squad were on a shuttle taking off from one of the many landing pads on the base having been ready to leave at a moment's notice since the base had been put on high alert status.

Across the plascrete inside the Cessna, Guardian and his team watched on the monitor screen built into the front panel of the passenger section. It was a live feed of what was taking place outside and they were itching to do something themselves, to get in on the action, to help somehow.

"What do you think is happening sir?" asked Hellcat.

"I'm not sure, but whatever it is, they're obviously sending some of our boys to sort it out," Guardian replied then added, "You don't have to keep calling me 'sir', my call sign will do."

"What is it?" she asked.

"Guardian," replied Cowboy.

She looked at Wayne then at Storm, her eyes wide in recognition. "You're Guardian!" she said.

"Yes, why?" he replied, a little confused.

"I've heard about you, your reputation is a legend within Recon Delta, sir. I'm honoured to be a part of your team," Hellcat gushed then immediately regretted it. She averted her eyes a little embarrassed by her outburst.

Guardian smiled a little self-consciously and then looked at the other two male members of his team. Cowboy held his hands up and said, "Don't look at me, I never said a word."

Hacker said, "Word has a habit of getting out Guardian, you know that."

At that moment they all felt a tingle at the base of their skulls where the NI was located, followed by an intense pain that forced them to close their eyes as their whole bodies went rigid.

"What the holy fuck was that?" shouted Cowboy when the pain and tingling sensation vanished as quickly as it had appeared leaving them all breathless.

Hacker said, "That was the upgrades... wow! For them to be that severe the upgrades have to be huge."

"Is everyone alright, no after-effects?" asked Guardian, concerned at the severity of the upgrades. He too wondered just what they had endured.

He received grunts or moans of affirmation that they were OK from all the team, and then he contacted General Sinclair once more over the same channel.

"Sir, we have just received the upgrades you mentioned and it was not what we expected," he said once he was connected.

"Yes, I neglected to mention that they would be a little more intense than usual due to the amount of data being transferred. It was necessary I am afraid, the package uploaded to your individual NIs had been preloaded with an increased security firewall which made the overwriting of existing codes a tad stressful," Sinclair explained.

"An overstatement, to say the least, sir," observed Guardian.

"Quite," Sinclair said, ignoring the sarcasm. He went on to say, "Now that you have received your upgrades I want you in the air immediately. A shuttle has left the base and I want you to shadow it. It is heading towards Tarsus II and I want you to take command of the mission. They were ordered to go as a routine measure but when word reached me it was too late to recall them."

"Copy that sir, is there any more you can tell us?" Guardian asked.

"Go secure," Sinclair said and Guardian gave a signal to the flight attendant – a finger up to his lips – to signify it was private and she left the cabin.

"Secure sir," he said, after switching to the encoded channel.

"There is a facility on Tarsus II which has been designated a Forbidden Zone. Twenty-five years ago an experiment was performed there in an attempt to produce a 'supersoldier' for want of a better term. Doctor Henkel was ordered to target certain areas of the brain using neural impulse stimulation from the test subjects' NIs. The impulses were to stimulate the release of natural testosterone to increase physical performance and endorphins to mask pain and hasten the healing process, but he was also ordered to increase aggression. In the program, he added a code that would transfer this program from one NI to the next to quicken up the process, but in his haste, he failed to put any safeguards in place.

"The program worked a little too well and the aggression factor took precedence, turning all the test subjects into homicidal monsters who will kill anyone close to them without a second's thought or hesitation.

"I do not know who or what has set off the alarm in the facility but if someone has breached it and enters they will become infected. If they open communications with anyone, that code will be transferred via that carrier wave and will infect anyone receiving it.

"When we learned of the severity of this situation it was deemed to isolate the facility and we have been working on increasing security on software protocols to prevent something like this happening again. The upgrades you have just received, boosted even further by RandCorp, mean that you and the Wildfire Team along with selected high-ranking personnel have the highest security available for your NIs. Unfortunately, the general population does not, so if one single person on Tarsus becomes infected with this code it will travel through the entire population at a staggering rate.

If the signal reaches the planet the satellite communication arrays would transmit it across space and we could be looking at the extinction of the human race within a few years."

Hacker said, "Sir, have you thought about using an EMP weapon against the facility?"

"An Electro-Magnetic Pulse, what are you thinking Hacker?" asked Guardian.

"Sir, they could direct an EMP at the facility and it would fry every circuit in the place, especially if the pulse was powerful enough and could penetrate deep into the facility. I don't know the schematics of the place so I'm assuming it would have to be a nuclear-powered blast to make sure," Hacker explained.

"We can certainly proceed with that assumption," Sinclair said. "OK Captain Storm, you and your team continue with my original orders and I will commence with getting the necessary EMP to your location. In the meantime, you are to try everything you can to prevent that code escaping the confines of the facility. At the very least you are to play a holding action until we can get the EMP to you; at the best, you eradicate the code. Take note though, if you have not succeeded with your mission when the EMP arrives you will have a limited time to get clear before the detonation, you understand?"

"Fully sir, you will not be able to delay the deployment to give us time to evac," Guardian said.

"You will be informed of the arrival, the rest is up to you," Sinclair said.

"We'll do our best sir," Guardian said.

I know you will, good luck," Sinclair said, and with that, he broke the contact.

Guardian looked around at his team; they had heard the conversation having been added to the call when he switched to the encoded channel and from their expressions they all knew how serious this was. He called the flight attendant and said, "Tell the pilot to head for Tarsus II, after that shuttle, I want to be behind it all the way."

"Copy that sir," said the young woman who disappeared into the pilot's section whilst the Red Team strapped themselves in, ready for departure.

"Let's go to work people," Guardian said, as the engines revved up prior to lifting off.

Sinclair had remained seated during the call to Captain Storm and his Red Team.

He could hardly breath he felt so stressed. A frequent nightmare of his had now come to haunt his waking hours as well and he could see death stalking him from the shadows.

Issuing Captain Storm his orders meant that he had probably sent him and his team to their deaths. Hacker's suggestion was an excellent one, but if they failed, the rest of the Confederation's populace would suffer the same fate and that was something he could not, no would not, allow. The EMP had been something he had considered but had been constrained from taking action by his superior's lack of good judgement and decision-making skills, but now he was in control and he could remedy that error.

He knew what the top brass were like over technology, they never destroyed something that could be made use of and this protocol had run throughout the Col Sec hierarchy over the past quarter of a century. He had become the very same officer that he had come to despise those twenty-odd years ago. Now it was he formulating the policy, it was his decision to conserve technology for posterity until it could be controlled or made use of. Now he was in a position to rectify his mistake. Now he could wipe out all those years of

384 • EXTINCTION - A COL SEC THRILLER

self-loathing for not acting when he should. Now he would act.

Accessing a comm. channel he called Captain Tyler Bennett on the Sparta, one of the oldest starships in the fleet and the nearest to Tarsus.

Captain Tyler Bennett was in his ready room after making his morning rounds of the ship; he was going over the orders for the day. He was considered young to have such an old starship, for the Sparta was almost twice his age and had seen far more combat than him.

He was average height at six feet one with a stocky build, which he disliked intensely because when he sat in the command chair it was more of a snug fit than he cared to admit. Dark hair curled around ears that lay flat against the sides of a square head. His broad shoulders, chest and thick waist gave people the impression he had been carved from a large chunk of rock. Thick eyebrows over dark eyes gave him a surly look, which could not be further from the truth. When his NI tingled to indicate a call was coming through he sat up straight and waited to hear who was contacting him.

"Captain Bennett, go secure," Sinclair said. Bennett initialised the encoding circuit.

"Go ahead, sir," Bennett replied. He had recognised the voice immediately and wondered what he had done to warrant a call from the great man himself.

"Captain Bennett, a situation has arisen that calls for drastic action. You are the closest vessel to the situation so I am afraid you are it," Sinclair said.

Bennett squared his shoulders and said, "Tell me what you want me to do, sir."

Tanya Wilde had been reviewing her father's work through the encrypted files he thought he had kept safe from prying eyes. What he had not taken into account was the increased intelligence of his new daughter, Tanya 2.0. She had his files open within a few seconds and when she saw the failsafe plan he had in place her heart jumped.

She didn't know which emotion was the strongest, admiration at such a fiendishly apocalyptic plan or anger at the stupidity of implementing it.

Once she had her emotions in check she realised she had to do something. She saw no sense in destroying the population of the entire galaxy; there was absolutely nothing to gain and everything to lose.

She had read all her father's files by this time so she was well aware of the potential of this organisation. She knew every detail of its assets so she came to a decision quite quickly about what to do.

She accessed a comm. channel via her NI and called the one person, the one clone, she knew she could trust.

"Apollo, I have a mission for you," she said.

Chapter Nine

Tarsus II

June 15 11.30 pm

Nikolas had approached the defence perimeter of the facility with absolute care. He had been given a universal code that was supposed to be able to unlock any security defence field. He accessed the computer controlling the perimeter field that was separate from any other computer in the facility. It had been set up so that it acted independently from the facility's computer, which had been isolated from all other networks because of the HADES code. Once he had access to the perimeter field computer he entered the unlock code and the defence shield was shut down allowing them to enter the facility.

He led the rest of his team of twenty, also large, men – so alike they could all be brothers – from the shuttle through the perimeter and up to the facility. They carried with them a large antenna array, which they hauled gingerly up on the outside of the facility and set up on the roof. Within minutes they had it erected and hardwired into a circuit attached to the door-locking panel. All circuitry inside the facility was connected to the main computer, which, although probably running in idle mode not having been accessed in a quarter of a century, was still capable of being connected to the antenna array.

Once this was completed they progressed into the facility. The door they had accessed was the main entrance and the outer door to the air-lock was soon opened allowing them to enter. Once they were all inside the air-lock the outer door was closed and the chamber was pressurised. After the pressurisation was complete the inner door was opened and they walked through into the facility itself. This entire action was completed within three minutes.

"We need to see if there is anything alive in here," Nikolas said and without anything further being said they spread out into groups of two and began their search of the interior.

He made his way to the C and C from where everything was controlled. It was there he intended to put their plan into operation. As they walked through the complex all the lights came on and they could hear the life support start to pump atmosphere through the vents allowing them to breathe normally. Heaters brought the temperature back up to normal working conditions. It was almost as if the facility had a life of its own and had just woken from a deep slumber. Pretty soon the men could discard the environment suits they all wore, as the facility would soon have habitable conditions once more.

Nikolas soon reached the C and C and looked around at the deserted area. On his journey through the entire complex he had not come across one living body, it was like a tomb. His team members had reached the chamber where the dead bodies had been left; they were nothing more than skeletons by this time. Twenty-five years of decomposition had eaten away at any flesh or organs those bodies may have contained leaving nothing more than bones behind.

He accessed the main computer via his NI and ensured the link between it and the antenna array was secure and that it was capable of transmitting what he planned to the nearby planet. The transmission only had to reach one person on that planet; the HADES code would do the rest. The extinction of the human race would soon follow.

Chapter Ten

Tarsus II

June 15 2.15 pm

Mike Ford saw the lunar surface approaching, the image relayed through from the forward view screen to the screen in the shuttle's passenger section.

"What's that facility down there?" he asked the pilot through the intercom via his NI.

"That sir, is your target," replied the pilot.

"What intel do we have on the place?" Ford wanted to know.

"None that I'm aware of, sir," replied the pilot once more.

The young captain accessed a subspace comm. channel via his NI and contacted Col Sec HQ, specifically, General Sinclair.

"Sir, what can you tell me about the facility on Tarsus II," he said, once the call was connected.

"Captain Ford, that facility is designated a Forbidden Zone. Someone has breached the security perimeter and you and your men are to stand by while Captain Storm and his team take command. You are to take orders from him directly, is that understood?"

"Perfectly sir," Ford replied.

"Good," Sinclair said, then closed the connection.

"Well, that was informative and rather creepy," Ford said. Turning to his men he gave them a quizzical look, "Did you hear that?" he asked. He had already included them in the call to save him explaining what was said.

He received nods of affirmation from his men along with expressions of deep concern. These men, although Recon Delta Marines, were to some extent, still raw recruits and had never had to face a threat under fire, but they were eager to prove their worth.

Ford did not like the fact that another captain would take command and steal his glory so he came to a decision, one that he would not live to regret.

"Let's do this," Ford said. Then to the pilot, he added, "OK, take us down."

As the shuttle containing the Marines prepared to make a landing on the pad outside the facility perimeter, the Silver Dart was approaching land.

Guardian said, "I don't like the look of this at all. What are those guys thinking?"

"I thought they were ordered to stand down?" Cowboy said.

"They were, they probably don't like the idea of us coming in to steal their thunder. This is probably their first taste of action, the dumb asses," Hellcat said.

"OK, let's get down there before those raw recruits disturb the hornets' nest," Guardian said with a cold look in his eyes.

Nikolas was striding around the C and C impatiently. Suddenly the confines of the room had become claustrophobic and he just wanted to get away from there.

"What is taking so long opening that chamber?" he said through a comm. channel via his NI to those of his men outside Lydecker and the other Marines' tomb.

"Sir, the access codes to the room have been scrambled. There must be millions of permutations," replied the soldier, attempting to get into the chamber. "I'm not sure I can open it in time, sir, I'm sorry," he added.

"Then go old school on it," Nikolas said.

"Sir?" inquired the soldier at the door.

"Blast the door open," he explained. As the facility's sensors indicated the approach of another craft he added, "And do it now, we're about to have company," this time with more urgency.

To the rest of his team, he said, "Prepare to repel boarders, I want the exits to this facility locked down tight. No one gets in here until we have that array operating, is that clear?" When he received affirmatives from all those he had contacted he stormed out of the C and C.

Time to get dirty, he thought.

Chapter Eleven

Tarsus II

June 15th 12.20 pm

Ford and his squad exited the shuttle once it had landed on the pad close to the first shuttle. They all wore environment suits with battle helmets beneath the large headgear integral to the suit. As Standard Operating Procedure, or SOP, they communicated with each other through the suits' integral comm. links until they had assessed if the communication channels available were compromised or not.

"What is that?" Ford asked, indicating the antenna array.

"It looks like a Type Four antenna array sir," replied Private Jones, their communications expert.

"What do they need that for?" Ford asked.

"I won't know that until we get in there and can question those inside, sir," Jones said.

"Right get that door open, I want to get inside but I

want two men stationed on that roof to prevent anyone util-ising that array," Ford ordered.

Jones said, "Sir, they could access it from the main computer, look they've already hardwired it to the door lock panel," indicating the wiring that ran from the array down the exterior wall to the door lock panel.

"Disconnect it now!" Ford ordered.

"On it, sir," replied two Marines, who began to climb the access ladder up to the roof. While they were climbing the ladder, Ford turned to Private Kelly, their tech expert, to say, "See if you can get that door open." To the rest of his men, he said, "I want flanking positions on the door ready to move in the moment it opens."

Everyone knew their jobs and quickly got into position, their assault rifles covering the doorway.

From the roof, one of the Marines said, "Sir, I doubt we can disconnect this array from up here. They've fitted it with non-tampering software; if we even attempt to mess with it it'll shock anyone touching it. I think our only option is to sever the connection at its source."

"Get that hatch open as fast as you can. Internal comm. units only Marines, as SOP," Ford said.

Kelly tapped into the door lock panel using a manual override cable. He bypassed the controls inside the panel and re-routed the power so that he could open the outer hatch to the air-lock. As the door opened with a 'whoosh!' of escaping air the two flanking Marines entered first to ensure nothing or no one was inside waiting to lay a trap.

Ford ordered his men inside using hand signals. Once they were all present and the outer door had been sealed, the air inside was equalised so they could discard their environ-ment suits. As soon as they were all ready to move he gestured for Kelly to open the inner hatch.

Everyone was on high alert status, their weapons up and ready to engage the enemy the moment they saw a threat.

Once the atmosphere had equalised inside the air-lock the door opened to reveal a long, wide corridor that ran from left to right. At each end were corners where the corridor branched off, ideal places to plan an ambush from.

Using the internal comm. channel Ford said, "Right people let's move it. We go right; you two watch our six. We go on three: one... two... three..."

Nikolas had reached the chamber where the bodies of the Marines had died a quarter of a century ago just as his men were about to blast the door open.

"Give me a sit-rep," he ordered quickly.

"The charges have been laid and are about to be detonated sir," replied the closest team member.

"Do it," he said coldly. Once this door was opened his mission would be almost complete. As soon as the array was in use transmitting the HADES code to Tarsus then his job here would be done and he could relax.

The charges were detonated and the door lock and the opening mechanisms were blown apart leaving the door ajar giving them access to the large room.

Nikolas stood to the side of the open door and said, "Get in there now."

The men standing in the corridor marched inside the chamber. He watched and waited to see what would happen.

The facility's computer was up and running so that the moment the men entered the chamber the code became active. Searching out active NIs, as it had been programmed through a wireless connection the code accessed the NIs of every man who entered the room, and because the door was open and the shield deactivated, it was able to access any NI in the building.

Nikolas felt the tingle of an incoming message and realised his mistake.

He too was infected.

Chapter Twelve

12.25pm

Guardian led the Red Team across from the Silver Dart parked next to the two shuttles. They all wore environment suits and ran as fast as they could given the lower gravity on the lunar surface. Each team member carried a Remm M25 assault rifle and the Sig P999 strapped to their chests diagonally, muzzle pointing towards the shoulder and butt towards the opposite hip, held in a sheath slip holster. This enabled the gun to be carried safely with easy access for a quick draw.

They reached halfway across and a stream of pulsed plasma bolts tore up the lunar surface in front of them.

Guardian ordered them to halt and contacted the two Marines on the roof of the facility who had fired on them.

"Halt your fire; this is Captain Tony Storm of Col Sec, you were ordered to stand down and wait for us!" he said urgently.

"Sorry sir, but Captain Ford ordered us to take command of the facility," one of the Marines replied. The other Marine stood at his side with his Remm at his shoulder, unsure of what to do or say.

"Why are you guarding the array?" Guardian asked, letting Ford's refusal to obey the chain of command go for now.

"It's been patched into the complex's computer, hard-wired into the system, sir."

"Oh my God, they plan on transmitting the code!" Guardian muttered when he realised the diabolic intention behind the invasion. "Where is the array pointing?" he asked.

"Towards Tarsus sir."

Once the transmission has been received the planet's communication satellites will transmit it to other planets, starships, stations, in fact, anything within range, just as the General said, he thought and then said, "Have you disconnected it yet?"

"Impossible sir, it's been fitted with a tamper-proof circuit. It'll shock anyone who messes with it. Captain Ford went inside to disconnect it at source, sir."

"Hacker, your job will be to disconnect that array at the source and I want you to eliminate this code. How you do it is up to you, you're the expert so that's your priority, we'll run interference for you, ok," Guardian said.

"Right let's do this," Guardian said and went to the outer hatch of the air-lock.

———

Ford and his team reached the first corner and turned into the corridor beyond. In the distance, at the far end of this space, they saw several large men dressed in combat suits aiming assault rifles in their direction.

Before Ford could issue any order the corridor was filled with a barrage of pulsed plasma bolts. The Recon Delta

Marines just had time to get back around the corner before they were all shot. Two Marines went down to the first barrage, shot and killed before they knew what had hit them.

Ford felt panic begin to take hold and his thoughts became harder to organise into a coherent order. He felt his mind suddenly assailed by something from outside. A pain in the back of his head, in the area where his NI was located, made it difficult for him to think straight. It took a herculean effort to shake off the pain and confusion to get his thoughts under control once more. He looked around at his men and saw the same thing happening to them.

By the time he had come to his senses, the intruders were close enough to take advantage of their inability to act. Three more of the Marines were cut down by pulsed plasma fire before they had the chance to defend themselves.

Ford saw the approach of the other soldiers and noticed they slowed their advance, almost as if they had trouble concentrating. He fired at the nearest one, his plasma bolts striking hard in the centre of the approaching soldier's chest dropping him like a stone.

What is happening? he thought as he watched how the other soldiers reacted and his own men too. Something was going on here and he didn't know what it was, but clearly, it was affecting everyone in the facility, albeit differently.

While he could still think clearly he tried to formulate a plan in his mind, to figure out what was happening. The opposing soldiers' appearance suddenly changed. They threw off their battle helmets as if they couldn't breathe, then their whole body language altered from being professional soldiers to that of an angry mob, an angry mob with a collective consciousness, because the only thought on their minds at that moment was the destruction of the Recon Delta Marines.

Before they knew what hit them the larger men were upon them, not bothering to fire their pulse rifles but using them to club and strike the Marines. Two of Ford's men went down instantly to the frenzied attack and it was clear these creatures would not stop until they were all dead. Was this what the General had warned them about? He managed to get free from one of the attacking Berserkers and shoot him in the chest. As he dropped to the ground Ford shouted an order to his men, "Fall back!"

They disengaged from the fight and retreated the best they could to the corner once more where Ford said, "Let's try the other way."

Kelly had fallen in the first barrage; Jones was at Ford's side while the two remaining Marines watched their six firing a steady stream of pulsed plasma bolts at the following Berserkers.

"This op has just gone to all hell sir, we could do with backup," Jones said, as they advanced towards the other corner of the corridor where they had entered the facility.

"Bit late for that soldier now, it's up to us," Ford replied, hoping to quell any further thoughts regarding defeat that his comm. expert may have been building in his fevered mind.

"We need to keep moving, sir, we can't hold these off for much longer," said one of the Marines, watching their backs. That made them increase their pace but as their minds were still being assailed by the invading code, trying to latch onto their NI's battling through the improved firewall, they were not thinking quite as clearly as they should. That, mixed with the panic they were also trying to tamp down, being untested Marines they rushed headlong into another team of the insurgents. Instead of trying to fight their way out of their situation they turned around in an attempt to get away but found themselves facing those Berserkers chasing them.

Their pursuers knocked the Marines to the ground and the others they had run into joined the onslaught. Captain Mike Ford and his men had been wiped out within ten minutes of their arrival.

Chapter Thirteen

12.40 pm

Nikolas tried to contact his men but it was no good. He wanted them to fall back and protect the C and C but the code had latched onto their NI's by this time and they had become the Berserkers he had been warned about. He knew he would succumb too; it was just a matter of time before the improved firewall uploaded to his NI was breached and he too lost all coherent thought. He knew exactly what he had to do. He had to get to the C and C and transmit the code to the communication array on the roof of the facility before it was too late for him. Once that was done his life was forfeit as the mission would be complete.

Shouldering his assault rifle he headed back from the chamber towards the C and C.

The Red Team reached the entrance to the facility having gone through the air-lock; the first thing they noticed as they were disrobing from their environment suits was the blood. There was a trail of it leading from the corner of the corridor on their left to the opposite corner on their right. As their eyes followed it they saw dead bodies on the floor.

"Looks like those Marines ran into something a little more than they bargained for," observed Cowboy.

"Yep, let's stay frosty guys until we know what it is we're up against in here," Guardian replied calmly.

"Guardian, is this the effect this code has on people? Is this what we can expect to happen to us?" Hellcat asked.

"Hacker, you're the expert, what do you think?" he said, diverting the question.

"The new upgrades must be working boss; you remember how intense they were when we received them. The new security protocols they installed must have upgraded firewalls so that this code can't gain access to our NIs," Hacker answered.

"Well, if they can stop the code getting to us then that means it can be stopped. Your job just got a whole lot easier Hacker," Guardian said.

"I don't know about ours though, boss, if those Marines were taken out that quickly it means we are up against some heavy-duty shit," observed Cowboy.

"Yep, but isn't that what we live for Cowboy?" Hellcat asked, with a smile.

"You heard the lady, let's do this," Guardian said, hiding the smile he felt creeping across his face at Hellcat's rebuke of Cowboy's complaint. *She would fit in nicely,* he thought.

"Which way to C and C from here boss?" Hacker asked.

"Well, we can't access the computer via our NIs, the fire-wall seems to be holding for now but we shouldn't take any chances on that score. What about other terminals? See if you can find one and bring up the facilities schematics," Guardian said.

"On it boss," Hacker replied. He spotted something that could be useful down the corridor and said, "Over here," and led them to it. It was a small monitor embedded in the wall with a touchpad beneath it for the manual input of commands.

"This should work," he said, as he got to work. He soon had the menu up on the screen and set about scrolling through the entire dropdown submenus until he found what he was looking for.

"Here we are, sir. This whole complex is built around a central hub that's sunk into the lunar surface. It goes down three hundred feet and has four floors. The very bottom is where the fusion reactor is that powers this whole place. There are corridors leading off the central hub on each floor that are joined by an outer rim of offices, rooms and storage places. The central hub is where the chamber is, one floor above the reactor, the C and C is on the floor above. We need to go down this way," he said, indicating the corridor following the blood trail.

Nikolas was on his way back to the C and C deck when he came across a team of his men wandering around. He stopped when he saw them look in his direction. They had hatred in their eyes and moved with a united purpose. He turned and went back the way he had come the second they gave chase.

He sprinted towards the nearest doorway and got it open as fast as he could. Once it had closed behind him he secured the lock. As he moved away the pounding from the outraged men on the other side was like the thunder of an impending storm.

Quickly he scanned the room for another exit. His

opaline green eyes landed upon another door at the far end of the room. His long legs powered him across the cluttered room to the door where he entered the code that would open it. Glancing outside he saw another corridor stretching out in both directions both left and right. He already knew which way he must go to reach the C and C so when he saw that the corridor was empty he set off.

His mind was getting increasingly confused and he found it harder to concentrate. He had to get to the C and C before he forgot what his mission was.

There was an anger building within him, which he had been told to expect and coached in how to control. He went through the mental exercises that would control it, subdue it down to a manageable level, but he had to get to the C and C before these exercises lost their effect.

He gritted his teeth and walked on increasing his pace steadily until he was running down the corridor.

Chapter Fourteen

12.43 pm

Guardian led the team to the end of the corridor where the bodies of the Marines had been found.

"Which way is it now, Hacker?" he asked. Before an answer could escape Hacker's lips a shudder ran through the entire complex almost shaking them off their feet. They saw the walls vibrate and the floor undulate up towards them.

Guardian fell against Hellcat, almost flattening her against the wall while Hacker and Cowboy reached out to steady themselves against the opposite wall.

As suddenly as it had started the tremor had finished and everything was still once more, almost as if nothing had happened.

They all looked at each other with startled expressions.

"What the fuck was that?" Cowboy said, voicing the question on all their minds.

Hacker looked at Guardian and said, "I think I may have an idea."

Guardian stared at him and said, "Go on then."

"I think because this place has been dormant for twenty-odd years the cold start up when the perimeter was breached may have caused a malfunction. I'm not an engineer so I can't be sure."

"So what exactly are you saying, Hacker?" Hellcat asked.

"The reactor is clearly faulty; I think this place could blow up and pretty soon."

Guardian looked around at the faces of his team and came to a decision.

"OK people, our job here remains the same or has it just got harder? Yes, it has, but we're gonna do it anyway. Any questions, but not from you Cowboy," he said.

"I was just gonna say that this is not just a job, it's an adventure. But I'm not gonna say it now," replied Cowboy, the usual complainer of the team.

"Good, let's move," Guardian said, with a wry smile.

In front of them as they rounded the corner, not more than four feet away, stood a group of three Berserkers. The moment they heard their approach, the three large men turned to face them, anger and something that could only be described as pure hatred showing in their eyes.

"Holy shit," Hacker uttered, as he was the smallest of the bunch next to Hellcat, and each Berserker was at least as tall as Guardian.

Before they could advance on them, Guardian opened fire on the nearest with his Remm assault rifle. The pulsed plasma bolts passed over the Berserker's shoulder as he dropped it to ram into Guardian. The force of the assault rammed Guardian's back into the wall of the corridor knocking all the air out of his lungs.

Guardian was bent double at the waist as he couldn't get his breath and only the Berserker's shoulder was holding him up. When he realised he still had the Remm in his hands Guardian slammed it down into the neck and shoulders of his attacker. This brought him some time and he managed to push the large man off him long enough to swing the butt of the rifle around into the side of his attacker's head.

A stream of blood was sent across the corridor by the blow to the head and the action sent the attacker staggering a few steps away from Guardian. Quickly regaining his senses, Guardian aimed and fired his Remm straight at the Berserker's chest. The high-energy bolts stitched a path across the large man's chest sending out small sprays of blood before the heat exchange from the bolts cauterised each wound. The salvo caused him to stagger back a few paces before dropping like a stone.

The speed and ferocity of the attack caught the others unawares and before they realised they were fighting hand-to-hand for their lives.

Guardian saw Hacker in trouble with a Berserker who was a head and shoulders taller than him. He struck the Berserker with the butt of his rifle opening up a cut on the side of his face right down to the bone. The Berserker's head was simply rocked to the side and he shook off the effects too quickly for Guardian's liking. He brought his head back around to stare wide-eyed at the man who had attacked him. He opened his mouth to bellow his rage at him and in the process sprayed Guardian's face with vile spittle. He then struck him a devastating blow to the chest that sent him sprawling into the wall. If he hadn't had his arms up to cover then he was sure the blow would have caved his chest in.

Guardian slammed into the corridor wall and his breath was knocked out of him again. For a second he was bent double as he desperately tried to force air back into his lungs. He thought that he couldn't take much more of this pummelling and had to end it quickly. He looked up and saw Hacker dodging beneath swinging blows from the

Berserker as he repeatedly pummelled the larger man's stomach with as much effect as a gnat attacking a dog.

Guardian came off the wall holding his assault rifle out and shouted, "Hey muthafucker!"

The Berserker turned his head to see the muzzle of a Remm assault rifle inches from his face just before Guardian fired.

The pulsed plasma bolt destroyed the Berserker's head in a gory shower of blood and bone. The headless Berserker's lifeless body crumpled to the ground, twitching, leaving Hacker standing covered in blood and brain matter.

"Gee thanks, boss," he said.

"Don't mention it," Guardian replied, with a smile when he saw the expression of disgust on the young Marine's face.

Hellcat and Cowboy weren't faring much better. The smaller and much lighter Hellcat had been tossed against the wall in much the same way as Guardian had but the tenacious young woman refused to surrender. She bounced off the wall and came back swinging her assault rifle like a club, first at the Berserker's legs behind the knee to topple him then the ribs and finally the head. Blood sprayed out across the small space from each blow to the Berserker's exposed skin. With a bellow of rage, the Berserker lashed out catching Hellcat across the side of the head sending her sprawling across the floor to collide with the wall opposite. The Berserker was on his feet and turned to face Cowboy who took a swing at the larger man. The blow caught the behemoth full in the face smashing his nose and sending blood cascading down his jaw. Cowboy rammed the butt of his Remm into the stomach of the man but the Berserker, instead of going down, lashed out with a backhanded swipe which landed across the side of Cowboy's face spinning him around and off his feet.

Hellcat dragged herself off the ground and leapt onto the

back of the Berserker and dragged her fingers across the large man's face, raking his eyes. The Berserker screamed out his rage at losing his sight and bent at the waist grabbing behind him snatching a hold of Hellcat's top. He pulled her free and threw her to the ground at his feet. She landed on her back and was momentarily stunned by the impact. She opened her eyes to see a huge fist aimed at her and nowhere for her to go. Cowboy rushed forward and placed his Sig P999 to the back of the huge man's head. The ensuing shot almost took the Berserker's entire face off as it exited his skull. Hellcat rolled free as the dead man collapsed on the floor where previously she had been.

"Well, now we know we're up against people so stay frosty," Guardian said, once he had taken a quick inventory of his team to ensure no one carried any injuries.

"How many more of these monsters are there do you think?" Hacker asked.

"Not sure, what bothers me though is in the original report it said those infected attacked anyone, even their own. These guys worked as a team almost, like we were the common enemy so what has changed I wonder?" Guardian said.

"Perhaps these intruders knew how to direct the code and make it work for them. I don't know how they'd do that without actually inspecting the elements of the code but I'm sure they must've done something," Hacker said.

"Well, it's obvious they couldn't stop the effect it has on people, you know, the whole turning them into rage-filled monsters thing, so perhaps they did what they could," Cowboy suggested.

"No they wanted the Berserker effect to remain, that's been their plan from the get-go. They want to infect every-one, hence the array on the roof. No, I think these guys have had a specific firewall installed into the software of their NIs to prevent them, and only them, from ripping each other apart. Think about it, they must've known we'd find out about the intrusion and that we'd send someone to investigate. They may not have been able to prevent these guys from getting infected but they made sure they would work together and fight off anyone who tried to stop them, at least until the array had transmitted the signal to the planet," Guardian said, to which he received nodding heads of approval from the others.

"It makes sense I suppose," Hacker agreed.

"Don't forget that code was invented around twenty-five years ago and I would presume that software security has improved since then," Guardian said.

"I agree, they've had twenty-five years to work on a solution to this problem, at the very least to come up with an improved firewall. Normal anti-virus software programs became defunct when the first NI was used. The danger to the human brain was considered too great should anyone be infected with a computer virus," Hacker said.

"I remember learning about the early trials of the NI programme; someone accessed a computer and accidentally uploaded a virus. It caused neurological problems that ended with brain damage. That's why they had to devise different protocols for security," Hellcat commented.

"Yes, it led to a whole new system of security programs for software which we take for granted today," Hacker replied.

"I think you're all missing the obvious thing here," Cowboy said.

They all turned to look at him with expectant expressions.

"Look at them, I mean *really* look at them, don't they all look the same?"

Guardian stooped down to look at the two nearest to

them. Both heads had been virtually destroyed so a facial check was out of the question so he checked their bodies. He stood up and headed off towards where the other Berserker lay. "There's one way to make sure," he said. He stooped down by the body and checked the eyes.

"They're clones," he said as he stood up. "They were sent by OMEGA," he added as he came back towards them, his face darkening.

"Holy shit, OMEGA!" Hacker said.

"Yes, there can be no doubt now as to their purpose here. This has just gotten a whole lot harder," Guardian said.

"Hold on, why is the fact they're clones important?" Hellcat asked.

"Because they're clones it would be easy to program them not to attack each other. These particular clones are probably from a specific batch and bred for this mission only," Guardian replied.

"Right, now that we have that clear, can we get back to it?" Cowboy asked.

Before the two of them could reply another tremor shook the facility, this time with more intensity. They were shaken off their feet by the suddenness of it. Once it was over they stared at each other in shock. Guardian reached out a long arm to steady himself against the wall. As he got to his feet he said, "Cowboy's right, let's move."

Nikolas reached an elevator and opened the doors. Once inside he pressed the manual control for the floor he needed, the next floor up where the C and C was.

The two tremors he had felt on his way from the chamber was something they had not considered. He knew what it could be but he tried to put that thought out of a mind that was already becoming clouded. It was one problem too many to concentrate on and if he reached his objective in time then it would be irrelevant anyway.

The elevator glided to a stop on the floor he wanted and the doors opened. As he stepped out his vision swirled around him making him think he would pass out. He stopped and leant against the wall to prevent himself from collapsing to the floor, then waited for the waves of nausea to pass. When he looked up there were two of his men approaching with murder in their eyes. Clearly, his designation as leader separated him from the rest of his brothers where the code was concerned; to them, he was just another enemy, not one of them.

They were coming at speed and for a split second panic took hold. He thought he would fail in his mission, then he remembered his pulse rifle slung on his shoulder. Quickly he brought it around and fired a burst at the first target. Pulsed plasma bolts tore open the chest of the first man, sending him crashing to the floor. By the time he brought the rifle around to find his next target, the man was already upon him, battering him with huge fists trying to pummel him to death.

Nikolas was at a disadvantage as he still had hold of the weapon, so for an instant, he was unable to defend himself. Heaving up with his powerful shoulders he managed to push his attacker away long enough to bring up the rifle and attempt to fire. His attacker was acting purely on instinct and sensed the danger the weapon posed. He grabbed it with both hands preventing his former commander from using it.

Both of them struggled to gain the upper hand, pushing and pulling at the rifle that was held between both their chests. They were in a stalemate as they were equal in stature and physical prowess but the Berserker began to gain the upper hand simply through ferocity fuelled by his rage. He began to force the muzzle of the weapon around close to the other man's face. Unable to stop the motion, the leader pushed the opposite end down as quickly and with as much force as his weakening muscles could muster, ramming the butt into the groin of his attacker.

The Berserker's face contorted momentarily in pain from the blow and his grip weakened on the pulse rifle. The leader wrenched it from his grasp and was trying to bring it around to fire when his attacker tackled him into the wall. The impact knocked the air from the leader's lungs and his strength left him. He looked up into the eyes of his former colleague and saw only hatred and the need to kill. He rallied himself; he could not fail this close to his objective. He pushed the man off him with all his strength then brought the rifle butt around slamming it against the side of the Berserker's head. The blow knocked his head sideways, opening a cut across his cheek, sending a spurt of blood across the room. He followed up his attack, as he knew he must, with a series of blows using the rifle butt to hammer at the Berserker. Somehow the latter managed to grab hold of the weapon as he was being hit and used his attacker's own momentum against him. He converted the force of a blow into a throw and before the leader knew what was happening he was flying over the Berserker's shoulder heading for the floor. This time the Berserker managed to turn the rifle around and fire. The bolt just missed its intended target instead it grazed the leader's shoulder in an explosion of pain that managed to focus his mind with a laser-like intensity. Instead of giving in to the pain, the wounded man lashed out with a foot sweeping his attacker's legs from under him sending him crashing to the floor.

Now Nikolas had control over the rifle once more and he didn't hesitate. The next shot struck the Berserker in the centre of his forehead. There was a momentary explosion of blood and gore over the floor beneath him then everything went quiet and still, the only movement was the twitching of the lifeless body at his feet.

The C and C was now within his reach and he could complete his mission. Pain from his shoulder and his other wounds inflicted during his recent fight suddenly became more than just apparent to him, it was overwhelming. He glanced at his shoulder and realised why. The bolt had struck his clavicle destroying the scapula behind it so that the humerus was hanging almost by a thread. His arm was useless. Taking a step forward and trying to put the pain behind him so he could complete his mission, the waves of nausea returned.

The next thing he knew the floor was coming up to greet him as darkness closed around him.

Chapter Fifteen

12.45 pm

Guardian reached the elevator first just as another tremor hit.

"We'd better hurry," he said and pressed the button that would bring the elevator to them.

"Where do we need to go, Hacker?" he asked.

"One floor down boss," Hacker replied.

As soon as the doors opened the four of them filed quickly inside the small cubicle and Guardian pressed the button that would send them down to the floor they needed.

As the doors opened Hacker said, "This is the wrong floor."

"What do you mean?" Cowboy asked, a worried frown over his eyes.

"They've blocked off the floor where the C and C is located, at least from this elevator," he explained.

"Where are we then?" Hellcat asked, picking up on the concern shown by her teammate.

"This is the floor below, where the chamber is."

"How the hell are we supposed to get to the C and C then?" asked Cowboy, his voice rising in frustration.

Before anyone could reply an ear-splitting scream came from behind. Hellcat turned and saw three Berserkers coming straight for them.

"Move, NOW!" she shouted, all pretence of subterfuge gone from their minds.

Cowboy dropped to one knee as he brought up his Remm assault rifle and took aim. He fired three rapid bursts at the onrushing Berserkers; the first salvo caught the lead man in the head, snapping him off his feet as his head exploded, the second burst caught the next attacker in the hips as he jumped over his fallen comrade dropping him onto the ground face first. As the last man came around the previous two, Cowboy was on his feet and ready for him, he brought the rifle up just as the man reached him and fired straight at his face. The Berserker's head was destroyed by the blast from the weapon and he dropped like a stone.

"Eat shit and die you fucker," Cowboy snarled.

Guardian walked up to the wounded Berserker who was trying to crawl towards them and shot him in the back of the head, stopping any further attempts.

Looking up and around them, Guardian listened, when he heard the howl of fury he said, "OK they know we're here and will be coming for us, Hacker, where to?"

"This way, I think," he replied and added, "We'll have to find an alternative method of getting back up to the C and C."

"What about service tunnels? They must have access panels for the tunnels they used to maintain the equipment," Hellcat said.

"That's what I'm looking for," Hacker said, as he looked down the corridor walls as he desperately tried to recall details from the schematics he had only scrutinised once.

"Y'know this would be so much easier if I could access the schematics through my NI," he groaned.

"Keep going Hacker, you're doing OK so far," Guardian said.

On the roof of the facility, the two Marines had felt all three tremors shake the building and were getting worried.

"What the fuck!" one exclaimed.

"They'd better get a move on before this place goes to hell and back and takes us with it," replied his fellow Marine.

"Try to reach Captain Ford and see if you can get a sit-rep," the first one said. When there was no reply he said, "What about those so-called specialists who came over from that shuttle? See if you can raise one of them."

He suddenly realised that the signal Captain Storm had used to contact them had been a one-way comm. link and he could not contact them.

"Shit!" he shouted when all he got was silence.

"Fuck, we're on our own," he said, as he looked at his friend.

"There's one," Hacker said, as he ran towards the place he had indicated near the bottom of a wall up ahead. As they neared it they became aware of the sound of running feet. Guardian turned in the direction the sound was coming from and saw two more of the Berserkers heading their way.

"Right people, Hellcat you cover Hacker while he gets that panel open, Cowboy and I will hold these bastards off," he ordered. Then he and his comrade turned to aim their pulse rifles at the onrushing threat.

As Hacker bent to the task he had been set, Hellcat stood guarding him while Guardian and Cowboy fired at the two Berserkers. A sustained volley of pulsed plasma bolts cut them down before they got more than a few feet from them and Guardian said, "Better hurry up with that panel Hacker, I've a feeling these two were not the only ones near here."

"Done," Hacker said, as he stepped back from the opening in the wall. He rested the panel covering against it and said, "Right let's go."

Guardian said, "Hacker you first, Hellcat you follow then Cowboy and I'll follow. Get ready with the panel cover, the second I'm through you get it snapped back in place. If they don't see us go through then it just might buy us long enough to get up to the C and C."

As they began to climb through the access panel into the wall behind it, Guardian kept a watchful eye on the surrounding area for any signs that more Berserkers would be coming.

Inside the wall, the access tunnel ran horizontally for admittance to the equipment positioned behind the walls and also vertically up through a hole in the floor to the top of the entrance level. There was a metal ladder fastened to the vertical section allowing access to other floors through the hole in the top and bottom of the horizontal tunnel. Hacker was standing by the opening holding the hatch cover while the rest of the team climbed through.

Hellcat had gone through and Cowboy was halfway into the opening when Guardian heard the screams.

"Get your ass through that hole," Hellcat screamed, as Guardian aimed the Remm in the direction of the screams. Cowboy felt himself being dragged through the hole in the wall by Hellcat and unceremoniously dumped on the floor by her feet just missing the hole. He had to catch himself before he slipped through and down the vertical tunnel to the bottom floor.

"Come on!" she screamed through the gaping hole in the wall at Guardian.

A Berserker had appeared running at the tall Marine, eyes blazing with fury as his mouth was twisted into a snarl of pure hatred.

Guardian pressed his back against the wall and fired his assault rifle at the clone. The pulsed plasma bolts almost cut the clone in half as they scythed across his chest. Blood spattered the wall as he crashed into it before falling to the floor.

"Now damn it!" Hellcat screamed once more when she saw the big Marine take care of the Berserker. Guardian turned quickly towards the opening and bent forward to climb through the hole. In his peripheral vision, he noticed two more of the hulking brutes come streaming down the corridor like express trains.

Hellcat wrenched the pulse rifle out of Guardian's grip and turned it towards the Berserkers. She aimed the rifle with one hand, firing blindly down the corridor as she tugged on Guardian's shoulder with the other.

The big Marine stumbled into the confined space behind the wall as Hellcat continued to fire but with increased accuracy because by this time she could hold the weapon with both hands.

"Hacker get that panel back on and sealed before any more of those bastards get here." Guardian snarled. Hellcat finished off the two that had threatened her boss and she ducked back inside the hole. Hacker came forward with the panel cover and placed it over the hole then took his Remm and blasted around the edges sealing it in place. Cowboy helped Guardian to his feet as they both watched Hellcat cover Hacker as he worked at sealing the opening.

"Good work guys," Guardian praised them. "Welcome to the team Hellcat," he added with a smile.

"Just doing my job boss," she replied, trying to keep a straight face. Inside she was glowing with pride that she had become part of the team.

"Right, let's climb," Guardian said, getting back to work.

"No rest for the wicked," Cowboy quipped.

Chapter Sixteen

12.55 pm

The climb was steep and because of their recent exertions, they began to slow as their arms started to tire. As they reached the halfway stage between the floor they had just left and the one they were heading for they heard a pounding coming from below.

Guardian glanced behind and saw impact ripples coinciding with every sound on the hatch panel. Someone was battering at it trying to break through.

"Pick up the pace people, they'll be breaking through that panel pretty soon and I'd rather not get caught on this ladder when that happens," he said.

His words urged them on to increase their pace even though arms and legs were beginning to feel like lead weights and it was a struggle simply to lift each one onto the rung above. The thought of the Berserker's breaking through made them ignore the pain from tired muscles and they climbed even faster.

"Hacker, can you open the panel to the next floor?"

Guardian asked as he saw the lead Marine on the ladder step off once he had reached their destination through the floor of the tunnel above.

"That may be a problem. It looks like they sealed off the hatch of this particular section, not sure why but I doubt we have time to get through here. I suggest we move on to the next," Hacker replied.

"Then we'll have to block this access point off at that level just in case those things come up after us," Guardian said as he continued to climb. Things were not going as smoothly as he'd hoped.

"Right move it, there's nothing to seal this access point off so we'll just have to find the next hatch and get that open, and fast," Guardian said when he saw the situation for himself.

"Right it's this way I think," Hacker said, which they all let go and just hoped he would get it right.

They began to crawl along the access tunnel in the direction Hacker had indicated. The tunnel was severely cramped and they had to crawl on their hands and knees. The light was low with just enough illumination to see where they were going. Dark shadows traced their path along the walls like spectres of doom that followed their every step.

"How close are we to the next hatch?" Cowboy asked. The strain of crawling through the cramped dank tunnel was beginning to tell on all of them.

"We're here," replied the young Marine. He twisted around so that he could reach the access panel and began to prise open the fastenings that held the cover firmly in place. "It might take a few seconds," he added, his voice a mere grunt as he strained to get the cover off.

"We don't have seconds," Cowboy said, then brought his Remm assault rifle in front of him and said, "Move!"

Hacker just got out of the way in time before his friend

let loose with a sustained barrage of pulsed plasma bolts at the fastenings on the cover. The heat from the shots raised the temperature inside the tunnel to almost unbearable levels but Cowboy would not quit until the cover was loose.

Hacker twisted around and gave the cover a hefty kick with both legs and sent the cover spinning into the corridor on the other side of the tunnel and they heard it clatter against the floor then the walls.

"OK it's open," Cowboy said, and he climbed through into the corridor followed by Hacker then Hellcat. Guardian brought up the rear and was glad to be free of the confined space of the tunnel especially as he had heard the Berserkers coming up the ladder as fast as they could climb.

"Seal that hatch quickly, they're on their way up," he ordered.

Hacker and Cowboy set about resealing the hatch cover over the tunnel entrance while Hellcat covered them with her rifle. Guardian stood at the side trying to get his bearings and his breath back after the long climb and the mad dash through the claustrophobia-inducing tunnel.

The two of them soon had the hatch cover in place and they reinforced it the best they could.

"Do you know where we are Hacker?" Guardian asked once the young Marine had got his breath back. Hacker looked around trying to spot anything familiar that he could remember from the schematics he had glimpsed. For several seconds he looked one way then the other and then back again as his mind formulated a virtual map in his mind with all their positions placed carefully on it.

"It's this way," he said, after a pause. They were all partially rested. They had taken the moment as Hacker got his bearings to relax a little and get their breath back.

"OK people, let's do this," Guardian said and they set off down the corridor.

Nikolas woke up to intense pain. His arm was bleeding from the wound in his shoulder and there was a puddle on the floor where he had lay after he blacked out. When he saw how much blood he had lost he understood why he felt like he did.

He looked up then carefully scanned the area around him to see if he was alone. There was no one else in the corridor where he lay and he could see the C and C in front of him, tantalisingly close. With all his failing strength he pulled himself off the ground using only his good arm. When he managed to get on his feet the room began to spin, sending wave after wave of nausea to wash over him like some unstoppable tide coming up the shoreline.

The blood loss was extreme; he had almost reached the point where it would incapacitate him. He was surviving on willpower alone by this time. His need to fulfil his mission was his driving force and was what kept him going. Even though that thought was failing, and failing fast. He was light-headed, nauseous and felt like he would pass out at any time. With all that going on he knew he had to move and now before it was too late.

Pushing himself forward he concentrated on putting one foot in front of the other, one step at a time. Slowly but surely he began to make headway towards his destination.

Apollo was a Rover5 and like the rest, he was six feet four of solid muscle and sinew with chiselled looks any model would give their right arm for. He was a match for the clones Jonas Wilde had sent to fulfil what turned out to be his last wish. Apollo had been given a name by his father – Wilde – and everyone saw him as their father because he and his two brothers had been special. They had been gifted with a certain amount of individuality that the other clones had been denied. It had been Apollo who had been the only survivor from the last mission OMEGA had undertaken against Wilde's mortal enemy, Col Sec.

Apollo's individuality had been the main factor in Tanya Wilde picking him for the mission she had sent him on. She had relied on him being able to think for himself when the time came to make instinctive decisions, the kind of decisions that any leader has to make when under fire.

When he had heard what the mission entailed he formulated a plan as quickly as possible and submitted his request for equipment to Tanya Wilde who agreed on the spot. He was soon leaving RH426 in a small but extremely fast starship, along with a contingent of Rover5s, his destination, Tarsus II.

***

Captain Tyler Bennett sat uncomfortably in the command chair of the Sparta, twisting first one way then the next trying his best to find relief.

"How long before we reach Tarsus II?" he asked impatiently.

"Sir, we're about to make the jump now," replied the officer at ops.

"Good, make the jump, time's running out," he said and braced himself for what they had to do.

Chapter Seventeen

1.05 pm

"Do we know how many of those clones there are in here?" Hellcat asked, a little concerned that every time they seemed to get closer to their objective another set of clones attacked them. She was beginning to think there was an endless supply of them or that somehow they were replicating themselves. It was slightly paranoiac of her but that was all she could think about.

"There's no way of knowing precisely how many," Hacker replied as he thought about it.

"We'll just have to keep killing the fuckers when they show their ugly faces then," Cowboy said, his words coming out almost as a snarl.

"Actually, there might be a way," Hacker said, after a moment's pause. "We could contact the Silver Dart and ask the Captain to use the ship's sensors to scan the interior of the facility for life signs. The sensors will be able to detect our trackers implanted in our NIs so he can eliminate us and anything else he picks up we either squash or avoid. It's as simple as that."

"Things are never that simple Hacker, you should know that by now," Guardian said, then added, "Besides, to contact him we'd have to access a comm. channel with our NIs and that would be bad, remember?"

"Hmm, sorry boss," Hacker said sheepishly.

"No need, if there was a way to contact him though, it would be extremely useful," Guardian said, and by that Hacker knew he had just been given a suggestion to come up with a way of communicating with the Silver Dart without actually saying anything.

Before Hacker had the chance to actually think about the problem an almighty crash rent the air as the hatch cover was torn off its fastenings by sheer brute force and thrown across the corridor.

"No time for that now," Cowboy observed, as the screams and shouts of several Berserkers were heard as they poured out of the hatch to come after them.

The Red Team began to run with no idea where to go, just aware they needed to get away from this latest bunch of psychotic killing machines.

As they ran down the corridor they saw a glass-walled enclosure to one side of them.

"There it is, the C and C," Hacker said.

Up ahead they saw an entrance to it, what caught their attention though was the large bloodied figure of a man struggling to get to a control panel.

"Who the fuck is that?" Cowboy uttered when he saw all the blood.

"Looks like he's had a run-in with our friendly neigh-bourhood psychos," Hellcat commented.

"He's heading for a control console. We need to stop

him," Guardian said when he saw where the bloodied figure was heading.

Behind them, the Berserkers were gaining on them. Guardian turned and sprayed a series of pulsed plasma bolts at them. The first figure was caught full in the chest with the high-energy stream. The kinetic transference of energy from the bolts stopped the Berserker in his tracks forcing the others to dodge around the flailing form as it fell.

Guardian did a quick headcount and there were still another eight of the homicidal clones rushing towards them.

"Find cover and fast," he said, and the rest of the team ran for the C and C.

———

Nikolas heard the gunfire and turned to see the Red Team advancing on him. He increased his efforts to reach the control console. Trailing blood behind him he dragged his aching and bloody limbs across the floor into the C and C. He saw the console in front of him as his vision began to swim once more. His efforts caused more blood loss, weakening him further. Every step increased his heart rate, which pumped more blood out of his body depleting his already low reserves.

Another tremor shook the facility, the floor undulated beneath his feet throwing him off balance and he stumbled and fell heavily on his side. Blood smeared across the floor where he landed and skidded a few feet. Pain lanced through his body threatening to overload his senses once more. He managed to remain conscious, gritted his teeth against the sensations smashing through his defences. When the floor stopped shaking he tried to regain his footing. His only consolation was that the tremor had slowed his followers too.

Stumbling to his already shaky feet he turned back

towards the console. The tremors had turned him around and he had fallen a few feet further away. He began to drag his dying body towards the console once more.

The Berserkers had been stopped in their tracks by the tremor also, which gave the Red Team a slight advantage. They regained their feet faster than their followers and were off towards the inner chamber of the C and C.

Every few steps one of them would turn and fire on the run with their pulse rifles, working instinctively as a team and each time they fired another Berserker would go down. By the time they reached the door to the C and C, there were still five of the hulking brutes chasing them with no sign of them slowing down.

"Get in there now, see if we can barricade it somehow against them," Guardian ordered.

They entered the room and immediately searched for somewhere to use as cover against the five Berserkers who were intent on killing everyone who was not the same as them. Cowboy aimed his Remm at the doorway whilst the rest sought out cover.

A Berserker appeared in the doorway, spittle flying from his slack-jawed maw of a mouth as he screamed in fury at them. Cowboy calmly shot him in the head, dropping the large clone like a rock.

"Here they come," he shouted, and the others turned and took up firing positions alongside him.

Nikolas heard the soldiers enter the C and C after him but he did not allow his focus to deviate from his objective. The console was right in front of him but by the sound of the running feet behind him, he knew he would not make it.

He felt despondency grip him like a vice as he realised he had failed, but then when he heard the voice shouting to warn them his heart leapt. They would have to defend themselves against his fellow clones that had been infected and all thoughts of stopping him would be forgotten for a moment. A moment though was all he needed.

Within a few more steps he would reach the console. It had already been programmed to transmit the code to the array on the roof of the facility. All he had to do was flip the switch.

Finally, he reached the console. He chanced a glance behind him to see all the Marines facing the opposite direction to greet the threat from his fellow clones.

With a sigh of absolute satisfaction, he reached forward to flip the switch.

Chapter Eighteen

1.15 pm

In space above Tarsus II, two things happened almost simultaneously.

Firstly, a hyperspace window opened and Sparta reentered normal space through it. She took up a course that would take her over the facility. The Sparta was a cruiser and fit for entering the atmosphere of a planet but with Tarsus II being a moon with no atmosphere it meant she could glide over the facility using thrusters only to act against the lower gravity.

Secondly, another hyperspace window opened and another, much smaller and faster vessel came through and made a direct line for the facility on an attack run.

On the Sparta, Captain Bennett sat upright in the command chair when he saw the other craft. "Who is that?" he asked no one in particular. "Hail that ship," he ordered then said, "And get me Captain Storm."

Apollo sat in the pilot's chair of the small craft. It was a sleek shuttle that had FTL capabilities. Based on an experimental design for a mid-range fighter that MaxCorp had been working on, it was new in OMEGA's arsenal. When the configuration was picked up by Sparta's sensors it was not recognised, causing their response time to not be as quick as it should be. It was an early design that had the Jump Drive engines built on struts to gain maximum output for the small craft. When the jump had been completed the Jump Drive engines or pods could be retracted into the outer hull of the craft to make it more streamlined so it could attain greater speeds.

Apollo had the coordinates for his attack run and his mission was simple. Re-enter normal space, travel to coordinates and begin an attack run on the facility. Continue the attack until said facility was destroyed then return to base. Under no circumstances must he leave the facility until it is destroyed and when he does he must ensure he is not followed.

At face value the orders were simple and concise; the execution of which may prove a little more difficult.

Apollo knew what he had to do so he took manual control of the small craft and pointed her straight at his target.

Guardian saw the wounded clone reach the console and he knew his intention.

"Hellcat stop that man," he shouted at her. As she was the closest to him she had the best chance of stopping him.

She turned and fired her Remm at the console. The pulsed plasma bolts scored a path up the console destroying whatever they hit in a shower of sparks and tiny explosions.

Nikolas moved out of the way by sheer instinct and roared his rage at not completing his mission after being so close.

The code had invaded his mind and he had fought it off with all his prodigious will but since being wounded his strength had waned to the point that his mental acuity was unable to fend it off any longer. He turned to face the onrushing form of the woman and by this time the code had him in its insidious grip. When his opaline green eyes saw her they were the eyes of a Berserker.

Hellcat saw the look on his face change and knew what had happened, but by that time it was too late she was almost on him. She leapt into the air attempting a full-length dive tackle that Nikolas saw coming but did nothing to evade; instead, he met it head-on. He stood his ground, all pain gone now as his brain refused to recognise it. They collided, Hellcat's shoulder striking him in the abdomen, the force of which slammed his back into the console.

He screamed in rage at being forced back and he slammed his damaged arm down against her back. The impact was minimal, as he had almost no control over the limb.

She brought the butt of her Remm around and upwards to strike Nikolas in the side of his head. The blow had enough force behind it to cut the larger man's cheek, sending a spurt of blood across the room as his head was turned. She followed up the blow by ramming the butt into Nikolas' face as he turned his head back to glare at her. Teeth and blood went flying in all directions from the impact and she was able to extricate herself from his hold. She took a couple of steps back from him and as he roared his fury at her and was about to launch himself across the distance towards her, she shot him full in the face at point-blank range. The shot blew his already damaged head apart in a gory shower that covered the console behind before his dead body slipped to the floor.

She breathed a sigh of relief, as she knew she had prevented him from transmitting the signal to the array and a smile played across her lips.

As she turned back to the rest of her team, suddenly remembering they were not out of the woods just yet, she saw Cowboy dispatch the last of the Berserkers.

The C and C resembled a charnel house as bodies littered the blood-splattered floor.

Guardian said, "Right Hacker get to work, disable the connection to the array."

"On it boss," Hacker said, as he ran over to the console. "That might be a problem boss," he said, after a cursory glance over the equipment.

"How so?" Guardian asked as he went over to him.

"The console has been shot to shit. I can't access the controls necessary to do it, not from here anyway," he explained quickly.

"Is it necessary, if the console is shot to shit like you say?" asked Hellcat concerned.

"We have to make sure that no one else can access it at a later date, just in case the EMP is not delivered," Guardian said.

Just then another tremor hit the facility. This one was the worst yet. The Red Team were thrown about like rag dolls in a blender. Guardian crashed into the wall, Hellcat was thrown back and landed on the dead body of Nikolas while Cowboy collided with Hacker before they too fell to the floor.

"Holy shit that was a bad one," Cowboy said, once the floor was stable once more.

"Feels like our time has run out," Guardian said, as he got to his feet.

On the bridge of the Sparta Captain Tyler Bennett watched as the sleek fighter headed down towards the facility on the surface of the moon.

"Why won't they answer?" he muttered.

"Sir, they're on an attack vector, we're getting weapons hot signatures from them. It's clear they're going to fire on the facility, what are your orders sir?" said the first officer, Commander Ed Crow, a stalwart of Col Sec Fleet and the most experienced officer on board.

Bennett turned away from the forward view screen that displayed the image of the craft heading for the surface and said, "Take it out."

Crow turned to the weapons officer and gave the order to open fire.

Apollo had one eye on the flight controls and the other on his sensors. He knew the moment the craft he had seen on his arrival at Tarsus II, had weapons locked on him and he threw the craft into a complicated series of manoeuvres, which he hoped would throw off their computer's aim.

His twists and turns threw his small craft close to the surface of the moon and narrowly avoided being hit by a strafing run from the Sparta's pulse cannons. Pulsed plasma bolts tore up the surface of the moon in the small craft's wake as they unsuccessfully chased it.

Apollo pulled back on the control stick which brought the craft's nose up from the surface scrubbing course he was on to fly up and away from the moon. He knew it was just a matter of time before the larger craft shot him out of the sky. He couldn't afford to allow his craft to be destroyed as it was still experimental and had not yet been fitted with all the necessary equipment.

On his way up from the surface of the moon he released two of the Hellfire MKIII's he had in his weapon pods. The two missiles streaked towards the facility on a collision course. Then he fired one more at the vessel that had been attacking him.

Bennett watched as his weapons officer tried in vain to hit the incredibly fast-moving target. When he saw the pulsed plasma bolts cut a trench in the lunar surface after a chase seemingly all through the sky over the moon, he thought they finally had him. Then he saw the sleek fighter twist around and begin to climb up into the rarer atmosphere over the moon. He ordered his helm to increase speed in an attempt to get closer to the fighter. He knew it was risky being that close to the moon but he had no choice, they had to stop that damned fighter.

Then he saw the missiles being released and his heart sank.

"Evasive manoeuvres and get me Captain Storm now damn it!" he screamed. The helm threw the ship into a tight turn hoping to evade the missile heading directly for them as he also activated the electronic countermeasures they had on board for just such an emergency. The countermeasures blocked the path of the Hellfire heading their way as it was given another target. The Hellfire exploded in a bright display of pyrotechnics that lit up the dark sky. The Sparta was brought under control once more and all the bridge crews' focus was on the other two Hellfires as they all watched the missiles streak towards their obvious conclusion.

Chapter Nineteen

1.25 pm

Guardian and his team had just got to their feet when he felt a tingle informing him of a call coming in.

"Captain Storm, you have two Hellfires heading your way. I suggest you brace yourselves," Bennett said through the comm. channel.

Guardian looked around him at his friends and his expression told them more than his next few words ever could. He said, "Incoming."

Suddenly their whole world went to hell.

Apollo turned away from the vessel following him as she dealt with the missile he had fired at her. He slowed down and activated his Jump Drive. The engines came out from the rear outer hull of the small craft and he initiated the jump into hyperspace.

He just had time to see the craft that had been following

him escape from the Hellfire he had fired at them before the window opened. As he entered the hyperspace window he saw the missiles strike the facility. As he disappeared through the window he was secure in the knowledge that he had completed his mission and the facility had been destroyed.

Now he could return home.

Inside the facility the explosions from the missile strikes were devastating. Even though Guardian and his team were over a hundred feet below the surface the shockwave caused a terrible amount of damage.

The roof above them began to crack as the whole facility shook from the double impact and subsequent explosions. Debris began to fall down in a frightening shower of plascrete and loose dust. Then chunks of the roof started to fall.

A piece of rubble the size of one of the desks fell away from the roof and smashed into the floor mere inches from where Guardian was standing. He threw himself out of the way but his footing was unsure due to the tremors from below and the shaking from the impact above. He stumbled and the huge chunk of roof narrowly missed him. He looked up as other chunks of debris started to fall. Hellcat pushed Hacker out of the way of a rather large piece and then she threw herself in the opposite direction to avoid being crushed herself.

Cowboy dived clear of the last piece to fall, for the moment anyway.

Guardian was on his hands and knees as were the rest of them. He looked around; he knew what had happened and what they had to do if they wanted to survive the next few moments.

He saw what he needed lying around on the floor after being discarded by the intruders once the atmosphere had been reactivated.

"Get an environment suit on fast," he said, as he indicated them on the floor around the room.

They got to their feet and quickly ran to the discarded suits and began donning them as fast as they could. All the time more and more debris rained down on them from the slowly disintegrating roof above.

"Hacker, which is the best way out?" Guardian asked as they gathered in the centre of the C and C once they had on the environment suits.

"I would suggest an elevator shaft but we'd better make it fast before they collapse and fill up with debris. If that happens we may never get out," Hacker replied.

Another tremor hit them, as the fusion reactor got ever closer to its own self-destruction.

"I think we have other problems to consider too," Cowboy said.

"The reactor is getting closer to blowing itself apart and us with it. We have to move now," Guardian said.

They ran towards the nearest elevator shaft as the floor beneath them shook from tremors caused by the reactor on the lowest level and simultaneously dodging debris falling from the disintegrating roof. It was an assault course the commanders of Recon Delta Boot camp would be proud of.

When they reached the elevator, the door was jammed open slightly. The tremors, plus the explosions from above, had warped the walls and forced a gap. They used the assault rifles as levers to prise the gap open enough for them to squeeze through. Once that was done they quickly filed through into the shaft. An access ladder was built into the wall of each shaft for maintenance purposes so they walked around to the one in this shaft and began to climb to the surface not knowing if they would be able to get out once they reached the top.

Tremors shook the walls of the shaft as they continued to climb. Even in this shaft, the walls were crumbling. Pieces of the wall and the roof began to rain down on them as they climbed, forcing them to pull their bodies close to the ladder so the debris would miss them when it passed.

It was arduous work especially as they were constricted by the cumbersome environment suits and by the time they were only halfway to the top they were covered in sweat.

Guardian had led the way and therefore was the first to reach the top. Luckily the door was ajar as it had been when they entered the shaft. Pushing an arm through the small gap he put his shoulder against the door and pushed with all his remaining strength until the door began to move. He forced the gap wider and stepped through followed by the rest of his team.

The sight that greeted them when they exited the elevator shaft was that of total devastation. The top floor of the facility had almost been levelled by the double missile strike. The outer walls had only fragments left standing, there were huge rents in the floor where it had collapsed down onto the floors below and rubble covered the ground and parts of the area surrounding it.

Carefully they made their way across the collapsing floor. A huge rent in the ground opened up right in Guardian's path. He stopped just in time holding his arms out to prevent his teammates from falling to their deaths. Slowly and extremely carefully, they walked around the gaping maw in the floor to a point where they could safely get clear of the devastation.

Guardian accessed the same comm. channel he had received the warning over and returned the call. "This is Captain Storm, to whom am I speaking?"

"Captain Tyler Bennett of the Sparta. General Sinclair ordered us to deliver the EMP strike to that facility down there. That seems to be a bit superfluous now though," Bennett replied.

"In more ways than you realise Captain. The fusion reactor is about to blow; it's been on a slow countdown since we arrived but I think the missile strike just may have speeded things along a bit. I would suggest you retreat to a safe distance which is what we intend on doing the second we reach our ride home," Guardian said.

"Copy that Captain. We will stay on hand should we be needed, Bennett out."

"Let's get to the Dart," Guardian said and he led them across the lunar surface, bounding faster and higher because of the lower gravity. They covered the distance in a few moments and entered the air-lock before entering the main hull.

As soon as they were safely inside Guardian told the pilot to take off. The flight attendant had a worried expression on her lovely face, but they could see the relief as she saw they were all safe and sound.

"Did you miss us?" Cowboy asked when he saw her worried frown. She smiled and said, "Have you been gone long sir?" with a smile.

They all took their seats even before disrobing from the clumpy environment suits, as the harnesses automatically strapped them down as the main engines powered up prior to take off. In a few short seconds, they were airborne and heading away from the lunar surface.

"Sir, I'm getting a massive radiation surge coming from that facility down there," the pilot said, over the intercom. "I think you'd all better brace yourselves, this could get a bit rough," he added.

Just as he said it they saw light bloom from the lunar

surface turning the deep black of space into an iridescent light in less than a second. The light was so intense they could see it even though they had turned away and screwed their eyes tightly shut. Seconds after the light came the shockwave buffeted the small shuttle as it tried to gain enough space between it and the following explosion. Like a leaf on the wind, the Silver Dart was tossed around, her main engines and manoeuvring thrusters were as effective in steering her as a gnat would be bothering an elephant. All they could do was ride it out and hope for the best.

The electromagnetic pulse from the blast washed over the shuttle and had the pilot not shut everything down in time all the circuits would have been fried beyond repair. The Silver Dart would have turned into a luxurious tomb for those inside.

Once the pulse had passed, the pilot rebooted the computer and restarted the engines bringing everything back online and finally got her back under control.

"That was a close one," he said, as he brought her back on an even keel.

"Well done Captain," Guardian said, over the intercom as they all breathed a long sigh of relief.

He called the Sparta, "Captain Bennett, are you and your crew safe?" he asked.

"Yes, thank you, Captain. That was some pretty impressive flying by your pilot. I thought you were all goners for a moment back there," Bennett replied.

"So did we Captain, so did we. I think our job here is done here, don't you? The facility is destroyed and the EMP from the fusion reactor blowing will have destroyed any trace of the threat down there. "

"It seems that way, and don't worry Captain, the General fully briefed us on your mission. It just leaves us with one question remaining though and that's, who the hell attacked you?"

"Are you referring to who fired the Hellfires at us?"

"Yes, they came out of nowhere just after we arrived and went straight for the facility. We tried to stop them but they were just too slippery. It was a design I'm not familiar with and it didn't register on the computer as anything we've seen before, so your guess as to who it was is as good as anyone's I suppose."

"Could I have a look at your sensor logs please, my team and I can have a look; it'll give us something to do before we get home?"

"I'm forwarding them now. See you soon Captain Storm and well done down there," Bennett said and the connection was closed.

Guardian used the intercom and spoke to the pilot, "Take us home please," he said.

Epilogue

Col Sec HQ

Nellis Base

5 pm

General Sinclair was seated behind his desk as the Red Team filed in. They stood to attention facing him. As usual, the General was looking at a monitor screen reviewing some detail in a file, his stoic expression giving nothing away.

He looked up at them, taking each one in his steely gaze. To their credit, none of them squirmed, not even the newest member of the team Hellcat, as others had been known to do under that laser-like intensity.

"I must congratulate you all on your sterling efforts in your recent mission, very well done," he said, his voice calm and even.

"Thank you, sir," Guardian replied.

"Any thoughts on who it might have been who attacked the facility and why?"

"None sir, it doesn't make any sense," Guardian replied.

"I agree, whoever it was seemed to be acting with the same goal as we were but who that could possibly be confuses me. As it confounds me as to why they would not identify themselves and to their purpose," Sinclair said, the confusion he was feeling was not evident in his voice or his manner. He could be an automaton for the amount of feeling he allowed to penetrate his hard exterior.

"Sir, what if they realised the extent of the damage that would be caused by their initial mission and decided to recall their men but were unable to?" Hacker suggested. It had been something he had pondered on the return flight to Earth.

"Interesting point," mused the General. "Are you suggesting that someone in OMEGA realised the severity of their actions, the utter madness of it all and decided to act against it?"

"It would explain why they didn't introduce themselves and why the computers couldn't recognise the configuration of the design of their ship, sir," Hacker agreed.

"Well, that surely gives us something to consider," Sinclair said.

"Good work all of you," he said, then went silent for a moment. When he spoke again it was with a sense of relief, as if a huge weight had been lifted from his shoulders, a weight that he had borne for years and was finally free of.

"It seems that the Red Team is fully functional now," Sinclair said, without a trace of a smile.

They all waited for him to start talking again.

"What you did on Tarsus II can only be described as exemplary. You prevented a catastrophe from destroying millions of lives but I am also afraid it will go unnoticed by the same lives you saved. It is a part of the job most people cannot understand except those who do it. I know this is no consolation but you have my gratitude and that of my staff, those of them who were in the know," he said finally.

"It comes with the territory, sir, like you said, we don't do this to get recognised, we do it because it's right," Guardian said, never taking his eyes from somewhere above the General's head.

"What might be some consolation though is that I have arranged for you to have two weeks R&R. I am afraid that will have to do."

"Thank you, sir," Guardian said, hiding a smile. He was immensely proud of his team, they were the best and he felt privileged to call them friends.

"OK gentlemen, that will be all for now. Enjoy your rest because I have a feeling you are going to need it," Sinclair said, to which they all gave a stiff salute then turned and marched out.

As Sinclair watched them leave he sat back and made a steeple of his fingers and rested his chin on them as he thought about Hacker's suggestion. It made some kind of sense. It brought up other questions though, like who authorised the first mission and who authorised the second counter mission? What would that mean for the hierarchy within the organisation? Does it mean there is unrest within the group and how would it affect its ability to function?

Sinclair had no doubt that these questions would be answered within the coming weeks and that the Red Team would take some part in it. For now, though, he took great comfort in knowing that for the first time in twenty-five years no nightmares would invade his slumber.

Fin

The Red Team will return soon.

About the Author

Jan Domagala was born in Staffordshire, England to a working class family where at school he discovered the joys of reading. Jan was a big fan of sci-fi books but would read almost anything he could get his hands on. His mother took him to join the local library as soon as he could read and from that day on, if it had words on it, he'd read it.

In the early 70's there wasn't much choice for employment where Jan lived so he ended up in an apprenticeship in screen printing for the ceramic industry. In the early years of his apprenticeship he had the pleasure of a trip on the schooner Captain Scott, a training ship as part of the crew. They sailed around Scotland and even up as far as Stornoway in the Outer Hebrides.

Jan is still in the same trade after a forty year career, but his passion is and has always been writing. After several abortive attempts, he started the Col Sec series, which is an action-adventure series set in the twenty fifth century.

Jan is currently working on the next book in the series.

Join Jan by subscribing today!
http://eepurl.com/dLM3gk.
Follow me on BookBub!
https://www.bookbub.com/authors/jan-domagala.
And on Facebook:
https://www.facebook.com/ColSecSeries